# TOXICATED DISTURBTION

# SEASON 1

# TOXICATED DISTURBTION

LJ PIERCE

PALMETTO
PUBLISHING
Charleston, SC
www.PalmettoPublishing.com



Hardcover ISBN: 9798822961517
Paperback ISBN: 9798822961524
eBook ISBN: 9798822961531

# WARNING!

The following story contains Violence, blood, gore, suggestive themes, nudity, nightmare-inducing fuel, and crimes against humanity. You've been officially advised.

# Table of Contents

# EPISODE 1: RAGE OF TOXICITY

## PART I

A young, dark-skinned 19-year-old African American/German/Korean boy with wild, spiky black hair is reading several journals with incoherent lettering scattered upon an old-fashioned birch wood desk in a dimly lit room. A single round dull orange light shines overhead from the dusty white ceiling. A desk so luxurious and stylish with many drawers and hidden compartments all exposed and showing their light tan bottom. Cleaned out and wiped down, their secrets are removed. The teen is rummaging through logs, notes & research books showing off the viewing of recorded words. Informing of what they know as they are scattered upon the long flat. Covering the brilliant wood. Loose papers filled with old ink and wrinkled notebooks seem to have scratches and folds that show damages from water.

A few seem to have been accidentally burned. Observing the knowledge, the teen checks over them with a careful watch as his black hair sways gently from the side and moves slowly in turn, facing slightly left. He places his white-gloved hands over a journal that touches a photo of an old man in the log, but it is unrecognizable as the picture is torn along with the page, hiding the face and headline.

*Grumbling* Annoyed as the teen tries to read the shredded pages. Bending down to check under the desk of the already open drawers and hidden compartments. He felt around in them as his gloved hands moved inside them, thoroughly inspecting for hidden secrets inside the drawer's top.

*Tap* *Tap* *Crumble* Feeling something is stuck, he pulls out of the middle right drawer of a taped up, crumbled-up envelope. Reading the big black and neatly writing, "I'm sorry." The kid sits back, feeling as if lost. Then turns it over and notices something is written on its back, "Protect the remaining." The teen then becomes more annoyed as he grips the envelope. Pondering whether to open it, with effort, his curiosity is lost to his will, and he then places it on the far-right side of the desk. Taking a silent breath as he removes himself from the room.

Now returning and wearing a white hazard suit, he sits back in the comforting chair. Checking the logs and notebooks once more, viewing the still-closed envelope. Putting the less important information aside, he now has a single logbook with dates, structured events, and observations. Common to a diary. Yet it's tattered and is barely capable of being even read at all. He then takes out a private device of a tablet that he pulled out from his right thigh pocket and places it on the desk. Checking the time on the tablet.

**The time is 3:44am of 07/07/3175**

Searching for the needed apps that are blurred and numbered. He then takes a picture of each page as carefully as possible. The device begins to decipher the incoherence from the log. All the pages can be read, but the torn, burned, and erased statements are to be of his imagining. Scrolling down, reading the old dialect, which, to his knowledge, is another act of treason.

As he reads from his tablet, his heart beats fast. Every new finding scared him. Focusing on certain words: "*Washington*" & "**БАРГУЗИНСКИЙ ЗАПОВЕДНИК**." He then turns to sight some other notes that have the same structure of information that is somewhere on the desk. Searching through a different journal. He hesitates to read it even though he often rummages through these papers. After reading through them, he places it back on the desk. Steadying his heart rate by calmly breathing. He gains some composure as he continues discovering more, but all that is left to read is the envelope. Curiosity takes full hold of him as he picks it up... *Notification* *Vibration*

He drops the envelope and quickly takes out a smartphone-like device from his left thigh pocket. He taps on the small handheld screen. Reading the messages. "Mission Objective: Find a good signal to establish a checkpoint base. Location Playground OR, Sector: 12. Time: 2:30pm" *Sighs* Feeling relieved that was the only message received. Continuing to scroll down, it reads, "Urgent: Due to your suspicious actions, you are to be judged at 4:30pm of 07/07/3175."

The time Is 4:54am of 07/07/3175

*Grumbling* Annoyed but not much as he swipes it away to read on. "Higher Ranks" Reading this section of the message got him frustrated as he read the long message. Gripping madly at his handheld. He puts it back into his pocket. Then gets up from the chair and turns to a corner.

Staring at the metal trash bin. He then carries it over to the desk. Piling all the notes and research that was once scattered upon the desk. All put into the metal trashcan out of fear and sorrow. He now has the envelope in hand as he stands over the trash can. Reading the words written on the front. **"I'm sorry too."** He says with a saddened tone, then takes the SD card from his tablet and tosses it into the metal bin. "**You can tell me yourself. I'll see you soon.**" Words spoken with a cracked voice. Shivering. Tears fall onto the floor as anxiety and fear dwell within him. He is on his knees, pulling out a white ash-like stick from his right pocket, then snaps the tip of it. It makes a spark, then slowly burns. Looking closely at the small burning flame of brilliant orange flickering yellow. Taking big breaths, calming his nerves. He then drops it onto life's work. Watching it all burn as it begins erasing knowledge. He is sitting next to the trash bin, hugging his knees. Feeling devastated as he watches the flame grow. Tired. Pained. Dread concurs about his well-being. Soon, the light dies, bringing back the dimly lit office room. Looking over the bin, examining only the ashes. He stands up but stumbles a bit while doing so.

He leaves the office and looks back, smiling sadly at the desk in the studies as if gesturing a goodbye. Then, turns off the light on the left wall. Pushes open the damaged door as there isn't a handle or a knob. As if it was burned and smashed off. Scorch marks and wood chips tell that it was. Walking towards the main entry of a furniture-less house with dusty white walls. Turning his sights to the left as he keeps pace. Turns his sight away from the many old photos; they are too dusty to recognize anyway. He exhales, then stops. Focusing on a particular picture that has the biggest rectangular thin gold frame. It is barely recognizable; he sees it in his memory as he closes his eyes. Annoyed by the dusty picture. Smiling weakly. Leaving the house. Keeping it unlocked as he steps out. Sighting above as he flinches from the bright light. A glass lantern housing a bright sphere but way dimmer than the sun, but it still has a warmth. No clouds but a quarantine bubble-looking ceiling kilometers high from the ground. Holographic signs, auto-driving cars, and a woman lying back as the screen on the windshield navigates to a location she is choosing. Homes look exactly alike. Forever autumn: trees & bushes are bright in a crimson/orange blend with a few browns. Normal animals such as dogs, cats, squirrels roam around but the mutts are leashed. He continues to walk, as most others are dressed the same way he is.

Glaring at those wearing hazard suits, agitated but calm. Soon, he reaches the end of the neighborhood and walks the long, empty main road towards the wide wall labeled **CAUTION BIOHAZARDOUS**. Three people wearing hazard suits with **"Rank N4E"** tagged above their right chest are blocking the gate entryway. Standing guard of the wide wall that is layers of concrete thick. It also has a tall metal door that can fit trucks. A code panel is on the right side; one of the people in suits stands firm in front of him, and the light-skinned boy stands firm, looking expressionless. The person inspects his uniform. Sighting his tag frame reading... **"VALCOMIX X2; RANK N2E".** They laugh, and the person removes herself from his way, granting him entry. One of the others is pressing buttons on the panel, and the door slides right after inputting the code. Valcomix begins to take steps, entering the barracks of white curved housings and seeing the huge curving of a dome as if placed inside a huge quarantine bubble. Walking his way, he pulls out his handheld and presses it, using his hands to play around on it for a bit. It is now showing a route and the...

The time is 10:47am of 07/07/3175

He follows the route precisely towards his barracks as they all look identical. Eventually, he makes it to the one where the handheld is showing him a pointed arrow that is now a circle. Seeing a door on the side of this building with a keypad lighting red on the right side of the metal door. Using his handheld, he puts it near the keypad and presses the circle. *Bing* *Beep* The keypad is now a violet color. It opens slightly. He pushes to enter.

Entering the living quarters, many children ages 13-17 walk about and talk, but a few are still asleep.

Sixteen twin-bunk beds evenly spaced across and rowed from wall to wall. Facing his bed and locker. "VALCOMIX X2" is in front of him but is placed to the right, which is on the left wall & fifth from the bathroom with a supply closet inside: four stalls and two urinals as it is located on the left from where he stands. People stop and see him as he tries to make his way to his bed. He is then accosted by a German/ Indian boy wearing the same clothing that appeared from behind the door. **"Rank N3E"**. **"Valcomix X2, as a C.O.A.T.S. soldier with a rank higher than yours, I am your superior. So, how many demotions have you had now? We got the message that you will be seeing a judge after your mission is complete. Since I am the one to escort you to them."** Coming from a boy who smells like onions & olive lotion. The guy is smug as he peers down on him.

Valcomix is standing without any emotion. Continues his walk toward his bed. The boy annoyingly follows him. Valcomix remains emotionless and calm. Then, he looks into the boy's dull brown eyes with white skin and brown hair and with his dead eyes... **"Your rank isn't important to me. You don't qualify to be a superior."** He tells the boy bluntly. The guy's face is shocked and agitated, turning away from Valcomix and leaving him alone. Valcomix then lays on his bed, closing his eyes. Trying to rest his mind.

*Murmuring* Listening to their arrogance. Ignoring them as he gets some rest. He wakes up abruptly, checking the time...

**The time is 11:42am of 07/07/3175**

It reads. Getting off his bed and goes to where his locker is. He opens the storage with a swipe of a finger from an app on the device and points it at the locker. It opens automatically, swinging open slowly. A single hanger and a gas mask were revealed on the bottom of the locker, not the shelf compartment. Grabbing his gas mask that has a single filter system on the left side. Along with his other mates in this barrack. Putting his handheld back into his left thigh pocket. He walks back to his bed to stand in front of it. Everyone else does the same as he is fully covered and stands silently and motionless in front of his assigned bed, minutes later, waiting. *Boom* Entering the building is a tall individual wearing a hazard suit and gas mask with his Name & rank reading **"Criyo Domony Rank: NQ6R"** as he opens it with a strong kick.

**"We are heading out to Playground OR, Sector: 12; you all have been given a mission to execute! So, let's go outside!"** He yells with a boisterous gullet. Seeing everyone check their missions and then line up towards the end of the wall. Opening a compartment where their rifles are. He then stares at Valcomix. Walking over to him and pats him on the shoulder. **"You're going to be okay. Just finish this rookie-type job and takedown Creates, and I'll convince them to get your glory back."** He says with a stern smugness. **"Domony, I accepted my terms. I'm on trial of treason. There are no gains in getting back old glories. Thank you for the thought."** Sounding defeated, he steps back from his officer and turns to pick up his weapon. As soon as Domony recognizes that everyone is prepared. Valcomix holds the door for him. Leaving out of the barracks as they are all lined up. **"Take care, Valcomix,"** Company says, feeling hopeful. **"You too, sir,"** Valcomix responds joyously, quickly returning to his melancholy.

Soon later. The unit is now in a helicopter. Valcomix is looking at the outside ecosystem. The sky is thick with dark grey clouds, the cities are in ruins, and there is a limited amount of light, a few lighter grays. Devastative structures of buildings that seem to crumble from just a simple touch. It is a gloomy sight as if this is an effect of a war. He closes his eyes for a moment. Convincing himself that the outside is similar to himself, he rests up again. Domony is worried about him.

They soon make a landing, and he startles awake, facing the hatch and lined next to allies packed shoulder to shoulder. There is a latch in the middle of this flying contraption. All are strapped with their rifle-type weapon as they hold onto them tightly. The Lead is sitting behind the pilot. Red-like ammo rounds placed in magazines are loaded into them. *Whirling* *Engine dying down* *Silence* **"All is calm, no Creatures in sight nor any other dangers! Safe to exit!"** The pilot shouts, and Criyo Domony unstraps himself from the seat and then makes his way to the hatch. It slides left by the pilot's work; the many in hazard suits are giving their lead their attention. Valcomix sees the ruined pile of rubble in the parking lot of the old city of once remembered as Salem. Seeing fields of rotted grass, trees of vile black trunks and branches with violet leaves. **"Go on! execute your missions!"** The officer orders with a booming volume through their mask. Everyone struggles to release themselves from their seats. Buddying up as they have exited. Valcomix and three allies remain on the helicopter, except he stares at the latch they're standing on.

**"You three need to proceed to execute your task."** says the lead with a serious tone. **"Yes, sir!"** They yell as they exit. Snickering as they gaze at Valcomix. The lead keeps the focus on the young adult as he pulls from the storage compartment of the aircraft a long red tool kit. He sees him check the inside of it: a long pole that looks like a high-tech javelin laced with wires

& a dish-type neck. There is a scanner and a cellphone-type iPhone model. He removes that and turns it on. It shows a low frequency of sonar on a blue screen with a white circle starting as a dot, then growing slowly, disappearing on the screen, and then becoming a new dot. He closes the kit. He walks to the parking lot. He places the scanner into his right thigh pocket. Then, he closes the latch, collecting his rifle, which is laid on the flooring under his seat. Then makes steps back to the parking lot. Outside, standing next to the kit. He straps his weapon behind him and secures it tightly. **"Valcomix. Will you be alright?"** The company asks, concerned about him. Valcomix just gives him a thumbs-up and walks away.

Checking the smartphone that he pulls out from his left pocket from the thigh. "Find a good signal to set up a base for a checkpoint. Location Playground OR, Sector: 12. Time 2:30 pm."

The time is 2:49pm of 07/07/3175

Reading the instructions on what to do with the kit. Finishing, he puts it back into his pocket and then digs in the other one for the scanner. Seeing it make waves, he picks up the tool kit and makes steps. From the city and onto the grass, sighting the old ruins. He traverses the roads until he is in a yard near buildings and narrow streets. The blue screen has many white rings centered by a vibrating white dot. He stops and places the scanner back into his pocket. Puts down the kit and opens it up. Pulling the pole out of it and forcefully putting the very pointy end into the ground. Stabilizing it by pushing it more into the ground. He checks to ensure that it's secure by pulling it up and pushing it around like a kid and a flagpole. He takes out the scanner again and is about to connect the ports from the javelin to the scanner. Approaching from a corner... *Dragging Steps* Valcomix knows these steps belong to...

A horde of melted skin and a deformed number of people are heading in the same direction, North. He aims his weapon at them as he got the target on the right, controlling his breathing to a slight silence. Then has a lock, knowing how much of a distance they are from him. Ready to fire...

*Boom* *Crssh* *Bones crunching*
A giant roach bursts through the underside of a building and munches on the many beings. Disappointed, he returns to a relaxed stance, breathes deeply, and kicks at the ground out of spite because his kill was just stolen from a pest. He finishes the act by securely strapping his weapon behind his back and walking back to the javelin-shaped signal. **"That roach stole my**

**kill."** He says with a small chuckle while connecting the ports to the scanner. The screen brightens a lime green color. He then sits down next to the finished work and stares above. **"I hope they just separate me this time."** *Sigh* Chuckling to himself, he continues to gaze at the sky. Remembering the message regarding his suspicious activities.

*Alert* The notification instantly pops up on his smartphone-like device as the screen lights his pocket orange. He then pulls out the device from his pocket. "Distress, Require Aid." He presses the message, and then it asks to... "Volunteer or abandon." Separated by click boxes. He presses the screen. Soon enough...

**"Everyone, this is the lead officer of barrack 23-E. All of you have received the distress message. Now, head back on the butterfly we're going hunting. All discarded missions will be forgiven. Hurry!"** Criyo Domony's orders sound firm. Valcomix leaves behind the kit in a rush.

The time is 3:51pm of 07/07/3175

**"Back to the butterfly! All C.O.A.T.S. back to the butterfly!"** Criyo Domony is now yelling through the sound piece located in everyone's gas masks. Arriving at the helicopter, Valcomix sees his lead rushing everyone onto the aircraft. He stands outside of it and tells them to keep low to the ground as the blades are spinning. Valcomix does so as he rushes closely to the craft. Arriving on it and standing up, seeing that the unit is waiting for him to sit down, he unstraps his weapon and sits down with his weapon between his knees for support so that he can strap himself in. The lead does a headcount to make sure no one is missing. At the same time, he walks to his seat behind the pilot. All is good as he shows the pilot that his thumb is up. The pilot takes notice of it. Then, the aircraft starts taking the. At a safe distance in height, the nose pitches forward. Hunting towards the location of the distress call.

# PART II

After some time flying, they reach their destination. Now, hovering over the location of the distress call. Criyo Domony is still in his seat, taking out his smartphone. He and the pilot are having a conversation. Then, the hatch slides open, letting in the air. All of them are seeing a city that is horribly filled with such creatures on the ground surrounding the unit in trouble. Another City in shambles that is destroyed by time & unnatural events. *Gunfire* Lowering the aircraft as it rolls slightly to the right. Backing up a bit to be over a clearing, Criyo Domony taps the pilot's shoulder as his other hand is on his given smartphone. Then as the craft is hovering, they all see built blockades randomly made from huge stone debris; also sighting below are allies fighting discombobulated and disfigured beings. A well-built man below is waving on top of the hill using his left arm, getting the attention of those above as his unit on top of the hill is firing at the many.

**"Who volunteered?"** Criyo Domony asks and sees that there is only one hand raised out of the many. He signals to Valcomix using sign language, well more like hand gestures... *"Change the frequency for private conversation."* Valcomix taps his forehead. Listening in... *Static* **"Tes..."** *Static* **"Test, test, test."** Now coherent. **"Received,"** Valcomix responds. **"Good. Are you sure you want to enter that hazardous zone alone?"** He asks worryingly about a fellow comrade. **"Yes, it's my job as C.O.A.T.S. soldier."** Taking in a pause as the two remember difficulties in the line of duty. Both show their appreciation, even if it's behind a mask. **"Criyo Domony, stay safe and take back our states. Thank you for being an ally through these hardships. See you soon."** Valcomix says with a proud voice, focusing on the horde.

Knowing fully well that Valcomix wants to do this as a proud soldier. Domony then removes himself from his seat and enters the cock pit on the right side, getting a rolled-up ladder. He carries it over to the hatch and unravels it. Letting down the ladder as it swings mildly. The well-built man below takes notice of the ladder and catches it from above. Then Criyo spreads it wide and hooks his ends to the concaves of the hatch using the ladder's hooks. The well-built man climbs up a bit and back down. All secure as the well-built man shows a thumbs up. Then Criyo Domony gives the young soldier a thumbs up. Valcomix unstraps himself from the seat, then stands, taking his weapon and strapping it securely over his shoulder. Then, he begins kneeling on the flooring and turning 180 to where his feet are facing out the door. Crawling backward and touching the ladder, he begins to climb down.

Four de-grips later, he notices a mound surrounded by strange, grotesque beings with legs. Staring at the sight with confusion, he continues his descent. Accidentally steps on the man's glove. The man lets go of the ladder and brings his weapon from behind his back into his hands in a firing grip and points it downwards. Then steps back away from it. **"You may resume your climb."** The huge man says boisterously. Following his orders, Valcomix does just that. Knowing that strong voice, he stares at his chest. **Diim Sourn: NQ7R** is standing six feet in height, and a gold star armband is wrapped near the right shoulder. They grasp hands excitingly.

**"Welcome to the lower grounds targeting practice. Show them how it's done and that any individual can become strong."** He orders haughtily as he slaps Valcomix on the shoulder. These hits were nostalgic as he remembers a certain individual who he rushed into danger. The one who got him much addicted to combat and strengthening. **"Then let me show off how we work."** Valcomix gives back the same energy as he turns around and notices that some of the creatures are reaching close to lower-ranked comrades. He moves carefully, trying to maneuver himself down the hill around the debris. Soon reaching the bottom, now behind his allies, he then pulls the two of them back.

His comrades are now away from the Creates, nearing the blockade. He quickly unstraps his weapon and has a firm grip. Bringing the buttstock to the soft part of his shoulder & chest. He brings it up to an aim and slows his breathing as the creature reaches for his throat. Calm & collected, as if he is at peace. *Rapid fire* Firing precise shots downing the discombobulated by the numbers with accuracy.

Everyone sees that a single soldier is capable of ridding a high number of creatures. Diim Sourn stands proud and then makes his way down the hill. Taking up arms. *Laughing* **"Like years before when you entered my platoon. Still, the little runt is doing heavy grunt work. Your accomplishments are highly worthy."** Proud and joyous as he again battles with the youngest member, whom he had ever completed difficult tasks with. **"Stay strong, Valcomix. Also..."** *Burst fire* Downing, all with perfect shots to what seems to be the head and vital points, and not one round is wasted as Diim Sourn is smug. Valcomix is agitated. **"Those were my targets! I thought you were in distress!"** The small C.O.A.T.S. soldier yells back. Valcomix shoots perfectly. The two begin to argue. It took only two soldiers to take down a horde. Astonished by their effort.

**"Sir, there is an occurrence happening."** Gaining the higher rank's attention is a lower-ranked individual. Diim Sourn receives a message and a picture from Criyo Domony. Valcomix looks at the picture on the device. **"Creates are gathering around a pile of rubble. Can you order your unit to fight behind me? Make it a mandatory cleaning. Criyo Domony, he can have your flanks. I'll go investigate the occurrence."** Valcomix says, determined and clear, as if ordering the one ranked higher than him. Convinced. **"Alright. But you're not going alone again. I lost a partner due to a mission failure."** He says softly. Valcomix pats the guy on the back. **"I'm here now once more. I will take a few weights with me."** Valcomix says proudly.

# PART III

## The time is 5:35 pm of 07/07/3175

The sky is darkening. Valcomix is now leading three Rank N3E's *Coughing* *Grumbling* All is clear through the alleyway. Everyone is armed and aiming in different directions. **"Why are we following you?"** Asks the fellow ally, taking the right. **"Sir, Sourn. I have a perimeter checker, N3E, complaining about his task. Permission to return him away?"** Valcomix is annoyed by the boy's complaining. **"Play nice out there. I left him as lead because he is experienced in these sorts of tasks. More reported complaints, I will make you do my workouts."** He warns brashly through their masks. Knowing the stories of his intensity is torture. Valcomix chuckles. "**Thanks, that should shut them up. Also, if you all want to climb the ranks, you will succumb to that torture as an NQ5E. Low ranks. I tell you...**" The three now understand that they're inferior. *Dragging footsteps* He hears them. **"Going silent, you three should do the same. Follow my signs, and we will be okay."** Becoming serious and taking a calm breath.

Valcomix leans on the wall and walks the narrow path. He then gestures to the one closer to approach.

He points upwards as he kneels, giving him a lift. The guy struggles to reach the rooftop. Valcomix pushes his feet hard. Now, the guy crawls and sees the horde from above. Aiming his weapon at the potential kills. Valcomix waits for a few seconds for a gesture. He then pokes his mask out of the passage and can see the white tip of the riffle. He then retreats, shaking his head frustratingly so. Now he signals for the two and points at the opening and to remain behind them. Valcomix then takes up arms and walks the narrow passage. The heart is still calm even though he is excited. He counted all the heads, and it was well over fifty as he remained upon the wall. Just a yard away from the passage. They're surrounding... Getting a quick glimpse as they ignore him entirely... a pile of rubble.

He takes strategic aim as he takes out the magazine. Counting. Twenty bright red ammo are counted for. There is one in the chamber. He nods and proceeds to take aim. *Burst fire* Five rounds spinning with celerity. Two headshots and the other three go down with force, causing many to tumble over. *Rapid fire* Walking through another passageway is more of them. Sighting this, he clenches his weapon better and takes a stance. Firing precise shots and changing out the empty magazine. *Groaning* Seeing them close up as he is surrounded. **"Fire at them!"** Annoyed and angry. The three are trying, but their shots aren't very effective. Valcomix kicks at the one trying to grab his mask. He then rushes towards the pile. Fighting his way as he stands in a better position. *Breaking* **"Return and be at a safe position."** Valcomix orders seeing cracks in the walls, shattered windows, and the doors seem to be dented & bent. He remains on top of the pile. **"Order received!"** Two were eager as they ran away. The guy on the roof isn't able to come down as the height is a bit scary for him. He remains there and continues firing. **"Don't fire. Save your rounds; a bigger target is appearing."** He suggests as he remains calm, keeping sight of the growing crack.

Now noticing it as well. *Hissing* Ignoring the sound and Valcomix as the Creates continue trying to dig up rubble. The sound gets louder, and Valcomix quickly lays on the pile, aiming at the made hole. *Crash* Upturned the streets as it ambushes the Creates to fall into the hole. Hearing solid meat turn to sloppy oatmeal. The crunching of bones becomes mush. All they can do is see that deformed, melted skin and bright-colored blood flesh sacs fall. **"This is one gluttonous insect. My guess stands that this is an adult Hissing Cockroach."** Valcomix says calmly and patiently. **"Valcomix, retreat, that is a threat level higher than your pay grade."** Says Criyo Domony out of concern. **"I will handle it. This will be the final time seeing the outside anyway. Let me get as much**

**excitement as needed. Besides, there is no rush; I missed my court time due to an emergency. At least that portion will be forgiven."** He voices back, loving the danger. He takes out his smartphone-like device and...

**The time is 6:27 pm of 07/07/3175**

Checking the notifications. "**Missed Court... Demoted to NU. hereby stripped of your rank and will be separated from...**" He puts it back into the left thigh pocket. Staring at the dark hole. The two are camping upon their respected high grounds. *Skittering* Finished its meal time as the sound dissipated. Valcomix then takes out his device and checks his location with quick fingers and shock.

## Playground WA. Sector: N/A

## The time is 6:29 pm of 07/07/3175

Smiling behind his mask. Knowing he is close to where he needs to go. This is his chance, but first, to exhume something that was causing such a disturbance. Putting his muscles to work to carry the top layer of debris and move it away. Creating loud sounds. **"It's not best to make loud sounds."** The nervous soldier suggests as he attempts to climb down**. "Use the night vision and heat signature mod of your gas mask and give me any warning. We'll regroup with the others at 6:50pm."** Valcomix says due to his own selfishness and curiosity. The ally does as he is told. Seeing green and dark spots. Nothing else except for the orange blotch standing on the green below him. After some minutes had passed, Valcomix could see a puddle of glowing black liquid. He continues to excavate the substance. Appearing on the lookout's sight is something red and is moving. He then stands up to see the figure. Then...

*Thwack* The sound Valcomix heard from inside his mask then... *Thump* It sounded heavy. This alerts Valcomix to keep a keen eye on the roof. On the street is a rolling helmet and now a damaged rifle. He runs and jumps, climbing the roof. Seeing that...the ally is belly up and groaning. Relieved that he is alive.

*Crash* Valcomix quickly drops, landing on his rear. Winces at the pain for a bit. He gathers himself and makes his way toward the pile of rubble... But the pile is gone. Noticing that there is a tall, muscular being wearing a hoodie and a pair of sweatpants. Seeing it reach for something. A metal cylinder similar to a thermos. Valcomix rushes angrily. **"Stop!"** The tall being quickly turns to Valcomix and takes a stance. He responds, holding his weapon firmly and aiming it at the joints. Setting it to a single shot.

The tall being moves forward with a single leap. Then attempts to punch Valcomix, then dodges down. *Shot fired* To no avail did it hit. The stranger then responds with a forceful punch to his torso. Yet, Valcomix blocks the blunt blow with his rifle. Still, that single pound was enough to injure him and dent his weapon. Now deemed unreliable. He tosses his weapon aside and gets into a fighter's stance. Calmly breathing. The stranger was quick to do the same. Moving slowly towards one another. Anticipating who will strike first. Valcomix is eager to put a combo in. The first hit was dodged, the second one blocked, and the third strike Was taken into the chest. The fourth one got Valcomix a strong left jab to his mask. His mask rolls onto the concrete. Dripping warm crimson from his mouth. He spits with a smile and again gets back into a stance. [Old dialect] Valcomix comprehends what the stranger said. ***"Exciting?"*** Recognizing the spoken language. **"That thing you and I are after is luring the Creates. Let me have it."** Valcomix orders grudgingly. The tall being glares at him. **"No. It doesn't concern you, and it shouldn't. Now, how do you understand my language?"** The stranger asks while intrigued yet confused and serious. **"I took a private session on all the historical language and other stuff."** Valcomix answers with a snarky attitude, and then he remembers the self-education.

The tall being then just walks to Valcomix. Standing over him and peering down at him. Valcomix glares from below with clenched fists. Now, seeing each other's faces. The stranger has brown hair, thick, strong, dried skin with a complexion that is red-brown and pigments of yellow under the cracks. Dull-gray pupils. Wearing: a light gray hoodie and a pair of black sweatpants, as well as black sneakers. The stranger then reads his nameplate, grips Valcomix's shoulder, and painfully squeezes him. The pain is throbbing. Holding back his voice as he bears it. Clenching his fists. **"What are you after?"** The tall guy asks emotionlessly as he digs into Valcomix's shoulder. **"That thermos, Creates are attracted to it!"** Valcomix yells loudly, answering fast. The tall guy releases the harsh pressure but still has his grip on Valcomix. **"How do you know of this?"** The stranger asks, and Valcomix... **"I don't know what that**

**is."** He answers with no reason to hesitate. **"Are you with them as well?"** The stranger asks angrily.

**"I'm a soldier! What else?"** Now, he is sweating profusely and burning as his shoulder is being punished. **"Really, I don't know what that is. I saw creates surrounding this area, trying to dig up a pile of rubble. I came to investigate and check to see what it was. Just finish this interrogation already!"** Grunting painfully as he tries to breathe and keep calm. **"You're not done being questioned."** The tall muscular being says and eases his hold. The pain in Valcomix's shoulder is just a common pinch now. Remembering his proud smiles and achievements. His tears begin to fall, yet he still smiles brilliantly. Showing this expression to the tall guy. He stares into his eyes, understanding he went through hardships no one should go through. **"Then ask all your questions."** Valcomix says with a vicious smile, as if accepting his new fate. The tall stranger then pinches his nerve. Putting Valcomix in a temporary stasis.

The tall guy then returns to the roof, takes out the smartphone device from the injured kid's pocket, and searches the apps. Pressing the distress signal; as well as damaging the device accidently from doing so. It begins to transmit. The stranger then takes out Valcomix's device and other items. Only seeing that he owned one full magazine, a device, and a bundle of white ash sticks that burn when the tip is snapped off. He reads his name tag as he breaks one. *Chuckles* Turning his sight to the dark glowing substance. Inspecting the thermos, and it is seeping out a bit. With a twist of the lid, seals it. He then has Valcomix upon his back. Now leaving the area through the opposite passage that Valcomix arrived from.

# PART IV

After some time, it's a new day. Now morning. Valcomix awakens with a stir. Trying to sit up as slowly as possible. Agonizing pain surges from his shoulder and head. *Murmuring* His way of speaking is slurred. *Snickering* *Teasing laughter* **"Relax. Our buddy here kind of gave you the worst treatment."** Looking to his right, he sees a girl with a healthy brown complexion that seems smooth to the touch sitting on a metal chair. Staring into her bright, shining violet pupils. She then smiles generously as she leans in the chair, resting her chin in her soft hands. Valcomix turns his gaze away from her and observes the room. There are gray, unpainted walls and bedrock flooring. Foldable tables with research documentation, logs, notes, a laptop, textbooks, and many other knowledgeable resources. A dusty bookshelf. Two old vintage oil lamps. Two mats lay evenly on the floor and a recliner that he is lying on.

Noticing that he is also nude and bandaged up. Indifferent, as his body aches, mainly his shoulder as it twitches. He then gets up from the seat. **"Where am I?"** He asks as he stands up, walking over to the two of them. The girl blushes upon the sight of his stature. **"TSinged, where did you get this one? Adorable, lost,**

**knows our language, and definitely not shy. Showing off is bad."** She asks keeping her eyes...

**"Hello."** Smiling and staring. The girl with long ocean blue hair that has a dark navy-blue gradient blend to light blue at the tips that reach the middle of her back says teasingly. Then she blows a chilling air onto his prided buddy. This makes Valcomix jump to the side and he glares at her. **"At least it got you some type of excitement. My name is TÖ-Slüdge. And do remember that I am the most dangerous of the group. Later."** She warns him in a joking matter, and Valcomix keeps glaring at her as she is wearing a thin, short black t-shirt and a medium black skirt that reaches her thighs. It flows and floats and has white wavey lines. A small, thin, stainless-steel chain is hooked to it. Leaving what seems like the basement, using the ladder. Valcomix still kept staring at the exit.

**"Don't keep that expression; it will only entice her more. Unless you want to keep being played with. Valcomix, this is our hideout left by them. Being affiliated with a soldier is disappointing. But you're unique. You can speak our language, and you seem calm around me. We have a young member who didn't care and another who wants to cremate you, but she says that to all of us. Just let her be."** He notifies Valcomix who barely understood any of what he just heard. Summarizing. TÖ-Slüdge is the pervert. One is an anti-social sociopath with a temperament issue. One is questionable. This guy is his only shield and means to survive if he answers to his authority. His own concluded gist of his predicament.

**"If I may get something to wear."** Valcomix requests, and the tall stranger turns and flinches as the guest is fully here... All exposed. The guy then leaves and soon returns by throwing a box of lost and found clothing articles below. There are some pants and a single jacket. Reluctant to put them on. The guy looks down at the box and then at Valcomix. Valcomix takes the box and himself to a darker corner. Putting on the silver pants with the sandals, then the graphic red jacket: a white car driven by a crow blowing fire. *Chuckling* **"That is bad."** The tall guy says with a smirk. Valcomix can't complain; at least he is wearing something. Still, he is annoyed. **"We will not allow you to wear a hazard suit or a lab coat. Here, we can be comfortable. Get used to this type of life. You're safe until you slip up."** He says reassuringly, but Valcomix feels as if this is his new prison with office space. He then takes a seat and rummages through the logs but isn't focusing as his mind wanders elsewhere.

He isn't allowed anywhere except the basement zone. Wondering about his two high-ranked battle brothers. Remembering the good times... *Laughing* Getting the guy's attention. **"Sorry, just thinking about my glory days and the mishaps as I tried more than the others. I was just a pipsqueak who wanted to climb the ranks."** He says sadly as he smiles on. The tall guy then stands up. **"I'll leave you alone with your thoughts. You can leave whenever, but you won't survive. Try to adjust here; it's better than being dead. If you are frustrated, don't hold back. I'll make sure no one disturbs you. My name is TSinged, so please use our names. Okay, Valcomix."** He gifts to Valcomix and leaves the basement with haste.

Now alone. Dwelling in silence. His entire life flashes before his eyes. Times he felt weak, days he mourned fallen comrades, seeing the fright in the strongest of warriors, and then red eyes above him. Agitated, agonizing, dread, fear, detest, happiness... Feelings swarm his mind. Every session of trials, whether it was by the judges or the outside world. Helpless, hopeless, and mainly weak. Knowing well that the choices he made brought him here. He asked for this, but it's not the way he wanted to go. His own curiosity led him down a path where he is labeled as treasonous. Remembering the long message as his ruling was final. **"I just wanted to be like you. Respected."** Distraught.

Angry and annoyed at himself, mainly because he was close to...

He clenches his hands as his eyes are shut, gritting his teeth. Trying to escape from the morbid thought. He takes a steady breath. *"I'm safe, I'm safe."* Repeating this quietly to himself, trying to calm down. Afraid still. **"You are safe."** Listening to a soothing voice as he slowly opens his eyes and turns to the direction of the voice. The girl with the deep blue hair is leaning close to him her shining violet pupils are mirroring Valcomix as he sees himself. **"TSinged told me you were down here alone with your thoughts. Not the best idea he had. Drastic changes can be much on the mentality and can lead a person to harsh things to others and themselves. For now, you are okay. TSinged may not approve of you going outside, but most don't agree to his terms anyway. He is just the nanny of our group."** She says eagerly with a generous smile flashing her bright whites. **"Let's go outside. This basement isn't the best to leave a guest at his lonesome. Just stay close to me, but don't touch me. I'm dangerous that way."** She warns him as her expression is serious but with a smile. Valcomix hesitates, quickly realizing that it will be best to have something else on his mind.

**"I cannot disregard his order. I have to remain down here."** Valcomix says as he is tempted to go but doesn't want to upset him. Holding his shoulder as he rubs the memorial ache. The girl then closes her eyes for a moment. Showing off a smile, but it twitches. Something has really annoyed her. **"Stay here for a tad moment."** She says reassuringly that she will return soon. Moving quickly out of the basement. Her expression was terrifying. Angry yet cute. Valcomix chuckles. That goes away fast by a single...

**"TSinged!!!"** Sounding scary with murderous intentions. Hearing heavy footsteps from above. **"What is it now? And be courteous to our new guests. He is studying down there."** He tells her as if mocking her with a fancy accent. Valcomix may not see what is happening, but he knows when someone has messed with the wrong person. **"Courteous? You don't even know the definition! It was just last night that you first kidnapped him without any reason as to why! Second, you get into a round of fisticuffs! Exchanging blows doesn't count as talking! Then you interrogate him, knock him out, and have him remain in the basement! Think about your crime... You will have a decent conversation with him as to why he is here. You're responsible for him, and you leave him by his lonesome in the dark, both metaphorically and literally!"** She is sound as there is no back talk. Then comes the punishment.

*Painful grunts and hisses* **"I get it; now please stop touching me! Wait... Stop, this is not a joke. Alright, I'm sorry!"** Listening to the troubled, tall, strong guy being handled by her small stature is a little funny, but it's highly terrifying as to what got him scared. **"You're apologizing to the wrong person!"** The finisher is here as the guy falls from above, landing shoulder-first upon the hard flooring. The tall guy looks above angrily then to Valcomix, who is confused and concerned. Seeing the menacing expression. TSinged change his attitude fast as he now is sitting up and holding his shoulder. Turning his focus to Valcomix. **"I do apologize for the actions I took. I didn't give you any type of reasons for me doing so. I will explain later when everyone is around. I do apologize."** Sounding sincere, Valcomix smiles not of happiness but of the altercation of the nagging women beating down the strongest men. It happens many times. Now, he feels sorry for the guy for having to take such a punishment. **"It's a deal, TSinged."** Valcomix reaches his hand out to TSinged, and he gladly takes it. Seeing them now somewhat buddies, she can't help but smile proudly as she observes from above.

# PART V

**"TSinged, I'm taking that pup outside."** She says excitedly as she points to Valcomix. They both turn their sights on her. TSinged is worried as his eyes are wide open. **"It's not safe for him to go out there!"** TSinged declares, not prone to the idea of Valcomix going out in the open. **"TSinged,"** Valcomix says his name stoically. Then, TSinged folds his arm, waiting for him to continue. **"She will protect me."** Saying this, determined and serious, he gazes into TSinged's eyes. Peering down at Valcomix, then spying on TÖ-Slüdge, who waves at him from above. Annoyed. He steps back. **"Go on. But do be safe; you're only a human."** Saying this as if persuading him not to go, and to think best about his choice. Valcomix smiles generously and with innocence. **"Now that you have permission, let's go, pup**." Deep blue says fast; with vitality, she races down the hall. Valcomix glares her way but is smiling. **"I am not a pup."** He isn't keen on the nickname. **"Yes, you are."** TSinged murmurs, and Valcomix chuckles. **"Later, nanny,"** Valcomix says eagerly as he continues. TSinged starts to chuckle. **"Have fun."** He tells his guest, but Valcomix is already gone.

Now above. Valcomix then breathes a sweet-smelling aroma into the air as he stretches. Flinching from the ache that lingers through his shoulder. Observing his whereabouts. Seeing that he is in a hallway and the entrance/exit way is damaged by an intense heat. Upon the sight of burn marks and soot. Outside is the plaza as he continues walking feeling the walls. A marble-stoned plaza with cracks and other disastrous damage shows proof of fighting. Surrounding the area are huge piles of rubble and collapsible buildings. Then ahead is a street beaten by nature. To the left is a town's remains. As if ruins called back to nature as moss and trees grow on them, on top of them, or inside the structures. Holding them intact. To his right is the woods with thick, luxuriant trees and brush with dark bark and violet leaves that are bearing a variety of fruits.

Quietly taking in the morning's new gift as he sees life with his own eyes. The sky is a bright gray where spots of light give the clouds a shining silver glow. Again, he takes in the sweet aroma with a smile. Then, he feels the gentle, chilling breeze, which causes him to shiver. **"The outside isn't the best place for Homo Sapiens. Due to many dangers that linger. Are you afraid of a little cockroach and cold weather?"** The girl asks, whispering in his ear, then blows into it. He again steps to the side frantically and glares at her. Seeing her mischievous smile along with those softly lifted pupils. His heart beats as he blushes. **"No, I have been a C.O.A.T.S. soldier for years and faced worse difficulties."** Saying this proudly with a smirk. She nods her head and walks past him as if not intrigued. **"Those times you had others and carried guns. Also, had security to call in for backup. Now you are a man not protected by the elements, no weapon, but all you have now is your pride."** She says the truth with a harsh but gentle annoyed tone. **"I'm not weak, and I can be crafty."** He says, glaring at her for that remark she made. He follows after her. Into the woods, they go.

Traversing through the path where, violet, and crimson leaves scatter from the blackened trees onto the cyan grass. Valcomix is bewildered at the sight of the vegetation as the old text didn't color the world as it was supposed to be. Staring above, not seeing what's in front of him. **"Valcomix!"** She shouts, frightened by his foolishness; he awakens, but... *Painful cry* His arm and leg get caught in a thorny vine. Both his ligaments are in pain. Then he sees that the flooring below him is thriving with these bright blue vines with orange spikes. Digging into his flesh. She comes rushing to his aid. Remaining calm as much as possible, not to jostle roughly but to better his position to use his hand. Then, appearing is her being. Her arms and legs are shining from a viscous clear coating. Staring at her skirt. **"I would smack you and end your existence, melting your frame. Eyes away."** She sounded serious, and he turned his gaze to her slender arms instead. The clear coating drips onto the vines. Causing a burning reaction. Now free, he then unravels his entanglement using his free hand, avoiding the bubbling areas.

**"It's best to pay attention to your surroundings and keep sight of what's in front of you. C.O.A.T.S. soldier. Peek at me again and I'll..."** She is agitated. Her eyes brighten to a pink color as her arms drip a heavy liquid discoloring the ground. Threatening. He follows her but at a distance safe for his wellbeing. Not letting him notice that she is blushing and smiling.

After walking some distance, they reach a pond colored like milk. Valcomix is awed by the sight of the opening hidden by poisonous plants. Mainly dark, slimy, rotten green colored poison: Ivy, Sumac, and Singing Nettles. Then, wrapping around the trees are vibrant orange with a white gradient long bell-like flower. Nectar drips from them, gliding down to the base of the tree. Valcomix is curious as his hand is reaching for the flower...

**"I never met someone that is willing to accidentally expire themselves for being attracted to deadly Foxgloves."** She warns him, and he draws his hand away. Admiring the flower. *Sighs* **"Listen up, pup, this outside world that you are exposed to now is dangerous, as TSinged mentioned. No human can**

**survive out here. Animals, plants, insects, and just the weather can cause the strongest of you C.O.A.T.S. a strange humiliation to die from. So, don't touch everything you see, and don't wander too much. Pay attention or lose the only life given to you. Now, turn around. I'm going to swim."** She says with concern that his curiosity will really kill him. He understands as he listens to every word. Noticing that she is uncovering herself, he quickly turns. But peeks a bit at her ebony back. It's only fair to see for he has been seen.

*Splash* Hearing the sound of something dropping in the water, he turns and sees ripples upon the surface only. The black t-shirt and skirt are tossed aside upon the grass. Now, back to the silence but only his own. *Rustling* Hearing animal movement for the first time during his walk, as there is something with fur over the brush behind him. Back to his thoughts as he sits upon the grass hugging his knees. Remembering the envelope. *Deep breath* Remembering the messages. Then, all the events of what transpired yesterday afternoon. *"What were those Creates trying to obtain? They are mindless. I'm exposed to the outside world without any protection. Dorm will not allow me in. I can't return anyway. I'm here as I wished. But how are they? I told Criyo that I would see him soon. I put even myself in danger. I'm sorry."* He says to his imaginative brothers and sisters that held him high. Balling his fists with tears falling on his face.

**"Depressed still?"** She asks out of sincerity and concern as she kicks the water, steadying her body above it. Resting her head, gazing at him. He lifts his head and gazes at her. Now, eye to eye. Saddened by the events. **"I just feel guilty, and I accepted the punishment. I'm at fault for abandoning them."** Releasing his frustrations. Seeing the tears fall from his frame. There is nothing much she can do to comfort but just to hear his cries.

**"What is it that you want to do? If you return to them, you will be..."** She mentions, as gentle as one can be when seeing a stranger is in a dire situation. He lightly rubs his neck, knowing of the consequences. **"I want to let those who were there with me through difficult days that I will be leaving and that I will be fine."** He says with a solemn smile. She sees that there is an intense despair behind his smile. She is terrified for him. **"Thank you for taking me out, but I want to journey back."** Requesting of her as he stands up, facing ahead on what he wishes to run away from.

**"Too much pride will lead you to disappointment."** She warns Valcomix, who wipes away his tears with the sleeve and then responds with a false smile. **"I'm a**

**C.O.A.T.S. soldier until I fully resign."** A brave persona lingering with doubt and fear. He is able to be seen through. *"Foolish."* Whispering a spiteful term as she gets out of the water. Putting on her clothes. After finishing, she glares at the irresponsible child, and he does the same. She then leads the guests to their return.

## Playground WA, Sector: N/A

## The time is 3:31 pm of 07/08/3175

Elsewhere, a C.O.A.T.S. soldier uses her device to pinpoint the last location where two soldiers were ambushed. **"We arrived at the prime area where our fellow brother became lost. A horde of Creates was here and was devoured."** She announces through the contact radio within her modified gas mask. The group of ten investigate the area. A patch of rubble and then a long-cracked flooring. **"Ma'am, you think our damsel is down here?"** A hazy voice as he and another shine their lights into the dark tunnel. The higher rank, N4E, blocks his light quickly. **"Remember the report."** She orders calmly, not to summon what may be below. **"One of our own was on the roof, viewing, then ambushed from behind. Still spared, and another is gone."** She tells the guy in case he has forgotten. He then turns off his light and his buddy's.

**"Ma'am. My hand is raised; we found certain items."** Hearing another soldier through contact. Sounding confused yet frightened. Turning her sights, she locates several C.O.A.T.S. gathering near the wall. One has their hand raised. She gestures for the two to follow after her. Now, all gathered and silently observe the removed mask. Close to it are the white ash sticks, bent weapons, magazines, and the device. The lead then inspects the helmet. Dried blood, small amounts of it near the filter. She then proceeds to turn on her light to a lower lumen upon her mask. Searching the area. **"Nothing else."** She alerts as if hitting a dead-end. Now tapping her forehead.

*Static* *silence* **"Sir Sourn, we found the damsel's belongings. His weapon is damaged, yet this is odd. All of his belongings are left organized against the wall. What is our next phase?"** Asking in monotone. Awaiting orders.

## ELSEWHERE

A tall-statured man ceases his movement, and those following do the same. *Sighs* Looking up to the gray skies above him. He then kicks at the ground, creating a dust lift. **"Return immediately. Our fellow man is MIA. Be wary of Creates; we have activity on these streets."** He orders without showing signs of emotion. Conflicted in mind to disembark himself from the mission as Valcomix would to aid others. Looking at the numbers behind him. **"Valcomix, he is entirely strong enough to hold his own. Stay alive just a bit longer, soldier."** Telling himself. Standing vast gazing at the obstacles of disgusting walking spoiled of meat. Seeing them journey ahead from yards away, clustered up together as if drawn to something. **"Everyone! Aim your weapons, and steady your breathing! Line the shot and fire!"** Yelling angrily as he readies his rifle. Others do as well, lining up next to him. Some sit down, a few of them lie down, and the rest keep standing. All ranked the same. N2E. Red bullets scatter, spiraling at the targets. Going through soft tissue and rotten bones as orange and brown liquid now color the tattered streets as they tumble over. The many in hazard suits fire hastily down this horde.

From over yonder on top of the roofs, someone is watching this event with a disgruntled expression. *Tch* Disgusted at the sight of their uniform. Moving sight to another point of view. Seeing that there is a collapsed building with those creatures huddling over, trying to unearth something. Approaching closer. *Cracking* *Skittering* Long hairy legs become bare underneath from where this individual stands. The temperature increases, becoming scolding hot. The hard material begins to glow and smoke. Close to the edge. Now falling. Spreading the intensity around. Causing the creatures to fall with visual burns. *Sizzling* The hairy legs retract fast. Giving them a burn. *Rumbling* The grovel of loose debris quakes. Something fast is approaching. Avoiding the impaction as one does to shelter themselves from harm. Then *Crash* *Smash* Large rubble scatters around. A roach bursts out with a sinister dark orange and green neon color mouth. The individual is close to it. Then stares at the huge cracks, hearing digging. Then, the individual hurries to retrieve a cylinder-like thermos and walk away. *Burst* *Hissing* Sloppy slurping sounds can be heard afterwards. **"Why would you scatter these about?"** A young woman's voice asked in a complaining tone examining the thermos.

# PART VI

## BACH IN THE BASEMENT

TSinged sees that his friend is agitated as her eyes focuses on Valcomix. He is immersed in the logs, ignoring all that is around him. Reading note after note, log after log. Documented knowledge added to his memory reservoir. His eyes are wide, just like a child discovering hidden clues and secrets. Smiling joyously. This agitates her much more as TSinged is uncomfortable feeling cold pressure in the warm area except the one who is causing this is... Turning his sight to Valcomix. She then gives up, showing a sad and complex expression. Turning away from seeing him, she lays her head on the table.

**"What happened? You both left with excitement and came back silent and grumpy."** TSinged asks concerned for both of them. Soft violet and sad pupils pierce his sight; causing a headache. **"Just talk about it."** He orders, holding back his impatience. *Snarling* Making such an odd sound confuses him. **"He wants to return back to being in their custody. How can someone know that they're in danger and still walk with a loose smile? It terrifies me. He terrifies me."** She says as she is conflicted, upset, and worried. TSinged stays silent and gazes at Valcomix. **"It's their pride as a soldier."** He concludes. Valcomix then stands up from the hard seat and stretches. Turning away and picks up the atlas, then moves the chair to the only laptop. He then begins to type.

Working for hours without a break, staring at the computer. Finally finished. Expressing a grandeur's smile. TSinged is elsewhere while TÖ-Slüdge is resting. A written note is in his grasp. Walking towards her, he lays the note beside her. Admiring her beauty as he blushes. Shaking his head. Now stern and upright. He climbs the ladder. Lurking in their hallways. Opening different doors. One room has a variety of potted plants, another is a fully equipped laboratory, then a shower/locker room. Now sights one with a plaque reading **"Biohazardous."** Opening the door, seeing metal containers similar to a thermos. All are organized in glass cabinets. Entering the room and turning on the lights. He looks around the room and finds his uniform discarded into the only trashcan he has seen so far. Removing his colorful clothing and puts the one thing that he is always going to be familiar with. Now clothed.

*Deep breath* He heads out of the room and walks fast out of the building. Figuring out his location. He then rummages through the debris. Finding rusted pipes, steel tubes, electrical wires, metal wires, and metal plates. Picking out what is better as a temporary weapon. He takes one of the rusted pipes and swings it onto the marble. *Bang* It snaps. He tries the same method with steel pipes that are less bent and formed. The one he holds has a sharp end. He chooses another one with similar characteristics.

Now equipped. He heads into the ruined city, not looking back. Just minutes of walking through the alleyways, he sees a small group of Creates. Gripping both pipes and rushes. *Thwack* Bashing the softest part of their skull. Down. He continues on. Looking above, notices that the limited light is fading. *Tch* **"I have to hurry."** He tells himself, annoyed at the sky. Now, jogging through the city. Turning corners smoothly. For a sudden moment, he felt warmth and saw an orange glow in the corner of his right eye. He is tempted to look, but shakes his head, and runs on. Slightly out of breath after a distance sprint. He walks on, putting both pipes into one hand to check his pockets. Wide-eyed and frantic. **"Where are they? Did he really take out everything from my pockets?"** He asks, afraid, as he searches around his area. He then quickly closes his eyes and takes a silent breath. Calming his heartrate and mind. Turning to the narrow alley. Using the passage to scale the buildings. Now, on top of a building. Feeling safe for a mere moment. He now looks around.

Carefully hopping from rooftop to rooftop. Measuring the distances with the pipes. After a while, he notices a glimmer of light below. Climbing down and dropping onto the hard concrete. *Splash* Walking on a puddle. He investigates a device belonging to a rookie soldier. There is a splash of crimson on it. Turning on its flashlight function. His eyes go wide, and he becomes furious. Silent rage. Seeing corpses of a unit, mangled bodies scattered around. Spilling out their vital warmth, now cold He then uses the device. "Emergency call." With no hesitation, he presses it. *Ringing* **"This is Diim Sourn of the base's field training functioning. What is..."** Instantly cut off. **"Valcomix here. Sourn, what is your location? I have a unit massacred and I can hear you firing rounds in the background. Send me your location."** Sounding upset as he barks his order with a sharp tongue. In an instant, he has their location. **"I'll see you soon."** He says fast and begins his rush, following the red line to the green dot.

## BACK AT THE PLAZA

TSinged is carrying a four-eyed deer with straight, massive horns. A bulk body in one arm and a backpack in his other. A bright orange light is approaching him. Coming into the visual is a girl with a healthy, light peach complexion, almost pink and glowing. Gradient of flame-colored pupils. Medium length of burning flame-like hair with a greenish tint flaming ponytail spiraling softly. Wearing a scarlet crop top, black polyester cargo pants, and black boots. Radiating heat that makes TSinged back away from her. Letting her enter in first. He follows her at a safer distance.

Examining the basement area. She sees that TÖ-Slüdge is resting peacefully; there is no one else. She then kicks the chair that TÖ-Slüdge is using. Disturbing her nap, she glares into a flame. **"He's gone. Where to?"** Brief question with a threatening tone. Glaring angrily as her arms are coated heavily in a clear liquid. *Drip* *Drop* The liquid colors the flooring and creates small holes. Turning to Valcomix. He isn't here. Confused yet annoyed towards the burning female. TSinged now enters the basement, putting himself in between them. Scolded on both sides as he pushes them from one another. **"You two cannot have a dispute when there is a human who is weak to your nature."** Sounding like a referee and tries to taunt Valcomix. He isn't here. Now both are staring at TÖ-Slüdge, whom they believe is guilty.

**"He was there typing; I was bored. So, I took a nap. Then now attacked and accused by her."** Pointing her finger to the other female. Both glaring with hate-filled spite at the other. Ready to rip a throat. TSinged is nervous. **"If he's gone, then it was his choice. I thought you accidentally killed him by finally wanting to touch a man."** A smirk upon her face as said that remark. Taunting TÖ-Slüdge who is whispering a term that is out of context. She is furious, and her demeanor becomes silent. *Rumbling* The room is now fixated on the trouble above. Now, there are more eyes upon the flaming female. Agitated. *Grunting* The flame exits the basement area to get away from their judgmental glare.

TSinged becomes relieved as she leaves. TÖ-Slüdge does feel guilty. **"Don't burden yourself with his leaving."** He says, assured, knowing well that the fault is the one who made the choice. He then sees a note. Picking up the written words and reads them. **"I'm going to find him. That fool is going to attempt to leave on his own."** TSinged is now furious. Slamming the note onto the table, creating a cavity. With a single jump, he clears to the above flooring. Surprised by his outburst and posthaste attitude. TÖ-Slüdge is curious about how a quick read got him emotional. She then reads it for herself. Written is:

Thank you for hospitality. I cannot leave those who have been there for me. I will be okay. When someone decides an action there are consequences. Even if it's unfair. I chose this. I don't know why there are *markings on the maps but I have checkpoints that all of you want. Download the information onto a device from the computer. Safe journey, I will be gone now. Live strong since a human like me can.*

Only by knowing him for a brief moment, she impacted by his goodbye. Such gratitude. He was a fun character. Just too proud as a soldier. Doubting that he will be okay. She knows his intention and the event he will face. As he mentioned, but so soon. Stricken feelings swirl. Noticing that her skin is becoming dry due to the interaction with that female's heat. She leaves the basement area and heads down the dark hall.

# PART VII

## ELSEWHERE

There is a fire surrounding the soldiers. Plenty of them shooting, others are feeding the flames. Now dark. Terrors of the night flood, infesting the Playgrounds are...

**COCKROACHES**: Giant car sized beetles that are mainly hungry most times. Night crawlers. Blind. Still is a boss insect ranked 4 on the threat level scale but are hard to deal with when in groups. Ambush type creatures and love to set traps. Light and fire is something that they avoid. Weakness: poke it in the stomach.

*Rapid firing* *Yelling* The fire is dying, and a soldier quickly pours oil onto the area. It doesn't burn so big. The soldier then throws a lit ash stick but misses it. *Gurgling* A roach makes it in, and all soldiers aim their rounds at it. No avail. *Terrorized screaming* **"Hold your fire!!!"** An excited yell is heard and they obey. From above, something comes from above. Landing on the back of the roach, stabbing its head with one of his pipes, it quickly fell underneath. Stabbing the belly. Warm, vile of thick magenta pools through from the pipe. Valcomix can tell that it's afraid. It's becoming wild and desperate for life. Now, it's just twitching. Valcomix stabs it over again and pulls the pipe he left within the head.

Everyone gives him attention. Covered in a thick magenta color. Then, from behind comes another, but Valcomix smiles at it. Then, he slides to be where it's vulnerable, pierces one of the pipes into the belly, and continues to thrust repeatedly with the other. Convulsing on the concrete as it leaves a trail, he pulls the pipe out of it and pushes it into the dying flame area. Walking over to a rookie soldier that was almost going to be mourned. He takes his ash sticks and oil from the person's pocket. Valcomix calmly, with a smile, pours the oil on the carcass and lights it ablaze. Then puts the items back in the soldier's pockets. **"Trouble with rookies."** Sounding boisterous and proud. *Laughter* A tall man from a part of the crowd stands and confronts Valcomix. **"Insanely wild! Brings back bad memories of a soldier that gets excited torturing the Playgrounds more than myself."** They clasp hands and pat each other's back. **"Listen up, Valcomix will be taking charge of our survival!"** Diim Sourn yells, and Valcomix stands straight, glaring at the many.

**"Weak, spineless, scum dwellers!!! Humans are stronger than roaches, so why do you cower seeing them!!! We are to exterminate! Take**

**in arms, aim at their plump belly, and make them bleed! Stay grouped up! Did we call for a butterfly?!"** He yells, standing vast, peering at his comrades. **"We have two of them taking flight, arriving in another couple of minutes!"** Sourn bursts quickly. Valcomix smiles towards the Soldiers, feeling nostalgic. **"Let's survive this and enjoy glory as well as a scrumptious meal. I am famished!"** He boasts as he really is hungry. *Victorious rant* Swarmed by a lot of them, and they're in high spirits.

## ELSEWHERE/DISTANCE AWAY

TSinged is rushing to find Valcomix. Serious as he even tosses the roaches or just throws them aside. Ramming himself through the many. Noticing that there is more than usual tonight. He sees that most of them are juveniles. **"Valcomix, don't be eaten already because I'm going to chew you out myself."** Rushing with a serious expression. While occurring at the same time TÖ-Slüdge is sitting in the shower room. Pelted by the cold water, clearing her mind, but it isn't hopeful as she whispers... *"Valcomix, stay well for a bit longer. TSinged do find him."*

As promised... *Whirling* Everyone Is looking above as if a helicopter is coming. Soldiers jumping and waving, getting the pilot's attention. Sourn gives

Valcomix the thumbs up. Valcomix aims his up high. After a bit of protocol, the ladder then comes down. Valcomix and Sourn hold it steady. Valcomix nods to Sourn. Both look above for a signal. Flashing light in a sequence. Showing both thumbs up to the one who notices it first. Valcomix. Then, a sequence of lighting commences. Counting each flash. He uses his left hand showing two open palms and then three fingers. Sourn then signals two fingers and waves them, followed by a steady open hand. Valcomix, with a concerned look, begins to signal what Sourn signaled to the one reading his signals inside the butterfly.

Valcomix then starts to pull each lower rank towards the ladder. Climbing one at a time onto the helicopter. Sourn then gazes at his comrade, but Valcomix smiles brightly and taps his shoulder, pointing to his own face. He is contaminated by the outside air. Now, labeling himself as filthy. Sourn ruffles his spiky hair. Both hug one another, for this is their goodbye. Sourn scales the ladder and Valcomix... Using the device. "Emergency call" Diim Sourn sets the emergency call to the conference. *Static* *Silence* Every C.O.A.T.S.'s receiver is ready.

**"This is Valcomix's last call and words. I am proud to have to have been a C.O.A.T.S. soldier. We are strong! No longer will we fear the outside world!**

**Claim back our lost states! For those who fought with me and those whom I joined in battle! Thank you! To all standing C.O.A.T.S..."** *Crying for a moment with happiness* **"IT'S BEEN AN HONOUR!!!"** Valcomix is joyous even when the situation is a bit of a predicament. He sits down, waiting for fate. His life flashes before his eyes. Closing his eyes and calm. Mild tears stream down his cheek. He was able to say goodbye proudly, but his end will be nasty and messy. *Laughing* The fire is dead, and the swarm is over him as he is prepared to exterminate. Their teeth sink in softly into his flesh.

*Growling* *Yark* Feeling a piercing wind. He got lucky once more as something just saved him. *Crunching* *Slobbering* *Chewing* Valcomix topples over, and the device's flashlight mod is still on. He can see teeth digging through the hard bodies of roaches, tearing them. Thick magenta drips through its gaps. It stops devouring and sniffs another corpse. Revolted by its scent. About to swipe Valcomix's putrid body away. Its paw is caught and then freed. The light and the scent disappeared. Feeling the rush of wind as he closes his eyes. Moments later. TSinged is carrying Valcomix's listless body. Covered in mucus, dirt, and blood. A smile still shines upon him. Laying him down gently outside of the hall of their hideout. TSinged sprints fast down the hall.

His sprinting echoes through the hallway. TÖ-Slüdge opens the shower room door. The dim lighting shows the flooring. Bloody shoe prints. Quickly putting on her clothes and rushing down the hall. Two others are already examining the fallen human. Indifferent while the other one remains in the dark, terrified of the sight. TÖ-Slüdge can see that he is smiling. So fragile, yet he remained prideful. He seems to be at peace. **"We'll have to bury him fast before he starts to have a foul odor."** The flaming female says, covering her nose. No respect. Coming out of the hallway...

**"Move."** Ordering with haste, he checks his pulse and a hand over his mouth. There is a faint pulse, yet no breathing. Not too late. **"Valcomix, are you giving up already? I take full responsibility for what will occur."** He announces to everyone and to the fallen warrior as he holds out a steel thermos. Opening it as a vapor seeps through.

The flame leaves, entering the hallway. A round silhouette rolls quickly, following after her. TSinged then turns the container upside down, and a small green and black hazy sphere quickly fuses into his bloodstream. It is too dark to see if it brought him life or just ended him entirely. TSinged and TÖ-Slüdge headed towards the basement, leaving his body exposed to the frigid air. Not wanting to disturb what may happen.

After some hours, the plaza becomes filled with grotesque creatures hungry for a fallen soldier. Walking slowly, reaching out with their disfigured hands. *Digging through flesh*

**TO BE CONTINUED...**

# EPISODE 2: INSTABILITY

## PART 1

Unbeknownst to his demise. There is no privilege of peace even in one's rest. Enraged with an intense surge of frustration. Digging through flesh and tearing away soft, rotted meat with teeth and claws. Surrounded by a horde of Creates that are easily downed. They try to reach for the newly formed; some do manage to grip its fur. The creature then rushes itself towards the wall and slams a sure number of them. *Crack* Not only damaging the surface of the wall. It snaps their bones. Rendering them unable to move and smashes in their skulls. It then picks a victim. Sharp nails violently tear apart the Create in half. Pooling its viscous existence onto the creature and onto the plaza. The creature is soaked in this vital carnage. Feeling calm, sensing a filled desire. *Inhale* *Exhale* Relief. Then, the feeling disperses. Snapping out of a euphoric state. *Growling* ***SCREEAHHHH!!!*** A scratching pitch scream pierces the area.

### BASEMENT AREA

TSinged jumps to his feet in fright and proceeds to take a stance. Others are also alerted. Looking at each other, confused. They remembered the corpse rotting on their plaza. At least, this is what the burning one recollects. **"Did he revive?"** TÖ-Slüdge asks curiously as she is afraid. TSinged exhales strongly. **"I suppose he did."** Answering her but not even certain himself. Just a hunch. He then ascends to the upper floor level. **"You are not going up there alone."** The burning one says with an upset tone and clenched fists. TSinged is calm and gently suggests... **"TÖ-Slüdge, remain here with Cretan. Fürthrived, please provide the light and, if necessary, fireworks."** He tells his team. The walking hearth radiates both with luminous orange and intense heat. Scorching the solid surface from where she stands. TSinged ignores her as he focuses above. Quick to leave. The burning one follows after. TÖ-Slüdge glares at her and smiles at the silhouette, who is the only one still able to sleep.

## BACK TO THE CARNAGE HAPPENING IN THE PLAZA

From Creates to now dealing with roaches. All partaking a feast upon the viscous orange substance soaking the plaza. The creature gouges the belly of the unaware few. Exposing the innards as it dissects them. Orange mixes with a deep magenta-like color.

The being squirms as the creature soaks its arms in its guts. Now, it has its jaws pried open, exposing its sharp white teeth and red tongue. Devouring. *Hissing* The insect is violently thrashing in pain but is rendered helpless. From the hallway is a light. The roaches eschew the luminated areas. *Hissing* Now, most are in pain as they are inflicted by radiative burns.

**"It's an infestation once again. Find his corpse if it isn't disposed of yet. I'll have to set myself to an intensity that will be rid of them fast."** She alerts him as she is already taking small steps and increasing her glow. The viscous orange is boiling and cleaned away. Now, leaving behind...

**"Foul odor, worse than the other time we had to clear them away."** TSinged reminds her as he steps away from her, not to be evaporated as well. He searches the wall to find where he had left Valcomix. Not there. Looking around the area; gazing through the dimness as the infestation is clearing away. Yet, something still remains. **"Our haven is going to have this stench for days unless the winds blow from the east to bring us the scent of the forest. I hate this stench."** She informs as well as wishes for it to go away. Having them scurry back into the dark, skittering towards the city. Avoiding to enter the forest. Smug expression, but that quickly disappears. Now, curiosity and annoyance are placed.

Both approach with caution as TSinged has his fists at the ready, and the burning one brightens the plaza. Scorching the surface and causing it to turn red. TSinged can feel his feet burning but chooses to ignore the sensation. Now fully visualized is...

# PART II

A single organism with black fur along with a thick curved tipped tail. Two long raised hairs as if they are its ears, which they are apparently. Its veins are scarlet red as they are exposed. Silver nails digging out meat from the roach's belly. The contents are questionable. Four sharpened, long canines shine as they begin to pierce the meat and fat. It is having a feast, leaving only a husk. Thick, dark magenta drools from its sloppy chewing. TSinged, and the burning one watches this disgusting behavior. The being is soaked heavily in meat and blood. Someone can no longer stomach such a sight. **"TSinged, you handle this thing."** Feeling quite nauseous as she covers her mouth and nose as if unable to keep things down. Walking away and dimming her light as she is weakened by the smell alone. TSinged watches her go towards the forest to erase the putrid scent of the plaza. *Retched* He sighs and then turns to the new creature before him. It finally finishes.

TSinged is now in a boxing stance, keeping sights and guard as a precaution for what it's about to do next. He doesn't want to be its next meal. The being finally opens its eyes, seeing a blurry vision but a hazy white blotch of a person that's in front of it. Tossing away the husk. *Silence* *Calm breathing* *Low growling* The creature is just standing there. Staring into its crimson irises. He takes a single step closer, realizing that it's shorter than himself. Short and skinny. ***"This creature isn't much of a threat. Every time I try to accost it, it steps slightly backward."*** Thinking to himself as he takes more steps forward, seeing that it is stepping back. But it isn't turning away. The creature is viewing a white blotch around the darkness. Then, it closes its eyes once more. Now, sensing two beings remaining in the plaza. There is a hazy blue figure in front of it and another one that is small behind it. It now notices a target.

TSinged takes another step closer, not even able to tell that the short and skinny being just lunged headfirst. Surprised by its speed. His right arm becomes a chew toy and a scratching post shredding away at his hoodie. Sharp nails pierced through his tough, hardened skin, as well as the jaw clamping hard. Quickly grabbing the creature by its head, it slams it hard onto the surface. *Bash* *Crunch* *Snarl* The creature's body is laid flat. TSinged holds his arm while standing upon the creature who doesn't want to yield. The creature sits up. *Footsteps* **"You have it pinned."** Says the burning one, who is still weakened by the scent of what lingers in the plaza. Then, she shines her light to have a clear sight of what is captured. Both glaring at the creature. It then opens its eyes, and its pupils shrink. ***SCREEAHHHH!!!***

Its banshee screech is causing them much more harm rather than its teeth and nails. The girl covers her ears while TSinged shuts its jaw. **"Turn off your light! This one has red eyes!"** Ordering her as he stops its horrid screeching. She obeys. She then uses her neutral glow that illuminates normally. Examining the being closely. The darkened sky is now becoming a light sheet of gray clouds. The creature scratches at TSinged's leg but misses. It then walks fast to the wall to where it once was before when it was disturbed. The same position, but the tail covers its eyes. Both now understand and realize...

**"This adorable thing, is that human?"** The walking hearth says in a confused tone. At the same time. **"Valcomix is alive."** TSinged is relieved that he wasn't called to an ending slumber. While the other is baffled, she isn't the only one who is. Raising his eyebrow as he looks at her.

# PART III

**"Really, you're into a furry?"** TSinged asked with a raised eyebrow. Then, he peers down at his arm. **"Can I ask you to watch over him while I go clean my arm?"** He asks as he walks towards the entrance. **"I hope he isn't an infectious type. I cannot deal with a virus again."** He mentions with an aggravated tone. The burning one just ignores his statement and complaining. Keeping sights upon the newly formed Valcomix. **"I just think most furs are adorable if it wasn't for their eating habits. Grotesque."** She comments, seeing the now calm and restful being. Petting his head softly. Smiling as the fur tickles her hand. Soon, TSinged returns with a sleeveless hoodie and bandages wrapped around his arm, covering the wounds that had been done. Concerned and disgusted by the new attitude she is showing Valcomix. She mostly never smiled but kept a smug expression occasionally when the two had unsightly arguments.

**"You're not being your usual self."** TSinged informs her as he stands behind her, peering down. **"I was just considering how TÖ-Slüdge labeled him as a pup. A kind of pet, and you took him in and announced that you were responsible for him. It will be best for you to put a leash on him before he bites more than just your arm."** She says with a smug smile that he recognizes. TSinged grumbles, then focuses on Valcomix. Knowing that the fault was on himself. Then Valcomix's paws grip the quick ligament, and his tail sways gently. Scratching his neck, he tries to open his eyes. The light stings them for a bit. *Grunting* **"Valcomix, relax; your body went through a change."** TSinged informs Valcomix. **"What?"** Confused as he is in tremendous pain and groggy. His eyes are burning, his head is throbbing, and his upper body feels crushed.

Slowly standing up using the wall for support. TSinged can tell that he is weak. Yet, considering what he was facing before the lights came on. He was lively and wildly active then, but now this is Valcomix. Both TSinged and the walking hearth have similar concerns. **"Why is it hard for me to see?"** Frustrated, he continues to rub the pain away, trying to keep them open. Unwilling to answer, as the answer should be obvious to him. Then, as a new instinct allows it, other senses are heightened/sharpened, but to no avail is it responding the information correctly. Getting a quick migraine. Now terrified, upset, and in pain. **"What happened to me?"** He asks as his memory plays what has transpired the night before. Now, calmly breathing and taking things slowly. He is still in pain, and he holds his head to ease his headache. **"I died."** Accepting the cause and knowing the circumstances of his actions. Shivering and feeling cold that isn't due to the weather.

**"Leave me alone with him for now, please."** TSinged pleads feeling responsible, and the burning one then stands up and pats his shoulder. Inflicting a painful burn. **"Taking responsibility?"** She asks with a serious tone. **"Yes."** He responds, and she goes away, leaving him a hurting shoulder. He now again focuses on Valcomix. **"Valcomix, listen to me."** He orders, and Valcomix has a smirk. TSinged can see that he is trying to remain brave. **"I am unable to do anything else at the moment. My body feels crushed, my legs are numb, and I am unable to see. I was at peace; I was ready to pass. I was done with dealing with this world! Every day was scary, protecting my fellow soldiers from danger! The only fun times I had was shooting Creates until..."** He yells frustratingly so, as he was willing to say goodbye. No more being afraid, no longer being an embarrassment to his fellow C.O.A.T.S. Nor, the responsibility of wearing the uniform nor the being that inflicted such fear into him. Listening to his shouting, TSinged knew that Valcomix had accepted his ending. Blaming himself and then receiving help is causing him pain. He is suffering right now.

**"Live for a new reason. I'm sorry that you are in pain, but keep living."** He says sternly. Heard words made his ear twitch. TSinged notices that he is listening. **"I don't understand your reasoning nor the reason for your choices. Help us, and you'll get to be free."** A pleading will from the tall guy as Valcomix heard an opportunity. **"We can aid one another."** Hearing TSinged trying to give him a reason to stay in a world he is terrified of. Yet knowing and remembering the many who still believed him. Those he fought with. Gulping down dry air and trying not to choke. **"I still owe a debt to the C.O.A.T.S. for taking care of me. I want to liberate the Playgrounds for them."** Valcomix is serious but has a shaky voice.

Anger, regret, pride, or maybe the type of fulfillment. But of this caliber? TSinged makes sure no one else is present as to what he said brashly. *Sighs* Understanding that Valcomix is getting more to the bargain, and it will cause more trouble to everyone else besides himself. Trying not to be influenced by his own selfishness. Remembering the comment spoken earlier. It's not fair on either side, but Valcomix still acts like a soldier and is also was willing to pass as one. Leaving him to himself will be the end of his second chance. Hoping that this is only his anger for having him become like this is talking.

**"I will allow it, but the others may not commigrate on your self-righteous mission."** He informs Valcomix. Then leaves the plaza fast to inform the others. Now, waiting patiently and, at the same time, getting used to his newly formed body. Moves his arms first to touch his face. Everything feels different, almost soft.

If only he could see what he has become. It is as if he is learning how to walk once more, taking simple steps while supporting himself along the wall.

**"What are you up to?"** He recognizes this mischievous voice and knows she is joyous, probably from seeing him struggle. *Snarling* **"Trying to walk again. Why are you not having your discussions with TSinged?"** He asks, trying to remove her from his presence. **"We already came to a close. We agreed, except for a certain individual who is upset about your terms. Now she is arguing with TSinged. I will inform you of this. Learning to use your abilities quickly won't be easy."** She informs him as he is annoyed, frightened, beaten, and still depressed.

Valcomix turns his head towards her voice. **"I just feel weak."** He admits with serious tone. **"You... You're not... Sorry, I don't have any words to say. Just survive longer this time. Also, stay positive; otherwise, we'll be dealing with another heated flame that I want to put out."** She says, trying to lighten his emotion, it's not much encouraging. Concerned about his well-being; he stumbles over himself. Seeing that he also has a dreadful headache.

Examining his fur and nails and how his form is prone to light. Understanding he is... **"You're not well**

**put in your element. Let me describe your mutation. You have black fur and red eyes. Suppose the light is bothering you this much. What are you adaptive to?"** TÖ-Slüdge hints as to what he has to know. He then confirms... **"The dark."** He answers with an exaggerated exhale. **"So, I must wait till the..."** He exclaims in a harsh tone. **"No, no, no, no. Stop with your 'I'm now pathetic attitude.' Other animals that are nocturnal can still traverse in bright regions using other senses. You just need to adapt to your new form."** Trying to reconcile with his emotions. Understanding that he went through a dramatic change that he hadn't requested. It was forced. Similar circumstances as done previously.

But his depression is just saddening. **"How do I do so? Every time I try just sniffing around or even tasting this toxic air, I get a throbbing headache, and my body feels even more weakened."** Smirking, but his words are filled with detest as if he is voicing to an enemy. Her fists are balled, and she readies to knock some manners into his noggin. *Exhale* **"Valcomix, understand that what you're going through is what we all went through. Let's move around a bit. Take easy steps. Step by step. I'll lead you around until you are comfortable. But first, I'm going to get permission."** She says, gesturing for him to stay but realizing he has trouble seeing. She just leaves. Once again, he is left alone.

## BASEMENT AREA

Incoherent: *Arguing* *Nagging* As TÖ-Slüdge enters in by a simple drop. *Silence* Gathering the two's very attention. Even the small one near the left corner of the room is paying attention. Her smile is bright, as it hides her intentions. **"Valcomix is having issues adapting to his new fur. Also, he must not remain nude any longer. So, he needs a location to adjust easier and a set of clothes."** She announces, and then quickly, something moves from the basement area to the above flooring. *Rolling* Then, a few moments later...

*SCREEAHHHH!!!* The high screech happened quickly. The three flinched but ignore the cry. **"I don't care what you two are bickering about, but keep that up in front of him, and I will solve the difference. We voted to leave. Prepare for the journey or be dragged out while screaming, alerting more of them. TSinged, get her to cooperate."** Warning them both with a passive-threatening tone. Also confirming that TSinged should act accordingly. He then scratches his neck, gritting his teeth. She then Leaves the basement area with only the two to stay alone together to sort out their issues.

Returning to Valcomix as he is rubbing his thigh. *Giggling* **"What is wrong with you?"** She asks mischievously. **"Something pricked me. It happened quickly."** He says while continuing to rub his thigh. She stares at him doing so and gets a glimpse of... **"We should really get going. We have to gather breakfast."** Sounding a bit flustered. **"I'm following you."** He says as if he doesn't have a choice of doing so. She then begins humming a tune while walking backward, staring at the sky. So, he is to practice following sounds. Silently chuckles as she hums off-key.

# PART IV

Now, after hours of walking some paths with a few stumbles. TÖ-Slüdge is joyously still humming her tune that is off-key. Leading Valcomix. His head still continues to ache, but he can notice his surroundings by just smell and touch only for a bit. **"Anything different yet?"** She asks him with a soft tone as she stretches her arms upon the stone grounds. **"I can visualize the area around me, but after that, it is an entire blur. My head is still pounding. Is it normal to notice every hair you have, as well as how heavy your nails are?"** He asks as he opens and closes his paws. Licking every tooth. **"I hope you're not sensitive when a single hair gets plucked. That is some intelligence, though."** She says with a worrying tone. **"It will be best to relax before we start our scavenging and hunting. Now follow the sound of my voice once more."** She orders with a gentle voice. Calming and soothing off-key humming.

Obeying her without a choice. Feeling the hard gravel of loose stones. Sensing a warm liquid as the tip of one of his nails is causing ripples. His fur tingles as he continues further. With half his body submerged in hot water, he then relaxes the rest with only his shoulders and head leaning onto the loose gravel. He smiles warmly. She is also smiling. **"Feeling better already?"**

She asks, knowing the answer herself. **"I do. This isn't a trick to have me take a bath or something?"** He asks with a low snarl. **"We have a working shower room."** She retaliates with a giggle. **"These are the hot springs we all use, whenever. Mainly to help us relax after hours of walking. You needed this. I don't know how it feels what you have been going through. TSinged, he doesn't mean any harm."** Telling him, trying to convince him that they're not a threat. *Snarling angrily* She then hushes.

**"Yesterday happened too fast. TSinged, and I have reached a compromise. I have a reason. There are things I should be able to do later on. If this will help ease your mindset about my situation. Let me say... Thank you. It will be pleasing to have allies at my side once more. Now, my head is still pounding, but this water is soothing. Let's just enjoy some silence."** He says with a bright smile so that he can think about the reason for wishing to be here. She chuckles silently. Both enjoy the silence as they bathe in warmth, relieving away the stress foreboding their mindset.

Sometime later. *Yawn* TÖ-Slüdge jostles awake and stretches; the clouds are a thickened sheet as the light is dimming. She then splashes at Valcomix roughly. He growls, **"What is it?"** Snapping at her. **"Try to open your eyes now."** She says excitingly. Reluctant to pry his eyes open. Looking down at the water first and slowly begins to use sight. Viewing himself through the reflection as his scarlet lit veins illuminating the water.

Antagonized by his new appearance a bit. Examining all that he has become. Getting out of the hot water with great celerity. Touching his long tail and the long hairs on top of his head. Checking out his new form with major curiosity. A few brief minutes have passed, and he is already dry. His form is skinnier. **"What did I turn into?"** Asking whomever is able to answer with a conflicted tone. **"There is no such organism from our knowledge. Are you ready to at least try out what you are?"** She asks as she gets out of the water. **"You certainly have a habit of exposing yourself."** He says quickly, turning his gaze towards the forest around them, avoiding her nudity. Flustered, she picks up her clothes and dresses herself. **"You were exposed first. Newborn pup."** Embarrassed that she was seen, she tries to tease him. Isn't working because seeing her blush this much is her defeat. Now fully dressed she walks pass him with a glare.

Now, walking the hilly pathway in an awkward silence. Valcomix stops as a sweet smell filters his nose. **"What is it, boy? Tell me."** Mischievously making fun of him. Valcomix then shows off his sharp canines as he snarls at her. **"A sweet aroma form over there."** He grumbles as he points in the direction. Walking past her but she takes the lead towards a shrub. Wildberries, a variety of warm colors and are shaped with a dent in the middle. Moss on trees and the lowland has fungi growing across its flooring. Wet cyan grass. **"Valcomix, we should go back. Don't touch anything. This is not the place you should be lurking in with your condition. South of this national forest belongs to dangerous wildlife."** She warns him but doesn't seem sound or convincing. **"All of the Playgrounds have dangerous wildlife. Such creatures, I had dealt with. I read in a book that survival comes when you are desperate to live. Consider this. Me, challenging them. Give me a list of what resides here."** He requests as he takes a breather. Tasting the air of mild fruit and of something that is questionable. A slimy, wet texture? Confused.

**"Mainly, this National Forest consists of poisonous plant life, a variety of berry bushes, and fungi for the animals that live here. There are, of course, newts, salamanders, squirrels, weasels, rats, mice, bats, and raccoons. There are insects, but mostly just mosquitoes located West. But you need to be wary of Elks, deer, bobcats/lynxes, cougars, porcupines, hares, and skunks. Now, please avoid coyotes, beavers, mountain goats, black bears, and foxes."** She informs him, and his hair raises when he heard the word 'foxes.' **"Why do you suggest**

**we be wary and avoid those you mentioned? I can understand that the fox is to be minded, but I'm not concerned about the others."** He says as he plucks a dark green berry from a bush. **"Skunks still spray, but it's a mist that may smell divine; our pal TSinged had a bad rash for a week with blisters. Hares and beavers are more about the group and are not easily preyed upon. Porcupines are half your size, and getting pierced by their quills can also cause blisters and infections. Elks, mountain goats, and deer are more about the alphas that will have your second chance ended. Mr. Flatlined by roaches. Coyotes and foxes may be smaller predators, but they're agile and quick. They hunt together against bears. They have the same eyes as you but are unpredictable creatures and highly territorial. Bears are ravaging antisocial giants. Now, do you understand?"** Informing Valcomix of the needed knowledge while excitingly acting out each animal. Those are threat levels he once took on.

**"That was adorable,"** Valcomix says, chuckling. not taking her seriously, but the gathered intelligence was well put. She then glares at him. **"Since you're more experienced. Can you please guide me through so that we may have something to eat tonight?"** He asks humbly. **"I shall guide our pup to become properly adapted to nature."** She says, plucking a berry from the bush. Causing the fruit to discolor and rot.

# PART V

## BASEMENT AREA

TSinged is napping on the recliner. At the same time, another is resting with her head upon her arms laid on the table while sitting in the metal chair. Tired from arguing and bickering. Both are softly snoring. *Rattling* *"TSinged. Hey. You need to see this. Come on."* Trying to get his attention but not to be rude for disturbing the other. TSinged waves his hand, shooing away the annoyance. Then mumbles. *Grumbling* As a final gambit...

Wet willie. TSinged is awake with an expression clenching his chair. Then, with a fist raised, he bonks the head of the perpetrator. *Yeesh* **"I have something that is fascinating."** A young, energetic voice says as he rubs his head. Then something rolls and then climbs up the above flooring. TSinged is displeasured from his nap. Looking at the individual who tired him out from their verbal wrestling makes him want to sleep more. But alas, someone wants his attention now.

Climbing the ladder and traversing the hallway toward the laboratory room. Stumbling a bit and tripping on his own leg. *Bash* His left broad shoulder makes contact with the wall. Leaving behind a dent in it. Rolling his shoulders, he shrugs. Resuming on. Arriving at one of the doors in this corridor. Opening slightly as cautiously as possible. **"TSinged, come over the counter; you have to see this."** Entering the lab room with plant samples on the counter. Hard stone tile floors and counters. A double sink in the back. Cabinets filled with needed utensils and instruments. A refrigerator. Also, a sewing table with two buckets underneath.

A smaller individual is wearing an animal-eared gray parka with three vertical white lines on the back and white cargo shorts. Gray and white boots with a black bottom. Showing off his shiny jet-black rough complexion with red markings on his legs and hands. Rummaging through the area and setting down on the counter is: a microscope with a set of lenses, some small containers from the fridge, a variety of colorful potted plants, suspicious discolored meat, and a water bottle. TSinged is waiting impatiently as he taps his left foot on the flooring. The kid then opens the small container with five different test tubes of various liquids. Using a syringe to take a sample of the darker liquid.

**"This here is that thing outside everyone seems upset about."** The kid says, intrigued as he examines the color. He then holds it to TSinged. **"You're really kind of creeping me out when you first did your experiments with our blood samples. It's inhumane to invade our privacy."** He scolds, but no voice that holds punishment. **"Says the one who got bit."** He remarks while seeing his bandaged arm and his sleeve repairing itself. **"She asked me to make some clothes, and so I needed its DNA, just like how I created your clothing. I made them for it as well. You and I are different from everyone, and we cannot affect anything. But the two girls have the ability to burn and poison, or at least its poison. Now, what will you label this?"** The kid asks. Now, putting a small sample drop on the meat and a plant. The kid smiles while TSinged is terrified. **"That is disturbing."** TSinged is disgusted by both the sight of his companion's behavior and what he just witnessed.

## THE FOREST

TÖ-Slüdge is rather anxious as she notices that the limitation of light is dispersing inside the forest. Valcomix is calm and checks out his fur and scarlet-lit veins. **"It will be best for us to return and try once more in the morning."** She says nervously with a chuckle. Valcomix ceases. **"You can go alone. I need to attempt to get used to this new. Time is limited."** He stubbornly sights his surroundings of black (darkness), gray (shaded areas), and white (trees, grass, and solid figures). The only color that is vivid is red. A number of crimson eyes are upon him from behind the trees. **"How is your vision?"** He asks TÖ-Slüdge while staring into a solid figure, a white blotch. **"I can see clearly, but you're still struggling."** She says empathetically, trying to make him regret this choice. Watching his eyes twitch due to anguish. Unable to bear such a headache, he clenches his head. *Groaning* *Coughing* **"You're in no condition to keep up with your bravado act. Now come on."** Worried about his condition and wanting him to return back to haven. Valcomix keeps his eyes focused on the red eyes. Ignoring her words, he remembers his days when he first became ranked as a soldier.

Thinking to himself and as he closes his eyes. Tasting the air as it is sweet yet strongly bitter lingered with iron. Sniffing the air, he has distinctive smells of a soft fragrance and other scents that he cannot tell but can trace/track. Feeling the wild breeze through his fur and softened earth that he is standing upon. Taking in much information that he has no comprehension of. His head is throbbing violently, and then his legs give out. Numb. *Heavy breathing* *Groaning* Unable to fully visualize his surroundings, and now everything is blurry, and his hearing has a lingering high-pitched noise. *Muffled yelling* Both his head and body is arching tremendously. TÖ-Slüdge is standing beside him, unable to aid him. **"Don't be foolish! You aren't even able to stand. Your action attracted them."** Ridiculing and scolding Valcomix as he withers, he kneels weakly upon gravel.

The red eyes lurk closer but are wary of the individual protecting their prey. Valcomix's head is throbbing violently, and he begins drooling. Looking more pathetic. TÖ-Slüdge sighs as she watches him. ***SCREEAHHHH!!!*** A piercing screech bellows out from him. Those that are near flinch from the terrifying sound of a banshee type scream. TÖ-Slüdge steps aside. *Chittering* *Snarling* *Hissing* Coming from behind the trees as they surround the two. One of prey. But the other is an issue. Rocks, pebbles, and sticks are being tossed at TÖ-Slüdge.

**"Seriously, throwing things again. Such annoying pests."** Frustrated and annoyed that the one who put her in this situation is unable to protect himself at the moment. Keeping watch as she is pelted by sticks and stones. Shielding her face as she minds the others lurking close by. *Chittering* Listening to them conversate, she is now more nervous as they're might be more of them lurking. She then moves close to Valcomix but makes sure not to touch him. She then adds a coating as before. Dripping a liquid upon the grass. Discoloring the cyan grass in a brown color.

*Calm breathing* Valcomix still has that migraine but is breathing normally again.

## DEEP IN THOUGHT

Remembering his days as a soldier of the C.O.A.T.S., Then a day of winter. Red eyes peering down at his uniform. Standing next to his mangled comrades. Frightened, weak, angry, pathetic. Weapon in hand but unable to fire due to his shivering. Then snow fell. He was sparred in the winter elements next to his fallen comrades. Angry, pathetic, and weak. Unable to pick up his rifle without shivering. *Crying*

Noticing its whimpering. TÖ-Slüdge sidesteps a bit, believing she is the one causing it harm. Then... *Snarling* Shocked as Valcomix is ambushed. Sharp teeth break through the fur and into the meat. TÖ-Slüdge acts quickly but to no avail. She is unable to rescue him due to the raining of rocks and sticks. Quickly dragging him away. Opening his eyes, he sees crimson. Seeing three of them as well as their teeth gripping his right hip and two into his shoulders. His head still has a raging headache. Remembering the same eyes from that event. Valcomix can only see anger. Clenching his sharp nails. Using the momentum. He scratches the creature at his hip, and then the two gnawing on his shoulders. He is getting a distance from them and now has a full visual of his adversaries...

# PART VI

**RACCOONS**: Dark blue fur, crimson eyes with silver pupils, a long spiraling tail showing off a light brown offset stripe. An ambushing type predator that lurks in darker areas and is nocturnal. Crafty, swift, and intelligent animals that work in large groups. As they only appear in groups, they are ranked as a level 6 threat depending on the numbers.

Facing off three of these beasts alone it's a lower threat level. *All Snarling* All four creatures have inflicted wounds. The team is coordinated against the new prey as it tries to stand. Quickly surrounding Valcomix and use the trees with ease. *Heartbeat* Valcomix is afraid and is in agony, now nauseous. Regretting his choice to be able to; and the historical advances that led him to his suffering. He cannot come up with a certain strategy to fight like before.

Then he feels a sharp cut to his left and right leg. Brought to his knees once again. Feeling pathetic. His body is suffering. Digging at the soil with his sharp nails. Taking severe attacks and punishment. His fur is disheveled, and his body is like a downed prey. There is no help this time; his second chance wasn't used properly. Giving up, as the pain is unbearable.

**REMEMBERING:** TSinged easily defeated him. He got his revenge and bit him. Then, before that, when he devoured Creates and roaches. *Chuckling* Valcomix laughs weakly. Lying upon the dirt like a dead animal. *Deep breath* *Calm exhale*

Realizing he agreed to fight for them once more and to lead a group across the ice. Fallen comrades and tears shared. "**STOP THINKING**." Throwing away the portion of reason. Feeling that sensation that his body felt when it attacked Creates and bit TSinged. To reclaim the same memory, he has somewhat of a recollection of. Letting his mind rest once more.

The raccoons have grown in numbers surrounding Valcomix. *Chattering* Huddling over their defenseless prey. TÖ-Slüdge emerges from the trees with bright pink shining irises. Calm demeanor but a furious aura. The raccoon's fur is standing. Inching close, they begin to arch their backs. Throwing rocks and pebbles. She smiles evilly and picks up one herself, coating the item with her substance, and throws it at the group. Hitting one and watching it squirm. Its fur sizzles, melting of the flesh. It runs away but dies fast as it leaves a trail of its warmth and bubbling vitality. The creature can smell it.

Standing firm to protect their meal. All attention is upon her. ***SCREEAHHHH!!!*** The piercing scream is loud and active again. Stunning the ones near as the livid creature who was ganged upon is thriving. It uses its sharp nails to tear through meat cleanly and then eat one, leaving only a puddle, but its fur soaks it up. With a smirk, it claps its jaw upon another. Lifting it by the use of its teeth. Skewering another with its nail. Soaking his fur in liquid warmth. Its scarlet veins shine brighter. Then, violently devours the smaller beasts hastily. Meat stuck between the canines. Then he gets piled on. Their hands slash through fur and flesh. Bringing it down on one knee. It then rushes at a tree by using a strong jump head first with a spin. Catching one of the beasts, pinning it to the tree with its arm. The unexpected Raccoon kicks and tries for its life. But to no avail is it given that chance.

The caught prey feels a hot wet warmth on its back when its jaws are agape. Smelling death and carnage as the poor raccoon tries harder for its life. TÖ-Slüdge is near this and witnessing this. Valcomix's back has plenty of slashes as its dark vile seeps from the wounds. Watching close hand on its eating habits. Fur, meat, and bone are devoured, leaving behind a mess that is soon cleaned up. The creature stands satisfied and sees her. An enigmatic expression lays bare upon her frame. It then turns from her attention and gives the remaining lot a hungry glimpse. Knowing it will be futile to fight both her and that other one. They scurry away frightened. She then sighs and examines the creature for its gnarly inflictions. There isn't any, and his scarlet veins, which were brightening the area, are now dull and calm. **"Valcomix? You alright?"** She asks with a calm and gentle tone. It then relaxes.

Called upon as it drops its guard and arms. Hiding its teeth. It shakes its head, and its tail sways gently. Relaxed, showing its big crimson irises. **"Adorable."** She says with a smile. *Grumbling* **"I am not. I became them. Another animal warped in violence."** He says while their taste lingers. **"It's called instinct fool. It's how all of them survive in their environment. Different behaviors used to fend for themselves or for their group."** She says educating the uneducated. *"It felt violent as I desired their taste more."* Whispering his impure remark. His headache has eased a bit, and his body feels lighter. *Exhale* **"You were right; I am not capable of continuing. It will be best to return."** Admitting his mistakes with an apologetic tone, he stares at TÖ-Slüdge and views how dirty she became due to his choice of action.

With a smug smile and folded arms, she stands vast. **"You had your fill and want to head home while the rest of us are famished. How cruel and selfish of**

**you."** She says in a sarcastic tone. Feeling ashamed as Valcomix has his head down exaggeratingly. TÖ-Slüdge laughs, and he does so as well. **"We're used to these types of nights. This is basically your first outing. You just need to get used to your new fur. Valcomix, you didn't ask for this life, but keep living and smile around me, please."** She requests with a gentle demeanor and soft eyes. Valcomix smiles a bit but still feels at fault. Not all his actions can be forgiven. He follows after her, lured by her kindness.

# PART VII

## BACK AT THE HAVEN OF THE PLAZA

TSinged is sitting patiently near the entrance. Feeling chilling winds and the frigid air. Soon after, he can see a dull light of scarlet. Standing a mere distance away from the entrance. Mission failed, as he didn't bring anything for them to eat. Valcomix can see the disappointment on TSinged. TÖ-Slüdge smiles. **"We weren't able to catch anything. We got ambushed by some raccoons and had to make way for us to escape."** She explains hiding the details. TSinged knows there is something she isn't going to say. Because Valcomix won't look him in the eye. He is fighting himself about what they went through.

**"TÖ-Slüdge, go take your shower; you look filthy. Valcomix, I want you to report on why you both came late and just as dirty."** He orders using a serious and punishing tone and truly means it. TÖ-Slüdge tries to intervene but is glared at. She has no means to stay and retreats. Valcomix then turns to meet his gaze. Wavering. He then gives a full, detailed report about their outing and the reason why they came late and empty. Reporting all of it. Valcomix feels ashamed of what transpired. TSinged's expression lessens into a smile, and then...

*Hearty laughter* The burst scares Valcomix and confuses him. **"Sorry, sorry, your story is not meant to be laughed at. You made it out alive, even when you were in that much agony. Now you return feeling like this. I'm not trying to make fun of you, but don't take it seriously. You managed to survive and win. We all had difficulty trying to manage our abilities. Valcomix, if you feel this way, it means you have morals and reason still. Take things slow and prosper on the use of your ability. I did the same and got run down by an Elk. My body was in pain for a few days. Yet you got bitten, dragged, clawed, and piled on, and all your scars are healed. I wish I had that ability. But honestly, I'm sorry for giving you this second chance due to my selfishness. If going a night hungry, I'll just have to cope with it."** He says with a prideful smile.

Valcomix still feels responsible. TSinged then pets his head. **"Want to learn how to use your ability?"** He asks with a violent smile. Then Valcomix meets his gaze. **"Of course."** Determined as he stands vast. **"Then you must keep thriving; don't hesitate. Relying on reasoning isn't an option. No one here has any idea what they are. In the morning, we hunt**

**together until you're able to do it by your lonesome."** TSinged teaches with a stern tone. Valcomix nods. Understanding that this is his new course of training and it will be on survival.

## HALLWAY AREA NEAR THE ENTRANCE

TÖ-Slüdge was eavesdropping. Relieved that there aren't any bad mixes between the two. TSinged is going to take responsibility and has forgiven the new member. Hopefully, thinking that Valcomix will be out of his depression. Still remembering their outing. She was scared for him. She then continues down the hallway. While outside. TSinged, and Valcomix clasped their arms forging an agreement that she didn't get to hear. Both staring at one another with exposed animosity.

## TO BE CONTINUED...

# EPISODE 3: RESILIENCE!

## PART I

### BASEMENT AREA

Here, everyone resides. Peaceful, quiet, and relaxed. Slumbering folks. But as for the outside, TSinged and Valcomix are in the plaza, both focused and awake. It's now morning, and the sky is dull grey. Chilling winds are blowing heavily. The thick sheet of gray has dark blue ripples. TSinged clicks his tongue while Valcomix is actually surprised his vision isn't bothered by the hidden light. Then he takes a strong inhale and tastes... **"I detest bitter flavors. And, it's a moisture-like mist."** Not so keen as he let his tongue roll out of his mouth. Then spits. **"You don't understand a natural occurrence that happens outside?"** TSinged asked with a confused, perplexed expression.

**"It's going to rain or storm today,"** Valcomix says, not liking the taste of the atmosphere right now. **"I'm not your adherent. You phrased it with a mediocre prediction. But you are coherently accurate. Also, you'll get you use to the taste of rain."** TSinged says with a strong tone with a drastic attitude. Valcomix has an eyebrow raised on what he heard from what TSinged said to him. **"What?"** That is all he could voice out. *Sigh* **"My bad, we have been up all night, and the weather... isn't in our favor. As you said, it will be a rainy or stormy day, also cold. I'm heading in for both rest and to hide. I refuse to deal with these types of days."** TSinged announces with a tired yet troubled expression. Heading into the hallway, slumped over.

Valcomix stays outside gazing at the eventful sky. His fur and tail sway due to the chilling, cold, heavy winds. Then, a stroke of light slithers across the sky. Soon comes the soft rumble of thunder. Feeling a drop of liquid fall onto his face below his eye. Then he holds his tongue out. Tasting the bitter and lightly salted drops and winces. It's not a favorable flavor, but the sensation is pleasing. His body relaxes. *Heavy rain & soft thunder* The ambiance of nature is calming to him. His headache is easing away, and so is his fatigue.

*Fast rolling* Sounding like a wet plastic bag being dragged in mud. Interrupted by this sound that is rolling excitingly around the plaza. Valcomix just watches a ball of plastic white leathery skin roll around the plaza. Keeping watch as it does what it's doing. Rainwater is carried by its body. It stops, then skips and increases speed. Accelerating at Valcomix, he catches the forceful being trying to run him down. Yet, he is still pushed away due to both the slick and slippery flooring and the being's force. The rolling menace is slightly pushed back but manages to keep rolling. It does the same thing again. Valcomix has his sharp nails at the ready. Before there was any damage. The ball unravels, shifting to a child that has round, sharp yellow eyes with a silver diamond common to a reptile. Plum-colored, spiky, unruly hair. Wearing an animal-eared gray & white parka added with white cargo shorts. He launches himself at Valcomix and exposes his sharp fangs.

At the ready, Valcomix punches the accosting brat. Changing his skin tone quickly to a dark gray with blue bumps. Knocking the kid in the forehead at the same time, he has cracked his fingers. His paw throbs in agony as if he punched hardened concrete. The kid rubs his forehead while glaring at Valcomix. He then changes his skin tone again back to plastic white leather. **"Why were you attacking TSinged!?"** The kid asks aggressively. Annoyed by his action, Valcomix was attacked first and now must explain to a child about his long, grueling training. **"Before you ask an enemy's/ foe's reasoning, you must give your name and rank."** Displeased by how brash he relates to TSinged by such actions, but this one is more aggressive. **"What do you mean by rank? My name is Cretan, and you're**

**the new mate that injured TSinged and attacked him mostly all night."** He says innocently with a glare filled with malice. Valcomix softly chuckles. **"Cretan. Is TSinged strong?"** He questions the child with a serious tone. Meeting this strange fur gaze as if looking at a dangerous monster. **"Yes, he is."** Answering with a smile. Valcomix then takes a knee. Putting a gentle paw upon this kid's shoulder. **"I'm not."** Admitting how he is. Noticing that he has red eyes. **"Oh, you just formed and trying to understand your abilities."** Understanding the creature's actions.

Both pelted by the rain while interlocked in awkward silence. Valcomix doesn't know how to handle this kid's pace. Cretan is trying to figure out if this being is of help or wants to attack TSinged again. *Sloshing* *Splashing* Noticing this sound, Cretan looks behind the being and sees her shining pink irises. Menacing smile. Captured by her by petrifying glare. He inches to hide behind Valcomix. Shivering. Valcomix turns his head. He looks backward and sees her mystifying eyes. Her hair is a shinier blue, like a shallow pool, with frost blue gradient tips. There are violet strands covering her right eye. Her complexion shines as if there is a thick coating of lotion upon her skin. She then folds her arms, smiling mischievously while glaring at Valcomix. **"Got anything to say for gazing upon me?"** She asks teasingly. Captured by her calm and haughty voice. He turns his attention to Cretan, who is more terrified as he is trying to speak but only releases a silent quiver.

**"Für..."** *Gulping* *Inhale* **"Fürthrived!!!"** He screams with all his power as it bellows out of him. Echoing through the hall. The kid who aggressively attacked by Valcomix is now exhausted just for calling out a name. The entrance is scorching as a bright light flares orange and flickers red. Water evaporates. Rain is no longer falling on the plaza only by her medium radius of burn. TÖ-Slüdge clicks her tongue in a rhythm with a brightened smile. Her clear coating is being depleted as steam rises from her body. The heat intensifies, coloring the plaza in a dim orange. TÖ-Slüdge walks towards the source of the walking furnace.

Smiling viciously, grabbing the hearth by her neck. Gently stroking it. **"TÖ-Slüdge, please cease. You're scaring Cretan."** Staggering voice pleading for mercy. **"He is in need of punishment."** She says with a half-serious tone. With a being in her grasp, she turns to Valcomix, but the individual hides behind him. **"You attacked our newly formed ally using the weather to your advantage. Come here."** She charges him rightfully due to his actions. Calling him over with a gentle smile. He steps back instead of forward. She doesn't show any more pleasantries. She then releases the hearth-like being and rushes at the kid. Rolling into a ball to make an escape, but to no avail was he able to. Received a full palm smack to the left cheek. Feeling the violent burning sensation as he tears up, holding his face.

Beguiled by her soft demeanor, she is more menacing than any other threat he has dealt with. Still charmed by her bright smile. **"Valcomix, it's not polite to stand in awe of someone if you don't have any compliments."** She says playfully, but her eyes are serious. **"You're fascinating."** He says with a nervous tone. *Giggling* **"Is that all? Pathetic."** Bored of his praise. She then stands over Cretan. **"You and Valcomix should get along better; go and gather some fruits."** TÖ-Slüdge orders with a threatening tone. Turning away from the two, she smiles generously at the flaming one.

Stopping midway, tapping her bottom lip. Switching sights upon Valcomix and the walking heater. **"Have the two of you been properly aquatinted yet?"** She asks the both of them. The burning one shakes her head, gesturing 'no' while Valcomix tries to gaze upon her but is bothered by the light.

Smiling mischievously, she laughs to herself as she thinks up a plan. **"Cretan, you will keep me entertained**

**while Fürthrived and Valcomix gather me some fruits. Do make haste, or else."** Flashing her bright, brilliant pink-lit eyes at everyone. Glaring fiercely, along with that empty threat, makes her more menacing. The walking hearth tries to voice out her opinion, but it is frowned upon. **"Want to speak?"** She asks slowly, alerting her that what she may say will have consequences. Witnessing her clear lotion-like coating getting thicker, and her heat wasn't affecting it. Then she looks away. TÖ-Slüdge is upset and forces her to give attention by lifting her chin and digging her nails into her cheek. **"Speak."** Serious tone and is coherent.

**"The ripe sour kinds that you so enjoy very much?"** Asking such a question sarcastically. TÖ-Slüdge does a brief exhale with her eyes closed to calm herself not to use violence. Opening her eyes slowly while gripping the girl's frame. Pinching her cheeks. ***"You know me well, if it's not ripe I will..."*** Whispering the fearful words into her ears softly. As the hearth's expression is frightened, TÖ-Slüdge smiles viciously and removes her hand. Moving limply as she is released, she rubs away the ache. TÖ-Slüdge smirks teasingly and smiles generously at the kid. He is frightened.

Valcomix rubs his neck nervously, bothered by her presence, mainly her glow. She is shivering. Uneased and scowls at him like some pest. **"Let's go fruit**

**picking."** She says with a dry tone. Seeing the attitude of the haughty one with brilliant bright eyes. Confused, worried. The candlelight is eager to obey orders due to harsh words. **"Come on, we have to... make... haste."** She says with a frustrated tone as it dies down to a surprised screech. Flustered. Someone is in full glory. The candlelight turns away fast as she cannot unsee his exposure. Valcomix isn't shy. *Laughing* TÖ-Slüdge teases her reaction. **"Cretan, give Valcomix his attire now. There is a pure female weak to a gentleman's stature."** TÖ-Slüdge says while giggling in a teasing manner, keeping sight of the walking hearth. Getting scowled at by those menacing eyes, but with that blushing face, she is no threat.

He quickly returns and makes a random right as he skids past Valcomix. Rolling cautiously. Cretan then unravels himself, standing in front of this stranger. Valcomix kneels down to be at eye level. Holding out slick material of silk and foam resembling a shirt and pants. Takes it from him and examines the material. **"All you have to do is put it on, and it will form to match your Deoxyribonucleic acid. As you put it on, it will change the shape, size, and color that you think it to be. Subconsciously though. It's not armor, nor is it quite indestructible. When torn, ripped, or even shredded, it will piece itself together. They are also adaptable to create shoes or any footwear. The form**

**it takes will become permanent. You can ask me to generate another set, but it is futile to wish for a new outfit change. It will remember the previous form. Trust me, I tried many times, at least for colors, but to no avail. That was unsuccessful. Put it on."** He explains with such high-spirited enthusiasm; proud of his own genius.

TÖ-Slüdge shakes her head, smiling. *"I hope you get to wear something foolish or embarrassing that you'll be likely to just want to be nude and exposed to the harsh environment that you'll get sick and have fevers from."* A harsh glare as he snickers to himself from what he whispered under his breath.

*"I hope you get severely punished for being a fiend. Children should be taught manners."* Valcomix whispers as he smiles. Putting on the slick yet soggy-like garments upon himself. Covering away his nudity. The material then becomes alive, moving like parasites underlying the skin. He was freaked by the sensation as it reminded him of his first week outside. The material begins to shape tightly around his body. A thick sleeveless shirt. Heavy pants with his tail given a space to be able to spiral freely. Changing the colors to a bleach white. Biohazard symbols on each leg and another appearing upon his back. Silver and gold lines run randomly through the clothing, forming squares.

Then he watches something forming upon his right bicep. A wrapped band. The coloring is bleached white with five black dots in the spaces of the centered gold star. Knowing what it used to mean. Including his clothing, he looks up to the scattering heavy rain. Clenching his fists. **"You got your wish granted. This is humiliating and absolutely embarrassing. TÖ-Slüdge, we'll get your fruits. Come on."** He announces with a determined tone but with a hidden emotion. Then, he orders the candle-lit girl, who tries to complain, but his expression is terrifying. Leaving the plaza, walking past her.

*Soft thunder* *Heavy rain* Cretan feels regretful as he thought his clothes were awesome at first but can tell it was terrible for Valcomix. TÖ-Slüdge's mood is disturbed as she clicks her tongue. Seeing the defeated, sad expression once again upon that frame. **"Fürthrived, make sure he stays alive. Do be nice; he is going through a lot and trying to prosper with these changes."** She pleads with a softer and gentler tone. The hearth exhales and nods, then follows after Valcomix. *Louder thunder*

# PART II

## WALKING A PATHWAY ON THE MUDDY GROUND

Valcomix's feet and pants get soiled by the moist earth. Focused. Unnoticing that he isn't by his lonesome. Feeling a tug. Pulled by his shoulder. Turned to sight that the candlelight was the one who halted him. **"You're walking too fast; it's difficult to keep up."** She tells him. likely causing a burn as her expression is surprised and apologetic. He removes her hand and turns away, showing his back. Gazing at the star symbol, annoyed. **"Slow down!"** She yells, walking at a faster pace. **"Keep up."** He says loudly. **"Does wearing the clothing upset you this much? Pathetic!"** She shouts, berating him. He then ceases his forward movement. *Growling* **"If someone wasn't so shy, like a pure maiden that first opened up a health class textbook, then I would be just fine believing that I was just some new creature! An animal, monster, or just a beast! I heard your terrible words when I was passing up my life! Don't speak to me about being pathetic; I already knew!"** He yells angrily, showing her his gaze, which makes her step back. She also becomes angry, trying to be brave. She is shivering, frightened by him.

*"The stench of a corpse brings pests! This one here has revived as such."* She whispers softly with a harsh tongue. No respect. Valcomix exhales. **"Understood."** He says calmly with a depressed, melancholy voice. *Sprinting & sloshing* Rushing to be away. The distance is already far. Lost sight of him instantly. **"What, he vanished?"** Confused, she frantically looks around. Then she realizes what she had said. Then remembers her words. ***"She is going to be furious."*** Saying to herself in her mind. She then looks down, sighting his footprints. *Deep breath* *Calm exhale* Trying to calm her nerves as there is hope of finding him. Yet the rain is washing them away. She shows a fearful expression and rushes straight.

Quickly heading deeper through the forest. The track is now gone, as the muddy prints have led her to the vegetative flooring. Medium-high grass reaching her shins. She can't return back. TÖ-Slüdge and TSinged will be furious, and if he is discovered fallen, then what? She was asked/suggested to be nice and aware that he is just trying to cope with this sudden change in his life. She lost him. Afraid. **"Valcomix!!!"** Screaming out his name while the rain, wind, and thunder is also quite loud. Cautious not to move forward as the forest can get many beings lost. Hesitating then trips on herself from moving back and forth. ***"TSinged brought this broken soldier and*** *was the one who saved him from dying. It would have been best just to be rid of him when he formed. TSinged wanted to be responsible, so why must I suffer? If you are worried for his wellbeing. Then TÖ-Slüdge should've kept him by her side. They want it as a pet, not me. So weak-hearted. I will just say he tried to eat me, and I defended myself if he's dead. This is annoying."* Complaining angrily. Berating the two and cursing the weather.

Then, she criticizes Valcomix for his own behavior. As she tells herself, feeling right about her judgement. **"Valcomix, return now!!!"** Yelling out his name, frustrated and angry. *Heavy breathing* *Fast heart rate* Going through a tantrum; unable to calm herself as scenarios in her mind play. Getting worse and worse. Her light dims, and she can feel the rain. *"It's all their fault, they're all..."*

As for the runaway. Holding a dark green fruit that he picks from a tree. The scent is pungent and is bitter. Using his sharp claws to pierce a hole into it. Dripping a yellow-colored juice upon his hand. Licking the fruit's flavor; tasting both the skin and juice. It's sour, but is mellow enough not to pucker his lips. It was not as delicious as he had expected. Trust that this will please her and calm her domineering mood. Chuckling to himself. Not to waste the fruit, he tosses it whole into his mouth. Chewing it and is indifferent to its flavoring. At least it's salable to be eaten. Taking a few more off the tree. Then, he sees the band on his bicep. **"You're a part of me once more. I don't deserve this honor, nor am I fit to."** He tells himself, feeling self-doubt.

He again picks a few more off the branches. His ears then twitch, and he looks to his left. Sighting big red eyes with teal irises. Staring at him. He doesn't sense any danger or hostility when he was ganged up against raccoons. This one is huge. *Rustling* Keeping sight of what is nearing. Its fur is thick, with a sturdy body and claws that are able to shred through a Valcomix with a single swipe. The animal is just a few feet from him, picks off a whole branch, and partakes in the fruits. Still examining and can now confirm that this is an...

**BLACK BEAR**: Boss creatures of most Playgrounds. Huge body color variation of dark purple to black. Herbivores as of late. A proud animal that knows its strength as the others don't compare. Violent when threatened. It is a threat level 8 due to its durability, strength, and violent temper when agitated.

Getting its fill, it leaves the area. **"Antisocial. Yes, they are."** Valcomix says with a saddened smile. Lying on his back next to his bunch. Staring at the dark, behaving sky through the vibrant violet leaves. Pelted by rain. Listening to the ease of soft thunder rumbling and the ambiance of nature. Lifting his right arm above and stares into his past through the band. Remembering his days as a soldier once again. He smiles brightly at how he attained such an honor. Remembering how he was congratulated. Perseverance, determination, and dedication were praised. Now a fallen soldier. Pathetic. Overwhelmed with the loss of both his humanity and the cause of stressful events. He covers his eyes. *Crying* Releasing all his pent-up rage from inside. Defeated, weak, and this reminder. Owing gratitude to many.

Unnoticing that he is being seen. As the being approaches and pets his head. **"You're okay. Cry as much as you want. You've been through a lot."** A calming, gentle tone spoke softly. She is warm. Covered from the hard rain. Soft strokes on top of his fur, calming his stress. His crying dissipates, and he gently falls asleep. Napping. Stroking his fur calmly with a gentle smile. Staring into a now calm and resting creature.

# PART III

## A BROOM CLOSET WITH A CHAIR AND DESK

TSinged is at peace with a huge goofy smile, studying certain rocks and reading books on geodes and geology. Enjoying himself as he hides in a cramped space that is surprisingly able to fit him inside it. *Doors opening* **"Where are you TSinged?! I'm bored dealing with Cretan! Come entertain me now!"** Yelling down the hall. TSinged puts down his book and opens the door. **"Bother Fürthrived like always! Leave me alone; there are some sour fruits in the main fridge; don't choke on them like last time! I do not want to deal with your mood today!"** He yells back. His voice is carried down the hallway.

**"Fürthrived is out with Valcomix gathering fruits! Also, you lie! I checked the main fridge, and there were only vegetables, most of them were rotten! So, I had Cretan collect more!"** Again, yelling back louder. **"Why is Fürthived paired with Valcomix!? She is unsympathetic towards him. Cretan should have been paired up to gather your fruits! How naïve can you get!?"** He yells, berating her choices. **"Woman's intuition! Everything will be fine! For now, I'm not okay and need attention pronto!"** Still yelling. TSinged is mainly annoyed as he grumbles. **"I refuse! Take a cold shower and entertain yourself in there! Then mope afterward!"** He shouts down the hallways. **"You heartless imbecile! I'll check your arrogant and rampant remarks later! Don't sleep tonight!"** She threatens as she slams the door loudly, finally back at peace. Now, TSinged is pondering on what is happening between Fürthrived and Valcomix as he is worried. His arms are folded, and he doesn't want to deal with TÖ-Slüdge nor wants to disturb her when she is showering again.

## BACK IN THE FOREST

Valcomix rests upon Fürthrived's lap. His tail gently sways. His eyes begin to twitch, and he refuses to open them. Feeling much more refreshed but still weak and confused by someone's kindness. **"Why be kind to me now?"** He asks, confused and wary of this nature of hers. The warmth is inviting. She is different than how she acted earlier. **"You seem scared, sad, defeated, and lost. I can guess your emotions, but I don't know anything about you. You're not what you want to be, but you were near the end. Now, you have to adapt to a form that you doubt is strong. We all had to cope**

**with our new skin. It's not easy, and it won't be; the best thing is that no one here is alone. Including you."** Sounding quite assuring as she smiles at him. Valcomix ponders on what is said. Minding that everyone here is surviving for each other. Just as when he was given a rank. He doesn't have anyone to protect. But of those who took care of him.

Gazing at his armband once more. Understanding of the uniform he wears. Looking up at the darkened sky. Standing vast. **"Thank you."** Opening his eyes to see an ally's appearance. Short, medium flame-colored hair that is vibrant orange with a greenish tint. Gold irises with a pinkish hue. A peach complexion that seems pink but has dullness and a healthy glow. Valcomix then glares at her. **"You get shy for having to see me exposed, yet your sense of clothing is immodest."** He says as if scolding someone for improper use of clothing. Seeing the indecency, a white top exposing her navel. Tan cargo shorts that are slightly unzipped. Getting a glimpse of her pink panties. "**TÖ-Slüdge suggested that I should wear it like this. She called this outfit adorable and cute."** She explains feeling doubt. At least she is wearing something. Imagining that woman, her attitude is indecent and has plagued this one's innocence. Staring down to see that she is wearing tan boots. Shaking his head side to side. **"Let's return. Candlelight."** He suggests with a smile as he carries the bunch he has gathered. Followed by a vibrant candle.

## PLAZA

Cretan returns with a variety of herbs and roots. He is quite filthy as if he was rolling in mud. *Sneezes* Entering the hallway. **"I'm back!"** He yells. Hearing the rushing of heavy footsteps. TSinged is tumbling down the hall; his shoulder dents another wall as he tries to rush. But recovers quickly. Now over Cretan. *"Keep it down, TÖ-Slüdge is showering. To remain safe from her, stay quiet. Put the things you gathered in the fridge after you rinse them. Then hide yourself until Fürthrived gets back."* Ordering him to do so as he is alert. Cretan becomes wide-eyed and nods. Traversing through the hallway cautiously. *"Also, clean yourself up as well. Tracking mud and filth, avoid the shower room and just hose yourself down in the lab. Do use soap."* He nags. Cretan is both agitated and annoyed. Unclear as to what he must do first. Wash up or load the fridge. Anyway, it would be best to avoid both of them.

***"That individual always returns dirty. I'm not a janitor. TÖ-Slüdge is unable to do any type of cleaning since she'll dissolve equipment. Fürthived burns hotter when frustrated, so I refuse to have her clean. Valcomix, maybe he can help out."***

Thinking to himself as he is annoyed but hopeful. Thinking about what may be happening between the two has him worried. *Footsteps* TSinged turns around and can see two individuals. One is playful, and the other is annoyed and snappy. TSinged is relieved as his concern was dispelled. Drastic changes to their appearance. **"Hey, we're back, nanny,"** Fürthrived says with enthusiasm. TSinged just brushes off her callout. **"TÖ-Slüdge is in the shower room."** He notifies by pointing down the hall. Not wanting to deal with this one, either. A winning situation. **"Best to entertain her now before she throws a tantrum again."** She says with an exasperated sigh. Yet she is joyous as she leaves the two boys alone after she a lemon from Valcomix.

**"I'll take those. Nice clothing, by the way."** TSinged compliments, but Valcomix isn't so fond of his outfit. **"What's bothering you now?"** Asking as Valcomix focuses on the band. **"I'm weak."** Admitting with a stern tone. **"No, you're not. You're just having a difficulty trying to cope and prosper with the sudden change. Being capable is all that you need to become."** He tells him as he takes the fruits from his grasp. Now, walking the hallway. *Low rumbling* Valcomix exits and gets pelted by cold, heavy rain. Clenching his fists. **"Then I will become capable. TSinged, when I return, I will be ready to leave with everyone."** Notifying him with a smile. TSinged is shocked by what he was just told. Understanding that Valcomix has to figure himself out. Swirling with emotions as he is. Maybe some time to himself will get him out of his head and be open. Swarmed with many questions but holds them back. **"Alright then, Valcomix, take care of yourself out there."** TSinged says, seeing the determination in his eyes. Valcomix smiles and nods. *Sprinting*

**"Best to inform everyone. Everyone here is a headache."** He complains with a bright smile. Walking the hallway, feeling upbeat.

### Elsewhere

*Splashing* Quick steps, leaving behind ripples. Remembering the first week of measurement tests as a C.O.A.T.S. soldier outside. Survival criteria. This is the outside world unknown to all. Now to retest. Closing his eyes. His headache throbs swarmed with complications. Mind and body are both aching once more, yet he smiles joyously. *"I will face the outside world until my end! All for them!"* He tells himself with might and focus. ***SCREEAHHHH!!!***

# PART IV

## SOMETIME AFTER

Sighting the alpha elk watching over its herd. Stalking them.

**ELKS**: Thick-skinned with tough meat. Brown and tan fur. Strong legs that can shatter bone into powered calcium. Their skulls are concentrated calcium due to their twisted gnarled horns. The muscular one with the largest gnarled horns is deemed alpha. Can see 180 degrees around their perspective. Protective of their young. Ranked 4-5 on the threat level scale, while the alpha is a 6 or 6.5 depending on their aggression.

Valcomix has a target of two of them. Smiling viciously, sitting upon the thickest branch of the tree. Exposing his teeth salivating. Hunger. Examining them graze upon this mountainous area. Valcomix drops from the tree. *Deep breath* Getting into a stance. *Growling* Making a quick dash straight and clearing the brook.

The alpha Elk notices Valcomix, and he turns to face him. Shaking its head wildly. Valcomix smiles madly at it as if taunting the creature. The herd begins to run, followed by the younger ones. The Elk stampedes forward to confront Valcomix. Using a quick maneuver to slide from the attack. Readying for the attack with his claws out. *Sharp, short exhale* The creature is rushing at Valcomix; he does the same, aiming low. Coming close as he gets kicked in the shoulder, dislocating it, but not without compensation. He has effortlessly scratched its hind leg and upper thigh. The creature has a hard time keeping balance. Grunting in pain as it attempts to stand.

Moving quick. Valcomix sprints, clearing long distances with a single breath. Catching up to the many passing the calves. Aiming low, dashing in a straight. Just below a fully developed adult. Spiraling with a pressed step. Sharp claws cleave cleanly through its neck. Pooling out its warm crimson liquid. Staining Valcomix's and the cyan grass. The herd keeps on. The felled prey is claimed by a predator. He then devours the creature, tasting its warm and sweet flavor. Chewing easily on its tough muscles and bones. Leaving no scraps nor the bones but the stained flooring. Satisfies his hunger.

*Sniffing* A bitter scent permeates the mountain. Curious as to what the culprit may be. He follows after it. Descending down the pathway. A variety of herbs is being laid down. Skunks rolling themselves around them. Then, hide away under the brush. *Rustling* Smaller critters are running past Valcomix. The cause soon appears. A pack of foxes and coyotes. Valcomix isn't bothered by them and begins to step. Traversing to pass them. *Growling & Snarling* Glimpsing at one another as if they're on equal footing.

Continuing his adventure on his lonesome through different areas of ecosystems. From wetlands to vibrant flora with diverse vegetation. To hazardous hostile zones. Trespassing different territories as the scenes are both of terror and gruesome devouring. Violence is a tool for survival. Using his abilities even when outnumbered and close to being beaten. Through perseverance, he is able. Looking at his band stained with dirt, filth, and dried blood. Then, it makes way to beautiful zones listening to songs. Ambiance of nature. Through harsh winds, heavy rains, and cold yet chilling nights which doesn't faze him. He is surviving. Smiling in his time of rest within trees that he marked with his claws. Taking time to swim in the fast-flowing streams, catching fish and other tasteful aquatic beings. Just by using his tail as a lure after witnessing a Platypus do so.

Walking around aimlessly or even running, he ends up further away from them. Not wanting to return until he is capable to complete his mission to alleviate the Playgrounds. There are hostile environments that have not been dealt with yet. But as it can bleed, it can be dealt with. Driven to become capable as TSinged mentioned days passed. He has to be the individual who was given an honor that is wrapped around his bicep. Reminded of the hardships and difficulties that transgressed from it. Remembering the defeat and drastic changes of keeping his title. Given a second chance at life. Bearing the clothes he now wears, acknowledging his choices. **"I still don't feel ready. But there is nothing challenging here anymore. Even the bears let me fish with them. But I won't be alone."** He says with a bit of confidence, noticing the filth in his fur. He looks to a distance, feeling slightly prepared to head back.

Stretching his body, reaching high. Closing his eyes. Using his heightened senses. He then kicks up dirt, sprinting. Moving swiftly and jumping high, clearing streams. Feeling the ground and checks the areas around him. He steps on trees and climbs upwards as he moves quickly through the forest above the top. Then, a branch snaps. Before impact, he rolls and then continues to sprint. ***SCREEAHHHH!!!*** Sounding lively getting attention from many critters that hear its screeching.

## PLAZA AREA

TSinged and Cretan are playing/working out. TSinged is rolling a Cretan around. Having tough skin plating that is dark gray with blue bumps. Having a hard time pushing him back to the opposite wall as Cretan is rolling forward trying to push TSinged. He then shifts to a jet-black rough-skinned complexion with red markings. Pushed hard; rolling into the wall. Unravels, ignoring the worried and concerned TSinged. **"He's returning."** Sounding excited. Turning to TSinged with a joyous smile. **"Valcomix is approaching!"** Alerting everyone.

# PART V

TSinged paces into the hallway. Jumping down into the basement area. **"We heard Cretan. TSinged, you and I are going to welcome the foolish whelp for making us worry. Returning after half a month. I thought the worst."** TÖ-Slüdge says, agitated with a furious smile. TSinged agrees. **"We should all let him rest first until he says we should leave,"** Fürthrived says openly. The two give her a look and then at each other. Believing that she has the correct approach. *Screaming* **"Help me!!!"** Cretan cries to be rescued. With no hesitation, they scatter to exit the area. TSinged jumps and lifts himself over. While the girls climb the ladder. **"Woah!"** TSinged yelps out. Spooked by the creature's attack. It jumps from the entrance's top. Landing on TSinged's back, knocking him off balance. Take down.

*Snarling* **"Valcomix?"** TSinged is concerned, thinking that he has lost the immobility of reason. TÖ-Slüdge has her arms coated with her dangerous liquid while Fürthrived is heating the flooring. Cretan is face down on the plaza. "**This is a bad joke. Cretan, we should cease this.**" He says feeling guilty then grabs TSinged's arm. Standing him up and receives a bonk on the head and a scolding look; while the girls are relieved. Cretan is annoyed that the prank didn't work. **"Sorry for leaving abruptly. I just needed to be alone. I..."** Valcomix announces with an honest emotion. **"Don't try to explain yourself. You were going through it. Did your fur grow?"** TSinged understands and then examines his tail and notices it got longer. **"I wasn't paying attention to it."** Valcomix notices as he plays with it. His fur did grow longer. His tail is longer. Swirling his tail to wrap around his body three times. Holding and stroking his furry ligament. **"That is adorable,"** TÖ-Slüdge says teasingly, and the guys are uneasy.

**"You seem much better now,"** Fürthrived says with a generous smile. Valcomix smiles back at everyone. **"I do, but I still have self-doubt."** He admits, but with a calmer attitude. TSinged scratches his head. Valcomix grumbles. He moves away and approaches Cretan. **"Cretan, thanks for the clothes."** Valcomix says with a smile. He becomes shy as he rolls into a ball and forms a sphere; his skin layers connect as if instantly. **"You're welcome."** Valcomix then turns toward the others with a serious expression. **"TSinged, I did say to be ready to evacuate this area when I return..."** Pausing... Waiting for any words meant to be said as he engages them. Fürthrived's facial expression is smug. *Deep breath* **"I'm going to shower first, check the device, and make a route to Playground ID. When I do, be supplied by then. We have to make it onto the ice from**

**Maine before Christmas. The journey is treacherous, approximately a twenty-five-hundred-mile hike or longer. But I will get us out of the Playgrounds."** He informs them with determination and no hesitation.

Giving him the attention and feeling uneased. Fürthrived begins to chuckle. Surprising everyone. **"Then get to it. Valcomix, you are filthy and you may have fleas. But you seem more fascinating; I trust that you can lead us abnormal beings."** She says to him with a teasing, playful demeanor as she scratches the fur on his head. Trying to remain focused. **"I may know the Playgrounds well enough. It's the ice and the other lands I'm concerned about."** Valcomix admits to them. **"Then we are the same on that thought. Our only option is to survive. Now go take your shower so we can leave at your order."** TSinged tells him with a disturbing smile with his arm out. Valcomix shakes that hand with a firm grip. He then walks past them and makes his way down the corridor. TÖ-Slüdge hesitates to speak as he walks past her. **"Best go claim something to eat before it gets any colder."** TSinged announces, walking up to Cretan. **"Fürthrived..."** TÖ-Slüdge calls out her name, holding her hand feeling uneasy.

## SHOWER ROOM

Well-lit with a wide area of tiled walls and flooring. A locker room on the side. Just like every other type, except the shower comes first and is a larger area without privacy. Removing his clothing as he opens a locker. Seeing a pyramid stack of six bars of synthetic detergents inside it. He takes the one on top. Entering the closest shower nearby. Turning the knob to the hottest setting possible. *Soft rain* Feeling the water on the back of his neck and then turning. Now leaning on the wall. Seeing the filth already being washed off. Closing his eyes and scrubbing his fur to enjoy his first wash after half a month plus a few days.

Moments of time pass. *Door opening* Valcomix's ear twitches, and then he has his sights on the invader disturbing his privacy. **"Something wrong?"** He asks with sincere concern. **"Not going to tell me to 'Get out, you pervert.'?"** TÖ-Slüdge asks with a smile but with a hidden emotion. **"I was already seen by you and the others. No reason to be shy. I had to shower with others once before. Besides this is your territory. I'm the trespasser here."** He informs, surprising her.

She then walks to the further adjacent shower. **"Why are we going to do the longest travel when we can just head north from here?"** She asks, truthfully curious and worried. "**TSinged didn't inform you**

**of what I told him before?"** He asks, knowing that too many questions won't answer the issue. **"You're going to be upset about the answer and may want to burn my flesh with your deadly touch. I'm going to do a final mission for the C.O.A.T.S..."** He announces coherently, and she bites her lip. She also folds her arms tight, trying not to berate him and remain calm enough to wait for his reasoning.

**"I'm going to be liberating the Playgrounds that has the most dangerous higher threat levels. I know that I may be labeled S.O.S. and that I am putting you all at risk as well. But there are those that I fought with, fallen with, and would die for. Not of my pride nor honor. But I still care; they're the only family I had."** He tells her with an honest mentality. **"The same family that will aim their guns at you."** She warns him, trying to give him a sense of reason. **"Yeah. If I leave now, I will regret it. But there is a location I have to reach."** Using a calm tone to get her to understand. "**You'll do the same for those three. I owe you four as well."** Striking her with words that angered her. Saying it so calmly.

Listening to his reasoning, she doesn't know how to stop him. **"I'm scared for you."** She tells him in a soft voice as she leaves the room, slamming the door behind her. Valcomix had heard those words before.

There is no comment as to what he could do to assure someone who can care about someone else's wellbeing. He says nothing to anyone, nor himself, but has a look of a being that seen hell and has to continues on.

# PART VI

## BASEMENT AREA

Valcomix is now focused on the computer and the handheld device, which has a full battery. Scanning the map app and seeing random but uniform movement across this Playground. Then pinches the screen. Widening his fingers and playing with it. Checking the notification and latest information. Researched for hours, watching the screen of the device in many locations. Stretching his arms high. Engaging the area. Sighting TSinged resting in the recliner while Cretan is rolled up near the candlelight. TÖ-Slüdge has candlelight resting in her lap. All of them are comfortable. Again, driven to continue to work.

Some hours pass by. Valcomix is smiling victoriously as he has his head nestled upon his folded arms on top of the keyboard. TSinged is peaking at him and begging the others to come to check him out. Silently making fun of his posture but relieved that he was alright. Now, he is the one looking comfortable. TÖ-Slüdge leaves the area and looks out at the plaza. Remembering, as she gazes at the light gray sky. Gentle breeze. *Inhale* *Exhale*

**"Are you alright?"** Fürthrived asks her in a soft tone, looking quite worried. Continuing to gaze at the familiar scenery from the entrance. **"I don't know. Just nervous and a little frightened."** She admits with a shaky voice. Fürthrived has her lean upon her shoulder and holds her hand tight. From behind them, TSinged's head is out. Sighting his allies having their moment. He returns below. **"We're leaving this area and going to a territory we know nothing about. We're all afraid. TÖ-Slüdge, I'll keep pace with you when you're hesitant. If I could, I would carry you."** She says jokingly yet sincerely. TÖ-Slüdge giggles a bit. Holding each other as they gaze at the quiet and pleasant scenery.

## BELOW

Cretan is impatient to leave above. TSinged is holding him back. Rattling and making a ruckus. Valcomix's ears twitch. *Yawn* Opening his mouth, showing off his sharp, jagged canines and other marble-white teeth. He shakes his head and then scratches his chest. Getting up from the chair and unplugging the device. Checking the screen and see movement on the device. **"Morning..."** He says to the two as TSinged has Cretan under his arm near the pit. Sighting the area. **"Where are the other two?"** He asks with a tired expression. **"Above, but they're having a moment. Leave them be for now."** TSinged requests.

Valcomix surrenders and returns back to sit down, gazing at the two.

Cretan is squirming, trying to get out of his grasp. Struggling. TSinged flicks his forehead four times. Cretan rubs away the ache, annoyed. **"Valcomix, help me out. Sorry that I attacked you before. TSinged here probably deserved to be bitten. Hey, did it leave a mark?"** He asks trying to get glimpse of where the bite mark may be. TSinged goes silent and enraged while calm. Cretan goes weak, not desiring to put up a fight, nor wants to speak. Someone was nonchalant about their behavior. TSinged then releases Cretan. He is upset and complains. Valcomix ignores them for a moment and checks the device.

## Some Time Later

## The time Is 5:21pm of 07/24/3175

Valcomix checks the time and his markings. Then, checks to make sure that they're prepared. Valcomix and TSinged both have backpacks. Filled with mainly their food supply. The sky is almost dark. Chosen the best time to leave as the roaches will take over the city soon. The five of them are standing in front of the building that was their haven. Scattered branches, sticks, dry leaves, and grass cover the hallway's flooring. Everyone is uneasy but understands the reason. TSinged looks to Valcomix, nodding his head. Valcomix stands firm.

Gazing at the temporary home of the four. **"Fürthrived, burn it. We must not leave any trace as to what nor who was living here. Nor can they have those canisters. Nothing must be salvageable from here."** Valcomix orders her and informs everyone that this haven will be part of the ruins. Cretan is crying, and TSinged is holding him tight. Valcomix stands firm, clenching his fur, knowing well he is destroying their home, along with the evidence like before. Burning her orange brightness, heating the area under her feet, and igniting the leaves. The flame grows and travels. The remaining papers are reduced to ashes. Each room is engulfed by such light. Scorching all as they witness it. Cretan continues to cry but isn't heard as the flame roars louder. Valcomix closes his eyes, not that they are hurting but to...

Ignore what he just saw. TSinged is smiling sadly as if his suffering was extinguished. Valcomix can see that the girls are doing the same. All relieved. The two are whispering their goodbyes, showing off that full, hearty smile just as bright and passionately as the flame is now behind him. Cretan turns and looks up to Valcomix with his tears wiped away and now focused.

Giving a brave expression. Valcomix then makes the first steps to the middle of the plaza. "We got to leave from here." Giving the order with a calm tone. The four hesitate to follow. TSinged takes his step, then Cretan. The girls follow just behind them together.

*Remembering The Speech of*
*The Well-Respected:*

*"The first step is always the most difficult. Knowing when to fall is a habit of learning. Falling on the first steps is the habit of learning about difficulties. Leaders are birthed through trials. Don't be afraid to fall; it will happen anyway."* Staring at his band, then looking behind him. Leading others once more.

**TO BE CONTINUED...**

# EPISODE 4: BAD WEATHER AND BEST STORM.

## PART I

After some hours pass by. Miles away from their starting point. Valcomix is leading them, checking the map, and realizes they're now in Shelton/Sector 43 of Playground WA. He is doing well, but the others... Checking behind him, they're keeping up with his pace as well as focused. Cretan is stumbling a bit, though. He slows down his steps. **"TSinged, pass me your pack. Cretan is having trouble."** He announces, and everyone gives the youngest their attention. Rubbing his eyes and silently yawning. He didn't even hear Valcomix speak. TSinged turns to meet Valcomix who smiles as he shakes his head. Fürthrived and TÖ-Slüdge are both glowing warmly, seeing that Cretan is, in fact, tired. Removing his pack and reaches them both out to Valcomix. Taking it and carrying both the packs with ease.

**"Cretan, get on my back if you're tired."** TSinged says, peering down. Cretan then smacks his fist. **"Not tired."** Stubbornly cries out. TSinged, and the rest are unable to respond. Not noticing that their pacing has slowed down. Valcomix has a smug demeanor. **"Let's take a break a bit. A few minutes to rest our feet."** He suggests as he points to a shambled restaurant covered in moss and a sign that is unreadable. Outside furniture of tables stand firm along with some chairs. But the inside is covered in moss with fungi growing. Fürthived heated glow exposes the vast takeover of nature. TÖ-Slüdge refuses to sit down in a chair that is extremely filthy as dust is piled upon them. The boys are sitting together. Valcomix minds his surroundings, TSinged is looking over Cretan, who has his head laid upon the table. Resting easily. Valcomix pulls out the device from one of the packs.

The time is 11:16pm of 07/24/3175

**"Cretan is now asleep. We can continue on."** TSinged informs Valcomix, who ignores him. **"Not yet; I'm checking the map right now. There are some Arrows swarming the next towns over. Olympia, Tumwater, and Lacey. We need to pass by undetected. Tumwater has hidden points. Concerning that, Fürthrived's heat signature may put us on their radar. From there, we can trek down to Playground WA, Sector 14, towards the hindrance of Mt. Rainier. Hopefully, we can walk straight to Spokane. Just be mindful of the Arrows hovering above."** He informs with a smile upon himself. Unnoticing that the three of them are gathered around him. Peering at the screen. Confused about the many movements and their functioning.

Looking up to see the nosy and curious allies. **"We can now continue on."** He says, showing the screen close to their eyes. Seeing a spot where the purple moving dots are avoiding to enter as he points to it. Putting away the device and then carries the two packs. TSinged helps Cretan stay rested. Piggybacking. Journeying more through the night. TÖ-Slüdge looks to TSinged, showing a similar expression. Doubt. Using facial gestures, they involve their eyes to silently argue. Glaring at one another. *Grumbling* TSinged is showing off his muscular form. With just a menacing smile...

She expels a translucent liquid, TÖ-Slüdge has TSinged frightened. Fürthrived is disappointed in their behavior as she had watched their back and forth. **"Valcomix, what are 'Arrows'?"** TÖ-Slüdge asks. **"If you can clarify, why are they dangerous?"** TSinged asks. Both were curious as they spoke at the same time, and the two were hesitant to ask themselves.

Valcomix looks to his band and then gazes from behind. Seeing how far he is from the rest. He steps backward and puts himself near everyone. **"Alright. Playgrounds are abandoned and lost states that are attached to Central America. Sectors are their cities. Arrows are tools, mainly our toys, engineered to map out environments and can detect desirable functions in the best of detail. Mods. Using the arrows, they read location, heat signatures, and radiation levels. Fitted with other functions that determine threats. Higher levels can become hindrances to their expansion to claim back the Playgrounds. Sending squads or teams to investigate that is directed."** Sharing his information while keeping eye contact with Fürthrived.

Turning away and facing forward. The three then look at each other, confused. **"Like an arrow pointing. But why go towards the dangers? Even the weather is a threat."** TSinged tells Valcomix with a vile smirk. Valcomix shows off his teeth. Angry. Upset by his kidding tone, the other two also find it humorous. **"It's not a kind joke knowing that it's true. Many lives were lost during the harsh winters and expeditions. How is that funny?"** He questioned them with a serious and frustrated tone.

Seeing the frustration in his eyes and hearing the terror of his tale. The three then lose their smile. Understanding his suffering. **"Sorry. But my comment still stands. Your goal is vague."** TSinged says to

Valcomix. **"Territorial beings that inhabit Playgrounds. Lost lands that certain animals claimed. I am going after them, the ones labeled as Black States. Since there are only two of them left."** He shares once more, and they are worried about him but keep silent as this goal is personal to him.

# PART II

Traveling the long distance of a road of loose rubbish and moss. Trees grow large along with fungi. Hours have certainly passed, and the chilling winds whisper. Thanks to Fürthrived's warm temperature and orange glow. Non are affected by the drop in temperature. *Yawn* TÖ-Slüdge is tired but mostly bored since no one is conversing. Valcomix stops abruptly with his arm stretched behind him before anyone can ask, sighting that he has his nail over his lips. 'Be silent.' Understanding this gesture. Valcomix's ears twitches, picking up the faintest of sounds. *'Adorable.'* All were thinking with a menacing teasing smirk. Ignoring their gaze. *Whirling* *Rustling* Reacting to the sound as he flinched? Unusual action. **"What is it, boy? Tell us."** TÖ-Slüdge says, bent forward, amusing herself from the phrase.

Closing his eyes. Silent breathing, heart rate slowing down. Just to hear his surroundings better. *Whirling* The sound gets louder. Yet no one else is hearing it. **"Fürthrived, dim your lighting and cool down. We need to move by the trees and stay hidden."** He suggests. Everyone else tries to see what he hears. Looking around, but nothing. *Growling* Valcomix then shows off his sharp canines and his veins burn scarlet. **"Trust me when I say move."** He says as no one isn't obeying his command, and his temper is raging. He then rushes off, leaving the packs behind. TÖ-Slüdge clicks her tongue. Fürthrived is worried and dims down. They do as they're told and hide underneath the trees.

Soon, Valcomix returns, jumping down from a tree. Looking around, observing a soft glow. Approaching them, while carrying a medium-sized broken... **"What is that?"** TSinged asks, trying to figure out what kind of machine he is holding. **"This is an 'Arrow' preferred name: drone. This thing hovers over playgrounds mostly through the night except in certain areas where signals are out of limit besides Freezones. Scouted by this, is exposure. We need to go. Hopefully, my brash attack didn't alert any sensors. To remain obscured, just listen to me. Until you're over the ice, I will not annoy you then."** He explains. Understanding that he shouldn't be taken lightly. Seeing him retrieve the backpacks and continue on. Following after their guide under the covering of the trees.

*Whirling* This time, everyone else can hear the buzzing sound of motors and micro propellers beating the wind. Valcomix takes out the device from one of the packs. Checking the map as the time is...

The time is 3:39am of 07/25/3175

Now located on the Westward side of Olympia. Many arrows hover over their heads. They all look at Fürthrived, who is trying her hardest to stay as dim as possible. Then, back to Valcomix, who shuts off the device and places it back into the pack. **"Good enough, we still have some tree coverage. TSinged, wake up Cretan so he can be aware. We're going to need to be fast as well as careful to tread to the opening down in Tumwater."** *Rustling* Interrupting his stratagem is a squirrel digging. Admiring it until...

*Firing* Multiple mini barrels deployed from under the drone and started spinning. Unleashing red ammo, brutally piercing it. Now smoking. Seeing it continue to hover. Shocked at how well it accurately deleted a small target from its location. **"Um. That is new. Our toys got an upgrade. That squirrel was given the C.O.A.T.S.'s wrath by an arrow. Anyway, folks, that will be us if we don't follow my lead."** He says to them, looking confident. Fürthrived looks sympathetic to the downed being. TÖ-Slüdge can't fathom what just happened. TSinged wakes up Cretan, who is slurring his words.

Moving on, copying Valcomix's treading, hiding in buildings. Then into thickets of trees. The arrows are growing in mass numbers as they get closer to Tumwater. There is a flock of them grouped by six to ten. Making rounds. Leaving only a slight window of movement. Valcomix counts the opening as there are only fourteen seconds of actual movement. Ducking his head to hide away from being their target. He moves to the group that is exhausted from all the stress, all to be unseen. Cretan is well enough. **"We are only a few miles near our getaway, and in just a few more hours, soldiers will be making their rounds as well. So, we have to sprint."** He suggests when looking at Cretan.

**"We cannot keep going like this. No more fast travel. We need a better..."** *Coughing* Seeing that they're out of place and the situation is dire. He takes the device from the pack. Turning it on, playing with the screen for a bit. Finishing setting up the map. Then passes it to the youngest being. Everyone notices that expression on his face. **"Keep this map open and head to this location. It's a twenty-mile tread from here. You're going to have to guide them there; you are the green dot following the red line."** He tells Cretan who stares at the screen feeling quite afraid that he has to lead. **"Valcomix, you are not going with that plan of yours. And why give it to Cretan?"** TSinged asks, trying to get him to rethink what he came up with. Valcomix smiles and stands vast. **"I will deal with the annoyances outside. Cretan is the best choice. Fürthrived will incinerate it; TÖ-Slüdge's hands are a no. Your hands are too massive to even consider**

**you an option. Cretan is the best choice. Seeing all of you like this is pathetic. So, I intend to do what you oppose of me doing."** He mentions, as he scowls, TSinged, who is ready to pound some reasoning into a being's brain cavity.

**"Then, he mustn't go alone. I am much more of a target than all of you. I am only tired because someone told me to dim down. That is much harder than you think."** Fürthrived says, releasing a surging heat and increasing her luminous glow. TÖ-Slüdge chuckles a bit after whispering a morbid thought. TSinged rubs the hurting ache in his forehead. Only to know that two adherent individuals are compromising. **"TSinged, I don't like this idea more than you do, but she will have us exposed soon. Besides, twenty miles isn't much. You two do what you can for a bit. Valcomix, if she is injured or feels as much as distressed. You'll be..."** She threatens as TSinged sweats, and Cretan is terrified. Valcomix smiles warmly. **"I don't want that to happen to any of you. But understand to give trust in one's abilities. I'm capable."** He says with a bright, adorable smile. She shakes her head defeatedly. TSinged begins to chuckle to a small laughing fit. Fürthrived admires Valcomix's smile. Remembering his self-doubt and depressed state. Now, she enjoys this new attitude. Instantly taking her hand and pulling her up to the rooftop.

# PART III

Cretan is holding onto the device with care. Checking the map constantly. Seeing the highlighted red path with a dotted end. Playing with the screen, minimizing the point to see its exact placement. Reading the red line carefully. Approached from behind, TSinged lays a firm grasp upon his shoulder. TÖ-Slüdge smiles gently, gazing at him and then tells him: **"You are intelligent and capable. Lead us out of here. This time, you're the boss."** Sharing words of encouragement, the kid smiles, liking the word boss. **"I'll get us there. No one has to worry."** Determined and confident. He stands in front of them. Smiling viciously.

## ROOFTOP

Valcomix is smiling viciously as well. Counting down the seconds as well as the next flock of arrows. Fürthrived is warming up feeling excited. Valcomix has her upon his back, piggybacking the gentle candle. With great celerity and precision, the two are about a foot over the arrows. Undetected. Valcomix is carrying Fürthrived, and she brightens up. Coloring the top layer of the machines a bright red to an orange glow. Then...

*Explosions* Warping the metal as it expanded, leaving them to smolder in pieces. Landing with ease. *Laughing* Fürthrived is enjoying herself. Seeing that Valcomix's fur is smoking and his veins light a pink hue, slowly glowing back to scarlet. **"You have a strange and wonderful body. I love the colors."** She says, scratching his fur behind his ear. **"You three can go! We'll be ahead providing you shade."** Valcomix announces sprinting onwards. Yep, they're having fun.

The three sort of understood the statement, but why use the word 'shade'? Cretan doesn't ponder on his type of logic. They are only certain that they need to go now. Making it onto the street. **"Having to keep running like this is a bit much,"** TÖ-Slüdge says, feeling quite tired. **"We mustn't run. We have to tread carefully and cool ourselves down. Valcomix doesn't want us to exhaust ourselves."** Cretan tells the two who are jogging. Taking time, TÖ-Slüdge can feel a slight pain in her legs. Constant distant walking for a consecutive number of hours. Seeing that the travel is about a two-hour hike.

The time is 3:56am of 07/25/3175

Cretan then sighs. **"If only he told us what time the C.O.A.T.S. make their rounds."** *Scoffs* **"They'll be the targeted ones. Arrows/drones, skies, annoying. They better be safe."** TSinged is muttering to himself as he holds his body. Using the hood to shield his face from the chilling cold winds.

Seeing that he is trying to keep his mind off the dropping temperature. Realizing that without Fürthrived, there wouldn't be any other portable heater. Yet they let her go with Valcomix. They then begin to walk near each other. But TÖ-Slüdge doesn't mind the cold. Seeing the two boys shiver from every gentle breeze is quite amusing. She gazes at the sky. Dark grey with a mixture of rough, deep blue circles and an ominous weather pattern. The boys see her thoughtful gaze aimed above, and they do the same. All seeing the sky sway and swirl. *"We need to hurry."* All are thinking the same thing.

## ELSEWHERE NEAR AN ABANDONED AIRPORT

Arrows are picking up a heat signature that is abnormal inside of the building. Counting approximately about 30ish. Standing behind the tattered windows is... **"We're in a predicament, aren't we?"** Fürthrived asks while stretching. **"I don't see that we are. They're about thirty or forty, maybe in between."** He notifies her while smiling. **"You have to say what you're thinking. I won't judge."** She tells him, singing her words. Gazing into her eyes. His voice is held back for a bit. **"I only got to break one for an example, and since I got us into this. I should be the one to get us out."** He tells her with a serious expression. *Sigh* **"Be honest. You want to break a few for your own enjoyment since I was having fun destroying most of them."** She says, and Valcomix turns away from her. **"I told you that I won't judge. But I do find it hilarious that you have a childish demeanor."** Saying so as she scratches his head. He snaps at her playfully.

She giggles. **"Go have fun."** Ordering Valcomix, who then rushes up the escalators. Kicking up dust behind him. Heading towards the bridge, and jumps on a platform below it. Walking along the weakly curved glass. Seeing the heavier dark movement from under the dirty, packed with grime and mildew-covered glass. He then goes to hang off. Viewing them as they're fixated on the heat signature. Valcomix drops down with a light foot. Extracting his claws/nails. He then jumps, reaching their height but above them. Slicing easily through the thin layers of metal, he drags his nails across their numbers. Using his tail as a whip, flexibility added with speed can put dents into them. But with accuracy, it can cause severe breakage. Now, he is walking towards the entranceways as the many arrows fall or crash around him.

**"That was reckless, considering your warning not to be seen by them,"** Fürthrived says to him as he realizes his action. Checking around him to make sure none of them are functioning. Relieved that they're all broken. *Giggle* **"Valcomix, you didn't have to take me seriously. Had fun?"** She asks with a gentle tone. **"I did, but there was no challenge."** He admits scratching his palms with his nails. His tail sways. Reaching out to pet him, he pulls away her hand as he witnesses the sky. *"Not this pattern."* Valcomix tells himself, also witnessing the mass change of the colored clouds. Frustrated, he snarls. Standing beside Fürthrived and lifts her up. Becoming nervous as she blushes from being held in such a way. Seeing his serious expression as he gazes at the sky.

Closing his eyes. He feels the heat upon the area of his body yet focuses on the frigid air on his back. Listening to the raspy howl of the wind, slightly becoming louder. A few gusts blow, but they're gentle breezes. **"Get on my back."** He orders her, trying not to sound harsh or paranoid. She nods while reaching for his neck and then swings herself to be upon his back. Valcomix secures her by supporting her thighs. **"Ouch, your nails are scratching me."** She tells him in a pained cry. **"Sorry."** He retracts his sharp claws. ***"You have a gentler touch now."*** She says, resting her head upon his neck and whispering into his ear. Valcomix chuckles softly as he bends over a bit. And then runs.

# PART IV

*Alert* Cretan hears the ringing and feels the vibration of the device. A message appears on the screen. He begins to read it. "Due to weather conditions, all outdoor activity will be postponed in the following Playgrounds: OR, WA, MT, and WY. Stay within your bases. Those who are in camps are to relocate to the nearest bases or return to Dorm. Until further instruction, take shelter." The two behind him have read it as well. Looking over his shoulder. But TÖ-Slüdge seems confused of what those symbols mean; Cretan swipes the message away. Pondering. Looking at one another in silence as if they have questions to ask. But must remain focused to keep on track toward the point where they're nearby.

The boys are shivering, searching for the placement on the map only to find a narrow road leading into a thicket of a vast forest. Cretan steps close into the vegetative mark. The device begins to act up. Glitching. The screen freezes and reads "Untraced Territory." The emergency app appears under the text. Cretan then steps away. The device performs its now as before: normal usage. Then steps forward again, and it freezes. Moving his arm this time. Playing with the functions until TSinged slaps the back of his head. **"This is the right direction."** TÖ-Slüdge softly giggling as she follows behind them.

The narrow road ends at a lake. An abandoned dam separates the lake's upper level, which is about a quarter amount of the surface layer. The water is flowing a milky white color and is glowing due to the algae. A water wheel on the other side is attached to a housing. All are operating continuously and functioning properly. Seeing lights through the windows and the trees over yonder. **"Do any of you have the feeling to leave this area?"** TÖ-Slüdge says while shivering, not from the chilling breeze but the sensation of the air is off-putting. Along with this eerie silence. TSinged can feel it as well. **"Let's continue on."** He tells them as he approaches the metal door.

It's locked. However, with the use of abnormal strength, the door is easily disregarded as if it were plastic. Cretan eyes widen with fear. TÖ-Slüdge holds her voice, disgusted by what they discovered. TSinged is indifferent.

Decaying bodies of fallen Creatures and mummified human remains are scattered about. But on the table is the most gruesome act. The bones of a man plated around four seated deformed shriveled up beings. Walking down the long path is nothing but a massacre. Cretan holds onto TSinged, forcing his eyes to stay shut. TÖ-Slüdge is still holding her voice. A frightening atmosphere. Then they reach the other door. Forcefully opening it. Then... a scenery...

Of such beauty. Awed by the houses merged with plant life and lighting as if natural. Small critters found this place formed a home. Even if there is some remnant of Creates on the flooring. The nightmare lingered for a few minutes. **"We should wait for them here."** TSinged tells the two, who seem to enjoy his suggestion. He puts down the packs and rests on the grass. The two do the same, but Cretan rolls up into a ball. TÖ-Slüdge is now concerned about her friend.

## UPON BARREN GRAVEL

Valcomix is swiftly moving ahead at his best speed. Arrows are attracted by the heat source that he is carrying. Due to the growing winds, they're not able to catch up, nor are they getting a glimpse. He sees that they're avoiding them...

Entering the forest ahead, they sort of glitch going into the out of bounds line where the signal can no longer reach. Gripping her thighs tightly and gritting his teeth. Bursting into a final dash. She wraps her arms around his neck tighter, not wanting to fall. Entering the forest. As he continues, he can hear rushing water. Trying to pull the breaks.

The wet grass causes him to slip up. Takes his hands off her thighs and removes her grip. Swinging her to be in front of him. Shielding her from the fall. *Splash* Valcomix and Fürthived are now floating. Both confused. Her tank top is up due to Valcomix's catch and support. Following where his eyes are focused on. She is now exposed, her lavish white silk bra that is see-through. Pink, he sees. She smiles mischievously and uses his chest to kick to the surface. She used both legs as she pressed off. Valcomix does an exaggerated backflip and looks quite annoyed. Then he swirls his tail, propelling himself to the surface easily. Taking a breath of air. Then sights a pouting Fürthrived.

**"Pervert."** Labeling him with a smile, she pushes him away slightly with her foot. Fixing her clothes. **"I wouldn't be looking if your attire wasn't so revealing."** He tells her while holding his arm out towards her as he swims with the use of his legs and swaying tail. Reaching for his neck, she chokes him for a slight second out of embarrassment. *"TÖ-Slüdge considers it to be cute."* A soft tone whispered in his ear. **"You're adorable."** He says with a serious tone. Only to be choked again. **"You're adorable. Soft fur,**

**perky ears, and a long tail that you wrapped yourself with while you were sleeping. Such a pup."** She tells him teasingly with a menacing smile. He grumbles while using his long tail to propel himself and the baggage at his side forward. Reaching the bank on the opposite side. Aiding her to have her climb out of the milky white water first.

Reaching her hand out with a gentle smile. Valcomix goes for it, smiling at her. Grasping her hand, she lets go. He falls, making a splash due to betrayal. *Laughing* **"Sorry, sorry, I don't get to play much often in the water. Sorry."** She shares with him. Seeing his expression, he is upset. Reaching her hand out once more. Valcomix splashes her and then decides to climb out using his own strength.

**"Don't trust me?"** She asks, feeling disheartened. **"No. I have something trying to drag me down."** He informs. Noticing that his nails are digging into the ground. Seeing the bubbles in the water and his tail moving about. With a single twist of his tail and a strong pull, he caught...

**CATFISH**: a long, medium-sized aquatic animal. Approximately about the length of a coffee table. It has no eyes and has six gills, silver-colored scales, and a pink underbelly. Not certain what their threat level is.

It Squirms around, Valcomix uses his sharp nails to dig into its neck and holds it still his tail. Slicing it open. Letting its contents spill out. **"Nice catch there."** Complimenting him. He then throws the aquatic being over his shoulder. Holding it by its slippery and slender tail with his nails dug into it.

Seeing lights flicker behind the trees. **"Come on."** He tells her, proud of his catch. She follows beside him. Following an opening of the lake's mouth, it moves to a wider area of the lake with a dam. Since they're on the other side, they traverse around the lake, sighting the nature-claimed houses. Accosted by small predatory animals. Pulling at his catch. Valcomix grumbles and snarls at them. They snarl back. Dealing with weasels and squirrels. Surrounded by the many. Ready to prepare to protect his meal. Fürthrived giggles softly and scratches behind his ear. **"Let them have it. Okay."** Gentle toned. Valcomix lays the catfish upon the grass. Glaring at them closely. A weasel snaps at his palm. Unaffected. He snaps back. It jumps back to avoid him. Valcomix removes his nails from it. Walking away. *Nibbling* *Scratching* The many predatory critters have surrounded the catch and take share.

Upon the bank, three individuals notice a familiar orange glowing light approaching them. Feeling relieved. TÖ-Slüdge rushes towards the light. Fürthrived holds her arms out. Receiving a tackle. Embracing one another. Valcomix keeps walking. Cretan gives him back the device that refuses to work. TSinged has his arms folded. A serious expression. Noticing the small text box on the screen. Skimming through it. He meets his gaze. **"Any questions you want to ask?"** He asks TSinged. **"They mentioned a storm coming. Also, what is this place? We saw something."** He asks, seeing the anguish in his eyes. Cretan seems shaken up; keeping close to the tall the stronger being.

Valcomix gazes up. Sighting the dark blue merge with dark grey. **"You went through the steel doors. I apologize for the gruesome sight. This is a Freezone, old habitants that refused to leave. Just be glad none of you saw anything worse."** Valcomix says, hiding his expression. Upsetting, he tried as he forced Valcomix to get him to explain. Seeing his eyes made him flinch. *"He saw hell."* **"Valcomix, are you alright?"** He asks, worried about this individual. Valcomix falls silent as if unsure of how to answer his question.

Cretan is confused but can tell when the atmosphere is uneasy. Soon, the girls return. Fürthrived is spoiling TÖ-Sludge, both giggling. Seeing Cretan in harsh silence, TSinged looks worrisome while Valcomix gazes up at the sky. **"What happened?"** Asking with a soft, annoyed tone. **"Nothing bad. I told TSinged that we had an opportunity**

**to reach the next Playground without issues, except for the hazardous weather. If the clouds coalesce any further, we will need to take shelter as well. Yet, we need to rest. Let's keep going a bit more. I don't feel at ease in this place."** Valcomix informs them. Gripping the device in one hand and a clenched fist with the other. **"I did agree to it, but I was uncertain about risking the others for such an opportunity."** TSinged plays along, remembering the look in Valcomix's eyes. **"I couldn't follow what they were saying. It was a serious conversation."** Cretan also lies, not wanting to know what Valcomix had seen that was worse. His eyes were terrifying. Now, the girls look at each other. TÖ-Slüdge shrugs her shoulder. Valcomix smiles, relieved, and approaches TSinged. Patting his shoulder. **"Thank you."** Expressing his gratitude.

TSinged can tell he bears a burden. He follows after him. Cretan then walks backward to stand next to Fürthrived. Traversing the vast forest, feeling an incline. A beautiful scenery of violets, sapphires, and growing fruits upon the trees. The breeze causes the vegetation to sing. Nature is lively and peaceful. Yet there is a potential disturbance as they look up and see the swirling, brightening clouds. Many animals graze upon this change of weather. After a long hike, they reach a wide-open area of a shallow lake with a cleaner look. Clear waters. A great view of a mountain. **"We should rest here for a bit,"** Valcomix says, stretching his arms high and rolling his fist. TSinged drops the packs and takes off his shoes. Placing his feet into the lake. TÖ-Slüdge takes off her shoes and then soaks herself into the water. Both are relieved as they finally get to relax. Cretan sits next to Fürthrived, away from the lake.

**"This is nice,"** TÖ-Slüdge says, fluttering her legs to keep steady. **"My feet and legs were aching. Also, Cretan is getting sleepy again."** TSinged mentions that, as he looks from behind himself, he sees that the youngest member is fighting his drowsiness. **"Better get him to eat first before he falls asleep."** TÖ-Slüdge tells TSinged. He nods and leaves, heading for the packs. Removing some contents of dried meats, fruits, and vegetables. She then looks to her right and sees Valcomix swirling his long tail across the water. Curious. *"Chilling his tail probably?"* Asking no one. The swirling stops, and Valcomix turns around, readying his claw.

A moment passes, and a medium-sized catfish squirms. Trying to flop back into its home. Caught. Valcomix begins to eat it. **"Nice skill you learned. Enjoy your meal."** Focused on another creature. Surprised. Noticing that he was being watched. *Snarling* Hiding away his catch. She then raises an eyebrow. *"I don't want your catch, insolent being. He isn't returning to a human acting like that. But he is adorable this way."* She says to herself, giggling softly. TSinged then returns with a few metal containers. **"Here is your share."** He says, placing the container on the grass near her. She then sits up. Picking it up and opening it. Seeing the variety of sweet fruits and vegetables.

**"Thank you."** Expressing her gratitude as she takes a bite of a pear. Excited from the first bite. TSinged shakes his head, smiling. **"I'm going to give Valcomix his share."** He suggests, and TÖ-Slüdge leans back to have him see that Valcomix is already feasting on certain fruits and fish. "**Wow, a few weeks of surviving, and he is this much capable. Now more of a beast than human.**" TSinged says, admiring his capability. Valcomix notices that their staring and hides away his food. TSinged has an upset expression. **"No one wants your share."** He says, but only she hears him. TÖ-Slüdge then laughs. Time passes, and they get some rest. TSinged, Cretan, and TÖ-Slüdge are huddled near Fürthrived. All sleeping warmly and at such peace. *Low rumbling* His ears perk up. Then settle down. *Wet Drop* Unconsciously sniffing the air. Awakening. Feeling a few drops of rain. He can see that the sky is twisting, and a few spots are lighting up. Fürthrived is warming the area around them, shielding her allies from the rain.

Approaching everyone with a serious expression. Not wanting to do it. *Inhale* ***SCREEAHHHH!!!*** Fürthrived awakens fast and covers her ears. The three wake up frightened. Then, see Valcomix pointing up. It's raining, and the temperature is lowering; sparks of light line across the clouds. TSinged hesitantly looks at TÖ-Slüdge from the corner of his eyes. Annoyed, she pinches his arm, causing a small burning sensation. He rubs away the pain. **"I'm still me!"** She yells out. Everyone is relieved, but Valcomix has no clue what she means. **"I can keep her sanity in check."** Fürthrived assures TSinged with confidence. TÖ-Slüdge, feeling embarrassed as she blushes, pinches her friend's thigh. **"Ow, why are my thighs getting punished by the two of you."** Giggling while holding her leg as she gazes at Valcomix and TÖ-Slüdge. Valcomix turns away from the menacing glare of her protective friend.

TSinged carries the packs, and Valcomix takes one from him after he puts the device away. **"We can reach the main highway and leave out easily since the C.O.A.T.S. are to take shelter. Again, we are rushed due to phenomena occurring over us."** He informs as he begins to walk. They have to follow. Cretan looks up to the sky. ***"Phenomena? That means many strange occurrences or events are going to happen."*** He says not wanting to expect what is going to happen. Fürthrived and TSinged heard him. Again, they look up at the darkening grey and blue swirling sky.

# PART V

The sky is unleashing its heavy rain, pelting those below and flooding the flooring. Drowning the soft earth. Strands of blue and white light scatter, reaching the mountain. *Thunder rumbling* Thanks to Fürthrived's ability, the rain and flooding don't affect her nor TÖ-Slüdge. Evaporating the moisture surrounding the two. The boys were left to be soaked by the falling rain and inches of flooding. TSinged is miserable. Cretan has shifted to another skin tone of white leather. Valcomix isn't bothered by the rain even though his fur has gotten heavier. Chilling winds bend through the trees, reaching them. TSinged, and Cretan flinched and shivered. Fürthrived is saddened by how the two are exposed to harsh elements.

Within time, the harsh rain of the sky lets up. But the temperature drops drastically as the two boys are really shivering. Finally, they reach the main road. Valcomix has the device in hand. The screen shows a warning as it brightens a red light. TSinged is shivering badly. Sighting his breath. Cretan's skin shows signs of frost bite. Fürthrived expands her radiative heat around her. The two get closer for warmth. All staring at his back. The only one left out in the cold.

His veins are a crimson color. Valcomix gazes worryingly at the sky's mass change. Feeling the freezing winds swirl around as they pick up speed. Showing his teeth, bearing anger towards the above.

Snow begins to fall. A single flake gently touches his nose. *Snarling* Valcomix shakes his head wildly from side to side. His fur spikes up and folds down. They enjoy his behavior as if watching a small creature take on the environment around it. Traversing the silent open road with only ambient sounds coming from the whistling winds, low thunder rolls, and the sound of their feet crunching the snow. Valcomix checks the device, but the screen remains a bright red light with a warning.

Noticing that they're slowing down and Fürthrived's heat is diminishing. He finally looks behind himself and can see that the four are near exhaustion. Frantically looking around, sighting that there is no cover nor a place of rest. Then, the screen returns to normal. Seeing that there is a camp nearby and seeing that they're not far from the bordering Playground.

**Time is 7:51pm of 07/26/3175**

He had them walking without a stop to rest for a full day plus hours. Determined to have them rest, going off a tangent of the highway towards the nearest camp.

Padded huge tents within a small town. No trees around, just empty roads centered by a pond. Relieved that there are no vehicles and that the lights are off. Justifying that the camp is empty. He enters one first to make sure. While the four are just able to stand. Fürthrived's heat is cozy but is losing its use as it is dimming. Valcomix exits and can see that they're definitely exhausted. They aren't talking to him, nor are they questioning where they are. They're so tired that they don't have an idea, nor are they able to argue. **"Go in."** He tells them with a brisk tone. A smile upon his face. They do as commanded. Entering into the huge padded tent. Seeing six air mattresses already blown. Nothing else is here but covers and mattresses. TSinged takes off his pack.

Taking the covers scattered about and then shoves them in the pack under the supply of rations. Using the remaining to overlay them with blankets. Hopefully, shielding them from the freezing temperature. Valcomix watches over them. His eyes begin to feel heavy as well. His tail wraps around himself instinctively, and his veins dim down. Now, he rests along with them, lying his head upon his tail. Bundled up by his own long fluff.

## MOMENT OF RECOVERY

After some time has passed, TSinged was the first to awaken. Holding his head. Gets off the mattress and then stands. Noticing that the one the girls are sleeping on is discolored and damaged. Feeling a throbbing pain that is unbearable, he sits down. Confused, groggy, and hungry while in pain. His body aches. Trying to think of his whereabouts as he looks around. Sighting that everyone is resting easily while bundled up. Then, he can see a ball of fur near the entrance. There is no collection of what transpired or how they got here. Only knowing that everyone was exhausted.

Listening to the muffled sounds of the weather and their soft breathing. Lulled back to sleep. TÖ-Slüdge awakens and can feel a throbbing sensation in her legs. *Groan* Clenching her teeth as she tries to get up. **"Don't try to get up. The four of you have strained yourselves from a distance, marching for a full day plus hours. We can rest more here since we are close to the next playground by a fortyish-mile hike."** Valcomix explains while continuing to stay where he is comfortable. TÖ-Slüdge inhales silently and winces as she tries to stretch her legs. Then, peers down as there is warmth close by. Smiling at the hearth, grasping her hand as she rests.

**"Valcomix, can you fetch me some fruits, please? I'm kind of light-headed right now."** Politely asking him. His ears twitch. **"Sweet, sour, or bitter?"** Asking her to pick what flavors for him to retrieve. Tapping her bottom lip, pondering on what she has a craving for. Then she smiles. **"Sour."** Eagerly making her choice. **"Very well,"** Valcomix says seriously. Turning to see his expression, he is serious and determined to carry out her plea. Opening the tent and entering the harsh blizzard. She watches, surprised at how he didn't even hesitate to go outside nor realize that they are still supplied.

**"I don't know why he went out there when we have supplies here,"** TSinged says as he remains bundled up. TÖ-Slüdge keeps focus at the entrance. **"Maybe he slightly forgot. How are you doing?"** She asks joyfully and sincerely at the same time. **"My legs and back ache at the moment, and I am famished. I want to get to the packs but don't want to move from where I am lying."** He informs her with a grumpy and agitated attitude. Looking at him with a disgusted expression. **"You haven't complained before."** Unfamiliar with his behavior. **"We exhausted ourselves following him this far. Yet he can just get up and go by someone's request."** He says, sounding quite jealous. TÖ-Slüdge looks towards the entrance/exit. "**Good recovery, endurance, stamina, and vigor. I want to know if his vitality is high as well."** Complimenting an ally while making TSinged uncomfortable. **"Ask**

**him yourself. I didn't need to hear your comment."** *Sigh* **"I'm kind of dizzy and hungry to listen to your depraved desires."** He says, staring at the packs. TÖ-Slüdge shrugs her shoulder.

*"I'm not depraved. Maybe I am a bit mischievous and needy, but I am not corrupted, nor am I wicked. TSinged, you're a bully."* She whispers to loudly while glaring at him with an expression of malice, which causes him to shiver. He refuses to give her attention. **"TÖ-Slüdge, be calm."** Fürthrived says in her sleeplike state, hugging her friend by the waistline. Resting her head upon her thigh. TÖ-Slüdge pets her head, letting her fingers brush through her hair. She smiles earnestly. **"Don't further your actions. I nor Cretan want to witness such activities."** He warns her with a sturdy tone. She then ceases. Holding back her urge to continue. Fidgeting. TSinged then attempts to stand up. Feeling a throbbing pain in his legs as he makes it to the packs.

Then the tent opens, and TSinged is attacked by the freezing winds, causing him to shiver. Valcomix has returned carrying a bunch of lemons and gooseberries. Vibrant colors distinguish of yellow with a red haze. Meanwhile, the gooseberries have a light orange and jasmine tone. Silently, he approaches TÖ-Slüdge and leaves the gathered fruits at her side. Being careful not to let them roll off onto the soft flooring or touch her. He then makes his way back to close up the tent. **"TSinged, it will be best to stretch before standing. Also, you need to eat. I had you walking for more than a full day. You might be dealing with fatigue right now."** Valcomix scolds him with a serious tone.

TSinged wants to hit him where his guts can scream. Valcomix searches through the packs and finds dried meats, a variety of vegetables, and a few fruits that have a sweet flavor. Not sure what to get out, he hands him the whole pack. **"Go back and sit down. Until all of you replenish and feel revigorated, I will be here. Just tell me what you might need."** He sounds sincere and caring. TSinged takes back his comment and returns to his mattress.

Valcomix remains at the entrance. Both of them enjoy their meals. Soon after eating, the two are bored. There is nothing to be entertained by. Their legs feel better now. *Silence* The feeling of boredom is annoying. TSinged is ready but doesn't want to make a step outside. **"I'm going to make some rounds outside. I need to check how the weather is getting."** Valcomix tells them as he is about to open the tent. TÖ-Slüdge removes her captor and stands, making her way next to Valcomix. **"I'll join you. Keep each other company."** She tells him, but he ignores her. Yet he smiles, not wanting to show her. **"Alright."** He opens the tent. Letting in the freezing air and snow into their shelter.

The tent is then closed after the two have exited. TSinged is left alone as the only one awake. Just as they have left. *Yawn* Cretan has risen. Stretching high then rolls his shoulder while circling each leg. Rubbing his eyes. He is still groggy as he looks around. Seeing that TSinged has the pack that holds food. He holds his arms out, gesturing, 'Gimme.' TSinged then passes him the pack. Now that he has received it, he reaches in and begins to eat. **"Where are we?"** He asks lazily. **"Near the border to the next Playground."** TSinged answers. **"Vague."** He responds maturely. TSinged is trying to figure him out. **"We will be leaving once everyone is well rested."** He notifies him. Cretan closes the pack and tosses it back to TSinged. Listening to the muffled winds. The tent is being rattled roughly. Cretan shows a serious expression as he chews on a jerky.

## OUTSIDE

TÖ-Slüdge is causing Valcomix an issue as he snaps at her. Valcomix ignores her as he turns his head from her. She tries to get his attention. *Grumbling* He then turns his gaze to the sky. His eyes grow wide. The clouds are now blended into a darkened blueish-grey, showing two swirling vortexes as the blizzard warps around one of them. The wind is pushing and pulling violently. Cretan and Valcomix can sense the change in the air. **"We have to go. Now!"** They both say, surprising the one close to them.

# PART VI

TÖ-Slüdge views the swirling snow and two vortexes expanding. Dark grey mixed with darkened blue. The wind accelerates, causing them to be pushed. Valcomix opens the tent. Rushing in and passing TSinged the other pack and then went to carry Fürthrived. Now piggybacking her once more. Cretan is ready as he puts one of the packs upon his back. TSinged is confused. **"Cretan."** Valcomix stares at him with a worried expression. **"Already know. Where is it?"** Cretan asks understanding the matter. Following Valcomix's eyes. Cretan approaches TSinged; jumping onto the mattress and searching through his pack. Rummaging through for a moment, and pulls out the device. **"We have to hurry. Stay together. Keep low to the ground, and don't slip on the ice."** Valcomix warns. Cretan nods, then heads out of the tent. TSinged is still confused. **"What is happening?"** He asks confused and serious. **"There is a bad storm about to commence. Save your oxygen and follow Cretan."** He answers him as if annoyed.

Outside and feeling the frigid air. TSinged begins to shiver. Looking up. The vortexes have thickening clouds reaching down to the top layer. They seem to be moving. They are being pushed away. Trying to stay balanced. **"What is that?!!!"** TSinged asks, as this is his first time exposed to a frightening weather condition. **"Summer's funnels!!!"** Valcomix answers. TSinged gives him a face that the answer is nonsense. Valcomix ignores him and TÖ-Slüdge then checks in with Cretan about the device. **"Guide your fingers to the dotted border."** Instructing him as he does so. A thirty-four-mile sprint. **"We are going to take shelter over at Playground ID!!! Cretan lead us there!!!"** He yells to sound louder than the heavy winds.

Rotating winds are picking up speeds as two vortexes bend. Blowing away trees and weak buildings. The weather of thick clouds is formed. This creates fog and mist, spreading fast across the state as the two swirling masses cause damage. Glass shatters, loose gravel, and other debris are lifted up. Spinning violently as the vortexes move forward while rotating around one another in a pattern heading in the direction of the East. The air feels wet and is freezing in temperature. TWENTY-EIGHT MILES LEFT TO RUN.

*Thin ice cracking* *Screaming winds* *Hail falling* The four of them are being pushed and pulled. Trying to maintain their balance upon the slippery, icy road. The fog blocks their vision as well. **"This is ridiculous!!! How can the weather**

**change this drastically so fast!!!?"** TSinged yells while listening to TÖ-Slüdge laughing seductively near his ear. **"Valcomix, wake up Fürthrived!!! TÖ-Slüdge's attitude adjusted to the abnormal!!!"** TSinged complains. Cretan has a smirk. Valcomix rolls his eyes for the first time. **"Deal with it!!! TÖ-Slüdge, how are you handling the situation!!!"** He yells in a polite manner. **"I'm doing well!!! Thanks to the fog, I'm no longer dry!!! Feeling kind of wet care to cure me!!!?"** She asks using a sultry voice. Valcomix regrets ever asking her. **"How much further are we from the border!!!?"** Valcomix asks Cretan.

**"Just twenty-two miles left!!!"** He yells, holding back his snickering. **"Don't ignore me!!! Valcomix, you're our pet, so you must entertain us and cure our loneliness!!! Especially me, do you understand, or do I have to train you until your arrogance is purged!!!"** She yells with a blushed, mischievous expression. Biting her lip. TSinged is embarrassed for having to witness that and to listen to her talk. Valcomix is growling. Feeling unsafe as of now. **"Handle it yourself!!! I don't deal with the needy!!!"** He shouts coldly and seriously. Fürthrived remains asleep. Cretan and TSinged are wide-eyed. The boys are thinking of the same outcome. *"He is going to be* *punished." "Harsh! Dear Valcomix, you are unkind, and it's unforgivable."* Speaking softly with a violent tone. Her eyes flash a light pale violet and shining pink color. Valcomix turns his head, seeing her vicious smile of bright whites. TSinged saw the flicker of color change. Frightened, he keeps his focuses ahead. Valcomix's heart is pounding.

## ELEVEN MILES LEFT

They feel that the air is warming up. The violent swirling is pulling them in. The fog is lighter. The sky is darker, and they can feel shaking. Cretan looks up from behind and can see clearly that one of the vortexes is nearing them. **"We got to move fast!!!"** He screams. Valcomix has already noticed. **"Cretan, it's alright. The leading one isn't our worry. It's the next funnel that will be trouble."** He tells the panicked Cretan as he remains calm. TSinged looks at him with a serious expression. **"How do you know? We're being pulled back by it!"** Misplacing his anger. TÖ-Slüdge shakes her head. **"We're being pulled in, and then we'll be pushed forward forcefully. This is the effect of summer's funnels. The secondary spins ahead of the primary. It's faster, warmer, and lighter. We are experiencing it now. The primary is heavier, colder, and slower. Exact opposite. The secondary is a natural gathering of air pressure and moisture.**

**Feeding the primary to become a category weather threat that will pass through some states or it will end up north again. I was a C.O.A.T.S. soldier. I earned my badges; one titled me as a meteorologist.** He shares with everyone to qualify that his reasonable answer is sound.

Amused, TÖ-Slüdge smiles proudly. TSinged grumbles. Cretan returns to keep his eyes on the device. The funnel is miles behind them, and they can feel the force pulling them. Cretan's skin tone changes to dark gray with blue bumps all around his body. Unmoving. TSinged puts all his weight on his lower body and holds onto TÖ-Slüdge. Bearing the pain of touching her. Valcomix kneels onto a knee and places a hand on the ground. Keeping low to the ground. Soon, the pulling subsides, and the vortex moves away. **"Alright, everyone, get to running and become as lightweight as possible!!!"** He yells, sprinting ahead. Cretan then again changes his skin to a plastic-white leathery tone. Rolling after him. TSinged and TÖ-Slüdge chase after them. TSinged is left behind.

The air around them drops in temperature, and thick fog commences its spread. The winds remain violent, and this time, instead of suction, it's a pushing motion. Lifting the four of them off their feet and carrying them inches off the ground as they are pushed by the strong force of winds. Cretan and TSinged are terrified. TÖ-Slüdge is smiling while Fürthived is relaxing in someone's arms. Valcomix is enjoying the moment.

## SEVEN MILES LEFT TO GO

A rough landing causes TSinged to tumble a bit. Cretan rolls on. Valcomix lands lightly as he continues running. TÖ-Slüdge catches TSinged and wraps her arms around his neck. Inflicting minor burns. They all look behind to view the approaching vortex, which is about four times the size of the previous one. Sprinting straight at their top speeds except for Valcomix, who remains near the others. Viewing his surroundings. The fast-approaching vortex is close in suction range.

Reaching the border. Almost there as the dynamic force of winds pulls them slightly. They then fall into a crevice with a cavity ahead. Fast crawling into the dark, narrow tunnel. TSinged is the last one to fall in piling on top of everyone. Stuck and uncomfortable; bearing hope. Taking shelter as the mass of clouds passes by after a while. Relieved as they laugh joyously. Soon, the softened earth gives way under them. They then fall on the underlayer. TSinged is on his back. Valcomix is on his side, tightly holding onto Fürthrived. Bright, fiery eyes staring, reflecting his. She is awake. Smiling comfortably. TÖ-Slüdge rubs her derriere as Cretan is in ball form.

**"We're safe, right?"** TSinged asks, sprawled out while panting. **"Mostly not. Yes, from the weather. But, we're in a tunnel system formed by something."** Fürthrived explains. Everyone stares at her, surprised. Valcomix gets up first and offers her his hand. Pulling her up gently. **"The device isn't working,"** Cretan informs as he gives it to Valcomix. **"It's working properly; it's just not functioning. There are no maps of Playground ID."** He tells everyone as he places the device into Cretan's pack. **"Are we going to climb out or do a whole detour and deal with what dwells down here?"** TÖ-Slüdge asks with a big smile.

*Growling* Valcomix's stomach rumble. Everyone then agrees by default. **"Alternative route,"** TÖ-Slüdge says shaking her head annoyed but smiling generously. Looking at the eastern direction. *Hissing* Just behind them. Fürthrived's brightness provides everyone the view of an eight-legged creature about the size of a house cat. Everyone is concerned, but Valcomix can no longer hold back his hunger and attacks it without hesitation or gives it time to react.

Devouring a light snack. TSinged pinches his forehead that suddenly aches. Cretan hides behind TSinged. TÖ-Slüdge is annoyed, grinding her teeth. Fürthrived sighs. "**Valcomix, you ate a spider.**" Telling him the obvious. Innocently confused, he blinks at them. Acting adorable. **"You ate one of them. We are intruders. You just become a predator. They will get rid of us!!!"** TSinged screams at Valcomix to have him reflect on such an action. *Hissing* *Skittering* **"Here they come."** Fürthrived is rested and full of spunk and excitement. Her comrades are annoyed as they prepare to retaliate. Valcomix's fur begins to shiver. Fürthrived notices that his tail has grown.

**TO BE CONTINUED...**

# EPISODE 5: TAINTED TREACHEROUS TERRITORY.

## PART I

*Hissing* Rhythmic song of the accosting arachnids. TÖ-Slüdge is smiling viciously as her arms are coated with a liquid. Dripping off her perfectly formed, clear nails. *Sizzling* A single drop corrodes the padded layer of dug earth. Fürthrived turns her gaze away from Valcomix and focuses on her left. Radiating a heat that causes the moisture in the softened clay and dug earth to evaporate and dry out. Cretan is hiding behind TSinged, who is in a boxing stance. Valcomix shows off his teeth and sharp nails. His tail sways gently about, and his ears are folded back. *Calm breathing*

Both sides are occupied by a lot of them. Reflecting five intruders from their numerous black beady eyes. Now, seeing a shine of white. Valcomix takes the first bite. Shaking his head violently. Releasing a half-eaten arachnid to be flung around. Jumped by many of them. His sharp, long nails leave a glare. He rips through them. Reduced to a clump of flesh exposing their innards. Pooling their warm crimson sour-smelling protein and iron upon the wet dug clay. Valcomix steps onto the wet red. Soaking his feet. Everyone witnesses his actions and cannot unsee what violence he committed.

Facing the opposite side of the tunnel. TÖ-Slüdge follows in with a single swing of her arm. Splashing her fluids onto their numbers. Hissing in agony as their skin begins to exfoliate and bubble. Fürthrived approaches them slowly. Burning them from her tremendous orange glow. The many brave ones climb around, trying to surround her. But to no avail. Her orange glow is causing them to cook within their exoskeleton. Sweltering. The arachnids are now cautious not to approach them on the other side. Valcomix is overwhelming them by his lonesome. Gory seen, as he has been slaughtering them and eating them. A voracious appetite that has not been sated yet. His veins are burning scarlet.

**"Valcomix?"** TSinged asks as he approaches him. Then, in a reflex, Valcomix turns his raged expression onto an ally. TSinged didn't react. Then, he pets his head. **"There aren't any more here."** He tells him with a gentle voice. **"There are plenty. There are numerous tunnels, and there is a pocket below."** Fürthrived informs her allies as she senses many heat signatures and feels the warmth that is natural. Weirded out by her use of skill. Valcomix closes his eyes. *Low throbbing* **"Can you guide us deeper below?"** He asks requesting...

Eyes filled with hate and malice. Everyone keeps silent. **"I can,"** Fürthrived tells him, reassuring his plea but gripping her arm terrified of his expression. But still supports his antagonistic work.

Traversing cautiously east of the tunnel, descending down by a slant, holding their nose as the air is horrid. It also causes slight headaches. Except for Valcomix. Then, entering a vast opening that is absolutely dark. Fürthrived's luminous glow shows that they are walking a narrow bridge. Valcomix's red eyes are open. Sighting numerous bridges connecting to proper tunnels. Common to an ant's colony structure. The air smells of mildew and rot. There is also a strong stench of decay. They see no bottom, yet they hear and feel something breathing coming from below them. **"Fürthrived, climb on my back."** Valcomix commands, and she does not hesitate. Eager to be spoiled. Wrapping her arms around his neck. **"Everyone, follow after me."** He commands. Cretan steps a bit off the bridge. Afraid and then clings to Valcomix's tail.

*Sigh* **"Don't grip too hard, and don't drag me down."** He tells Cretan, trying to comfort his unease. He is clenching his eyes shut while his arms are holding onto his furry ligament.

TÖ-Slüdge looks around and can see something glistering along a thin wire. They're also moving and vibrating. **"Wait."** Calling out and getting her allies' attention. **"We are in the arachnids' house. There are thousands of webs surrounding us. They already know we're here and probably planning to get rid of us by the numbers. If we can find their central web that is guarded by a queen, we can disconnect all of them from one another. We should devise a team to deal with the opposition. But the queen will be guarded by goliath-sized spiders or durable poisonous ones. I am hoping for a goliath since our muscle here can handle it."** TÖ-Slüdge informs while praising TSinged for his strength. **"How big is the queen?"** Valcomix asks, seeking more valid information.

**"Uncategorized. It was written in some notes, but the queens weren't discovered. Valcomix, what are your intentions?"** TSinged asks, and Valcomix keeps focus, glaring at the below. **"I told you. I am removing all high-level threat s for the C.O.A.T.S. This playground is a hazard zone for them to claim back. Thank you for the information. If my actions are unsettling, then**

**don't intervene to aid me."** He expresses his gratitude and readies to jump. She shrugs her shoulder. TSinged can see he is determined to give grounds and territory for those people. Valcomix then jumps to the bridge below them. TÖ-Slüdge follows the light, and TSinged chases it.

Running along the narrow paths and then jumping. The stench becomes thick, creating a fume that is inches above the flooring. Landing in muck. Viewing that this is a feeding ground. Rotting bones and webbed animals as if mummified. Decay has lingered. TÖ-Slüdge becomes nauseous. Feeling sick. The floor is flooded with crimson protein that has moss growing from it and bacteria swimming in it. Fürthrived's presented ability causes the vile mixture to boil. *Hissing* *Sloshing*

Valcomix notices everyone is uncomfortable and quite sick. He quickly jumps up and has Fürthrived and Cretan upon the bridge. TSinged follows him as he carries TÖ-Slüdge. TSinged has seen a notable change. Valcomix's has four spikes protruding out his back; brightening crimson as well. Unleashing his claws and teeth. **"TSinged, this area is vile."** Cretan says, complaining about the bad smell. TSinged silently agrees. *"It's a fitting place for that thing."* Mocking the creature as he saw it smile with that expression.

*Splash* Landing with all four limbs soaking within the putrid compound. His veins are heating up, and his heart is pumping calmly but loudly. Something is moving fast. Leaving ripples. Remaining calm and patient as his long tail sways and his ears folds back. It tries to kick Valcomix, but he dodges to the side and bites hard on the leading leg. Pulling it with a yank. The arachnid hisses in agony, falling to its side. Trying to stand, but only splashes. Its six eyes see white and a gluttonous throat. Its jet-black, shiny body reflects the ugliness of hunger. *Spray* Saved as the intruding creature is webbed. Tangled by the ambushing others. Three more. One is brown, another is a dark shade of blue, and the last is a skinnier black.

Trapped in their web. He struggles to remove himself. The skinnier one steps over him; its sharp legs pierce one of his paws. Now hinged back, exposing its dripping fangs. Hissing out victory. Finds Valcomix's head and drops its fangs. Valcomix's tail swirls, having it to get bit instead. Everyone above is witnessing his deadly end. **"Those designs on their abdomen."** Cretan is worried as his fear becomes wide. Panicking. TSinged clenches his fist. Fürthrived's heat is increasing. **"Why is he smiling?"** TÖ-Slüdge realizes that the creature is having fun. Then, the others see him as well. **"He is fighting against True Widows."** Cretan and Fürthrived announce as they fear for him.

**LATRODECTUS**: Commonly known as True Widows, sighted as black, brown, and blue. Distinct markings of hourglasses on their abdomen or other bright colored shapes upon it. The dark blue one is dull in color and hairier than the others, with a silver ink blotch-like marking. The skinnier black arachnid that is injecting its venom into the tail of the intruder has four orange circles for its marking. The tan-brown type widow has a red cross marking. The one unable to balance is the commonly known Black Widow that most are familiar with due to red hourglass marking.

**CONTINUED**: Residing near the master/ central web. They are weaker than goliath spiders. They are highly potent in their use of venom. The first bite is painful, followed by seizures, and then the nervous system shutdown. Then death. Fatal ambush predators to wandering trespassers. Mostly table-sized or a fraction smaller. Scaled as a level 10 threat when grouped and when confronted in their home. If flushed out, their threat level is equivalent to that of a roach. A measly 4.

Valcomix can feel the cool liquid of its potent proteins being injected into his bloodstream. He uses his sharp nails to free his paw. Piercing through its soft underside. It lets go of his tail, thrashing in agony. His sharp nails are tearing open its underside due to him keeping hold of the arachnid's innards. Feeling the warmth of its wet disturbance. Its thick crimson coats him and the web. Causing it to loosen. Valcomix, who is now free, has his other set of nails at the ready. Swipe. Slicing its head; removing its fangs as they are flung away. He then bites its head. Adding another ingredient to the vile flooring of muck. Desecrating the carcass by standing on it with one foot. ***SCREECHING LAUGHTER*** His veins are now brightening a scarlet shine. Skin crawling scene.

# PART II

The four are disgusted. Noticing the disturbing movement of his veins bulging, deforming his fur. But his back is increasing movement. The four bumps are brightening to a luminous scarlet color and growing thinly out. His nails are also increasing in size, and his canines are sharpening. Everyone is witnessing that...

Valcomix is evolving. His body is even growing. Then, it suddenly condenses. His tail is longer and curved at the tip. His eyes have brightened as well. Then, something emerges out of his back. Four long flowing scarlet-like whips. They touch the flooring, acting like straws. *Rejuvenated snide* They then touch the carcass. Causing it to decompose fast. He is feasting. Cretan looks at TSinged, and he stares back. Shrugging his shoulder.

Closing its eyes. Hearing the loud breathing more clearly. Feeling the complication of his made shifted form. Lighter. Turning to face the common widow. Easily clearing the distance with only a few steps from a sprint. Testing the sharpness of his developed nails. Slicing perfectly into its abdomen. Releasing its meaty contents. He can feel the warmth of crimson being fed into him through his fur. Just standing in the muck of this vile compound is replenishing him, satisfying his hunger. On cue, his four exposed veins enter the opening, draining everything inside. Leaving just a shell of the exoskeleton. The two other arachnids are backing away from him. Noticing the slight movement from them. With a single breath, the creature proceeds with violence. Moves swiftly, takes apart its legs, and then puts itself on top of it. Bending it back by grasping its head. Revealing its two sharp appendages. Using its other paw to grip one. Then pulls it off.

Fürthrived turns her sight from it, holding her mouth. Disturbed by its cruelty. **"That is so cruel. What is Valcomix doing?"** TÖ-Slüdge asks as she watches him disrespect a natural life. Holding back her tears, seeing him cause meaningless animalistic torture. TSinged only sighs. **"Valcomix is fighting a war for them. Unleashing his resentment on them. The queen will be given the worst treatment if he manages to bring it down."** He tells them, that he as well is disturbed by how it treats them. Cretan is concerned. *"He is tearing them apart. This change of his is quite frightening."* He tells himself as he watches Valcomix torture the arachnid, draining its innards through the use of his exposed thin whip veins. The arachnid screeches and hisses while in agony. Trying to crawl, only inching forward as its warm fluid spills from its torn abdomen. Hanging loose are its organs. Touched by the flailing whips causes them to melt. Feeding the main body of its usurper.

The arachnid slowly stops its struggle and falls. Now, another being that is decaying in its own territory. Claiming an easy victory as the violent being drains it dry. *"Ironic."* Cretan mutters. Knowing that spiders drain their victims while alive. Merciless creatures lay their eggs in the stomachs of their victims. Witnessing Valcomix commit the same action, except he doesn't lay any eggs within them. All Latrodectus/True Widows have fallen. Now just empty husks drained of their contents. The creature remains unsatisfied; its warm, pulsing veins coil around the carcass of the arachnid. Desecrating the exoskeleton by slashing. Opened its form only to feel a moist heat that was trapped within. He then does the same to others. Only to be given the same conclusion.

It is not safe to go down from the bridge they're upon, knowing how that creature is roaming. TSinged takes the initiative. Leaping down. The creature notices him and has TSinged as a target. Feeling a sense of déjà vu. Confronting Valcomix. He doesn't want to be bitten by it again. *Crack* Cracking his knuckles from his right hand. *Pound* An instant direct hit to the being's face. *Groaning* Not knowing what just happened; Valcomix has regained consciousness and reasoning. Feeling a throbbing headache as he is kneeling up while soaking in muck. Sighting the four exoskeletons bathing in the vile crimson compound, then the serious standing TSinged. He approaches Valcomix. Offering his hand. **"Paw."** TSinged orders Valcomix with a mischievous smirk.

*Snarling* **"Preposterous, you pompous naïve contentious muscle-bound creep! I am not your pet!"** Valcomix tells him as he detests his way of ordering but still takes his gesture to stand up. TSinged smiles heartily as Valcomix's reasoning is restored; also, someone knows how to obey. Valcomix's expression is wide-eyed as he is already standing. Sighting that the two are holding each other's forearm. Quickly taking back his hand. *Grumbling*

**"I wouldn't have to do so if someone didn't lose their mental state and went full animalistic. Just look at yourself. As long as you can obey, you can change form and become wild anytime you want. Don't become a threat to us."** TSinged warns Valcomix as his long ears perk up. Listening. Then he turns his sight to the bridge. Clearly, he did something that made everyone aware of him. No collection of the cause. Valcomix inhales softly. **"TSinged, keep this premonition to yourself. When it happens, I won't be returning."** Valcomix requests of him as he feels different, and his thoughts are disturbing. Sounding melancholy, TSinged wants to talk to him more, but the three have jumped down.

Cretan admires Valcomix's new look from a better view. Up close. Valcomix is trying to gain back his personal space by backing away. But to no avail, Cretan and Fürthrived are both touching his softened fur. Silkier and smooth, and his tail is rough. Trying to get a feel of his exposed veins, swaying away from their hands. Valcomix looks to TSinged for aid. He and TÖ-Slüdge are discussing something. TÖ-Slüdge stops whispering and takes notice of the annoyed Valcomix. Watching Fürthrived all joyous while being wrapped around by his tail. TSinged focuses on them as well and holds a smirk.

**"That is enough. We have to get out of here. Lingering more in their home is not a place to frolic."** TÖ-Slüdge says, interrupting everyone's fun. She may be smiling, but she is agitated as she is focused on Valcomix and Fürthrived. The two-step back from the fluff. **"It's going to be a long climb."** TSinged says as he gazes at the darkness above. Fürthrived and Valcomix both have their eyes closed. She can sense a large pocket of heat close by. He can feel faint vibrations in the room, a faint rhythmic thumping coming from below, and movement nearby. **"There is a passage**

**over there,"** Fürthrived says while pointing towards the east. Giving each other a cautious glare.

Valcomix takes steps to find the source of the vibrations. Now standing underneath a ball of woven white threads suspended under the last bridge. TÖ-Slüdge stands next to him. Then the others. **"That's is the master web. Every arachnid of this home is connected to it."** TÖ-Slüdge says as she is fascinated by its size, color, and shape. Approximately has an 8.25ft radius, a lustrous white, and a perfect sphere. Meaning its volume is about 2352.07cu/ft. The others admire such a thing as it is their first time seeing one so close. Watching Cretan form up to a ball; heaviest skin. Dark gray plates with blue bumps: which has a volume of about 65.45cu/ft. They stare and wonder at such a creation. Yet, Valcomix has a blank expression focused on the dangers it can cause.

**"Fürthrived, burn it for me, please."** He pleases. She looks to TSinged. Not giving her much restriction to not do it, as he nods. Agreeing with Valcomix. She then looks to TÖ-Slüdge. **"Do we have to do such a thing? We have already invaded and terrorized them."** She says to Valcomix, who doesn't seem moved. His expression remains blank. **"I'm removing all potential threats. Eradicating their numbers and eliminating the queen is the goal here. I told you already. I'm removing all**

**difficult threats."** Valcomix reminds everyone. **"That was the agreement to have him guide us."** TSinged, reminding all about the verbal contract. She has no choice but to fulfill an outrageous request. Cretan is worried that the spiders will be vanquished.

Valcomix bends down, exposing his back to Fürthrived. She then wraps her arms around his neck. He leaps to take hold of the master web. His arms become tangled and stuck to the sticky threads. Fürthrived increases her heat. Temperature rising, causing his veins to brighten and the web to melt. The individual loose threads connected begin to burn. The two drop down to see the work of their action affect the area. A beautiful sight of the threads catching fire. The whole room is glowing. A few spiders are falling overhead to their sudden expiration. Cretan protects his head. The glowing dims down, returning to the vast darkness. Now considered finished work. Valcomix heads towards the next passage. The others follow.

# PART III

Walking through a vast passage that is filled with clumps of wet dirt. Soon, finding connecting passages. They keep straight, and then curve down. Valcomix begins to become uneasy, and his veins flicker from a scarlet color to a crimson hue and then back. He stops, unable to move forward. **"Valcomix, you alright?"** TÖ-Slüdge asks worryingly. **"No."** He answers as he is afraid of what is coming. The ground begins to shake. **"Everyone, move out of the way; something is coming!"** Fürthrived yells as she alerts her comrades. Feeling that the ground underneath them is giving way. Valcomix's legs have failed. **"I hate...**

**GIANT PALOUSE EARTHWORM**: The huge body of this creature reaches the size of a bus. Mucus covered thick, soft flesh. A single eye that is blue or cyan on the spot above its head. A mouth filled with eight rows of curved teeth. Prey cannot escape as it takes in rocks or dirt within its massive body to keep prey down. Weak to salt, vinegar, hot water, and a lot of other things that contain alcohol, sodium and/or heat that is over 210°F (98.89°C). Just don't divide it. A threat level 6. But to Valcomix, all types of these beings are just dangerous and are a threat higher than the scale can measure.

**"Worms!"** He yells his final words as he is just swallowed from below. Everyone witnesses his demise. The creature returns downwards. The massive body of this gross sight of a creature causes the flooring to give way. The four hitch a ride on it. Bearing the speed as it digs around. The body is sticky. TSinged is disgusted as he picks his face off from it. Lingering a connection of viscous slime. The girls are sick just from the sight. Cretan is laughing hysterically, taunting his ally. The worm thrashes about and ceases its digging. Breaking the flooring underneath. The four bear the sense of falling. Falling from a great height. All are closing their eyes.

*Splash* All submerged within clear water. Cretan is aided by TSinged. Fürthrived is aided by TÖ-Slüdge. All swimming to the shore. Now gathered together. Cretan is breathing hard. TSinged is upset. Fürthrived is frightened, and TÖ-Slüdge is angry. **"What just happened!?"** The sudden event has TÖ-Slüdge confused and angry. **"A giant worm came from under us and fell from up there,"** Cretan answers her as he tries to catch his breath. **"Valcomix was eaten,"** Fürthrived says as she watches the worm's body float. *Tch* **"Everyone, on guard."** TSinged orders them as he sees legs and eyes coming from the many holes surrounding the area.

They have sighted the many insects crawling from the exits. **"We were just in a spider's home; now we're**

**in some nest?"** Cretan distinguishes as they're two separate infestations. Then he notices that the insects are different. Roaches, centipedes, silverfish, crickets, termites, and other species. **"This isn't a normal nest."** Cretan informs everyone. They even know that this nest is a new-found nature of insects under another nest.

*Muffled screaming* All focusing on the bulging area coming from the lifeless worm. Its skin is ripped violently as thick fluids pollute the water, turning it a yellow color. Exhumed from the length of the being is another creature. *Tearing* *Sloshing* *Splatter* Creating an opening through the soft flesh by the chunks. Carving its way to the outside. Sighting the many insects. ***SCREEAHHHH!!!*** The high-pitched scream bellows out of the worm. Echoing. Taking its step onto land, feeling solid ground. Fürthrived and Cretan are smiling. Relieved that he is alive. TÖ-Slüdge and TSinged are shocked but can see the anger from him. **"Infestation. Exterminate all."** His expression is blank. Then, with a dashing leap, he makes the first bite.

Going on a rampage, quickly reducing their numbers by tearing through bodies with his sharp nails. His veins and tail sway. The insects try to attack to defend their home against this intruder. Same as he did with the spiders. The bigger ones are quickly dealt with by his fast use of clawing. Their underbellies are pooling their contents to be seen. Leaving with carnage. He gets bitten, he bites back, and his wound heals. Replenished by their meat and iron. TSinged, and the others can only hear the cries of the tormented beings. Many of them abandon their nest. Valcomix laughs viciously as his body is layered with contents of deep crimson. Claws lingered with torn and shredded skin. His teeth have their remains. He held no mercy. Quick work of the mass number of the nest. The exposed veins clean him off, including his teeth, as if the violence wasn't caused by him.

*Rhythmic thumping* The loud sound is heard where TSinged and the others stand. While Valcomix can actually feel the thumping from already being within the tunnel. **"Remember that large pocket of heat I mentioned? It's near, and it seems alive."** Fürthrived tells her allies. Perplexed expressions. **"Valcomix is heading towards its location."** She continues, and TSinged stares off into the darkness, where the creature had entered **"Lead us to it."** He orders her. She nods and begins lighting their way.

Warm, moist, eerie, and putrid scented passages. Traveling the various crafted openings. The thumping causes the walls to shake and affects their heartbeat. The feeling is strange and quite ominous. Soon, they arrive in a vast opening much like the spiders', yet this one has fine moss growing. The stones are glowing. A small pond. Humid area. Above is a type of amber placed in the cracks. The four examine the room. **"There is something in the next room."** Fürthrived tells them. A single passage with a massive opening. Annoyed by how there are many chambers beneath this Playground. **"How far deep are we?"** Cretan asks as he gazes above. No one is able to determine the distance.

They make their way to the next room. As the passage descends, the air becomes thick and vile. Entering the hot area where the crimson compound is boiling. In the center resides a huge mound of greyish-white quaking flesh. The thumping is its heartbeat. Throbbing skin with numerous tentacles slurping up the muck. Disgusted and terrified as they are in the lair of the queen. TSinged and Cretan are sweating. The heat is sweltering. **"We must be deep underground where magma chambers are found. Stepping into that pool can cause severe scalding. What insect is that, and how is it able to handle this intense heat?"** TSinged asks, keeping himself at bay by not touching the boiling muck slightly.

**TERMITE QUEEN (ABNORMAL)**: A regular Termite Queen has a white sheen sbody. They can reach the size of a bus. Mostly, they live in thick forests with flourishing roots that are nutritious. Thrive in modern climate. Their threat level can reach an 8 to a 10, depending on the size of their nest. This one is highly mutated. Three times the size of the regular/ normal. Eight tentacles, dim white body. Thicker skin. Eyeless. Able to withstand temperatures up to 1450°C (2642°F). Its threat level is categorized as unknown. Has just been discovered.

**"It will be best to just leave it alone,"** TÖ-Slüdge says. Everyone else is in agreement as they make their way back up. *Sprinting* Something came in fast, glowing red. *Splash* Without any hesitation, it entered the boiling muck. All are turning their heads. **"This can't be real,"** TÖ-Slüdge says with her eyes open along with the others. **"I'm just as stunned as all of you."** TSinged shares with everyone. **"Heh, what is Valcomix?"** Cretan asks as he witnesses him make his way towards the slumbering massive lump of white flesh. "**He isn't going to do something mindless, is he?"** Fürthrived asks as he is now close to the queen.

Valcomix is in range of his target. A depraved smile. His fur is glowing scarlet, and his veins are surging brightly. His tail is lined with a scarlet spiral. Curved at the tip is a crimson point. His sharp nails are glowing, and so are his teeth. Gaping his mouth. Strands of saliva are connecting from each of his canines. His tongue flicks to the underside of his jaw. Releasing a vapor from his breathing. Everyone gulps. Hoping he isn't about to do what he is going to do. *Snap* *Bite* *Tear* Squish* A fast bite.

Valcomix has torn off a clump that is bigger than his jaw. *Clicking* The huge insect turns around. Then stands on six huge, sharp legs. It blinks. It does have eyes. Twenty dark orange round-like mirrors. Reflecting the creature chewing on its torn piece. Now, seeing eyes to eyes. Valcomix gulps down the chewy raw meat. *Burping* The insect belches showing off its wide, caved mouth that can easily eat Valcomix as a snack. Its slob escapes from its cry. Coating Valcomix with its saliva. He turns to face the creature. *SCREEAHHHH!!!!* He cries back.

*Laughing* **"Valcomix bit off a chunk from her butt."** Cretan shares. They just look at him, not amused, but can't help but smile and chuckle. The queen swallows the vile, boiling compound as she tries to devour her attacker. Its tentacles are pointed at him. Swinging them down fast. The muck splashes about, causing it to undulate. Valcomix is dodging while scratching at each one that comes close. Finally, his nails get stuck into one and is taken above its body. He lets go and drops upon its bouncy top flesh. Sliding down from its side. He takes his sharp claws and teeth.

Tearing through its soft flesh, as he falls. Dropping into the vile. The creature sees him and swipes her leg quickly. Managing to evade her attack. He was surprised as he was able to. She then stomps around while swinging her huge tentacles.

Not noticing that he is climbing her leg. He then slashes the softer meat, connecting it to its underbody. Its pink ooze spills, and Valcomix takes a drink. *Burping* The insect is in agony as it loses its back right leg. Managing to keep up using its others. Standing on his gain as his exposed whips melt the ligament. The insect uses the muck like a wave to toss him about. The area is getting hotter, and the muck is rising and glowing more. Both feel uncomfortable. Valcomix's fur and body are steaming. The insect's body is doing the same. He has the chance to use his speed as an advantage. Valcomix notices that his heartbeat matches that of the queen. Calming his breathing. Focusing on its wounds.

The queen's legs are melting down a bit, and Valcomix's feet are burning, running through the intense boiling of the muck, using his tail to wrap around a leg. Jumping from leg to tentacle, then to the top. Quickly biting off chunks of her flesh and slashing it. Pink hot ooze drains from the open wound. Inflicting more pain as his exposed veins squirm inside the queen. Continues his slashing as his nails dig through layers of flesh. *Burping* The queen begins to hit herself desperately, trying to get rid of a pest. Thrashing about. Then Valcomix smiles evilly, inserting his tail into the newly inflicted dug wound.

Infecting it as its white flesh begins to brown. Spreading a disease slowly into its bloodstream. Releasing the venom that was stored in his long-furred ligament. Rotting its skin, which is now easily peeled off. The rising temperature is painful to it. Thrashing around. Loose boulders, dirt, rocks, and clay fall. *Burping!!!* Releasing its tortured cry before going silent. *Sizzling* Valcomix makes his exit from the room towards his teammates. His body is burning up. Quickly dashing towards them. **"Don't touch me!"** He yells as he passes them as he ascends. The four are worried, impressed, and frightened.

# PART IV

## ENTERING THE ROOM OF THE HUMID CLIMATE AND OVERGROWN MOSS

Valcomix is soaking himself in the pond. Cooling down his heated body. *"That threat would have been highly difficult to deal with. Even if they send their best soldiers, none of them can survive the temperature of that area. That is one threat removed. But there is another one residing above. The apex of Playground ID. I'm not ready to take it on just yet. I'm still afraid."* He admits to himself as his hands are shaking. Relaxing himself as he closes his eyes. *Breathing calmly* After a moment. The four have now entered the room. Searching around. TÖ-Slüdge smiles and chuckles a bit as she stumbles upon something adorable floating in the water.

She waves her hand, getting the other three's attention. Holding a finger to her soft lips. **"He was just gruesome and violent since we came down here. A menace to the arachnids and insects. He took down a queen, and all of his actions had no empathy, just driven by carnage. Yet he remains adorable."** Cretan informs his comrades and mainly himself that the nonsense needs an explanation. *Giggling* **"As long**

**as someone or something is cute, all troubles are forgiven."** Fürthrived tells him. TSinged and TÖ-Slüdge do not agree with that logic. She already sees the two as adorable and cute and still deserves much-needed punishment for any bad behavior. TSinged follows Valcomix and finds a place to rest, taking off his pack. He lay on the wet moss with his hands behind his head, gazing at the glowing ceiling. *Yawn* He also closes his eyes.

Cretan puts down his backpack. Rummaging through it and then peers inside. The food supply is scarce. Fürthrived is lying upon TÖ-Slüdge's lap as they engage in conversation. Enjoying some downtime. Everyone is now resting easily after their events of physical and mental strain. Valcomix definitely needed to rest. Just floating comfortably in the pond. TSinged is only just resting his body as he is up studying the rock structure and admiring the glowing stones embedded in the walls. Soon, the area around him gets dark.

Knowing that this is impossible. He turns his head to look behind himself. Sighting red and gold fur attached to the front leg of a huge, statured beast. A long narrow face. Huge slanted, vibrant crimson eyes. Six long black whiskers. He turns away from the creature agitatedly. *Deep breath* **"Can we relax for**

**a few more hours?"** TSinged asks, as there is another type of animal that they must deal with.

**"Are you the one that ended the reign of the queen?"** TSinged is asked a question and is confused about who asked. Looking around. Seeing the huge animal and searching for any human-like being that is able to speak. **"Let me reinstate my question. Are you the being who fell the queen that reigned here?"** TSinged is shocked. This animal is politely asking him while speaking the old dialect. **"Uh. No. I wasn't the one that caused her to fall."** TSinged answers it, confused. "**For what reason are you down here? These were her chambers; since the one who ended her has claimed her territory, it may not be kind to trespassers."** The being warns TSinged. He gazes in the direction where Valcomix rests. **"May I ask what you intend to do to the being that now rules her territory?"** TSinged asks politely. Then, the animal gets to eye level. **"You are in league with the next competitor to claim all."** It concludes with a serious tone. TSinged is again is worried over Valcomix.

**"I just want to ask a serious question. Depending on the new ruler's mindset. Does it want to claim both territory or to reside mainly down here?"** TSinged is unaware of how to answer its question. Pondering on the best answer, as Valcomix did mention. 'To take back the Playgrounds and get rid of their threats'. But he is tired right now. This creature seems to be polite. TSinged stands firm and is eyes to eyes with it. **"He is resting right now."** TSinged informs the fox. It looks around, noticing a few others. The girls are gazing at him, and a smaller being is surprised but still continues to snack on some jerky. Checking behind itself and just underneath its twin tails. Resting so peacefully is, a creature of black fluff.

**"This being is puny; how can such a thing, such as this, defeat that queen?"** The fox asks as it dangles a paw, exposing a sharp nail over him. **"He did defeat the queen! Valcomix did it all by himself. Took out many of the insects and arachnids as well!"** Cretan shouts, praising his ally's feats. The creature snickers as it removes its paw from over Valcomix's torso. **"If you claimed to have earned the lower grounds, then I must tell you to remain down here. I rule the top."** It informs Valcomix menacingly. Awakening fast, he stands firm. Making eye contact. *Snarling* Determined. **"Not much longer. I want you out of the Playgrounds!"** Valcomix tells it. The fox blinks twice and then smile. Noticing this creature is trying to be brave. Watching him shiver. **"Are you no longer afraid this time, brat?"** The fox asks Valcomix using the combined language. Remembering a snowy day as he was peered down. Gripping his claws. Angry and torn. Tears fall from Valcomix. The three of the four are confused. **"No,"** Valcomix answers using the combined dialect. The fox walks past him and moves swiftly out of the area.

TSinged is seriously listening while the others are confused as to what transpired and why Valcomix began to tear up. Worried about him as Valcomix hasn't said anything else yet. TSinged notices something is off; he then jostles his shoulder a bit. Impressed and concerned as...

**"How do you faint standing up?"** TSinged asks him as Valcomix is blank. Even his tail is stuck. Just a statue standing firm. Picking up his lightweight body to the water. **"Is he alright?"** TÖ-Slüdge asks TSinged. **"I don't think so."** He answers, ridiculing their exchange of words while splashing water on Valcomix. He finally blinks. Holding his head. Sitting up and putting a hand on his right knee. Seeing his hand shiver. **"I'm afraid."** He says aloud. Everyone heard him. He realizes and looks down. Fürthrived scratches his head. **"Care to explain so that we may understand?"** Asking him with a soft, gentle tone. They are gathered around him.

*Exhale* **"That monster took the lives of my unit."** He tells them. Clenching his knee, he is angry. No one interrupts; just let him continue of what qualms he has. He stares at the band.

**RED FOX (ABNORMAL):** Apex beast of Playground ID. Highly agile, clever, and brilliant. Its fur is light red with gold mixed in. Compared to a normal and standard fox, its size is abnormal. 4.5m (15ft) tall as it stands on all fours. 11.25m (36.91ft) From nose tip to tail end. The length of its tails is 3.75m (12.3ft) long. Uncategorized feature except it can speak fluent old dialect and the combined language. But only a single C.O.A.T.S operative knows of this. Its threat level is 11.5 due to the major difficulty of hunting it. But to Valcomix, a threat not wanting to challenge.

# PART V

Valcomix's paws are shaking. Feeling his heart pound violently. The stomach is squeezing tightly. Closing his eyes and only envisioning the red snow and that creature peering down at him. *Choking* Fürthived pats him on the back. *"Symptoms of trauma."* TSinged, Fürthrived, and TÖ-Slüdge notice what he is going through as they are concerned. **"Breathe slowly and deeply."** Fürthrived tells Valcomix as she pats and rubs his back. Easing out his coughing fit. Now, able to breathe normally, and the shaking subsides. Gazing into her bright glowing eyes and seeing pathetic weak creature. *Grumbling* Valcomix turns away, feeling more pathetic.

He tries to stand but staggers back onto his right knee. Fürthrived catches him before he falls over into the water. TSinged lends a hand out to Valcomix. Turning away his gaze from them with a stubborn attitude. **"I'm alright."** He tells them as he stands back up, tottering a bit but is able to walk. TSinged shakes his head, knowing that Valcomix is upset with himself. He just leaves him be. Cretan stares at TSinged and gazes over to where Valcomix is headed. Worried. Fürthrived gestures for TÖ-Slüdge to go talk with him by using her eyes and head movement.

## IN THE CHAMBER WHERE THE BOILING MUCH BUBBLES

Valcomix stares at the melting mass of brown muscle. Hugging his knees and closing his eyes. Only visioning crimson splattered upon piles of snow as he is peered down from above. Burning red eyes. Fear overwhelms him. *Coughing* Haunted by this awful image of that day as tears fall from his face. His body shivers. Hugging his knees tighter.

Someone sits adjacent to him. TÖ-Slüdge watches over him and then sighs. **"Please speak to us. You're definitely pushing yourself knowing that you are unwell."** She requests only to be snarled at. It's not convincing for her to be turned away or even threatened. Seeing the glare of hers. *Scoff* **"I'm still terrified of it. To take back the lost states, I have to fight that one. Also, if I cannot manage to face these apex creatures, then I certainly won't be ready to go across the ice. I just know how to get there, but surviving out there is unknown. I have no type of resolve."** Valcomix admits as he pushes each word out forcefully.

Remembering him letting go of his life to find peace. Complaining to himself as weak. He has a burden that she may be unaware of. Valcomix is completely defeated. Staring at his kill as he accomplished such a feat on his lonesome. Yet a fox of similar status is affecting him. That animal caused an indelible memory to him. TÖ-Slüdge opens her mouth but cannot say a good phrase. Pondering for a moment.

**"If you're afraid of going on, that is okay. You don't have to tell us the full details of how you got this way, but we're willing to listen. Living out here is scary enough, but with allies nearby and good friends, we survived this long together. Valcomix, I'm afraid of you. You alone subjugated these chambers and its queen. You have the ability to push onward, just manage to stand, and we'll push you. We are strong, too. Just ask for our assistance. We should persevere altogether."** She says with a softened smile. Seeing him stare at his victory with brighter eyes and a wry smile. Understanding he isn't alone in hardships; they're just uncommon.

TÖ-Slüdge chuckles as she sees his tail slightly swaying up and down. Valcomix can see her chuckling, but as to what? Following her line of sight. He quickly holds down his tail, embarrassed by its wagging. Now, after a while, they remain in silence. Valcomix is smiling as he continues to watch the lump of flesh being cooked. *Low rumble* TÖ-Slüdge heard his stomach growl. Valcomix laughs nervously. **"It's looks delicious."** He tells her with a smile. She gazes at the lump of flesh being boiled and witnesses a bubble form from the underlayer of the skin. *Pop* Disgusted, she holds her mouth. **"You enjoy that. Also, open up to us when you're comfortable."** She says to Valcomix, who nods his head. Now alone and feeling better. His stomach has been grumbling for a while now.

He then stands with a serious expression. Stepping into the boiling bright crimson of this putrid soup. His fur brightens up and smolders. His veins are lighting up, burning a scarlet color. Making his way to the lump of melting flesh. The four whip-like veins slurp up the liquefied boiling brown muck and white chunks of muscle and fat. Feasting on the chewy and softened up mass of flesh as pieces are torn from the use his jagged teeth. Savoring its flavor as its eyes are closed. Euphoria. The shadow upon the wall shows the terrifying action of a creature ravaging its meal. Then it's changing. A form of a monstrosity.

Valcomix heaves heavily as his body is in pain after devouring the remains of the queen. Upon exiting the vile soup with smoldering fur... *Inhale* *Exhale* Inhale* His tail swirls rapidly, and at the same time, his bloodstream begins to brighten vibrantly. Exposing the scarlet veins burning a newer hue. A stable shining pink. His nails are flushed to a scarlet color. His crimson irises widen. *SCREEAHHHH!!!* Unleashing his victorious cry after digesting the queen's melted clumps of flesh. Showing its blackened hot crypt that leads to an insatiable abyss.

## THE OTHER ROOM

Startled by the sudden screeching. TÖ-Slüdge blinks twice. Looking at TSinged, he shrugs his shoulder. **"Sounds like he is enjoying himself. TÖ-Slüdge, what did you say to him?"** Fürthrived asks with a gentle chuckle and joyous smile. TSinged scratches his cheek, staring at his ally quizzically and curiously. TÖ-Slüdge is feeling uncomfortable. **"That he is not alone anymore."** She says, blushing. Putting a hand on over her face to cover her embarrassment. Fürthrived and TSinged stared at her, just smiling. Openly teasing her. Cutely pouting as they do.

Cretan is resting with a joyous grin near the tunnel leading to the remembrance of the fallen queen. Grumbling and rolling to the side to avoid the light approaching. The others notice the glowing passage. All sighting Valcomix's new color change. Entering the chamber. Valcomix stares at the ceiling. **"Are we ready to exit?"** He asks, and they are shocked by his new brightness.

Trying to hold back their snickering. Yet TSinged bursts out laughing... **"Why are you pink!?"** TSinged asks him. Valcomix refuses to answer with a serious stare. **"You are too adorable!"** TÖ-Slüdge shouts. Fürthrived is holding her sides as she laughs. No one is taking him seriously.

*Growling* **"Are we ready to exit?"** He asks again. **"Are you still afraid?"** TÖ-Slüdge asks him, and he remains staring at the ceiling. Closing his eyes, the same image resides. Touching his armband. Then he remembers what TÖ-Slüdge has mentioned. **"Yes, and a bit nervous. Knowing that I'm not alone, I have to refine myself to become better. I won't run."** He tells them with a smile. TSinged nods his head and goes to retrieve one of the packs. Fürthrived taps Cretan lightly to awaken him. He awakens abruptly, rubbing the minor burn. She apologizes multiple times as he gets us up and picks up the pack near him. TÖ-Slüdge sees that everyone is prepared, so she makes her way to the exit.

TSinged follows after. Cretan and Fürthrived make their way as well, careful not to bump into one another. TÖ-Slüdge looks back to Valcomix. **"We're going, so move your pink-lit furry mutt butt as well!"** Shouting at him. He awakens from his daydream and takes the next step, leaving behind a black, wet footprint. The moss around it begins to rot...

**TO BE CONTINUED...**

# EPISODE 6: POISONOUS BLOOD EXCHANGE!

## PART I

### PLAYGROUND WA, SECTOR: 10. WITHIN THE BASE

The time is 5:19am of 07/28/3175

Control room. A certain office with desks, flat top cushioned chairs with three wheels, high-tech laptops, and needed utensils. Modified game controllers on the right side of the desks. A screen covering the north wall is in front of the double railing stairway with a deck. Double doors with a rectangular window. Seen through it are personnel C.O.A.T.S. soldiers unmasked, marching down the corridor. The double doors are pried and held by two. Coordinated walking by two lines of people walking down the stairs and entering their assigned desks. Standing in front of them.

Soon, a single woman with red-colored hair, pale tan skin, brown eyes, and wearing her uniform enters in. "**Good morning, Ma'am!"** The two holding the doors say. They then excuse themselves to go to their assigned desk. Holding the rank of NQ6R. She watches from above, supervising her employees, all of whom have the rank of N4E.

Rubbing her eyes, she puts on her slick square glasses. **"Morning to you all. The bad weather has dispersed and is continuing towards the east."** *Groaning* **"I don't want to work just as much as you don't. Our outfielders need us to report any statuses. Damages to campsites, blockades that need clearing, and more stuff."** She says, leaning over the rails. Taking out her device. Seeing the mission as directed. *Groaning* **"Let's do our job."** She says with a yawn. The desks are now occupied.

As their laptops have visuals of the outside. Yet many of them are showing "Signal lost." Many of them scratch their heads or just gaze, annoyed at the circumstance. Even the boss lady is losing patience. **"The funnels must have got to them. Those factory workers said they upgraded them to be much more efficient and smarter. Those with operating arrows that are live, proceed for mission clearance. Everyone else figure that mess out. Check the recorded visuals, and do something until break time."** She orders, feeling bored.

Checking the recordings. Many of them are surprised, confused, and curious. Checking the readings on the diagnostics for reasons for 'Nonoperational.' After a few hours, most of the workers stand. They then walk to the side. She watches them discuss whatever is needed as long as it isn't personal. After a few minutes, they return to occupy their desk. Soon, they have a clear reading of the failure and recorded visuals. The screen on the wall flares up. A black screen with white-worded coded diagnostics from the many with similar structural damage caused by... "Overheating." She is wide-eyed as she reads the screen.

**"Is there a temperature reading? If there isn't a battery or core corruption, then that is the manufacturer's fault."** She tells them as she stands firm supervising. **"Ma'am, I have found a visual. The location is Playground WA, Sector 22. It is not far from the Freezone. Permission to play."** He requests, trying not to stutter. **"Just do it. I told you before that no one has to ask to use the big screen. These are our toys provided. Just have fun with the busy workload given."** She tells the individual, while smiling.

Most of the employees begin to chuckle. Feeling like the odd one. **"I wasn't informed. I was just relocated to this base the week after I was granted my rank up."** He informs, and she smiles at him. **"Well then,**

**now you know, under my watch after the hallway and behind these doors. Relax. Chat with your fellow operatives on the laptop. You're given toys such as arrows and control them as needed. Race them, play with them. See a target, shoot it. Also, considering that you have been promoted. Congratulations."** She orders him with a serious tone. Generously applauding him as the others join in.

Feeling bashful. **"Thank you. I will do my best to uphold the dignity of the C.O.A.T.S."** He says with enthusiasm. Everyone is disgusted and cringe. She acts like there is a bad taste as if she ate something nasty and heard something horrible. **"Don't ever say something like that. Yes, we follow routines and guidelines. You are outside in the Playgrounds, meaning you play. Clear missions, get points, and reach rank. Celebrate. Just because you were taught a strict form in Dorm, well, that doesn't apply out here. Enjoy your time; it won't last long."** Smiling with a morbid tone. Everyone has similar feelings as her.

He now feels responsible for the heavy atmosphere. She chuckles as she watches over the brat. **"My suggestion. Show that attitude within Dorm and rank it to eight for an easier life. We'll be having more fun out here. Now share with us this visual."** She orders the brat with her arms folded, trying to sound serious and appear bossy. He then turns around, places a sit in his chair, and then presses some buttons.

The video shows a recording with five minutes and a twelve-second time span. The screen displays the enhanced visual with its 4K UHD imaging of the abandoned and filthy airport window with something behind it shining beside a blurry crimson glow. He presses play. There is no sound. Then, after the minute and forty-three seconds mark, the crimson blur moves fast out of the screen. Now, it's just the image of the shining thing behind the dirty, damaged windows. At the four minutes and fifty-one-second mark. *Glass shattering* *Metal scratching* The screen goes back to black. Then, he minimizes this video and expands an another but it's an image. Enhancing the image of a being wearing white clothes with green blobs. She studies the image. **"Enhance the image of the green blob and get us this suspect smug face."** She orders with a serious tone. Executing the order. A square with dotted lines appears on the screen. The blob is seen. Enhancing the image as much as possible. A blurry image of the recognizable symbol is shown. Then, another enhanced image of the being's stature, but it's dark with a crimson glow.

Everyone is stunned and then murmurs. Collaborating with one another. **"Ma'am, we're going**

**to the location to check the damage."** A soldier informs as she plays with the controller. **"Treat the area as a hazardous zone. Be cautious. We may be dealing with one of our northern comrades. Newbie, great job. You have our gratitude. Send those images to the main junction and post it as important."** She orders him as she glares at the images on the big screen. Staring down at the C.O.A.T.S.'s new target. *"I'll have to call this in. If this is their retaliation, then they'll be excused. If this is a transformation of one of them, that base will be given the might of the C.O.A.T.S. faction. This one will have to be done with the issuance of S.O.S."* She tells herself, standing firm and with a serious expression.

# PART II

## PLAYGROUND 10, UNDERGROUND TUNNEL

The distance pathway is lit bright with warm. Cretan walks near to TSinged. Fürthrived takes her steps with TÖ-Slüdge. Valcomix guides them. Showing off his new glow of pink. His fur is still smoldering. His ears are perked up, and his tail sways lively back and forth. Hearing some taunting giggles. Fürthrived tries to catch it. Feeling the soft and smooth brush by a graze from her fingertips. *Low growling* Annoyed as he holds his tail out of their reach. TSinged is serious. **"Stop playing with his tail. You're disturbing his focus. He may be cute and cuddly, but that doesn't mean you should pet him when you feel like doing so."** He says with a kind tone. *Snarling* Valcomix tries to sound convincing, but due to his new scheme of color, it's not.

**"TSinged, looks are deceiving,"** Fürthrived says, smiling at Valcomix. **"When something is bright, colorful, or even just beautiful, they're to be considered the most dangerous. Remember the raccoons and the thorn rope from a certain plant. Fürthrived and I are adorable and cute, but touching**

**one of us can lead to serious injuries. Even Cretan, who is meant to be innocent, can be a little difficult to handle. Now, the addition of Valcomix, who is cuddly, colorful, and adorable, is a danger. Careless behavior has gotten you bit twice."** TÖ-Slüdge informs TSinged with a twisted glare, taunting his very being. Menacing.

Remembering his naivety as he rubs his left arm. Scowling at TÖ-Slüdge, who smiles innocently. Cretan snickers at the situation. **"It won't happen again."** TSinged says in an annoyed, angry tone through his teeth. Fürthrived chuckles. Valcomix smiles and shakes his head. TSinged notices. **"You want to comment?"** He asks with the same tone. **"I'm just another adorable animal wanting to survive outside. Guiding four individuals to unknown lands."** Valcomix says, claiming the new nature of his life with a smile directed to TSinged. Fürthrived scratches the top of his head. Cretan laughs. **"This is fun."** Cretan comments, sounding pleased. Everyone just smiles.

After a while, a bitter-sweet aroma wafts through the tunnel. All smelling the soft sweet yet but bitter scent of nature as it tickles their nose. **"Not far from the exit,"** Cretan says, enjoying the calming aroma. Then, Valcomix notices the cold air carrying a bitter fruit aroma. A pleasant taste even if it's cold. Soothing his mind. Valcomix closes his eyes. The chilling breeze settles his fur to simmer down. The girls hold their hands together. Cretan gets closer to the warmth. TSinged begins to shiver a bit. Reaching the end of the tunnel. The heavy grey light dimly shows the exit.

Valcomix has his eyes closed. Feeling the mild freezing winds upon his fur. *Crunch* His shins are enfolded by a soft and chilling substance. His ear flicks from something that fell onto it. Opening his eyes slowly. Sighting blue sparkling snow overlaying lush violet leaves attached to the trees. Some are bearing fruits with warm colors that are easily spotted. A small stream that is frozen. The sky is still a dark grey with light snow falling softly. **"Wow,"** Cretan says, admiring the view. **"This kind of scenery always fascinated me,"** Fürthrived says, melting the snow around her and exhuming the cyan grass. Plants' life of vibrant colors rest under the piles of snow. Some are in full bloom. Jasmine, red, and gradient white with orange radiate their colors above the snow. **"Yeah, it's amazing and cold. This happens every year, and I feel as if it is getting worse as they pass. Fürthrived, please warm me up more. I'm shivering."** TSinged alerts her with his teeth chattering. Holding his body tight. She then provides the warmth. Feeling his body warm up and seeing Cretan's legs shaking, he pulls him close to get him out of the cold.

TÖ-Slüdge looks around the area with her guard up. **"This forest is a bit eerie. If there are plants in full bloom and ripened fruits scattered around the trees, there should be a variety of animals taking advantage. Not even a footprint or markings."** She says, examining the trees and ground flooring. *Frigid wind* Listening to the sounds from the air and sky. **"It is snowing. When it snows, animals would seek shelter and bother no one. Seeing the sky as it is now, it may become heavy again. Unleashing another blizzard, most likely."** Valcomix informs with confidence. They all look at him, confused.

**"I thought you were more of shooting everything that isn't wearing a uniform kind of soldier,"** TÖ-Slüdge says with a hand on her hip. **"I thought I mentioned that I was taught many skills as I had the badges."** He reinstates, making her smile. Cretan eyes sparkle, anticipating that he wants to be told the story of how he managed to obtain them. TÖ-Slüdge can see what he wants to say.

**"Tell us about your days as a soldier and how you obtained such skills."** She orders, and everyone listens. Valcomix smiles, looking for a pathway to take. Heading Northeast. He then starts to walk by her side, just a few feet apart... **"I took my missions seriously and studied the outside on my downtime from higher**

**ranks. Combatting against those considered a threat. Our respected brother saw me of code, and he had me train to do more difficult tasks. I cleared those missions."** Valcomix shares, then laugh. Such a proud demeanor.

TSinged isn't amused. **"That is kind of cruel. Ordering you to fulfill difficult missions."** He tells Valcomix. Fürthrived nods agreeing with him. **"Just as I thought, you all are just serious, uptight, it's no fun having humans that just fire at anything that walks on more than two legs. Keep going."** She orders sounding intrigued after berating his code. He smiles and laughs knowing they are concerned.

**"The tasks I was given were not really that difficult. Except, I was close to being ended by the apex of Playground NY. But that was my selfish request. I was praised for all my feats and accomplishments. He gave me this armband..."** He says, smiling, but it begins to die. Stopping. He finishes and shakes his head to remove the image of that scene from his mind.

Cretan is astounded, holding no reason to doubt after listening. TSinged ponders a bit and focuses his attention on the ground covered in snow. Fürthrived has her attention to the variety of colors of blooming flowers. TÖ-Slüdge is silent with her eyes closed.

**"Valcomix. Don't fall into depression."** She orders him with a gentle grin. **"I don't consider doing so."** He says, snarling at her. Her violet-lit pupils flash him a glare. **"I have to stay strong with my second chance. Also, to stand tall knowing that I have another team that cares this much."** Valcomix says with a bright smile that is truly aimed at the four.

TSinged is surprised, and Fürthrived's face is red. The glowing becomes intense, and her warmth increases. TSinged notices himself getting cooked. Cretan smiles back. **"Valcomix, you're such a..."** TÖ-Slüdge says with an annoyed, embarrassed, soft tone. **"Dog."** Valcomix smiles at her finishing her remark. **"What happened to calling me a pup?"** He asks with a serious tone but smiling. She refuses to answer. TSinged cannot stand the heated space of Fürthrived. **"Valcomix, you can't go say something such a thing. Especially to the girls. Fürthrived is easily emotional."** He complains as he is being cooked. The two glare angrily at him. Continuing their voyage.

# PART III

After hours of traversing the forest, they reach a frozen pond. Walking around it through deep snow. Fürthrived melts the snow for easier passage. Soon, the Sky brightens, unleashing a bending light striking a tree nearby. The blue spark shined their eyes as they witnessed the wrath of the sky. The wind blows wildly, creating a howl. Violent rain falls then slowly turns to small fixtures of hail. Exposed to the weather. The sudden changes are ridiculous. All five of them are being pelted by the wrath of the storm. *SCREEAHHHH!!!* Aiming his anger at the sky. They cover their ears along with their heads except for TSinged, as the hail doesn't matter to him. The sound is carried by the wind, and the echo is produced. The high-pitched scratching screech is heard.

*Howling* *Screaming* The sound is called back. Received. Valcomix gestures a halt and to be silent. Listening to the ambiance of the eerie nature around them. Closing his eyes. Feet placed firmly upon the cold grass below the snow. His ears are perked up. Feeling the wind and slight vibrations that quickly disperse. Changing to random locations but approaching their whereabouts. Valcomix open his eyes, seeing teeth connected by saliva. A red tongue is lying on the bottom jaw. A dark, wet, narrow chasm further inside. Getting the best view of the mouth of a certain creature. It snaps its jaw fast, then snarls while peering down at the annoying trespassers. Valcomix's mental state replays the same memory from before. TSinged, and the others aren't threatened. Valcomix snarls back nervously, confronting the fox.

"**You want to challenge for my territory now? In these weather conditions?"** It asks menacingly. **"No, I won't claim your area yet. Since we're neighbors, can we share homage right now? I'm being pelted by ice out here. As I am humble and respect the rules, please take us in for temporary shelter!"** Valcomix yells, glaring at its crimson eyes. Its red and gold fur becomes erect. Ready to swipe Valcomix from its sight. "**Such an insolent whelp. I can give your subordinates shelter. But, for you, I don't share my territory. Come."** It orders, using its tails to shield them. Then Valcomix walks alongside it. They're confused and curious as to why and what just transpired.

Valcomix keeps his attention on the fox's stature, and being confident. Feeling a bit creeped out from being stared at. **"You own the underground routes now; why exit out of them in the harsh overworld?"** It asks as it is curious and annoyed. **"Because you reside here, and I want you out. When the snow stops falling, I will claim**

**it."** Valcomix says, focused on the creature. **"That is some grit you got there. Then let me tell you now, I don't want to die."** It says with a smug smirk. Valcomix's heart pounds madly as his anger pumps his blood.

He then sees the four and calms down a bit. **"I won't hesitate nor shiver as before because I don't want to die again."** He tells the apex threat with a menacing glare. The territorial abnormal fox does the same. They both smile as two predators compete to claim. The four notice that Valcomix is shivering still but holding strong to his bravery.

After leaving behind traceable prints in the snow, they reach a huge mound with a dug hole. Fürthrived senses many heat signatures within. The fox enters and yawns. The four were allowed to follow into its den. The owner blocks the deeper reach. They are meant to stay near the entrance. Given only shelter from the harsh storm, not the warmth and comfortability.

**"Valcomix, are you coming in?"** Cretan asks as he puts down the pack and sits beside Fürthrived and TSinged. TÖ-Slüdge lays against the opposite opening. **"I am not welcomed inside. You all take shelter. We'll move on after the bad weather."** He tells them, and the fox scoffs at him. Cretan's eyes are heavy, and he quickly begins to rest.

TSinged follows suit. **"Well, rest easy to all of you,"** Fürthrived says to Cretan, TSinged, TÖ-Slüdge, the hospitable fox, and Valcomix. The fox growls at her, and she just smiles. Only agitating it more. Inhaling gently, then exhales. The fox chuckles and has its attention to its hostile contender that rests outside. TÖ-Slüdge may not understand what is happening, but they have a certain air about them. This causes her to smile and be concerned. The fox covers its face with its long tail. Valcomix rounds himself up and uses his tail to cover his face. *"You're both adorable; Valcomix is cuter, though."* She admits as she watches them. Remembering his words, she blushes and glares at him. Bothered. After battling with unneeded thoughts, she begins to rest.

The sky continues its merciless release of built-up moisture. The mist covers most of the territory. The thickness of it isn't even penetrable by light. The air is warmer, and the lightning strikes upon the land, only causing minor damage. The snow melts slightly.

Fürthrived attempts to shine through but only can have a visual of Valcomix, who remains slumbering. TSinged and Cretan are quite famished. Rummaging through the packs and only finding nothing. **"We have to resupply."** TSinged informs the team. Valcomix ears perk up. **"Sir fox,"** Cretan says, requesting the owner's audience.

*Growling* **"My name is Sevulix."** Sevulix informs them as he focuses on the individual resting on his porch. Sensing the individual who is faking to be asleep. Sevulix smiles, knowing the creature's quiet temper.

The four are confused as to why it has given them its name. Cretan then gazes at the fox once more. The three watch him with a raised eyebrow. **"Sevulix. Can we gather food from your territory?"** Cretan asks humbly. Sevulix peers down at Cretan, snickering at his attitude. Young and innocent. **"You all may replenish your needed appetites. But the challenger outside may not get to feast."** The others now think that this fox needs to be dealt with. Realizing the tension within his home. **"Got a problem?"** Sevulix asks the three who do not want to agree with his standing. **"Stop. Everyone, go enjoy your downtime. I have eaten enough, I'm still full from devouring the queen."** Valcomix says, with his head raised, then rests again.

The three then draw back their disrespect. Seeing him actually just resting. Sevulix himself doesn't want to deal with them either. Both of them are unmotivated to move from their spot. Granted that they can go scavenge for supplies and replenish their appetite. TSinged and TÖ-Slüdge are conflicted that Valcomix won't challenge it now and confused about how they are even given temporary sheltering.

Granted to feed themselves and roam freely in its territory. Fürthrived smiles openly along with Cretan. The two of them stare at Valcomix and Sevulix. Both have unique names and similar sleeping habits. These creatures recognize one another. Fürthrived then grasped the hand of TÖ-Slüdge, intertwining their fingers. She now smiles, and TSinged throws his hands up, giving up on his questions as this situation is confusing, and these two...

**"Fürthrived, and I will go out to gather supplies,"** TÖ-Slüdge informs TSinged, who becomes serious. **"How, most things you touch rot or melt. Fürthrived, same with you. This causes our supplies to be reduced to cinders, which are charred, burned, or dried out. Both of you cause our food to become inedible."** TSinged says to them, and TÖ-Slüdge scowls at him with a menacing glare. **"You and Cretan can go out to do the chore while the two of us will..."** He doesn't want to deal with her when she is in this type of mood. Holding his hands up and backing away. **"Alright."** That is all that TSinged says. Picking up the packs and carrying both. **"Citrus fruits, right?"** He asks, guessing. Surrendering his reasoning. TÖ-Slüdge nods. He leaves quickly to be away from the two of them.

The girls leave as well, heading in the opposite direction from TSinged. Cretan is left alone with a rumbling tummy. Valcomix's ears perk up along with Sevulix's. Listening to his hunger echo, trying to hold back his starvation. The fox gets up and heads down to its den. Soon after, it returns with a variety of fruits. Not a lot, but enough to hopefully shut up his hunger. **"Thanks, Sevulix,"** Cretan says his appreciation. Sevulix returns back to his resting position. Smiling for a bit, but now Valcomix has a conflicted expression.

# PART IV

## A FIELD OF SNOW SURROUNDED BY TREES

The air is warm, and the grass is slippery. The familiar scent of when they exited the tunnels permeates through the air. Carried by the winds. Following where the sweet aroma is strongest. *Giggling* **"TÖ-Slüdge. Stop. No, not yet."** Hearing Fürthrived's soft cries trying to whisper. Noticing a hand placed at her hip. TÖ-Slüdge rests her head upon her warm shoulder. Reaching down to her waist with her other hand. Fürthrived is shy and blushes. Squirming, trying to escape her capture. **"Now, please."** TÖ-Slüdge's irises are burning a dim pink glow. Smiling seductively at the bashful Fürthrived while hugging her. A gentle touch brushes her cheek.

Listening to the rush of TÖ-Slüdge's heartbeat. **"Not yet,"** Fürthrived says, trying to resist. TÖ-Slüdge uses her right leg to cause Fürthrived to fall backward. Now pinned with her wrists tightly gripped. A knee placed at a sweet spot. Her frame blushes, trying to hold back her voice. TÖ-Slüdge smiles mischievously and then whispers into her right ear. *"I thought I told you 'Now'."* TÖ- Fürthived blushes more. Frantic, she forces her eyes to shut. Seeing that her ears are red and her body is becoming warmer than before. Listening to her groan. TÖ-Slüdge then starts nibbling on her left ear softly. *Moist seductive cries*

## BACK IN SEVULIX'S HOME

Cretan is bored as he waits patiently for any comrade to return. Valcomix remains in the spot unmoving and sleep. Sevulix is doing the same. At least they're still breathing but slowly and almost silent. Soon after, some hours before the darkening of a day's end, TSinged enters the den. Cretan has such a wide-grin smile. Puts down the packs and tosses the young member of their group a plum. He catches it and devours it whole; the juice drips down his chin, and he wipes it off with his arm. Noticing two of the beasts slumbering; his head pounds. Confusion and curiosity rile his thoughts with questions about the situation.

He takes out some ripened fruits from one of the packs and lays against the wall to ease his mind. Filling up his hunger. Cretan rolls up to TSinged with jet-black skin with red ink blotch markings. **"How bored are you?"** He asks and gets lightly tapped on his shoulder by his rounding. **"Alright. Change fast."** He says quickly as he lifts Cretan and throws him towards the den's ceiling. Changing his skin to a slippery grass green and lime green skin tone. Slimy and sticky, he is stuck onto the ceiling, dripping fluids. TSinged dodges them joyfully. Then he changes once more into a rougher skin tone that is dark gray with blue bumps. Dropping fast, TSinged has his arms close to his chest. Ready to catch him.

He catches Cretan but is slammed onto his backside, splashing the green goop around the entrance/exit. *Snarling* *Growling* Their noisy play upsets the two once-slumbering beasts. Both show off their teeth and glowing red eyes. Focused at TSinged. Cretan unrolls himself into a plastic white skin tone and snickers silently. TSinged is agitated by both these creatures and the amused Cretan, who is at more fault than he participated. Valcomix and Sevulix return to rest, knowing that there was quietness... Gone!

*Giggling* Hearing the familiar sound of joy. Valcomix raises his head with a mischievous smirk. **"Enjoyed yourselves?"** He asks without any tact. Fürthrived blushes. *Grumbling* **"Go back to sleep."** TÖ-Slüdge orders him with a twisted, menacing smile. He yawns, unfazed by her attitude. **"Now you act shy. We shared a bath, and you were the one that blew on my..."** Valcomix reminds her with a smirk. TÖ-Slüdge face blushes and grumbles, not used to being teased. **"Want my affection as well?"** TÖ-Slüdge asks with a threatening glare dripping her hazardous translucent liquid from her hands. TSinged is annoyed, and Cretan is innocently confused and lost from their conversation.

Fürthrived, who is watching their interaction and the other comrades' expression. **"No violence. Aren't you embarrassed by what you two are saying?"** She asks with a mild tone. Valcomix ceases his crude mannerism, then lays his head onto his paws and covers his face with his tail. Fürthrived shakes her head, smiling. Seeing that the packs look full. TSinged notices that they're staring at the packs.

He then goes to take out some lemons and gooseberries. Passing them to Fürthrived. She shares and hand feeds TÖ-Slüdge. Cretan is bored and rolls around a few times. Soon, the entryway grows quieter as the dark grey becomes dark.

The sky finally settles to its dark grim of smooth clouds that form streams. A moment later, the sky dims to a darker grey. The new morning is unleashing gentle and chilling winds. The snow has melted, creating a glistening dew upon the vegetation. The resting Sevulix and the slumbering Valcomix nose start to twitch. The two yawn and begin to awaken and stretch. The storm has subsided, and the weather is fresh and calming.

Valcomix's venous system burns hot with a pink hue as his scarlet eyes focuses on the fox.

Hearing the restful mass of life around them. Valcomix steps backward away from the den. Sevulix treads carefully as he walks towards the exit. He peers down at Valcomix and gestures with his head to move. They walk side by side to another location. The four who remained at the entrance were awake as well. Following them quietly.

# PART V

**"Valcomix, why do you want to challenge me again?"** Sevulix asks him, focused on the distance ahead. **"I want you out of the Playgrounds,"** Valcomix answers with a stern tone as his nervous heartbeat pumps rapidly. **"Explain, more of a reason will suffice."** Sevulix requests as he side-glance at his challenger. Remembering the tragic event. **"You are a threat to them,"** Valcomix says with a serious tone. Sevulix stares at Valcomix, now glaring at one another. **"Does that mean you are no longer of their flesh?"** Sevulix asks as if Valcomix admitted to something.

Seeing his expression mixed with anguish and sorrow. He got his answer. **"Why do you want me out of my own territory? Are you trying to satisfy your vengeance?"** Asking a valid question to his challenger. Valcomix begins to tear up, remembering that day when he encountered Sevulix. Then he remembers what TÖ-Slüdge said to him and then the day he took it upon himself to rescue his allies many times. He soon wipes away his tears.

He now stands vast with a remaining nervous heartbeat. **"I am fulfilling the words and mission of a fallen soldier."** Determined but with a shaky voice that is non-hesitant. His nervousness isn't settling. Sevulix focuses ahead, given the answers to his questions. The four that are following them through the thicket and brush witness them having a serious conversation but without audio.

Traversing uneven grounds for a few hours. Arriving at a loose gravel flat that seems to have been a parking lot; it has moss and grass growing between the cracks. They face one another. **"Do you want to challenge me!?"** Sevulix asks again but loudly with a menacing glare as his tails sway, slamming down his right paw. A memory plays in Valcomix's mind. "**Yes. I want you out of this Playground.**" Valcomix declares with his heart beating faster. This sound is annoying, Sevulix. *Growling* **"Are you going to do it!?"** Sevulix asks, digging his claws into the ground. His bristled fur stands sharply; its tails grow to a longer length. *Snarling!!!* *"I'm afraid."* Valcomix yells into himself as the same event plays vividly from memory.

His rifle aimed at it. This time, he doesn't have the tool he carried for years. Seeing that his claws are sharp and his veins are brightening. Remembering his tussles with many other creatures and him devouring them. He has a new arsenal resembling non-human-like traits. Feeling the rush of battle as both a C.O.A.T.S. soldier and an abnormal beast. Searching within for such courage. He himself fell a queen and reigns the underground passage ways. Unsatisfied he wants more and the looking at band wrapped around his bicep...

*SCREEAHHHH!!!* The four thin veins emerge from his back, and his tail sways wildly. He then stands on all four limbs. Getting into a recognizable stance.

From the side. Four familiar individuals are peeking from behind the trees. Eyes wide in shock. Sighting the drastic changes of two beings. TSinged knows that stance, along with TÖ-Slüdge, who recognizes it as well. They see an image of a raccoon. TSinged rubs his arm, and Cretan snickers at him. The two are careful of each other.

Not wanting to make sudden attacks, just yet. Circling one another. Valcomix remains low, putting the weight on his back legs and his right arm which is bent under his chest. Sevulix makes the first move. He attacks with his teeth to catch Valcomix's lagging tail. Launching himself with a twirl to dodge away from the jaws and counter. First bite. Valcomix's sharp teeth pierce through skin and try to dig into the tough meat of the front left leg. Gripping tight. Sevulix rolls to the side. Putting Valcomix under his weight for a second.

*Coughing* His fur is dirty, and he is putting himself back into the stance. To no avail, the fox bites down, clamping the creature's right shoulder. Using its claw to scratch the gums. The fox flinches from the pain. The creature bites back on the lower jaw. Wailing its other claws. Managing to scratch the nose of the fox. It releases the creature. *Screaming* *Barking* The fox's tails swirl and sway madly. The fox spins its body. Valcomix gets side-swiped. Flown across quite a few meters. Landing on his side. Quickly recovers and swiftly dashes about. Reaching the tail. Biting down on the rough fur. Taking in its warm red fluids into itself. The tails thrash around into the ground. The creature hangs on tight. Digging its claws into the tail as well. *Snarling* The fox had enough of the creature's teething. It jumps up as high as possible, rolling its upper body, then slams its tails onto loose gravel. The creature whimpers and stands again after being slammed but still lands fine on its left shoulder. The fox lands its front flip.

The creature's left arm is throbbing. Managing to stand up on both legs. The fox does the same. Standing upright meters tall. Its claws shine as they come down upon the creature. The being jumps back. It didn't evade fully. A huge gash is diagonally open upon the creature from the chest to the hip. Black ooze seeps out of it. Leaving a puddle. Soaking its hands, tail, and feet. Panicked. The fox sniffs the air. A vile, putrid scent emanates from the creature.

Distracted. The creature bites the fox's left leg hard. Reaching the meat, taking wet iron from it. Piercing the leg with its claws, the four veins squirm through the openings. A few drops of its blood mix with the fox's. The heavier content spreads a virus from within. *Crying* The fox's leg becomes numb. The gash has closed up. The fox uses its front leg to lift up and toss away the annoyance. Sending the creature into ropes of thorns. Tangled and trapped in agony as they pierce its flesh. ***SCREEAHHHH!*** Screeching in pain as it struggles about. Only making it worse as they sink into its flesh deeper. The fox smiles. Cretan and TSinged are terrified, along with the girls, who are worried.

# PART VI

They worry over Valcomix. The fox walks to him, dragging his leg. Valcomix remains in agony. The thorns are soaked with his black blood as the many nettles pierce through flesh and meat. Soon enough the entanglement feels sticky...

Becoming their blight, the ropes begin to rot, turning into brittle brown strings. The grass, taking a drink of his vile ooze, also rots. The trees of beautiful, vibrant colored leaves shrivel, forming a brown and rotted mix of weak yellow, and start to stink of mildew and old mold. Scattering as dead rain over him. The lively vegetation around him becomes an area of muck that is bubbling black. Like tar but with a potent scent of...

**"Why do I smell a strong scent of lemons bathing in mint?"** Cretan says, and the scent bothers him as it is concentrated and potent. Burning their sense of smell. TSinged covers his nose as the scent kind of burns and itches his throat as well. Fürthrived falls, and her head is aching. TÖ-Slüdge inhales the aroma. **"It's better than any other fruit I've eaten."** Enjoying herself.

The fox shakes its head, unable to think clearly. The blackened compound seeps into the soil and slowly infects other surrounding vegetation. Valcomix is slowly returning to the dim crimson glow. Becoming lighter and relieved by the removal of the extra weight. His veins emerging from his back are lit scarlet and then become dull. A dark crimson hue. They lie on top of the muck. *Slurping* Drinking in the thick, viscous pool of muck and rot. After a few minutes, his fur is similar to that of a fox. Soft, firm, sharp, and tough. **"His tail grew again."** TSinged isn't surprised as his head is throbbing in sheer pain. Trying to keep focus on this battle. Sighting his two allies who are suffering and choking.

Valcomix rushes at the fox, headbutting its chest. His needle-like fur is injected into its flesh. *Crying* The fox falls, sliding its chest against the loose gravel. Feeling a burning sensation within its chest flowing throughout the upper body. The red fur of the fox is discolored to a dimmer color of orange. Dripping a clear liquid from its body.

Valcomix can smell salt. Sevulix is now in agony. Opening his eyes, he sees the rotted life. Closing them again relies solely on the vibrations, holding his breath, and slowing down his heart rate. **"Valcomix."** He says angrily as for what he felt. The forest he rules over and this habitat he resides in is dying. Valcomix takes a knee and lays a gentle touch upon Sevulix's narrow part of the nose. Valcomix takes in the sight of what is happening as well. Remorseful. His comrades are in agony as well.

**“Sevulix. I want you out of this Playground. Go North, towards the vast snow and ice. You didn’t have to spare me that day. So, let me spare you.”** Valcomix tells Sevulix with a defeated tone. The large fox picks itself up, dragging its leg. Heading into the decaying lands. Stepping into the muck, tracking the muck throughout the territory. Valcomix is not victorious nor defeated. A threat wasn’t responsibly dealt with, but he managed to have it leave as he intended. He had to upkeep the words spoken. *Exhale* Rolling his shoulder.

# PART VII

Valcomix makes way to those suffering. Fürthrived is being watched over by TÖ-Slüdge. Staring into her eyes with a serious expression. She steps aside, and he puts the 'candlelight' onto his back. Tapping TSinged's shoulder. He glares. TSinged stands in front of him. **"Where to?"** He asks with an upset expression as his head is aching. **"The hazardous zone of Playground WY. C.O.A.T.S. won't enter there, and there are no signs of life."** Valcomix informs everyone. Noticing they are dizzy except for TÖ-Slüdge. Valcomix aids Cretan and TSinged forward. TÖ-Slüdge walks behind them. Valcomix takes the device from the pack. Nothing is readable. Looking around, and manages to sight violet clouds with an orange gradient over yonder. They head towards them at a comfortable pace.

## ELSEWHERE, PLAYGROUND, WA SECTOR: 22

### The time is 6:43am of 07/30/3175

A squad of soldiers investigate the area. The scrapped Arrows are scattered in front of the abandoned airport, as shown in the images. Similar damaged markings. **"They seem to have been clawed.**

**I've seen attacks with similar damages. While others seem to have been hit with a blunt object, due to the dents."** A soldier with a husky voice says, examining the damages done. **"It's wearing the separated uniform. We are making it a priority to question our secondary bases. No numbers are missing so far. They have reported loss and many deaths this past week. Rogues, perhaps?"** A strong female voice informs the squad questioning about a group. The squad inside the airport flash their light and notices black dust. Walking closer to it; it's a black scuff mark. A soldier outside looks up. Examining the glass. Then, a picture plays in his head. **"This is an intelligent being. It attacked from above."** He says with a serious tone.

## SPOKANE/SECTOR: 13 OF PLAYGROUND WA

Everyone works diligently investigating the areas. Some are near borders. The footages play in real-time. Many of them are focused on their screen. Then, the large screen shows the video. The supervisor is wide-eyed and standing vast. **"Share this with all of the C.O.A.T.S."** She orders, and it is executed.

*Notification* The sound spreads to all devices that are within a signal across Playgrounds and within Dorm. Reaching even the soldiers **Ranked: NQ7R** bearing a similar band as Valcomix. This also then reaches important desks of different factions of Dorm. Now reaches a silhouette of a man with a broad stature having a meeting with an elderly lady inside his office.

## SOME FULLY EQUIPPED GYM

*Notification* A white-haired person that has a muscle-bound stature and green eyes. A French/ Caucasian male standing at 6ft, pale peach skin tone. Wearing a tank top and white shorts. Picking up the device. Checking the footage. He then takes his personal device out. A screen saver image of him, some other individual, and the human Valcomix all at a wing restaurant wearing chicken bucket hats. Laughing at the image. He then makes a phone call. *Ringing* **"Criyo Domony speaking."** He introduces himself. **"Playground ID is now obtainable. Join me in claiming back our lost state. I could use a wing buddy."** Diim Sourn says, smiling.

# TO BE CONTINUED...

# EPISODE 7: OUR PRIDE LOST, WHICH THEY GAINED.

## PART I

### PLAYGROUND WY: HAZARDOUS ZONE

TSinged takes a seat on a boulder. Cretan rubs his neck and coughs softly. TÖ-Slüdge stands and stares at her allies, seeing them recover from what was ailing them. **"My throat kind of hurts,"** Cretan complains as he continues to rub his aching esophagus.

TSinged is groggy as he rummages through the packs to obtain mellow-flavored fruits and passes a few pears to the younger member. Carefully taking a few bites and partaking their juice down to soothe the aching, Valcomix is calm; no longer bright nor shining. His veins aren't exposed as they were minutes ago. Still carrying the passed-out Fürthrived, who is resting easily, as she is lying against his back.

TSinged takes a deep breath and chokes midway through the inhale. The burning sensation still lingers.

He rubs his eyes to remove a buildup of them watering. Holding his head up, he tries again. *Calm exhale* *Sneeze* **"A'ga-za."** Valcomix tells him. **"Thanks,"** TSinged says, pinching his nose and then breathing through his mouth deeply.

Itching and burning are much more tolerant now. Also, his headache is better. He stands up from the boulder and does dynamic stretching. Taking in the view of soft violet clouds as others are gradients of gray and pale blue. Noticing the temperature and air pressure. **"It's wet and warm here,"** he says as he looks around the barren ground.

**"Hazardous Zone of Playground WY. There are no signs of life here. This area is mysterious and consists of pH at level eleven. Mainly bleach. That explains the clouds being violet and blue,"** Valcomix informs them as he sniffs the air. The scent of a cleaning agent tickles his nose. Everyone gazes and above, sighting the gathering of the violet and blue clouds rising. Then Valcomix's ears twitch, hearing the muffled sound of an engine Fluttering, he then carefully moves his arm to view the device. Not functioning still.

**"We're moving on,"** Valcomix orders, and TSinged is not liking this. A mental alarm is sounding for him not to keep going. Cretan stands near TSinged, having a similar thoughtful feeling. TÖ-Slüdge remains in the back and notices her skin complexion. It feels soothing as she rubs her fingers together. Her eyes are widened as she can feel herself taking in moisture. Willing to speak up but goes back to silence.

# PART II

Traversing the barren land's rough grounds for a while, TSinged takes another few steps and realizes it got smoother; however, some spots are still jagged and rough, similar to fish scales. The flooring is covered by a strong mist that is strongly smelling of bleach, and the air is hot containing heavy amounts of moisture. He wants to take the situation seriously, but...

*Giggling* **"Valcomix, your fur is sagging a bit much. Feeling heavy?"** TÖ-Slüdge asks with a snicker as she teases Valcomix. Valcomix's fur is absorbing so much moisture that it is dripping water. Cretan himself is enjoying the funny situation. Annoyed but he remains focused with a gentle expression, trying to hide his smile.

TSinged stops abruptly; he is excited. Valcomix steps away from him as he is murmuring to himself. Cretan's eyes are wide, taking in the awe. TÖ-Slüdge herself is amazed at the sight...

Hot springs, rivers, waterfalls, pools, and mounds. The ground area is colored in a red or orange stream. The rock formation of the waterfalls is a crystalized topaz-like color. The sight is beautiful and wonderful.

All of them stand to view such a sight as steam rises from the bubbling blue centers. Wide in range. The ambiance of boiling, sizzling, and gentle cracking travels the air. Clouds are being bleached as they gaze at the steam staining them.

TSinged's excitement is at its peak. "**We're standing near active volcanic activity. The hardened yellow crusty rocks are limestone. But it should remain hardened or stasis or frozen unless the heated water is carrying out the dissolved limestone known as calcium carbonate. Reading upon a lot of geological research, the area should be acidic. Especially if there is this much activity yet the reaction is a base color.**" TSinged informs them as there is a mental alarm going off, but his excitement is tuning it down.

Valcomix is making eye contact with TÖ-Slüdge as he points to TSinged. **"He likes rocks, volcanoes, and earth,"** TÖ-Slüdge answers as she smiles at TSinged, seeing him enjoy a passion. simplifying his love for geology.

Valcomix is impressed that he knows about a certain science as well. He turns to focus on the route pictured and displayed mentally. **"Are we really heading that way?"** Cretan asks as his heart races. **"Yes, it's not the best option to traverse here. But we can avoid more**

**trouble this way."** Valcomix answers him with serious tone. Cretan stands near him, terrified by each step.

**"TSinged, stop staring at the hot water. We're leaving!"** TÖ-Slüdge yells, and he wakes up. Now hurrying to make his way to the others. Ignoring the sharp pain in his head. Informing him that there is danger ahead.

# PART III

Journeying past steaming streams, pools, and mounds, Cretan is holding tightly onto Valcomix. TSinged is still entranced by the wondrous sight of the bubbling mud. Walking on a red path way four hours now. No sign of trouble nor danger. Cretan is terrified. Fürthrived is still resting against Valcomix's back. Missing out on the scenery. TÖ-Slüdge is getting annoyed because all she sees is hot water and mud puddles. TSinged is still fascinated by such sights. Taking in the beauty of such hot springs. Valcomix himself is smiling watching him being entertained.

Soon the ground is now smoother and more slippery. They all are making precautious steps onto oddly morphed surfaces.

Cretan then ceases, being reluctant to step forward. Everyone is watching him. **"I'm scared."** He says refusing to move on. Even TSinged's feet don't want to move. He isn't terrified but something is bothering him as well. Looking around the vast open barren earth. There are boulders and rocks scattered about. But the land ahead is flat. Besides what TSinged notices... Dark holes...

**"Valcomix, is something in there?"** he asks, pointing at the ominous shapes in the flooring. They now notice it as well. Volunteering to check the nearest darker hole, Valcomix stares into it and listens... remaining silent... No one speaks... Valcomix is peering down in the deep made circle...

*"What's in the hole?"* a voice tickles his right ear, causing him to flinch, and he jumps backward with a frightened face. *Laughing* Then, there is a soft kiss on his right cheek. **"You can let me down now."** Fürthrived tells him while petting his head, easing his sudden fast heart rate.

Valcomix then lets her off, and she stretches. Reaching high, he is staring. TÖ-Slüdge is glaring menacingly, and he feels that cold glare. She approaches the two to show them her expression. Just wanting attention as Fürthrived kisses her cheek as well. Valcomix just leaves them be.

She is now focused on the two that won't make another step. Opening his mouth, but no sound from him is heard as his voice is overlapped by... *Rumbling* *Gurgling* Feeling the vibrations of the ground. All the dark holes have water rising out of them fast in a sequence.

All heads turn as their attention is given to the sprouting buildup pressure of water released from the holes. Releasing heat up within the atmosphere, carried by the wind scattering through the air. The heated water now falls, raining upon: Fürthrived, TÖ-Slüdge, and Valcomix. Showering the three along with the flooring they stand within. Their bodies are steaming. TSinged and Cretan are terrified by the increase in temperature and also by how the three are not even bothered by it. Valcomix is drenched and begins to make his way to the two.

**"They release hot water,"** he informs them, both raising an eyebrow. They stare at each other and back to this soaked and violent furry creature. **"Yeah, we just witnessed it,"** they say in unison.

TSinged tosses the packs to this genius. He catches them and puts the device within one of them. TSinged turns to Cretan and orders him as he strongly pats both his shoulders, **"I'm going to carry you across. So, get into your lightest form."**

**"Thanks, TSinged."** Cretan can feel the quavering from the stronger individual, knowing that he is terrified as well. He then rolls up and changes. Forming a ball, distinct in a pale yellow with a dull grey pattern that lines down through the forward.

TSinged carries him under his right arm. Taking a deep breath, he plunges his feet into the scalding temperatures of the liquid. **"We should rush this,"** Fürthrived mentions, witnessing the agony on strong-armed TSinged's face. **"They can't complain about being cold now,"** TÖ-Slüdge says, disturbed by his change of pained expression. Changing his expression to anger and agony due to TÖ-Slüdge remark. Fürthrived pinches her cheek hard. **"Bad."** She informs her. TÖ-Slüdge just shrugs her shoulders as she rubs her left cheek. Valcomix sighs silently

**"Let's just keep moving. My feet are burning!!!"** TSinged screams angrily as he is pain. They look to Valcomix. He quickens his steps. TSinged is at his side then moving on first as each step is difficult for him. The girls take their time walking behind them.

# PART IV

*Rumbling* *Gurgling* Dodging the boiling and bubbling areas, the scalding water falls, and TSinged braces himself for a regrettable shower as he tries protecting Cretan, holding him tight and bending forward. *Scattering rain* His body is unharmed except for his feet.

Valcomix's long bush brush tail gave him cover. TSinged gives him a nod with a smile expressing his gratitude. The sky is darkening once more defeating the present day to become a tomorrow. Finally, they reach the end of the barren land of heated earth and can view vast overgrowth of vegetation.

Filled with a spire of hope, TSinged makes his way fast to finally cool down his feet. Accidentally, he loses his footing as the earth is on a slant, and he trips into...

*Plunge* *Splash* Before rolling hysterically into cold waters, he tossed Cretan behind him. Assisting him is Valcomix, who catches Cretan but falls backward, and cushioning himself withs his tail. The girls hurry and locate TSinged, who is splashing about with a tortured expression.

**"This water is freezing,"** TSinged says, shivering. The girls look at him with pure animosity and disgust. **"How are your feet?"** TÖ-Slüdge asks with a menacing, cold smile, hiding violence that is certainly exposed. TSinged backs away from her.

Valcomix chuckles a bit, carrying Cretan, who isn't unraveling himself. Valcomix shakes him for a bit. *Slumbering* **"The kid is resting,"** he informs everyone, gathering their attention, then looks around the area and notices islands.

Aided by the candlelight luminous body, TSinged and TÖ-Slüdge view small banks of lands like islands surrounded by a stretch of murky waters. Valcomix is remembering what these areas are called. **"We're in a swamp?"** Valcomix asks mainly himself as he has no such idea where they are located. **"Are we lost, perhaps?"** Fürthrived asks with worry.

**"No, I was confirming my knowledge. I have some bad experiences with areas such as these. Let's all rest up for the night on one of the islands. I don't trust murky depths during the darker hours."** He shares reluctant to even touch the medium. Looking at TSinged, he says, **"When settled on one. TSinged, remove your shoes and dry your feet."** He then turns to Fürthrived and orders her, **"Fürthrived, warm him**

**up and check his injury. And TÖ-Slüdge, climb that island near your side first."** He gives them orders like some type of commander, strong and stern.

TÖ-Slüdge clicks her tongue and begrudgingly does as she is told. **"Oh. Sure. So, bossy"** she says rolling her eyes annoyed. Such attitude. Then sticks her tongue out at him. Valcomix just smiles. He hesitates to enter the water, but he has to do so anyway and gets the bottom of the packs wet. He holds Cretan up above the knee-deep, murky, dark medium in the solid night.

TSinged then aids Valcomix by taking Cretan and rolls him toward Fürthrived, just nearly touching her. He then pulls up Valcomix. Valcomix checks himself all the way to the tip of his tail. Relieved. The bank is bigger than he thought. He aids TSinged to remove his shoes. **"Fürthrived come here, please."** Valcomix requests with a serious demeanor.

TSinged is in pain by just trying to take them off. They both check out his injury, and TÖ-Slüdge is curious as she stands up to take a peek. TÖ-Slüdge doesn't want to be left out and is curious about his scalded feet.

The huddled three smile at the... **"It's not as bad. When I accidentally burned your back. That left a**

**mark. There's nothing noticeable."** Fürthrived says with a giggle. TSinged is not amused and rubs his back, removing the mental agony as he remembers it physically.

Valcomix even cringes a bit. **"Keep them cooled down. It may not look bad, but the sensation of the soles would be uncomfortable. By morning if there is a sign of softness. Inform me."** He tells TSinged with a gentle punch to the shoulder. TSinged chuckles. **"Yes boss."**

All watching him go towards the only tree and then leans against it. Doing what she is told. Fürthrived stays near both TSinged and Cretan. To help warm them both.

Valcomix has put himself where he can watch everyone as he is under the tree. TÖ-Slüdge sits beside him, sighting a wonderous smile. **"Got your flare back?"** she says with a teasing demeanor.

**"Explain."** He says as he is if giving an order. **"That. Your attitude. Taking charge like an outstanding soldier."** she says, and Valcomix chuckles softly with a hint of sadness. TÖ-Slüdge then gazes him into his eyes. **"Do you miss being a C.O.A.T.S. soldier?"** she asks out of concern, as her voice is sad and honest for him.

Gripping tightly at his armband, he says, **"I do. But I realized something. I was constantly afraid for them. If I can help this way and disappear, then my mission to code of arms will be fulfilled. Humans are weak, but they're resourceful. They can claim the states to build better weapons and occupy difficult areas such as this, then they can handle the fox. Honestly, I survived another encounter with that fox, Sevulix. I could have been killed again."** He shares with an upbeat expression as his tone is lively. He smiles his brightest canines.

*Giggling* **"You're finally opening up. Hopefully, you can tell us your war stories. Cretan loves a good tale. Goodnight, fur C.O.A.T.S."** TÖ-Slüdge says, nestling near him against the same tree but avoiding physical contact.

Valcomix remembers his time in Dorm. A sad smile appears on his frame, trying to picture what his human form looked like before. Only can see the fur and claw raised over his head knowing that this is his paw. A brand-new nature that is confusing and sometimes difficult to handle. **"Have a well slumber, to everyone, and sorry."** A single tear falls from him., and TÖ-Slüdge slightly regrets asking him such a question. Both of them rest with thoughtful emotions.

# PART V

The sky welcomes a better morning, as the thin sheet of grey clouds is calm. A gentle breeze flows past, causing the trees to sing. *Croaking* *Hissing* TSinged is stirred awake. Now fully awake because there is a frog upon his chest. Just there. He doesn't know what to really do. On his left, he sees a blue snake, which is focused on Fürthrived. He moves over slowly and sits up. The frog hops off him but remains close.

Standing up and feeling the ache from yesterday, he views behind him Valcomix and TÖ-Slüdge, having a conversation while eating apples. Wrapped around by three snakes is Valcomix. TSinged expression shows off his disgust. The furnace is still resting. Those two are talking... realizing.

**"Where is Cretan?!"** TSinged yells frantically, startling the two, almost awakening Fürthrived. **"He's playing on the island. Look to your right."** TÖ-Slüdge answers calmly, pointing her thumb at the location.

TSinged sees the kid chasing after the frogs and snakes. The small creatures aren't even annoyed and easily get captured by him. Seeing the kid enjoying his time playing, TSinged feels relieved with a smile. But is still disgusted by being around such animals.

**"Stay off your feet."** TÖ-Slüdge orders with a smug expression. TSinged doesn't like her attitude and tone on how she commanded him. He does so anyway, sitting up. Cretan sees no challenge in chasing these small creatures if they don't resist. Soon, he hears...

*Ripples* The water is awake, and there is a dull, dark, bulky line floating from the murky medium. *Splashing* Now, it rolls to the side, exposing its pink and orange bottom with brown bumps. Valcomix's ears twitch and he then sees Cretan leaning over. Gritting his teeth, he jumps over to the other island, clearing it with ease. He manages to yank his parka back, surprising him as he falls onto his backside. Wanting to slow down, but the moss is slippery and causes him to topple it.

*Thrashing* *Splashing* "Help, Valcomix is in trouble!!!" Cretan screams, unable to do anything else. Frantically watches the dark water being stirred roughly by the creatures under medium struggle.

Fürthrived awakens abruptly, kind of groggy as she searches the area. TÖ-Slüdge answers his cry, rushing over to where they are. Sighting bubbles and many ripples, she frantically looks for something, but to no avail. *Growling* The sound is muffled. Then, soon after, Valcomix breaks through the medium, splashing about. There is a bulky creature trapped in his shredders. Biting with might, gripping the creature. Seeing the pink and orange surfacing, sticking its brown bumps onto Valcomix's back.

Using his claws to scratch at it with relentless vigor, the thing unravels from him and floats. He then swims to the bank, tosses the thing onto the island, and climbs up. Agitated, but he laughs silently. **"I hate leeches!"** he shouts, laughing at the fallen parasite.

**LEECHES***:* A long and bulky parasitic animal named by many as the water worm. No mouth. No eyes. Blend with the dark swamp waters with their dull black plastic textured back. But their underside is a brighter color to entice and lure prey. Orange, yellow, pink with brown bumps. The bumps have needle appendages working like teeth and tongues to drain blood. A Threat level 3. They can drown their prey or over excessively eat causing blood loss. Maybe tough muscled, but they are soft tissue. Great use as bait for higher threats. Rich in protein.

Valcomix begins to devour it like a tough noodle. TÖ-Slüdge turns her sight away as the scene is horrifically disgusting. Cretan watches in amazement as his feasting habits are beastly. Finishing up a meal with a satisfied expression, by slurping up thinner end. Staring at Cretan, and checking him up and down, Valcomix asks with a concerned tone, **"You alright, Cretan?"**

**"Yeah, I'm okay."** he answers, petting his head. TÖ-Slüdge has a mischievous smile, taunting him but relieved that the boys are alright. They all go back to the other island. **"Valcomix, what happened?"** Fürthrived asks, concerned and curious as she rushes to see him closely, eyes to eyes.

**"It was just a leech,"** he informs her, smiling and laying a hand on her shoulder. She smiles as well. He then approaches TSinged, his arms folded, staring at him with a serious, blank expression.

**"I'm feeling better. So, are we going to continue moving on, or is this our New Haven?"** TSinged peering down at Valcomix. Sizing him up and glaring seriously at him into his crimson eyes. Both of them glare at one another. The girls are confused as to why these two want to fight now. Cretan is worried. **"Valcomix, you seem better. Mentally. Are you?"** TSinged asks seriously with a smile.

**"TSinged, thank you for saving my life and giving me a second chance. I'm getting comfortable in my fur. But I'm still lingering with doubts."** Valcomix says with a conniving smile, showing his violent intention. Then, it becomes a bright smile showing his canines.

TSinged pets his head. "You're welcome, teammate," he responds, knowing his new attitude is open. Valcomix grumbles due to everyone petting him. TÖ-Slüdge smiles seeing their joyous attitude as Valcomix then snaps at them.

**"Everyone, we continue. I have to guide you across the ice as agreed after I liberate the last Black State. First, we get out of this swamp."** Valcomix informs, gathering their packs and putting one to himself as front cargo. Then, he passes the other to TSinged. Valcomix makes his way to the water, and the snakes and frogs move where they don't get stepped on. He puts himself in the murky medium up to his waist and walks around a bit, watching the top for any ripples. **"The water is asleep. TSinged, carry Cretan once more. It's a bit deep for him."** He orders while watching for any wakes.

Soon, TSinged has Cretan on his shoulders just pounding at his head. "Keep it up and I'll dunk you," TSinged says with a half-threatening tone as he stands firmly in the medium near Valcomix. Cretan laughs childishly, enjoying the view.

TÖ-Slüdge jumps in, splashing the boys. Valcomix is not amused, nor is TSinged, but Cretan laughs hysterically. They just watch her swim around them while she taunts her teammates brashly. Valcomix can see that Fürthrived is hesitating to join them. He then shows his back. **"Get on."** He says and then she holds on to his neck excitingly.

**"Good boy."** she says affectionately, and he feels embarrassed as the others smile at him. He ignores them, trying to hide away his joy. He then leads them, making cautious steps through the murky water.

# PART VI

## Playground 10

### The Time is 7:55am of 07/31/3175

The sealed massive door of Dorm opens. The first to step foot is a C.O.A.T.S soldier with many vehicles behind him. Bearing the name: **Curesed Kiel, Ranked: MD9QR**. Having many badges and medals. Wrapped around his right arm is an armband with three gold stars.

Appearing from the door is another soldier rushing to stand beside his leader. This soldier's tag reads his name as: **Trenton C. Calhous, Ranked: NQ7R**. Wearing a similar armband as Valcomix. **"Sir Kiel. The scientists are placed at the center in the best-armored truck. All equipment loaded. The bases near the black state have cleared their expedition mission. Considered it as safe. Also, the individual who destroyed most of our toys is still unknown. Not a member of the separated base. Considered a rogue. Maybe a lost one of theirs. Perhaps."** Calhous informs, facing the rotting area.

Now, given the information, Sir Kiel looks behind himself with a slight turn of his head. **"Keep up the**

**investigation of the individual. For now...**" he says with a raspy, serious tone. Then presses his helmet. **"Claim back our lost state! This is my order!"** He yells to everyone with a commanding and booming voice. The vehicles begin to sound off with honking. Him and his soldier enter the first truck. All are making tire tracks as they enter the Playground with excitement.

## The Time is 11:24am of 07/31/3175

Drones are swarming over the Playground. Many C.O.A.T.S. are in units and squads at the ready. *Notification* Sighting the message: "S.O.S." Rifles are drawn. Precautious for any type of danger. Butterflies are flying over. Building perimeters and loose camps. Clearing the way with fire, enjoying a victory, as many are laughing. *Firing* Rounds piercing through lower threatening animals, hunting everything in their sight that isn't of their rank. Completing their mission as they put to end such creatures on sight.

The Playground is in such disarray. Once a natural home to thrive in as the trees and grass were lush in the spring. Fruits and other vegetation would grow vastly for all to have. Roam, feast, sleep and play. Now a sight of fire, rot, carnage and masses amount of filth.

On the northern bordering mountain formation, there is Sevulix and the rest of the surviving animals that inhabited Playground: ID. All are witnessing it being stolen and becoming wasted. ***"Sacrilege, our land is being burned and stepped upon, disrespecting my once proud territory. Valcomix, you shouldn't have spared me."*** It tells itself while growling angrily as its tails sway about. Its eyes are burying a rage, sighting these putrid beings in C.O.A.T.S. *Crying* *Screaming* Moving away from the disastrous scenery as the fox heads north. The surviving animals follow after their apex.

The calm weather grows darker, and the wind drops in temperature. After some time, the C.O.A.T.S. are camping around the Playground with a few others, just near where the cause of the rotting is a specialized armored vehicle. A few people wearing hazard suits leave the vehicle. The soldiers encircle them. Flashlights are shining bright. Using the picture from their tablet, they have stumbled upon it. **"The pool of a mysterious substance,"** one of them says, getting out a few test tubes and scooping up samples. **"Mark this place. We attend to return with our better equipment."** A joyous voice is heard coming from the regular hazard suit wearing person. They then walk away, returning to their vehicles.

## ELSEWHERE. WHERE THERE ARE VALLEYS AND PLAINS OVER YONDER.

Swarmed by mosquitoes upon a wooden dam blocking the rapids, causing the flooding within the swamp behind them, Fürthrived heats up, acting like a bug zapper as she reduces their population to cinders and ash. Cretan and TSinged have the beavers down. They seem the same, with no evolutionary traits. But the creature that Valcomix is facing is the...

**PLATYPUS***:* An excellent fisher. It bullies other beings that are smaller than its size with fearlessness. Dark brown fur that has hidden spurs filled with a cyanide-type poison. The sharp green bill can inflict piercing damage. Its long wire whip tail acts like a fishing line with a lure-tipped tail that luminates to attract fish. It's a lazy animal and sleeps long hours with its tail mainly in the water all day. Provoked, just get away. They have weak eyesight. Near-sighted, blue bead-like eyes. Mainly surrounded by beavers because of the control of the water. They could have been true apex predators if they chew their food. Nerfed by eating prey whole, they choke themselves. They are quite active when swimming. Threat level 6-7, depending on their awareness. Also, no threat if they are asleep. Heavy sleepers

This one is awake and focused on Valcomix. The beavers are occupied. Mosquitoes eliminated. TÖ-Slüdge is beside him. As he takes a stance, his expression is smiling menacingly, salivating at this massive creature as his stomach rumbles. Finally, he kicks off his hind legs, launching himself at it. *Rip* *Tear* *Chewing*

**TO BE CONTINUED...**

# EPISODE 8: IT'S A NATURAL THING.

## PART 1

Valcomix's stomach is rumbling, targeting the boss creature known as a Platypus. Its beady blue eyes stare at Valcomix. Smiling menacingly, Valcomix lunges at the animal with his powerful hind legs. His teeth and claws dig through the fur, skin, flesh, and meat of the plump sized animal. Devouring its fat and muscles. The creature didn't even put up a fight or even resist. Because it was sleeping.

Everyone just listens and witnesses another eating habit of their monstrous teammate. TSinged is disgusted, amazed, and curious about how he is able to eat the whole thing. Then, Valcomix's four scarlet-like veins help take in the raw crimson fluids that drip near his feet.

The girls leave him to his late dinner. It only took a moment, and Valcomix's hunger is now satiated. Returning, his scarlet-lit veins causing him to dimly glow. *Relieved sigh*

**"We're finally out of the water"** TSinged says with an annoyed grin. TÖ-Slüdge is also gratified that they're no longer in the murky medium. Grotesque and viscous mud mucks. At least most creatures weren't interested in them besides the swarm of flies and mosquitoes. *Yawn* Fürthrived becomes tired after exerting her heat just to be rid of the swarm around them. Cretan is silent and staring at the clouds.

Over the bright cyan grass fields and vibrant flowers of violets, whites and green that are being blown by the calming winds. The sky is a soft sheet of dark gray; allowing small spots of light to pass through. The wind isn't an issue nor is it the cloud formation. But the weather seems strange.

Cretan stares at the sky along with Valcomix. The two are thinking alike as they conversate with their eyes. The girls along with TSinged are making their way off this dam to be on much solid earth. Sighting the vast gardens closely. But the just now notice that they're being left.

Catching up with the girls and their muscular companion. All walking the hills, traversing through the plains' low, dull, pale blue grass that shin height. The area lacks a scent. The flowers in full bloom should smell like something. Valcomix isn't smelling anything.

Getting close to Fürthrived and gets a whiff of the side her neck.

*Giggling* TSinged is surprised. TÖ-Slüdge is glaring angrily at him coating her arms with dangerous clear lotion. Cretan keeps his eyes in the clouds. **"Valcomix, stop your tickling me."** She says trying to push him away. But is enjoying the attention. Just her aroma is kind. Realizing that he is kind of close to her.

**"Sorry. I was just making sure that my sense of smell isn't lacking. But you do smell very sweet."** He says with a serious demeanor as he is still close to her. Blushing due to his words. **"Pervert."** She says teasingly as she takes a firm hold on his tail. **"You're so soft."** Now with mischievous tone as she plays with his furred ligament. Valcomix grumbles.

TSinged shakes his head; not wanting to listen nor see them like this. TÖ-Slüdge bumps her elbow in Fürthrived's arm. Not understanding, Fürthrived backs out and puts them close. The two begin to play: eyes on, eyes off. Just a childish game where one looks at one another without the other noticing. Catching each other and staring into crimson and violet.

Both smiling. Now closing the distance as they walk beside one another. A nice gentle quietness of such a calm scenery. TSinged is glaring at them. Fürthrived is joyous seeing them interact close. Cretan is still searching for the source of his uneasiness in the clouds. Valcomix then looks behind them noticing the uncomfortable TSinged. TÖ-Slüdge is annoyed.

*Yawn* Fürthrived covers her mouth and starts dimming. Now gaining the attention. And can see the concerned expression of TSinged and TÖ-Slüdge. She silently apologizes and TÖ-Slüdge takes her hand.

Cretan is saddened by Fürthrived's frequent signs of tiredness, noticing her stagger for a while and also realizing how late it is. **"Everyone, we're going to take immediate rest,"** Valcomix orders by sitting on the field of grass first. Cretan follows, and TSinged nods to TÖ-Slüdge. She then pulls Fürthrived away from the others so they can have their privacy.

**"What's wrong? Feeling in the mood once more?"** Fürthrived concludes her question, blushing while smiling shyly. TÖ-Slüdge shakes her head and remains silent, gazing into her eyes, attracted. Both close their eyes as they close in for a passionate kiss. TÖ-Slüdge hugs her close and then rests her head on her glowing, warm shoulder. **"Good night, Fürthrived."** she says with tears as she smiles. **"Rest well."** Fürthrived tells her true friend.

## Where the boys remain seated...

**"Fürthrived is changing again. Valcomix don't mention anything that is going on between the two of you."** TSinged says with an annoyed, upset, and serious tone. Valcomix is confused and is being glared at. He nods. Cretan pulls up some cyan grass and open his hand and it's carried by the wind. A sad expression upon his frame. **"Also, your flirtatious behavior..."** He was about to mention until... *Steps*

The two have returned holding hands. TSinged can see that TÖ-Slüdge is tired as well. Annoyed about the next day that will come. He then gets up and walks away to lay near everyone but at a distance. Valcomix can see that TÖ-Slüdge wants to be next to her companion. And Cretan, taking shelter under his tail. Valcomix allows it. He is shivering and uneased. TÖ-Slüdge remains by her friend's side. Valcomix stares at the sky and something about the weather is unsettling.

# PART II

As everyone rests before him, Valcomix gets up. Rummaging through the packs for the device. Turning it on waits for it to be fully functional. Now plays with the screen to get a clue about their whereabouts.

The time is 3:41 am of 08/01/3175

The last known location was Playground WY, Sector: 13, and then, notified 'Off Grid' and considered lost after some time. They all pass the Hazardous Zone and kept east, remembering the swamp and then the that creek that led them to the dam now in a mountainous terrain. This is a vast area where they have reached: vast hills, plains, and valleys of vibrant pale blue grass.

Valcomix checks for the compass app. It functions correctly with the detailed accuracy of a full sphere displayed as a two-dimensional use. Aiming the device directly east, he has the direction pinpointed. He then checks the battery life. Sixty-five percent. He powers it off.

He then closes his eyes. *Strong inhale* He takes a whiff of the air's scent, there is no smell but the cold feeling entering his immune system. It doesn't smell like a storm, nor does it have that light mildew scent of rain.

But the air does feel different. Noticing they're high in altitude, he checks the hairs of his fur. No sight of it rising. *"Then, why is the air pressure different somehow?"* He questions himself as he stares at the complete darkness of the windless skies. Noticing a pinching sensation happening, Cretan grips his tail tightly, sleeping with an agonizing expression. Quivering, he continues to gaze up, expecting something to happen.

**"Val, Valco... Valcomix."** a strong voice calls out to him.

Valcomix opens his eyes, and for some strange reason, his neck won't turn correctly, as it is painful to do so. TSinged notices this. **"Alright, relax. I'm going to fix you,"** TSinged says as he holds Valcomix's head firmly. *Crk* Sound of a bone snapping. ***SCREEAHHHH!!!!*** Sound of Valcomix crying. His onlookers understand his pain.

Rubbing his neck and wincing, TÖ-Slüdge has her hands on her waist, peering down at him. **"Weird position to sleep in with your head up facing the clouds."** she says, confused while sneering at him. TSinged shakes his head. **"You and Cretan both. Cretan has been anxious and started rolling around, muttering about 'bad weather.'"** He informs as he is holding a certain individual rolled up and quaking. Showing Cretan's behavior to him.

Valcomix himself can't understand this situation. The sky's change in pressure has him bothered as well. Looking around, he sees that Fürthrived remains asleep. He gently picks her up and settles her upon his back. **"We need to find shelter. This weather is bothering me as well."** Valcomix's voice is anxious, but he still doesn't have any idea why he has this strange sense.

TSinged and TÖ-Slüdge look at each other, feeling worried about this sudden change in his behavior. Then, they focus their attention on Cretan, who looks frightened. They then focus above, viewing the dark grey clouds. Same as it was yesterday.

They walk for some time and reach a flat land field with yellow and silver flowers. TÖ-Slüdge admires the beauty that she is surrounded by. Now having her attention upon Valcomix. Walking forward but frantically searching for something... *Growling*

Valcomix stops, gazing angrily at the clouds and grips Fürthrived tightly. Cretan becomes more unsettled, trying to get out of TSinged's grasp. **"Too late."** Valcomix growls. Then, they witness the uneasiness of these two. The sky brightens a crisp blue and white light over the vast area... *Crackling*

# PART III

They all are standing in this field of yellow and silver flowers upon a valley, and there is a bright blue and white light above them. Valcomix frantically searches for anything to cover the others and himself, but to no avail. *Crackling* Valcomix's ears twitch, and Cretan squirms. TSinged's heart is beating faster. TÖ-Slüdge is worried.

Valcomix clenches his teeth as he has his eyes shut, waiting for its wrath. Nothing, no sound, no smell, sight; just the sensation of him standing in a field of flowers. *Crackling* Opening his eyes, TÖ-Slüdge and TSinged are witnessing a phenomenon. Many bolts and their strands are attracted over the hill in front of them. Bending as the sky strikes this hill with all its built electrical energy.

*"Lance."* Valcomix whispers with an amazed expression yet boding with fear. He then looks behind them and takes a gulp. **"We have to keep going where the lightning is striking."** he informs them. The two first hesitate to follow Valcomix but settle to have him guide them. After some time leaving the field, TSinged says within himself, "**There hasn't been a sound of**

**thunder yet**." He openly mentions, and TÖ-Slüdge agrees to his statement.

**"Lance doesn't make a thunderous sound. It just continuously strikes, releasing neutron-charged ions. This lightning isn't like the snakes that travel the length of the clouds or the normal. Lance is silent and unpredictable and strikes from the ground to the sky."** Valcomix explains with such meaningful details. Reaching the summit of the hill from the steep drop, staring ahead is...

**"Bighorn Iron Pass."** Valcomix says watching the mountain region of composites, stone, rock, mostly iron, wood, brass, and trees that are shining white be struck. The striking continues for a while, and they are more in awe as they witness the scenery of hazardous nature dancing and lighting the mountainous region in a blue and white electrical glow. The white trees' leaves scatter, gliding through the windless air. The dark clouds swirl and brighten a sapphire light.

Shaking away the distraction, Valcomix takes a leap and runs down the steep hill. TSinged slides down the hill. TÖ-Slüdge carefully takes the step onto the steep slope of this grassy hill. Making a misstep, she rolls horizontally all the way down. The two have a smirk, taunting and teasing silently with their gaze. Covered in grass and petals, she growls at them with a menacing glare. The two cease and shut away their smirk.

Valcomix guides them through the mountainous path. Their hair is standing on end following the currents. The area is surprisingly harmless. Feeling the sensations of small shocks that do make one flinch but it's more of an annoyance.

Cretan is now calm within TSinged's grasp and slips out. He sees the sight beside him of the storm striking its might on the highest peak receiving some jolts as well. Seeing the blue glow, his eyes are open, and he points eagerly at each stroke of lightning bending. TSinged smiles joyfully, knowing he is alright even when shocked by such strays.

Now, the mountain is behind them, and ahead is a city-sized fortress with a dome, a gate, and iron blockades. Valcomix's facial expression becomes dull. **"No one should worry; that base is abandoned. It's still operational, though."** Valcomix shares as he keeps his eyes forward, avoiding even a glimpse at it.

Everyone else stares and wonders at such a construct. **"Why was it abandoned?"** TSinged asks curiously. **"Lance. That base was built way too close to the mountain. It was our mining expedition target**

**for our gains. Then most times huge power failures and communication interferences began to happen constantly. We had to stop and relocate. Too many lives lost, a risky task for search teams if no one can predict the next storm."** He explains, answering TSinged's question with a serious morbid expression.

**"How is it still operating?"** TÖ-Slüdge now asks her question. *Sigh* **"Once they have a better study of some unpredictable weathers, they can return to the abandoned bases and adjust them accordingly and turn the power back on."** He finishes answering her question with a crestfallen expression. All while gesturing flicking a power switch off and on.

After another set of kilometers forward to the east. *Murmuring* Valcomix's right ear twitches. Nuzzling against his neck and stretching her arms straight, Fürthrived feels that her legs are restricted, and she opens her eyes slowly. Unfamiliar location of just a flat land surrounding her. Then, she notices she is being piggy-backed by some strange being. Remembering its violent spree of events. Terror shows on her face. **"Put me down! Hostile creature!"** Fürthrived screams as she punches Valcomix with a strong left hook.

Valcomix drops her. TSinged and Cretan are surprised and rush to aid the victim, helping him catch his balance. TÖ-Slüdge confronts the wailing and loud member. **"Shut up!"** she yells with anger and annoyance.

Fürthrived ceases her actions and views her surroundings. Everyone is here with an added menace. She glares at Valcomix, and he meets her gaze, then ignores her and turns to TSinged. **"I'm getting out the device."** He says, rubbing the ache away with his thumb. He retrieves the device and plays with it.

Fürthived is annoyed and accosts them. **"Where are we?"** she asks with a heated temper that makes TSinged and Cretan back away. Valcomix doesn't give her any attention and walks off. **"I'm checking that out now,"** he answers her question, keeping focused on the now functioning map.

**"Where are you taking us?"** Fürthrived asks another question, ready to burn away the entirety of his being. Intensifying both her heat and glow. Valcomix's veins also brighten to a scarlet light. Unfazed by her heat. TÖ-Slüdge intervenes, mediating for Valcomix's safety. **"Dim down,"** she commands with a deathly tone held with malice.

The two begin to argue and bicker. Getting louder as they become less coherent and sensible. Cretan covers his ears and backs away for both safety and to keep his sanity. TSinged sighs, and Cretan hides behind him. He isn't do anything. So, in his position, Valcomix is calm...

*SCREEAHHHH!!!!* Screeching out his piercing yell. Everyone is covering their ears. Bearing the pain of such a sound. Unfair to Cretan. *Crack* The device's screen has been damaged as a line stretches and diagonally across the screen. Now there is... *Silence*

**"No clashing. Fürthrived, if you have any complaints, speak of them now."** He orders with uncaring eyes. She clicks her tongue and chooses to be silent. TÖ-Slüdge folds her arms and glares at him. TSinged commemorates on how well he handled those two. **"Fürthrived changed again."** Cretan says with a saddened expression and a frightened tone. He also notices that her clothing scheme has changed—black polyester cargo pants tucked in her black boots, a scarlet crop top, and a black belt without a buckle fastened about at her waist. Better appearance but a disgusting personality. Witnessing that the girls are again despising one another.

# PART IV

## Back in Playground 10

### The time is 6:10pm of 08/01/3175

People in hazard suits are gathered by the black muck ooze pool, this time with a quick and easy transport lab. Computers on top of foldable tables. Test tubes, beakers, microscopes, tablets, and measuring tools.

One of the people pokes the pool with a stick and witnesses its sticky content strongly pulling it. **"This is strange. Our database can't categorize this substance."** One of them announces, intrigued as he steps back from the computer and jots his research into his tablet.

One of them studies a sample using a microscope connected to a monitor and it's wirelessly connected to her tablet. Zooming in, the monitor shows her thousands of lines clustered together, forming a complex structure, using a split screen. The split screen scrolls through hundreds of these complex structures but of different a color and pattern.

They are immersed in studying this complex singularity. Its origin doesn't match any of the other complex strands, yet it has the chemical structure of amino acids. Readings of high consistency of collagen. Reasoning its viscosity and density. Reaching her conclusion...

**"It's a pool of proteins. I ran hundreds of other structures; it doesn't match any of them, but it has a similar structure. This protein has a higher rate of collagen than any other contents categorized."** she says with an excited and coherent tone. Her team applauds her for her discovery and well-spoken research.

**"That does explain its density and viscosity. But how does it explain that this substance can kill plant life?"** The head lead scientizes genuinely asking the question, not wanting to base it on some hypothesis or even a theory.

Two scientists step back as they pour a bit of the substance onto a brilliant blue shining flower. The substance causes it to quickly wilt and rot, dripping a brownish liquid from its petals. Now dried. While under a drone, capturing it frame by frame motion. Recording. The scientist diligently working near the two scoots away from them as she witnesses that disturbing phenomenon.

She tests the samples within a scrambler. It spins the test tube, sorting out its contents. The tablet then has a pie chart shown on its screen.

- 11.4% Iron
- 10.8% Salt
- 6.1% Water
- 20.2% Zinc
- 3.3% Technetium
- 48.1% Unknown

Surprised by this reading, she stops the machine's rotational process, takes the sample, and sets it near a Sievert scale. Getting out a Geiger counter instrument, they both begin making a sound and measuring for radiation exposure. After a minute, 56Sv is the accurate read from both. The regular animal and plant life is at least 20Sv- 31Sv. Yet, that "Unknown" percentage has her gripped to figuring it out.

All scientists in her team are working, researching, and studying this substance. The source of Playground ID's dying forests. Using plenty of microscopic lenses. Noticing the different shapes of blood cells: a black cylinder with blue light, a black sphere that has a scarlet hue luminating from its cracks. And black viruses with a crimson tint moving freely. The viruses bounce into the cells and seem to cause them to brighten and have them grow.

She moves from the microscope, removes herself from the table, and says frustratingly, **"Sir, I have to announce that I'm giving up. This is too complex to even study. I'll label it as biohazardous with radioactive properties."** She walks away jotting down the occurrence on her tablet with her stylus.

The lead watches as she leaves and places his sight through the microscope. Witnessing the same phenomenon, he backs away. **"Everyone. We have to take our findings to the lab. For now, we'll consider it as a blight. Our fellow scientist discovered something that even I can't comprehend."** He announces to all and continues to stare at the phenomenon happening. Given the order to postpone they all begin seal the test tubes. Also, other samples.

After a while, they start to clean off their equipment, electronics, and instruments with alcohol spray or wipes and store the samples in a secured chest. The lead then takes out a flask, gathers up the substance from the pool, fills it up about halfway, and seals it. Then, he places it into a steel box, setting it into the truck. He then pulls out his device. *Ringing* **"Well, this is Suviron Arc speaking. I have to tell you**

**to be patient. Claiming Playground ID will be later set. We don't know what caused it to become the way it is."** He informs and hangs up. *Hopefully, they won't act brash like last time.*" he wishes. He then climbs into the truck with his team, and a C.O.A.T.S. soldier drives them away. The lead scientist places a marker on their location.

## WHERE THE OOZE POOL IS

The wind blows violently but soon calms down. Hours pass, and the rain soon falls onto the rotting lands. Splashing upon the black ooze, the water slides off, flooding around it. From its dense center, there is a blue light, and from it comes a glowing, twirling plant. It dims.

# PART V

## FARMLANDS WITH AN EERIE GREEN MIST RISING FROM THE GROUNDS

Taking shelter from the outside inside a white deteriorated farmhouse is the five. Cretan sleeps beside TSinged. Fürthrived rests up against the furthest corner trying to be away from everyone. TÖ-Slüdge rests near Valcomix. Who remains awake due to his growling stomach. Agitated, he gets up and heads outside.

TSinged notices his reasoning as he watches him exit. Valcomix returns quickly and retrieves the device trying to be quiet as much as possible. He then exits again. After some hours, TSinged fakes a yawn and stretches high as he stands, loosening and limbering up his body while making loud sounds.

Cretan grumbles. Fürthrived remains asleep. TÖ-Slüdge takes a breath. **"He hasn't returned yet?"** she asks with concern. TSinged answers by shaking his head. He then heads for the exit after pointing at Fürthrived and gathering the packs. She glares at him and continues to do so even when he has left.

Searching around, sighting the many houses with acres of land. Gardens, farms, decomposing animals, and other needed resources. He then sees a figure hiding above the mill behind the house where they sheltered themselves. He approaches his teammate. His ears twitch and he then looks down and jumps.

TSinged can hear the low rumbling from his torso. **"We're up and ready."** He tells Valcomix, patting him on the shoulder. Valcomix takes a whiff of the air. **"I smell burning wood."** He informs his muscular teammate with a serious and confused expression.

Confused, then surprised as TSinged's eyes widen. Sighting smoke fuming out from the house. He rushes to the front. Valcomix follows after him. They both see that Cretan is rolling about, hearing muffled yelling as two individuals are arguing while they are exiting. The house is engulfed in flames, but the two walk out casually, glaring menacingly at one another. Valcomix growls menacingly and readies to...

Fürthrived prepares to cover her ears. TÖ-Slüdge quickly confronts him waving her arms as if wanting him to be screech. **"No, she just wouldn't wake up. I tried light jostling but that was ineffective. I began shouting and she pushed me away and started complaining. So, I put my foot to her face forcefully."**

TÖ-Slüdge admits with a smirk on her face. TSinged only sighs and shakes his head annoyed by such an action. Valcomix is furious as he glares at the two for such devastative behaviors.

Fürthrived is angry. They can feel her radiating heat from where they stand. Seeing Cretan roll must have been a way for him to cool down. **"I was being cooked alive! TÖ-Slüdge, you know how easily you can provoke her! TSinged, why didn't you wake her up like most times?! I'm always the victim of their fighting! Valcomix, your screeching harms everyone! Not very effective!"** The youngest member has lungs. Valcomix is proud that someone can say something.

TSinged looks at Cretan with apologetic eyes and whispers... *"Sorry."* The girls separate as they were scolded. Valcomix is surprised by how loud his voice is. Fürthrived dims down, walking past TÖ-Slüdge forcefully ignoring her. TÖ-Slüdge was ready to punch her in the lower back. Valcomix catches her and shakes his head looking quite furious.

She drops her fist and waits for her not to be nearby. Her eyes widen as to what just happened. Cretan walks beside TSinged. To be away from those two. Valcomix approaches TÖ-Slüdge. **"You just scolded by the kid and you still want to antagonize her. Keep provoking her, I'll let her settle the difference."** He warns her with a harsh look of such disappointment.

She then sticks her tongue out at him. Now smiling, and stares at her wrist. Hoping she understands as he goes to be at the front. Smiling warmly at Cretan who is still upset. He then faces forward and playing with the device's screen that is slightly damaged. Then has eyes upon Fürthrived, who is glaring at Valcomix. But Valcomix has no idea what he did that got her upset, and he focuses his attention forward. TÖ-Slüdge is smiling at her wrist. *"Soft fur."* She tells herself remembering the sensation of his grip.

The time is 3:54pm of 08/02/3175

Playground WY, Sector: 37

Checking the map Entering the thicket of trees near the marked tower: 'C.O.A.T.S. lookout' is read northwest from their location. *Dragging* Valcomix listens in, knowing that sound. His stomach rumbles louder, and he turns his attention behind him. **"Everyone, you realized a lack of some beings lately?"** Valcomix asks and no one has any clue to his question.

Walking at a steady pace as he continues, he reaches a mountain pass with silver peaks and vibrant blue grass. Valcomix smiles greatly and quickens his pace to be at the top of the passage. The others appear and are shocked and bewildered by the droves. **"It's a horde of Creates."** Fürthrived alerts as her eyes sight the many. TÖ-Slüdge can understand why she squeaked. Cretan is not liking this at all. TSinged is ready for combat with that serious and mad expression. Valcomix's stomach rumbles, and he begins to salivate, getting excited as he has his sights on the plumpiest ones.

They feel uncomfortable except for TSinged. "Go eat." he orders with a smile. Now, Cretan is joyous as he gets to witness another feasting. With no hesitation, Valcomix rushes down with his four scarlet veins emerging from his back. Unleashed as he swiftly makes it down, sighting a target, and showing off his hot, moist, abyssal jaws.

Valcomix clamps his first prey as snaps a strong bite. As bright orange and heavy yellow liquid drips from his closed jaws. Euphoria. Enjoying the sensation of devouring, his veins drink in the leftovers. The horde approaches him silently, dragging themselves only to be downed by his gullet; becoming his meal. He relentlessly scratches at them, biting and using various techniques like some known animals. Flesh, corpses, stains, and himself are what remains for now. His veins drink in as he uses his jaws to devour the bigger chunks of leftovers.

His claws brighten to a scarlet hue, and pink color luminates his veins and eyes. He finishes and inhales with a satisfied smile. Cretan is rolling down the passage and slightly misses him then unravels. **"That was wicked! Just like you did with those true widows! But this one was more carnage and instinctual. You must have been starving. The first attack had me stunned!"** Cretan sounds lively as he sees the return of Valcomix's pink glow.

TSinged carefully makes it to them, followed by Fürthrived. Seeing Valcomix's color scheme and his form, she blushes. **"Cute."** she says with a serious tone. Her said word only makes him insecure. TÖ-Slüdge hesitates each step. **"Don't trip!"** Fürthrived warns her with a gleam in her eyes.

The three boys know well that is what she wants her to do. TSinged goes to help her. Getting injured for doing so, his arms and sides have some scald marks, but they clear up in seconds. **"Thank you, TSinged."** she says, showing her appreciation with an innocent smile. He flinches at her unusual way of her showing gratitude. **"You're welcome."** he says, gazing at her expression.

The five continue their voyage through the passage, reaching a waterfall with a steep staircase on the side of it, and scale down it carefully. Dur to the cracks and wet moss. Then, they walk the cement bridge that is damaged, vegetation grows from the cracks. Traversing this spectacular area and admiring the beauty of such nature as the waterfall is next to them. Then comes a view of a city claimed by nature.

Creates occupy the fallen structures. Ruins. The winds feel warm. TSinged touches the air. So does Cretan. The sky is brighter than they have ever seen, with light grey sheets of clouds. **"Playground SD. The Creates' house. The next state over belongs to giants. That is my last hunt."** Valcomix shares as he views the lush, vibrant blue grass trampled by disformed beings with a menacing glare.

# TO BE CONTINUED...

# EPISODE 9: GIANTS & HEAVY HITTING!

## PART 1

**"He's leading us towards that horde!"** Fürthrived yells frantically, pointing at the mass of disfigured beings wandering around as they drag themselves. TSinged sighs as he cracks his knuckles. **"You're intending to power through them?! TSinged, understand we'll be surrounded!"** Fürthrived nags with anger trying to warn him and others, but he ignores her. **"Listen to me. That creature is only going to get us and itself killed. TÖ-Slüdge, please. Stop these insolent boys. We need a plan!"** Fürthrived shouts begging for them to have reason.

TÖ-Slüdge puts both hands on her shoulders and pinches them. **"We survived a nest with tougher beings. We protected our haven from those Creates and roaches as before. It will just be a prolonged front."** she says to her with a serious gaze. **"We have abilities and a wild loose Valcomix."** Cretan mentions, stating the obvious. Valcomix then punches the brat in the shoulder. Then ponders. **"TSinged what is your**

**ability?"** Valcomix asks with true curiosity. TSinged shows off his muscle excitingly.

Fürthrived swipes away her holding and then uses a surge of heat to punch TÖ-Slüdge into the torso. Surprised and in pain, Fürthrived peers down at her with anxiety and anger. TSinged glares at Fürthrived. Cretan is concerned for TÖ-Slüdge as he stands beside her. Fürthrived readies herself to burn them both with a blank, hateful expression.

Valcomix now stands in front of Fürthrived and slaps her. TSinged is shocked and so is the other two. **"They did nothing. This is all my idea, don't like it? Speak your opinion and take that frustration out on me. Go on."** He says with an upset tone, keeping his attention as she rubs her cheek. Looking quite surprised.

Now angry, Fürthrived unleashes her fury. Intensifying her het. Doing so the three back away. Valcomix has his arms folded with a serious expression. Also attracting Creates as they reach for the source of such warmth. She goes in for a left hook aimed at his face. Valcomix stops her attack by pulling her to him. Putting his bent arm upon her above her chest. Then trips her up with his light leg. A swift motion that happened too fast. The three remain shocked. As he has her...

Pinned on the ground. She wails about and he flicks her on the forehead many times. She ceases her tantrum. Looking quite defeated as she tries to her attitude. *Growling* **"You don't hit your comrades. I was taught to voice my opinion to the higher statuses or directly to the person in charge. So, dim down and raise your malice elsewhere. Do you comprehend?"** Valcomix asks her with a serious and frustrated tone.

Defeated, humiliated, and upset, glaring into his eyes, seeing herself through them, Fürthrived whispers *"I understand."* Avoiding eye contact and becoming meek. Valcomix then removes his grip from her neck and helps her to her feet. He looks back at her as she bites her lip. Upsettingly so.

TSinged admires Valcomix's handling, admitting to himself that the situation would have been worse if he had interfered. Seeing him now take a knee in front of TÖ-Slüdge, he says with a smile, **"When she becomes that unstable, back away from her. If you start a situation, I'll use TSinged's hands to punish you."** TÖ-Slüdge begins to giggle. TSinged regrets admiring him. **"You can count on me to come to you if there is trouble."** Cretan says brightly. Valcomix gives him a thumbs up.

TSinged continues to watch Valcomix's actions. He was no longer that sympathetic meek being when he first met him, remembering his fight with Sevulix and how he acted to that fox. Now, he seems confident and capable. Valcomix again accosts Fürthrived. She glares at him. **"What?"** she asks with a threatening tone filled with defeat.

**"We're going through the masses. It's a straight shot to my final goal. Then, I will focus on getting you and your comrades across the ice. I'll play it safe then. For now, you have to stay close to my side. You have a bad temper"** he voices to her in a calm tone that hopefully eases her. To no avail was it successful. Wanting to voice her opinion but reluctant to make a sound, she just nods while biting her lip.

Sighting that the Creates are no longer approaching them as they were before. They just walk pass them seeing them drag their soft fragile gruesome formed body around without making any kind of sound besides dragging themselves.

# PART II

Now entering their domain, the Creates stop and turn their heads, facing the approaching five and dragging themselves as they reach for them with a single arm stretched out. Fürthrived begins to shiver and snivel, gripping her arms tightly.

Valcomix recognizes this quivering because he himself went through it. **"Close your eyes and cover your ears."** He tells her calmly while his fur flares a bright pink. His veins waver and undulate as they emerge from his back. TSinged gulps and then straight punches a group, stretching his arms at such a distance. Scattering the many of them with such brute force.

Valcomix is wide eyed. **"Your arms stretch far and with that much impact."** Sounding surprised and bewildered. TSinged has smug smirk upon his face while showing off his strong arm. **"This isn't all my power."** He says and punches more of them away. Valcomix is impressed. TÖ-Slüdge is not amused, shining due to her liquid coating, dripping hazardous fluids onto the concrete, and it cracks. Splashing at the numbers. Their flesh begins to bubble and melt. Reduced to a yellowish-orange puddle

Cretan changes his skin into a tan color. Then rolls around as spikes emerge from his skin. Piercing them and shifts his skin tone to a silver & pale green diamonds centered by brown shiny ridges. Rotating with such speed as the once attached flesh rotted bags are sent flying. Fürthrived remains silent bearing the fear of the action around her. Noticing this...

*Tch* Valcomix rushes into the city, claimed by the new nature of plant growth. Quickly slaughtering the Creates as they are not given a chance to retaliate nor respond. Digging his nails into their soft tissue and muscles, ripping through flesh easily and effortlessly. Spilling yellow vile all around. Coloring the concrete and growing life with viscous dull yellow and orange.

TSinged is punching them, crunching fragile bones. Cretan rolls into them, piercing their plastic-like skin with spikes jutting out the darker spots of his tanned skin. TÖ-Slüdge continues to splash them, causing them to melt or decompose at a high pace.

Fürthrived opens her eyes and witnesses everyone fighting with ease. They look bored. Thick puddles of orange and heavy yellow seep from the fallen bodies. Common scene of a massacre. They continue forward, brawling against the mass and reducing their numbers.

Not far from Valcomix, he rips one of them in half, making it rain a vile collection of heavy mixed colors.

Sickening. He isn't even enjoying it. His facial expression is similar to everyone else's. Bored. Remembering how shooting it was more fun as he kept aiming for their heads and competing with comrades.

They're slow-moving, unable to retaliate quickly. Their threat level is a basic two. They each had expectations, and none of them met their criterion. Disappointed, they continue through the city, seeing them sluggishly accost, reaching out for them.

Cretan snickers as one of them touches TSinged. Annoyed, he uses a strong slam, splattering the Creates' contents onto the ground, tossing away the disfigured. TÖ-Slüdge touches them herself, causing them to dissolve where they stand.

Valcomix slashes through the mass approaching the front. Soon, they exit the city and reach a road like a highway. Creates still lurk about, but they don't approach them; they just stand and point east. So still. **"This is a bit ominous."** TÖ-Slüdge says as she sees their disfigured lifeless expression being silent and acting mannequin-like. Just pointing.

As they continue for some hours, TSinged and Cretan feel a bit dizzy. Valcomix notices the two have been slagging a bit. **"You two alright?"** He asks as he turns and aids them. **"It's hot."** TSinged complains. Cretan is miserable as well. Valcomix takes out some fruits from the packs and offers them. **"Hydrate."** He orders. As they take some bites of the succulent and sweet mild flavoring helps cool them down for a brief minute, Valcomix takes the packs and carries them. Relieving TSinged from the extra weight.

They move on and sight more hordes of Creates. TSinged and Cretan don't have the energy to defend. These Creates are focused on something. Every single one of them is on their knees, swiping at the ground, digging, or feeling the hardened earth. Odd behavior. But, as long they're not being a bother. The sky turns darker. Fürthrived along with Valcomix is luminating the way. The two boys who struggled through are feeling much better as calm, warm winds breezes pass.

After some time, they reach another area with buildings. A town. No sight of Creates. Walking through the town of slightly damaged buildings caused by time and natural weathering, Valcomix sights an old-time fire station. He breaks the door and checks if it is safe. **"Clear, everyone. We rest here for the night."** he announces.

Cretan enters first, and Fürthrived follows after glaring at Valcomix. TSinged holds out a hand; Valcomix passes him the packs. TSinged then enters inside. Valcomix remains outside as a lookout, leaning against the wall by the entryway.

TÖ-Slüdge sits close to him. He smiles, enjoying the company. She rests fast. TSinged comes out holding some lemons and pears. Valcomix takes them. **"Make sure she eats those."** TSinged tells him, and he nods his head, understanding. His ears start to twitch, and he looks around to trace the source of that sound; the sound kind of hurts. Nothing. He stares at her sleeping face. Admiring.

# PART III

The sky shows another day of a sheet of light grey clouds. Calming warm winds pick up the dust scattered on the grounds. Valcomix shields TÖ-Slüdge using his tail from the dirt whisked by the winds. He remained awake, holding onto fruits, listening to everyone's soft breathing as they slept.

Most times, there is the sound of... *Faint metal scraping* The sound causes him to flinch. *Deep breath* *Yawn* TÖ-Slüdge is reaching high as she stretches, eyeing her navel as she does so.

**"You're staring too much. Have a thought?"** TÖ-Slüdge asks with mischievous tone as she smiles evilly. Valcomix stares into her gaze with an innocent grin. **"It's an inappropriate idea."** he tells her and passes her a lemon. She giggles softly and takes a bite of the sweet layer of the skin to drink the sourness that is within. With each finished fruit, he passes her another. **"Stop staring."** she orders with a soft, annoyed tone.

He turns his gaze to the entry of the old-time fire station. Cretan makes an exit, rubbing his eyes with his thumb and middle finger. *Sneeze* He then inhales fresher air. **"It was dusty in there."** Cretan complains.

**"A'ga-za."** TÖ-Slüdge and Valcomix both say to him with a smile upon their frame. **"Appreciated."** Showing mannerism as Cretan does some stretching. **"TSinged is doing his morning stretches. Fürthrived remains asleep. She is always the last one to rise."** He informs them agitatedly.

Concluding that everyone seems to be willing to leave already, but Candlelight wants to sleep longer. Valcomix enters the office area of the fire station. He finds her resting comfortably on top of the marble desk with her head resting on her folded arms. TSinged leaves after tapping his ally on the back and showing him a thumbs up.

*Low growling* Directly into her ear. She mumbles angrily and tries to punch the creature while still sleeping, and this causes her to roll off the desk. Waking up instantly, she sees Valcomix and notices she is being held by him. She finds Valcomix grinning and this infuriates her. She intensifies her heat, and Valcomix's fur begins to smolder. **"Put me down."** She orders him with such cold hostile tone. But he refuses and just carries her out.

TSinged raises an eyebrow. Seeing her become heated, Valcomix isn't bothered by her temperature nor her temper. **"Put me down,"** She orders grumpier than the last one. **"We continue on."** He announces to his teammates, ignoring her completely. Making sure that no one else in the radiative area.

TÖ-Slüdge has a smirk, seeing her humiliated once more. Some minutes pass, and Fürthrived keeps up with the nagging and threatening. TSinged groans, having to hear her mouth. TÖ-Slüdge is enjoying the view, seeing that she is helpless. Cretan is actually smiling, knowing someone has the ability to handle her temper and temperature. Valcomix avoids her hitting and nods at her words. Her yelling is less annoying and painful than the constant sounds he was hearing before.

Reaching a massive eight car lanes bridge of and walking across it. Fürthrived yawns and is a lot more tolerable. No longer wanting to put up a fight. TSinged is surprised. **"He outlasted her nagging."** Witnessing such a feat as Valcomix still continues to carry her. "Cretan is relieved. **"She finally is quiet."** He says with satisfied grin. **"Tired?"** TÖ-Slüdge asks and Fürthrived is embarrassed. Already being carried in such a position. Valcomix glares at her.

**"Do not provoke her. Next time, I will use TSinged's hands to punish you."** He says with a serious expression. TSinged doesn't agree with that idea.

**"Why my hands?"** He asks, and Valcomix says with a normal and obvious tone, **"I'll lose an arm if I touch her."** Cretan nods his head, agreeing that will happen. But TÖ-Slüdge remembers what his fur felt like as she rubs her wrist.

*Metal Scraping* Valcomix flinches at the horrible sound, but this one is louder and more continuous. *Rumbling* The bridge begins to shake violently and sway. Valcomix puts Fürthrived down. **"Everyone, hug concrete!"** Valcomix yells as he drops himself onto the bridge. They follow. Except he had to pull Fürthrived down, cushioning her fall with his long tail.

TSinged is too close to the edge and hangs to the railings. Splashed by the water, the weak railing snaps and pokes a hole into one of the packs. Causing supplies to spill out. After some uncomfortable minutes, the rumbling and the sound of metal scraping disperse, and all is silent.

Valcomix helps Fürthrived up. She turns her sights from him. This one is alright, and he then checks Cretan and TÖ-Slüdge. Cretan gives him a thumbs up. TÖ-Slüdge is alright. TSinged is not alright. One of the packs has gotten ripped, and all of the items inside are lost. He checks the other one, which is a little wet inside, and the device remains. Valcomix turns it on.

**The time is 10:14am of 08/03/3175**

It works and has a forty-three percent battery life left. He puts it back. **"Sorry,"** TSinged says, feeling responsible for losing most of their supplies. Valcomix shakes his head. **"We're uninjured, and the device is somewhat undamaged. There's plenty of fruits remaining. An earthquake happened, and that is what I'm blaming it on."** He tells TSinged and pats him on the shoulder assuring his comrade. It's hard to take this pup seriously when he looks adorable.

They soon cross the bridge, walking the distance of the highway. The air feels colder, and the winds become more hostile as they enter the zone where it is raining heavily. They can see a waterfall stretched far and huge boulders. They climb over their slippery obstacle, helping one another up to the top. Massive rubble and debris are filling this zone. Valcomix becomes more serious as they soon reach a massive reinforced curved wall. **"This is the last black state. Playground IA. Domain of giants."** Hie shares as his eyes flare with rage as his fur brightens a pink fire.

# PART IV

TSinged has his arms folded and stares at the constructed wall, seeing its vast length. **"How long is this wall?"** He asks with curiosity, trying to size it. **"It's a whole state, 30meters high and 1,553kilometers long or approximately 965miles long."** Valcomix answers with a surprised tone. Informing everyone as he sees their expression. TSinged is surprised and amazed. **"What animals are these 'giants' anyway?"** Fürthrived asks, curious as to why they will block a whole state off.

**"I don't know. They got some footage and some measured damage from scales connected to the drones. Heavy as a tank was our answer."** He answers her question, unsure himself. Just passing on what he was informed. "**How do we enter?"** Cretan asks the right question.

Seeing if he is able to scale to the top and over the wall, the trees are too short for that, and TSinged won't be able to do so anyway. Pondering on how to get in. *Bang* TSinged is throwing Cretan at the wall and creating dents.

Fürthrived steps toward the knuckleheads. **"You can't just bend metal to break it. Cretan will**

**be injured after a few more attempts. Let me try something."** Annoyed, she murmurs to herself angrily complaining about these two imbeciles. She brightens up, intensifies her heat, and touches the metal wall, coloring the metal from silver to red, then orange to a bright yellow.

Her heat is melting a hole through the wall, burning the ground around within a radius. Her body is bright, causing everyone to turn away their eyes from her. She enters the state of Iowa and then dims down. Valcomix ducks his head to go through the opening. The others follow. Their eyes are wide open taking in the view. **"We're the first group to ever set foot in this Black State."** Valcomix says sighting...

The vast area has a variety of fruits growing from vibrant and lush trees. Blue grass with patches of orange and white flowers. Almost as if a jungle then a forest due to the overgrowth of trees and moss clumped like vines. Already hearing the animal sounds and rustling as the ambient heavy rain and low thunder generate music.

They now traverse and see stags, raccoons, squirrels, and bears near streams. Then, a herd of boars over the hills. This area is a habitat for them to thrive. Valcomix remembers Sevulix's territory and then those of equal status. Bearing the armband and as to what he promised to them. Clenching the same armband. Feeling uneasy. TSinged and TÖ-Slüdge can see that he is troubled. Concluding that he may just be nervous.

*"Forests and valleys dwelled by nature; all states belong to them, absent of humanity as it once was."* Valcomix says within himself unsure to believe that. But he has to complete his mission. They keep on moving through the thicket. After several hours, the sky again welcomes the night. **"Valcomix and Fürthrived stand out. Knowing that giants lurk and they are in their territory, it is best to hide."** TÖ-Slüdge says while mumbling.

TSinged heard her. He agrees. **"Valcomix, Fürthrived, we cannot continue to journey within these unknowing lands with a potential number of beings with a status similar to Sevulix's. Especially in the dark. Everyone should rest, including you, Valcomix. I'll keep a lookout."** He suggests as he rests, leaning against a tree.

Valcomix does not agree with his suggestion because there isn't a place to hide. Knowing that they journey for quite a while. He gives up and leans against a different tree. Cretan stays beside TSinged.

Fürthrived is near Valcomix but not close, despising him. TÖ-Slüdge also rests near him. TSinged pinches his forehead from what he is witnessing. He is thankful that...

**"TSinged, if you feel that you're in need of rest, wake me."** Valcomix tells him with his eyes closed. TSinged nods his head. Now, he watches them sleep. Some hours pass. The clouds swirl in the sky with their dark gray and dense color, and soon it begins to lightly rain. The area around the forest still remains beautiful, and the animals are still out taking a drink.

They continue, but this time, Valcomix leads them through the thicket. Black roses with a violet light are growing in the patches of wild thorns. There is a stream of water. Treading carefully. TSinged lifts up Valcomix, not wanting of what happened before to repeat. The other three agree. Putting Valcomix out of harm's way from the thorns.

They reach a swampy area. Huge fish are taking in algae. After a while... *Sniffing* Valcomix takes a whiff of the air. He knows this scent: a pungent smell of rusted iron, rotting meat, and fat escaping. Decay and decomposing. The heavy scent of death. Just like many other creatures to ward off small challengers. Queen's nest, the bear's lair, and the bird's tower. Now it's the giants' domain. He gets serious and moves through the stream that descends with a wide mouth at the end, where water falls into a deeper hole from a three-foot drop. There was a hill on the side. Which the four are using. They now smell the air, and it is worse than the queen's nest.

Valcomix exits the water, reaching the shallow part. He sees scattered bones with rotting meat of boars and stags piled on top of the other. They seem to have been half-eaten. Their eyes remain open and lifeless, dripping thick crimson from the corpses and mouths. There are plenty of bones made into a road. **"This a not an animal that eats what is needed. They're mainly hunters counting game."** Fürthrived says from horrid sight as it frightens her. Causing her heart to beat loud. Valcomix's ears begin to twitch. They all notice and can feel rumbling. Now hearing such a set of heavy footprints. **"TSinged, find a spot to hide."** Valcomix orders as he gets into a stance.

Fürthrived is scared, and TÖ-Slüdge drags her near the hill. Cretan follows, and TSinged stays with them. He covers his ears, and they do the same. Fürthrived closes her eyes and covers her ears. *Silence* *Heart beating* *Inhale* Valcomix takes in air into his lungs... then... ***SCREEAHHHH!!!***

Unleashing his loudest screech. It echoes through the forest.

Everyone is anxious. *Booming Roar* The return call is followed by rumbling that causes the ground to shake. Valcomix smiles evilly as his veins emerge from his back. Shining his brilliant pink hue.

TSinged squints his eyes as the thumping of its footsteps grows louder and closer. It is approaching. His eyes are in shock; he stands frozen by the sheer size of such an animal. Sevulix was a lucky triumph. **"Valcomix is not going to win against that."** TSinged hesitates to say. Then, they all see it and are completely afraid. Peering down at its challenger is a...

# PART V

**AFRICAN BUSH ELEPHANT**: 12.08meters (39.63ft) in height by shoulder to shoulder. Weighing 33.62tons (US), or 33,499.55Kg, that is 67,240lbs. Even heavier than informed. A heavy beast called 'giants,' the apex of the African savannah.

**2**-Their trunks are tougher skin with hard tissue plates. Their robust body is layered with the same plates of tissue fibers and condensed muscle. Each leg, especially the back ones, is thick boned. The back legs can weigh up to 4.93tons each, and the front legs weigh at least half that per leg.

**3**-They lost their tail. Their tusks are condensed ivory that is whiter with a brilliant shine and doesn't stain. Completely solid, and a single incisor can weigh up to 145kg or 319.67lbs.

**4**-Their jaws can open wider due to the head being narrow. Carnivorous creatures with ivory teeth, each tooth is sharp. It has a bright smile. When it does so, it is going for violence. Navy blue with a greyish gradient skin complexion and dull green round eyes.

**5**-Threat level ranked at 17-20 depending on their mass and age. The thickness of their skin can measure their age. The threat level of this one: Unclassified.

---

It sees the trespasser and quickly brings its trunk high to the left. Showing off its bright, flawless smile and swings it to hit Valcomix, who dodges and tries to bite the front leg. The tough and rough texture is unaffected by his weak attack. The beast kicks Valcomix off, causing him to land in the pile of corpses. Valcomix then recovers and rushes to be underneath the massive predator to enter blind spots, avoiding its teeth, trunk, and ground-shaking stomping.

Seeing the lesser dense skin hanging, Valcomix ruthlessly slashes the skin. After some ferocious scratching, he inflicts a wound, but it's not deep enough. *Bellowing* The massive being tries to walk over Valcomix but misses him. Exposing his four veins, Valcomix swiftly gets under its huge face.

It again thrashes its trunk around and steps off the ground using its hind legs. *Bellowing* Using its weight to slam upon the ground, the giant beast creates a crater, causing Valcomix to be pushed away by a few inches. Knocked off balance and readies to take stance... *Grunting* Valcomix gets charged from the side and splashes within the water. Now appears is the other giant...

**BLACK RHINOCEROS**: Standing at 8.04m (26.38ft) tall. Weighing in at 4,248kg or considered 9365.24lbs, just 4.68tons (US). Just a seventh of the African Bush Elephant, this creature is much faster, standing on both its hind legs with a toughened, limber body. Now adapted to consume both meat and plant life: omnivore. Its eyes are sharpened with better peripheral vision. They have ivory plates on their arms. Their horns are long and can pierce through the elephants. These two giants are built to kill the other. Armored skin, the same characteristics as their rival. Their heads are flatter, with a wide forehead curving backward. Bright green oval shaped eyes, gray and black skin. Threat level is 14-18 depending on weight, environment and agitation.

TSinged is frustrated, witnessing a battle that was unfair already. Now, a sneak attack by another huge animal. TSinged doubts that Valcomix would survive a strike from either of them. **"That head bash caught him off guard."** He informs just watching a small contender face off against beings that are way beyond its weight class.

*Splashing* Valcomix comes out of the water and gets into a stance. *Grunting* *Bellowing* The two giants begin stomping about. Valcomix's tail begins to sway. He looks behind himself and smiles at his teammates. Smiling. Then focuses on the giants. ***SCREEAHHHH*** His screech was weak. He attacks first but trips up on his front right arm. The rhino punches Valcomix in the shoulder, using his tail to wrap its neck, pulling himself with his jaws at the ready. The elephant swipes away the small fur using its massive trunk. Valcomix is sent near the bones, and he uses his tail to cushion the fall. He takes a stance again.

**"TSinged, can we help him?"** Cretan says with anger in his eyes, concerned for a comrade. TÖ-Slüdge nods her head, agreeing with him. Fürthrived stays silent, witnessing his stupidity and continuing to fight a battle against creatures that are in a different weight class than his own. Taking brutal hits from the both of them. **"He needs to stop."** Sounding a bit worried as she is frustrated that she is watching him taking a beating and being tossed around.

TSinged drops the packs and rushes. With brutal force, he uses his might to punch the rhino in the side. *Crk* Cracking a bone within its ribcage. *Painful Grunting* the rhino squirms in agony, falling to the ground.

Valcomix smiles at TSinged. Only seems exhausted, no wounds nor signs of bleeding. Just ruffled up fur and signs of exhaustion. **"Thanks, TSinged."** Valcomix says with a shaky voice. *Coughing* Trying to stand; and manages to but his legs are weak. Now both focusing on the massive being. The elephant prepares to trample them both. Feeling something roll into it, Cretan smiles mischievously.

The elephant prepares to swipe away this one. TSinged punches it, stretching his arms. He then gets closer. The massive giant can feel the force of his pounding, but they're just annoying. It then hops off the ground and slams, knocking them all off balance. Valcomix goes to stand on all fours. Bearing the quaking as he grits his teeth. TSinged took a knee, while Cretan is

is the first to recover and rolls fast toward TSinged. Changing into his white plastic skin, he then picks up the lightweight and tosses him high. The elephant tries again and swipes its trunk at TSinged this time. He catches it but the power has him on his knees. Gritting his teeth, trying to keep it from moving so much. No avail. He gets lifted. Cretan comes down; dark grey with blue bumps as his new shift. Heaviest form. *Bash* *Bone cracking*

The impact was audible. Smashing into its face, slightly missing TSinged.... Cretan rubs his back and has signs of cracked skin but is smiling viciously while TSinged is kneeling proud with a smug grin. Valcomix is shocked but amazed. The elephant lost one of its tusks. It remains intact on the flooring, with the root of it fractured. *Bellowing* Angry, it rampages at Cretan, charging at him and swinging its massive trunk.

TSinged then rushes to get him but to no avail. He twisted his ankle during his fall. Something blurs pass him. Valcomix pushes Cretan into the water. Almost getting his leg struck, he trips up and lands into TÖ-Slüdge. Her heart is beating... *"Valcomix."* Whispering his name. He isn't waking up, and his body is dimming.

Cretan is injured and breathes heavily while holding his side. TSinged is furious as he witnesses this elephant attacked his teammates. **"Cretan. Valcomix."** Tears in his eyes as he approaches the giant. Remembering a certain scenario that he wants to forget. **"Duvuin."** His eyes become a dull grey. The skin on his arms begins to contract into thin plates and color to a dark greyish-brown color. The underlayer starts to glow orange. *Yelling* TSinged cries.

# PART VI

TSinged is enraged with tears. Cretan can see that he is different. The elephant charges at TSinged. He gets into a boxing stance quickly. Then, he launches the first punch, striking it in the face, causing it to look left, leaving a crack upon its hard skin plates. He then launches another, aimed for the jaw, having it bleed a bit. Quickly, he gives it a combo, aiming for the head this time. *Bellowing* It then forces its body to go forward. TSinged remains where he stands, punching with newtons of force.

The combos soon become more violent and random. Now, a barrage of punches. Some of them explode on impact, sounding like cannon fire. *Barrage of impacts* TSinged's expression is nightmarish. His dull grey eyes are filled with such hate and anger. That Cretan himself is afraid. TÖ-Slüdge turns her head not wanting to see him. Fürthrived is terrorized as she is solid and unmoving by fear.

The skin plates on the elephant are majorly damaged. It just now stands there taking TSinged's rageful fists. His relentless attacks soon become slower and weaker. *Breathing Heavily* TSinged's arms are shaking and feel heavy. His knuckles are dripping hot crimson onto the solid earth. Filling the cracks. His eyes return to a lighter gray, and his skin reverts back to a dark tan. He feels hot and exhausted.

The elephant remains standing and then drops and falls to the right, releasing hot, thick crimson onto the flooring from its face. Soaking itself in its wet, hot iron, TSinged falls over as his body is hot, feeling dizzy, and each blink is longer than the last. Forced to rest and is breathing hard.

Cretan still holds his side as he lays in the shallow part of the water. Valcomix remains in TÖ-Slüdge's arms. Feeling hairs brush against her thighs. *Murmuring* She is confused, seeing him move his tail to cover his face. She starts to smile.

Fürthrived witnessed the aftermath of their brawl. Seeing the rhino still squirming, she approaches it and then burns its very existence, leaving only ash and cinders. **"I'm glad for you that he is alive and can manage your touch. But all the boys are injured and tired. Help me attend to them."** Fürthrived orders sounding reasonable but is annoyed by their stupidity.

They first carry Valcomix and lay him beside TSinged. Then, they go get Cretan, yet he is crawling while holding his side. **"Cretan."** TÖ-Slüdge says worryingly. He smiles. **"I just cracked a shell again, right on the long, hard white spike on its face. Is that a bone?"** He asks as he rubs his side while in pain. **"It's a tusk, and it's a harder substance than bones, known as Ivory."** TÖ-Slüdge informs while smiling.

Cretan snickers and has prideful grin. **"Well by skin is tougher than ivory, but it still fractured my toughest skin."** Yet, he feels annoyed at his injury. After some time, Cretan is better and helps tend to the two exhausted members. TSinged's body is heating up. Valcomix is no longer glowing pink nor scarlet. **"There is a dead elephant for him to eat. Not much to do to help. Our effort may cause more harm. Just let them rest."** Fürthrived says with annoyed tone. Frustrated that they ended up like this. The two do agree but they also agree that her attitude is ugly.

As some time passes by, TSinged's body cools down, and Valcomix's stomach begins to rumble. TSinged awakens first, rubbing his forehead and feeling quite groggy and is shivering. He sits up, sees a massive elephant corpse, and remembers what happened. He was punching it with brutal force. He stares at his arms, which are now dark tan and no longer glowing. He mentally feels hot, and it is excruciating. He gulps down his saliva and rubs his chest. **"Thirsty."** He sees the pack near his person, takes out some fruits, and chews them slowly.

Then, he notices Valcomix. Upset with him, he is worried and thankful. Swarmed with a mixture of emotions, he has no idea if he should: scold him or commemorate his promise. Slowly standing to his feet, he searches around and doesn't see the other three.

As TSinged focuses harder to search for them, he spots TÖ-Slüdge and Fürthrived at the top of the hill. Rolling his arm, he can feel his bones pop. Now, he makes his way to their location. TÖ-Slüdge is the first to notice as she interrupts their serious conversation, turning her attention to muscles. **"Are you well?"** she asks concerningly.

TSinged sighs. **"My arms hurt, and I feel heavy. Just restless and need to move around. So, don't tell me to relax. What are you girls up to, and where is Cretan?"** He asks as he is curious and also wants to distract himself from the discomfort. **"We were discussing the action of you boys, but since this was Valcomix's idea, that was dangerous and bullheaded."** Fürthrived says with a sneering tone along with spite and detest. Not an answer, he didn't want the cause.

TSinged has a slight headache from her nagging already. **"I agreed to his terms. This is also the end of it. Remember what he told you. Now, we're going to focus on getting out of the Playgrounds."** He tries to tell her calmly, but the discomfort is aggravating, and she is making it worse.

**"She kept repeating it, and I told her the same thing. As long as we are okay. It may be worse out on the ice and further."** TÖ-Slüdge says, annoyed by such a conversation. **"Cretan is with those algae-eating fish."** she informs him. He raises an eyebrow, confused and, at the same time, curious. He then walks past the girls and returns to the river ending area.

He now has Cretan in his view. He is shivering near a built fire pit. TSinged knew that he was resourceful, but this surprised him more. He approaches him and takes a seat on wet moss. **"Cretan, why aren't you near Fürthrived to get warm?"** he asks with a gentle smile. **"She kept calling me bullheaded. I know what she meant to call us. Idiotic or stupid. Know the definition before speaking. Valcomix is the one who is stubborn, but brave. I couldn't be around her. She ridicules everyone else and complains to be right. I'll return once he's awake so she can be silenced once more."** He says, pouting, putting some dead leaves on the medium-sized flame. It grows a bit.

TSinged chuckles, knowing what he meant, remembering where that individual tripped. He slaps his face. Cretan is shocked and stares at him. *"He is unaffected by her touch."* TSinged closes his eyes, hoping he doesn't wake up too soon.

## WHERE THE FALLEN GIANT LAYS

TÖ-Slüdge got away from her bickering and nagging and is now attending to Valcomix as she is petting his head, smiling and giggling. Setting him on her lap. **"Your fur is soft. I was trying to avoid hurting you until you caught my wrist."** She says with a pout while lightly pinching his ears.

**"Thank you for caring about me."** Valcomix says in a soft, melancholy tone, enjoying the gentle scratching. Noticing something is ailing him. **"Speak."** she orders, and he smiles with a sad expression. **"TSinged, once again saved my life. Defeated the apex giants of Iowa and got injured for it. Both Cretan and him were injured. TSinged managed to fall these creatures and that... I feel pathetic. Weak."** He voices out with a snarl. Upset.

TÖ-Slüdge has a serious expression and glares into his eyes. Ten pinched his cheek. **"It's not about being weak. We all have different strengths, if reasoning.**

**There were two of those massive beings."** she tells him, and Valcomix closes his eyes and exhales. **"It still feels like I lost my hunt to the better."** he grumbles.

She pinches his ears, annoyed by his statement. **"You boys did a team effort. You were already beaten up, and Cretan injured himself by removing a tusk. TSinged went and bombarded the massive after you two became unable."** TÖ-Slüdge tries to tell him as gently as possible. *Grumbling* He remains upset and dissatisfied about the outcome. She clicks her tongue and removes her hand from him. **"Face off with TSinged if you got something to prove."** She spat out with a vicious tone.

# PART VII

Shall you speak a name, so shall they appear. **"What's happening?"** TSinged asks with a disgruntled tone as he peers down at Valcomix. Cretan backs away from him. TÖ-Slüdge then excuses herself along with Cretan to leave these two alone. Valcomix then stands up, staring at the stolen kill with a complex expression. TSinged calms down and has a serious frame. **"Your concept of strength is simple-headed. You were incapable of taking down that creature, then it became impossible after the second one entered into your challenge."** he tells him.

Valcomix becomes more upset, snarling lowly, showing off his teeth, and feeling self-defeated. TSinged focuses on him. **"Dispose of the word strong. Replace it with capable and inform yourself with capabilities. You alone eradicated a nest and devoured a queen. Unaffected by the touch of two certain individuals. You're fast and agile. I'm not. My arms are still in pain due to that brawl. Here you are, standing after a beating. You're capable, but learn how to be resourceful of being so. Make that an advantage."** He informs Valcomix, noticing his temperament is a little more relaxed.

Cretan and TÖ-Slüdge smile. TSinged approaches Valcomix but gets glared at. **"I'll do so. But you managed to fell this creature mostly by your own effort. Yet, you didn't take the first bite."** Valcomix tells TSinged. He is surprised and disgusted.

**"No, you can have the whole thing."** TSinged offers the kill to him. **"Its skin is tough. My teeth are incapable of puncturing through."** Valcomix says with a snarl. TSinged chuckles and then goes to pick up the heavy incisor. **"Then, become resourceful."** he says with a smile, carrying the tusk.

Valcomix can see that he is struggling with it. He hesitantly puts his grasp on it, pulling it to his chest, and TSinged lets go of it. Bearing its weight and letting his legs stand in a firmer stance. He takes each step carefully as the tusk is heavy, holding the pointed end part over the corpse's belly. He drops it, and it stabs through the skin, reaching the meat. His four veiny-like whips emerge from his back. They reach in, taking in the moist crimson fluid. He gazes at the sky, satisfied. **"We should leave him to his feast."** TÖ-Slüdge suggests, making her way to the river up hill. TSinged nods his head, agreeing, and follows suit. Cretan remains to watch. Fascinated.

## SOME HOURS PASS

The night returns. The four enjoy a wholesome meal of fruits and fish grilled by the radiant heat of Fürthrived. They are above and away from the area of decay and rot but closely located by the river. Hearing the water flow. **"When do we continue?"** Fürthrived asks, holding a plum and drying it out by immense glow yet she is dim.

TSinged finishes up his meal. "**Valcomix didn't say. I don't believe we should keep going just yet anyway. Cretan is still sore, and my arms are still hurting. Also, I want to know how I got them to glow.**" He tells her, curious about the takedown he committed.

**"We should just make our way as early as possible."** Fürthrived refuses his recovery. **"The boys need to recuperate, and it's best to have some downtime once more."** TÖ-Slüdge says, smiling honestly at the flowing stream down the path of where the watering hole is being filled.

Fürthrived glares at them both. Her meal now tastes bile and is unsavory. She then turns to Cretan. He flinches, then returns to calm, knowing someone is able to shut her up. He then turns to TSinged. **"I want to help. Those punches were quite powerful."** Cretan says excitingly. Disappointed and angry, Fürthrived then stands and walks away from them. The three are just relieved that she didn't intend to argue.

## THE AREA OF THE REMAINS

The massive creature is now of scattered bones. Valcomix is resting unwell as he squirms around a lot in pain. He then crawls to be under the skull, clenching the tusk that was given to him shining a bright pink color and flashing scarlet. Putting it close to his sharp teeth; agonized by the strength of the massive creatures and a beast. Valcomix rests unpeacefully fighting all of them. Red eyes of dark shadow-like creatures beating him. Still, he stands against them with a smile and attacks with claws and fangs. *Biting*

**TO BE CONTINUED...**

# EPISODE 10: RESTRICTED? UNBOUND & LIMITLESS!

## PART I

Cretan yawns, reaching to the dark, swirling clouds, then winces as his side stings and burns. TSinged rubs his arms, and then he opens and closes his hands, flinching from the uncomfortable throbbing. TÖ-Slüdge may not be able to see them much, but their pained breathing and grunting are unsettling. A new morning and they're definitely feeling the hurt from yesterday. She sees from a distance Fürthrived lying down, refusing to go near her and wanting to get away from these two.

She stands up, and then from her side, she can see a blurred scarlet glowing. Smiling and giggling, she carefully traverses the sloped path. Lurking closer and seeing the mess of massive skeletal bones, she climbs over a few; this time, her touch doesn't melt or cause them to deform. Maintaining their dull white color. *Biting*

She then finds the perpetrator causing the sound and the glow. Which is burning a brilliant scarlet; he is gnawing angrily on the tusk. She bends down and watches the pup act like a whelp, inching closer. He ceases. *Giggles* **"You're such a pup."** she says, smiling mischievously as she reaches to pet its head. Its tail reaches out and snags her arm, then wraps around her waist, pulling her into an entangled embrace against his side.

She is surprised and then tries to pry herself free, but to no avail. Unable to stand, she is forced to only have her head rested upon his side. Soft fur. She continues to struggle. *"Valcomix."* TÖ-Slüdge whispers, annoyed and angry.

Valcomix continues to chew on the tusk. After struggling for some time, she gives up, feeling warm and drained. She can hear his soft heartbeat and feel the creature expand and contract due to its calm breathing. This lulls her to sleep as well.

## NEAR THE RIVER AREA

TSinged splashes his face with the cold water. Still groggy upon awakening, he then opens and closes his hands. A dull throbbing sensation spreads through his arms, but it's not as bad as yesterday. He then attempts some pushups, managing to do his normal without any issues except having to feel this weird throbbing. Now he stands, sighting that Cretan is resting comfortably holding onto his side. Fürthrived is still radiating. He then makes his way toward the place where the giants once claimed.

Moving the scattered heavy bones as some post work out, he shakes his head as he stumbles upon a sight. TÖ-Slüdge is resting peacefully nestled against soft fur while covered comfortably and warmly by his long tail. Valcomix remained where he rested with the tusk under his paws. *"You two are apparently comfortable. Underneath a skull, though?"* TSinged whispers in a serious tone as he rolls his eyes, then notices Valcomix shifting a bit.

Valcomix now opens his eyes, inhaling deeply, then exhales. **"Morning. Now, what has you disturbed?"** Valcomix asks in a restless tone. **"Morning. Just an awkward sighting of two individuals."** He answers, viewing TÖ-Slüdge rest with a smile upon her frame.

Valcomix looks to the side of himself. He then chuckles and slightly moves his tail to provide her more coverage. Now, he focuses back on TSinged. **"Don't let her get attached to you."** He warns him with a serious tone. Valcomix smiles. **"She is, apparently."** He says enjoying watching her sleep. Then smiles mischievously. *Scoffs* **"We're going to need time**

**to recuperate. Cretan is still injured and..."** TSinged suggests forcibly with an annoyed tune.

**"Alright, it will be best to relax for some days and a few nights anyway. The rest of the states belong to the C.O.A.T.S. We need to act cautiously to get to any type of beach and hope it's frozen over."** Valcomix informs TSinged with a serious expression. TSinged nods, understanding the circumstances, and walks away. Leaving the two be.

# PART II

He returns to the deeper portion where the huge catfish swallowing algae. Sighting small riverine islands within the middle of the long stream of flowing water. There are trees, flowers and moss growing on them. The chilling winds cause the leaves to sound, creating an ambiance. TSinged shivers, trying to focus on the wrath he used to defeat such a massive being and remembering the emotion of anger. But to be calm and soothing as he watches such a scenery. Many large fish have surfaced. They're mouths are fully open swallowing in algae.

TSinged now stands, then copies that expression of hate; he aims his punch at one of the fish. *Splash* He misses. It sunk itself down. First effort. No discouragement. Just try again. After a while, all the fish had sunk themselves or swam away. He feels furious as his arms are heavy from being over-stretched and exerted, while that throbbing sensation remains dull.

*"What was it that I did? I felt anger, and then my arms felt a little warm, and then my punches were explosive. Every punch felt as if there was an increase in power. I want to do that again."* He

wants of himself with determination, driven to keep attempting but not while his arms are aching. Then he sighs, viewing the calm water's surface and then looks to his right. His eyes are wide open and surprised as well as confused. There is a bright yellow ball rolling as it skids across the water. That yellow ball then changes its color to black as it reaches the base of a tree of one the islands. Unravelling itself is Cretan, and he is upset.

TSinged hesitates to enter the cold and deep waters. Seeing that Cretan is bothered by something, he leaps into the water. Not knowing its depth, he struggles and then hastily swims to where the youngest member is. Getting out of the water, he is shivering. **"Cretan, you alright?"** TSinged asks with a concerned tone.

Cretan sits himself up, rubbing his eyes. **"Fürthrived, she burned my arm. I accidentally rolled into her, and she judged it as an act of violence."** He sniffles and shows TSinged the red burn mark hand print upon his forearm. The mark looks as if she grabbed him for a while.

TSinged's eyes and expression are furious. Upset, he makes it to the edge and is ready to step back into the dark depths. When he does make the plunge, he quickly swims to the bank side. Climbing out, he begins running and sees the individual who is hopping on one foot and wincing. **"Fürthrived!"** he yells, spatting out her name with anger and disgust.

Fürthrived looks in the direction of where she was called. She is frightened and heats up intensely to defend herself. The moss and cyan grass reduce to cinders within a 4ft radius**. "He ran over my foot! I retaliated wrong! I was just sleeping and..."** Fürthrived says, trying to share her side while yelping as she is frightened. He is approaching unfazed by his own skin being burned. She backs away. Raising her arms over to shield her face. **"I did nothing wrong!!"** She screams

Hearing the screams, Valcomix is sprinting fast and arrives. Pushing TSinged back to be out of her surging heat. He shows his back to Fürthrived and gives TSinged a calm expression. "What is happened?" He asks seeing Fürthrived shaking and steam from her face. Noticing that she is crying.

**"Valcomix, move aside."** TSinged oddly and coldly tells him. Valcomix doesn't do so and slightly turns his gaze to the frightened candlelight. **"You'll be burned before even touching her. We should listen to what caused this situation."** He suggests as he backs away from TSinged entering further in the radiating heat.

TSinged folds his arms, still furious with a blank expression. Valcomix then sighs. **"Fürthrived, explain what happened."** He orders her while still keeping sights upon TSinged. **"Cretan was rolling around in his heavier skin and then accidentally ran over my foot. I was asleep, and I screamed because of the pain. I did yell back, and out of spite, I grabbed him by the arm and told him what he did was an act of violence. Then, he started crying and rolled away."** she explains while terrified, covering her face and looking weak.

TSinged calms down a bit. Valcomix rubs his forehead. **"Sounds believable. Still, it was an accident. You did hurt the kid with your touch and caused him to cry. You two are both at fault. TSinged, you attend to Cretan. I'll dim the flame of candlelight."** Valcomix suggests; disappointed on how all this transpired. Knowing that Fürthrived is violent when you disturb her sleep. Cretan is a wild kid. **"Let's find calm grounds and separate for some time."** Valcomix suggests with a calm mild smile. TSinged nods with a serious and upset expression aimed at Fürthrived. Then, he makes his way back to where he came from.

**"What are you going to do?"** Fürthrived asks using an angered voice. Valcomix aids in removing her boots and notices that there is swelling. He lifts her up like cargo, using his tail to tie her legs so that she isn't able to kick, and then carries her boots.

Approaching the stream's mouth, descending into a clear pool, he smiles evilly as he jumps. Keeping her head above the water and using his legs to kick, he then sits her down on the shallow end. She is surprised. Valcomix, with a smirk, says, **"Keep that foot still in the cool waters and reduce that temper of yours."** Fürthrived glares at him and he flicks her forehead, feeling humiliated once more.

TÖ-Slüdge then appears. Valcomix informs her about the situation. She then casts a worried glance behind at the walking hearth. **"Let's leave her be."** Valcomix suggests and leaves the area to explore. TÖ-Slüdge joins him to give Fürthrived her peace.

# PART III

Finding an abundance and varieties of fruits growing from the trees, a stag stands on its hind legs to reach for them. Valcomix is already showing exhaustion as he is carrying two of the tusks. One given and the other tusks was pried by force. It took a few tries. He is struggling to just lift his arms.

TÖ-Slüdge is awed by how he is even managing to lift even one but is travelling with two of them. He then drops them. *Breathing Heavily* **"Why are you even doing this?"** she asks concerningly. Valcomix is disappointed as the stag has run away from the tusks that are now laying onto the soft earth.

**"Cretan is rolling in his heaviest skin. TSinged is bothered by something. He came at Fürthrived, ready to enter her heating. It's a crazy disturbance that a lot of us go through. I attempt it every day."** Valcomix informs her. Now, TÖ-Slüdge is more confused. He chuckles. **"Becoming more capable."** he says with a smirk, answering her question.

She sighs. **"Those two should be healing, and you should be..."** She then starts to nag and Valcomix smiles close. Seeing her reflection in his scarlet eyes, he says,

**"TÖ-Slüdge, we're going across the ice. I don't know those lands, nor am I informed on how the wilderness is. Unknown regions can be terrifying. It may be malarky to most. But we're going to have to become more capable. I'm not satisfied with the outcome of losing to those two, nor with Sevulix. Until we feel ready, we continue."** he voices to her while smiling.

She then understands, turning away from his soft and meaningful glare of determination. Blushing while annoyed. Valcomix then turns around, taking a knee as he grips the tusks in each hand. *Strong exhale* He then lifts the heavy tusks and swings them to have them placed on his shoulder, walking off-balanced for a bit. TÖ-Slüdge's violet eyes shine for a moment realizing a crucial moment they're in.

## WHERE THE SCATTERED BONES RESIDE

TSinged is boxing around the heavier femur. *Thwacking * The sound of each pounding is precise but isn't causing it to crack as he is anticipating to do. Cretan is walking toward Fürthrived hesitatingly so, and she notices him. He sees her foot is slightly swollen, and she sees the dark red handprint she inflicted.

**"I'm sorry, Fürthrived."** Cretan says with honest remorse. She doesn't show any emotion. "**Thank you**

**for apologizing. Cretan, I do apologize for your arm, but you must be careful of who you're rolling into."** She warns him with disappointed tone. **"I'll do so."** He says, upsettingly and annoyed by her attitude. He then leaves her by her lonesome. He changes his skin to dark gray with blue bumps, struggling to walk as if gravity has increased.

TSinged smiles at him, knowing that he is serious. After some time, Valcomix and TÖ-Slüdge return before the night makes an appearance. Sighting the exhausted Cretan and TSinged, Valcomix approaches the two. He staggering a bit. Then, he accidentally drops the tusks. They each sit up and read each other's expressions, smiling.

TSinged begins to chuckle, and then Valcomix. Cretan then begins to snicker, and the three start to laugh. TÖ-Slüdge smiles at them and shakes her head, not understanding the boys.

# PART IV

## A NEW MORNING

Valcomix sniffs the air while TSinged and Cretan are waiting for him. He then lifts TÖ-Slüdge, who remains asleep resting on his shoulder, and sets her gently within the skull. Then, he adjusts Fürthrived on the opposite side. She fights back as a reaction disturbed as she rests. He now picks up the tusks. He stumbles a bit as he walks, traversing through the thicket where there is an opening.

TSinged and Cretan sight the stag reaching for the fruits. TSinged takes down a plum and a few kiwis and passes two of them to Cretan. A moment afterward. TSinged is lying on the grass. Cretan is doing the same with his silver and pale green diamond skin centered by shiny brown ridges within each diamond.

Valcomix knows this positioning as he follows after TSinged with the heavy tusks on top of his back. **"We each go our own pace, reaching the goal of one hundred."** TSinged tells them with a serious attitude. They now commence to do pushups. TSinged finishes first with ease.

Cretan is at fifty-two, and his arms are shaking. He then takes a knee. Valcomix reaches forty-nine and is breathing heavily. He struggles as well. It now rains lightly, and they finally finish after some time. At least they managed. Exhausted already. TSinged then punches the both of them. Cretan rolls up to defend himself while Valcomix takes the hit, smiling menacingly.

## ANOTHER DAY

The sky rumbles, releasing its droplets of rushing water. Pelted by rain are the boys. Valcomix dodges each punch while carrying the tusks, but he is unable to get closer. Cretan tries to roll into him but is set back. TSinged tries to hit Valcomix. Cretan is receiving brute contact and is pushed further away due to his barrage of punches.

## NEXT DAY

The boys struggle to stand. The ground level is covered in a cold mist. They do some dynamic stretching. Then, they return to the area. TÖ-Slüdge smiles at them, shaking her head. As the three return to their training ground, they start the day eating fruits and doing their paced pushups. Today, TSinged and Cretan are determined to stand firm against Valcomix.

Cretan rolls first with his white plastic skin tone, then quickly changes his skin to dark gray with blue bumps. Valcomix sidesteps. TSinged follows him, unleashing his barrage of punches.

Surprisingly, Valcomix manages to defend himself from the brutal connections. Not noticing a wild roll midair. Finally moves out of the way only to receive an impact to his stomach. Dropping the tusks and is laid onto his back, staring at the leaves.

TSinged stands over him with his arm reached. He then grasps it and is pulled back to his feet. TSinged pats his shoulder. **"Valcomix, you focus too much on how to counter or making the first strike. You were tossed around by those giants and Sevulix, literally. Don't limit yourself to just your teeth and nails."** TSinged shares his advice with a violent smile while pointing at his tail.

Valcomix stares at his tail, measuring the length by sight, moving it about while checking its flexibility. He then puts down the tusks, focusing on his claws, and then pricks his thumb on his sharpest tooth.

Cretan accosts TSinged with a roll, connecting directly at his side, causing TSinged to kneel and wince in pain. Caught off guard. *Snickering* Cretan smiles victoriously. TSinged then recovers, glaring menacingly at Cretan. And Cretan glares back. TSinged approaches the young menace and holds onto his head. Squeezing.

**"TSinged, I give! Avdul! Mercy!"** Cretan cries out helplessly as he tries to pry away from his holding. TSinged then releases his hold and Cretan turns his sight upon Valcomix. **"What's he doing?"** He asks, confused and curious, watching him move his tail. TSinged focuses on Cretan in a boxing stance. **"He's figuring himself out."** TSinged answers his question.

## NOW, A WINDY NIGHT

Fürthrived provides warmth for TSinged and Cretan while TÖ-Slüdge rests beside Valcomix. They are gathered around each other on the flat near the river area. Valcomix's eyes are open, and he sees his teammates resting and a friend beside him. He is careful not to awaken her as she is removed from him. Picking up the pair of tusks. Returning to the training ground, which is now occupied by squirrels, boars, and raccoons, he watches them and examines their movement.

He notices how squirrels scratch a raccoon as it gets too close to their tree. The boars are huddled together, aiming their gnarled tusks at the approaching bandits.

After watching their movements for a while and seeing that there was no success for the raccoons, their sneaky heist and hunt failed tonight. Valcomix approaches. The boars aim their gnarled horns at him and squeal with such hostility. The creature uses its long tail and swipe them away. They scurry into the thicket. Valcomix now rubs his long attachment, feeling mainly muscle structure and a bony end. He remembers his encounters with many beasts and a variety of animals, definitely Sevulix and his experience with the raccoons and his beating from the giants.

## THE MORNING ARRIVES

TSinged and Cretan wait for Valcomix, but to no avail; he does not wake up. They leave without him.

## A FEW DAYS PASS

Valcomix hasn't been training with the two. TSinged smiles and pets his head. **"Keep doing what you're able to do."** he says, encouraging him as he remains asleep. Cretan is disappointed.

After some hours, they return with bruises. Fürthrived is disgusted by their appearance and for wasting time and their attitude toward their situation. She is annoyed, but she doesn't want to say anything.

Forced to prepare grilled catfish caught by Valcomix for everyone. Cretan asks, **"He's been doing a lot of fishing lately. When will he join us in our brawls again?"** TSinged just smiles. **"He will, soon. Just like I've been doing, he's trying as well. Once he figures himself out, we can brawl again."** TSinged informs Cretan, who is only getting more confused by the same answer, not understanding what he's implying. The two then feast upon the fish.

TÖ-Slüdge is as much concerned as Cretan is, thinking he may have given up on training and is depressed. TSinged is annoyed as she stands up, looking toward the direction of the river ahead where the islands are. Just behind the trees. **"Leave him be."** TSinged warns her. Looking quite crestfallen by his suggestion, he sighs and shows a serious expression. This is upsetting his appetite. **"This is similar to him leaving for weeks before back at that place. At least this time, we know that he's close and returns daily."** He tells her. He mutters angrily to himself, not able to convince TÖ-Slüdge to remain stationary.

**"Do what you want. Just don't interrupt him. Curiosity may get you bit."** he warns her as he rubs his arm, feeling a memorable pain. She then smiles and traverses ahead where an individual may be. Fürthrived is angry and glares at TSinged. TSinged then scoffs, staring at her with a calm demeanor. Cretan is annoyed and uncomfortable due to their silent arguing.

TÖ-Slüdge walks upon the slippery moss, hearing movement. Her eyes are relaxed, and she smiles, listening in on the creature. *Snarling* *Growling* As she witnesses...

# PART V

Valcomix is staring at the tip of his tail with a malicious smile, circling it around himself; his long tail bends and sways. Then, it twitches, striking at his face. Valcomix manages to move, but his shoulder gets struck, creating a small hole. His tail tries to stab him many more times. Each strike is unpredictable, swiping a few away and evading major wound inducing strikes rather than small inflictors.

His scarlet-lit veins emerge from his back and burn bright, emitting a pink light. His tail bends and wraps around one of the tusks. It curls like a spring, pointing at the back of his neck. The four scarlet veins surround him. Valcomix sights all five threatening attackers, envisioning them as dangerous creatures. Using his claw, he swipes at one of the veins as it rises and repositions itself.

Valcomix is then attacked from his side. *Snarling* He evades it but is led into a series of relentless hits, leaving marks on his arms and legs. The tail then falls while uncurling itself, aiming for his head. Preoccupied with taking hits from the four, he sidesteps fast, evading the kill strike. Catching the ivory spike with his teeth and hurting his jaw, he releases it, unwrapping the heavy tusk into his hand. He smiles and winces from the pain he inflicted upon himself. Approaching the deep, dark depth, he sinks his tail in the murky medium. A moment later. Feeling a nibble, he quickly pulls his tail out of the water, catching a catfish. With haste, he devours the huge fish.

He is now replenished, revived, and healed. All his wounds now only have the lingering sensation of pain, like a bad memory. *Yawn* He lies down underneath the nearest tree. Playing with his tail and controlling it to curl, he bends and sways it, doing the same with the four whips. He makes them focus in different directions and then quickly has them centered on a single point. He then stands up.

*Gentle breeze* *Inhale* *Exhale* He relaxes his body and closes his eyes, relying on his acute hearing, causing his ears to twitch. Listening to the gentle flow of water, he inhales and exhales softly a few more times. He is feeling the ground and smelling the air. He then drags his tail around the grass while he remains stationary and sees the surrounding area in a blue haze picture. Black smudges are above him and through the thicket. All is blurry and steadily enhanced. Only getting a range of his tail a perfect visioning.

His head is burning and begins to throb. *Growling* He tries to keep the focus up, but it disappears. A sharp pain pulses in his head. He immediately holds his head to subdue the pain and inhales and exhales raggedly, rolling his temples as he sits down.

TÖ-Slüdge is watching him train just as seriously as the other two. She thought he was playing with himself for a moment as he was chasing his own tail, questioning how he just gave himself a severe migraine.

After some time, the sky begins to darken. Valcomix checks himself for any type of cuts or bruises. None. He gathers the tusks but then decides to let them remain where they lay. He smiles mischievously, sighting the area where someone is hiding.

TÖ-Slüdge realizes Valcomix has seen her and steps out into the opening, smiling shyly. **"I was concerned about you since you weren't doing the regular routine with Cretan and TSinged. You're not a being that should be left alone."** She explains her reason while standing on guard as her eavesdropping is justifiably right.

Valcomix approaches her. She remains still and glares at him. Now, standing close in front of each other, they stare into each other's gaze, sighting their own reflections. Something like an intense staring contest. She then looks down. Her eyes widen, and she is now in the same predicament as before. But this time, he is awake and using his tail skillfully lifting TÖ-Slüdge off the ground. Binding her, where her arms are bound to her waist side. Captured once again by his tail. **"You're really abusing it."** she tells him while glaring menacingly at him.

**"It's a useful ligament. It's also capable of carrying heavier things that my arms aren't used to."** He informs her with a smirk. Gently tightening his capture, she yelps in a seductive cry. She has her head turned from him, upset and embarrassed, blushing pink.

He remembers all the times he has been teased by TÖ-Slüdge. **"TÖ-Slüdge, you're not getting away."** Then, he remembers her being concerned and caring from then and now. Noticing that his gaze is gentle, she smiles, blushing more and her body warming up. **"Well, we're alone, no witnesses."** She says shyly with a seductive attitude. He releases her binding but only allows her hands to be freed. He removes her black t-shirt and her light blue swim top, exposing her light tan skin shoulders and perky c-cup breasts with cute bright soft pink nipples.

Quickly hiding them as she blushes. Valcomix admires her expression. **"What are you going to do now, pup?"** she asks, trying to be brave with a mischievous grin, trembling.

Valcomix then holds her close and whispers in her ear, *"Thank you. Now, try to relax. This time, I'll take care of you."* She tenses up as he tells her so, removing her clothes and his own while seeing the change in her expression of being scared and embarrassed

As she pulls his neck toward herself, her moist violet eyes blink slow. They engage in a passionate kiss and embrace as mild warmth turns hot mixed with a light sweetness. They are enjoying the night as they are joined by lust.

# PART VI

Cretan is asleep, and Fürthrived is furious with TSinged. He only ignores her and avoids conversing with her. She is glowing dangerously bright, causing the grass to become burned and dry. The light may wake up the kid, and her expression will probably give him nightmares.

TSinged faces her but does not try to blind himself. **"Say your animosity before you burn us up and yourself out."** he orders as she continues to overheat. **"You three are wasting time out here! We're finished with his mission, and we should be heading onto the ice to go where you and TÖ-Slüdge want to go! We left our haven, our home, for your reason!"** she yells furiously.

TSinged stands up, peering down at her. She dims down, feeling helpless and scared. Her heart is beating fast, seeing TSinged's expression as the same as she remembered. **"That wasn't my home. It wasn't."** He says with a calm hatred.

Fürthrived is trembling with fear, hiding herself from him. Protecting herself as she burns up more explosively. **"Please, TSinged, calm down."** she says, crying. TSinged realizes that his anger and annoyance are seen once more, and he sees his arms brightening a bit. This sensation was the feeling that had ended the massive creature. Hearing her cries and knowing her sensitivity. Cretan remains resting which is good. He then relaxes his expression into a serious, apologetic one.

**"Fürthrived. I'm sorry, but that place you call a haven is no such thing."** He tells her. She dims down gradually, placing herself further from him. He exhales, rubbing his forehead as the heat in his arms fades away. Now, he regrets how he got his arms to glow. Cretan has rolled up and still remains asleep. TSinged is relieved but annoyed that he let his temper get the better of him. *"Duvuin."* He shakes his head to remove a bad memory.

## ELSEWHERE

TÖ-Slüdge is nestled up to Valcomix, covered by his tail and enjoying his embrace with a blissful smile. Valcomix rests his head upon her shoulder, sighting their clothes laid upon the wet moss. **"We should return before they come searching for us."** TÖ-Slüdge says, feeling slightly embarrassed and drained. **"Can you stand properly?"** he asks, concerned for her as he smiles joyfully. **"Then, you should carry me."** She suggests with a mischievous grin. *Giggling*

He then lifts her up into his arms and dresses her and then himself, pulling on his neck to have him closer. *"Take care of me from now on."* She orders as she whispers into his ear. **"Of course."** He tells her with a sincere tone now making their way to where the others are.

TSinged sights a scarlet glow approaching. He can see that those two have gotten closer. He sighs. Fürthrived and Cretan are resting. Not wanting to interrupt their peace, he remains silent. However, he yields to the swirling of anger, spite, and impatience, swallowing the taste of disgust so that he can speak calmly. **"Valcomix, are you ready to continue?"** TSinged asks as his heart violently beats louder; seeing them comfortable is unsightly.

Valcomix notices that something is ailing him. **"Just a few more days. Give me three more. We'll have to travel by night since we're going to be entering their claimed states."** Valcomix requests. TSinged has a serious expression, and Valcomix notices a twitch from his frame. **"TSinged, are you alright?"** He asks, concerned for his teammate.

TSinged nods his head and leaves from their view. He then lays himself to rest. TÖ-Slüdge glares at him. Then, she stares at Fürthrived, who is shivering in her sleep as if cold. Valcomix lays his tail upon Fürthrived's back to ease her. TÖ-Slüdge is confused and a little jealous. ***"How are you able to show someone kindness when they despise you. Valcomix you are strong."*** She commemorates his mind set. Nuzzling her head against his chest. Closing her eyes. Valcomix follows suit.

## A FREEZING MORNING

TSinged is off by his lonesome, shadowboxing while remembering the event that happened before and Fürthrived's reaction from his attitude. He feels anger and hate build up within him, and his punches become more powerful. His arms start to glow a dim orange, releasing an explosive hit that heated up the air.

Feeling the increasing speed and power, he feels a jolt in his arms. He ceases his attacks as his arms begin to hurt. *Breathing heavily* First, he felt quite heated as the temperature didn't bother him. Now, he is shivering cold and makes his way to the others.

Cretan is awake, eating a prepared meal of a grilled catfish. Fürthrived's expression is blank, providing the young member with warmth. TSinged approaches, and Fürthrived flinches. He then stops where he stands. TÖ-Slüdge shows up dripping wet. She has replenished her skin in a healthier tone as she returns from her swim. She sits close to Fürthrived. Sighting TSinged, and then shields candlelight from seeing him.

Thankful as TSinged approaches close and cautiously. He enjoys the prepared meal but struggles to gulp it down. The night appears, and Valcomix rises. TSinged folds his arm, grumbles, and goes to lay himself down to force himself to sleep. **"Valcomix, can I train with you?"** Cretan asks. Valcomix stares at TSinged. **"You may."** he answers him. Something is disturbing him. Fürthrived is too silent and doesn't have any type of expression. Blank. TÖ-Slüdge keeps her company. Giving Valcomix a kind smile. He nods his head and takes Cretan with him.

## ANOTHER FREEZING MORNING

TSinged awakens first. Valcomix opens his eyes and sees the facial expression of TSinged. Surprised. His eyes were like his own before. It frightens others and causes oneself to be alone. Reluctant to follow after him as he promised Cretan to give his attention. Valcomix himself has a serious expression.

TÖ-Slüdge witnesses his glare aimed at TSinged but doesn't want to speak out. The day ends, and again, they rest without any kind of conversation. The next morning is cold and frozen water droplets fall gently. TSinged is again the first to rise. Same expression as yesterday. Valcomix approaches him. The two silently traverse pass the scattered bones and through the thicket. Reaching the opening where they first trained. The two face one another.

Valcomix lets his four scarlet veins free. TSinged's arms are dim but glowing an orange color. Both of them are blind to such rage seeing a regretful past. Yet their expression is scared, anger and sad. They both have seen hell. Lighting up.

# PART VII

TSinged gets into a boxing stance, only seeing the past. Valcomix stands on all four limbs, visioning his past. They both rush in to attack the other. TSinged punches Valcomix, releasing an explosive hit. Valcomix cushions the attack with his tail and uses his series of swipes from his veins onto his opponent, but a few connect only to his arms and sides.

TSinged then sends a barrage of forced power at Valcomix. He evades a lot of them easily. Getting closer in, he receives a strike on his left shoulder. He sends his tail straight at him, stabbing his right leg.

TSinged takes a knee while Valcomix's arm is unable. Both are angry and frustrated. Tears well up in their eyes, remembering their loss and the feeling of being weak and pathetic. They both stand and attack the other, brawling violently, causing the other harm. TSinged unleashes strikes that have more power than the last.

Valcomix is getting pounded but shielding his face with his fast-moving tail and claws, refusing to yield as he continues to push forward. Soon, TSinged's hits become slower. Valcomix leaps at the opportunity and punches him. TSinged manages to block it. Tripping him up with the use of his tail, Valcomix starts thrashing at his opponent.

TSinged takes the hits while trying to block with one arm and is punching his opponent in the face. Crimson and black ooze splatter on the snow and mix. They continue their thrashing for a while, refusing to yield. They get slower, and their strikes lose force, becoming just taps. Blood dripping warmly from their ruthless bout.

Both are angry and growling but exhausted and beaten. Frustrated. Then their eyes have become heavier. The two now rest with their energy depleted. After some time passing. They awaken looking beaten up. Gazing at the snow falling. **"You want to talk about it?"** Valcomix asks with an annoyed and frustrated tone. **"No."** TSinged answers with no hesitation. **"Do you want to talk about it?"** TSinged asks with an angered yet calm tone. **"No."** Valcomix answers.

**"Thanks."** TSinged says with a serious and sincere tone. **"You saved me twice. I owe you this."** Valcomix tells his teammate. TSinged stands first and lends Valcomix his arm. Valcomix takes hold of it and is back on his feet. **"We're leaving tonight. I'll get you and**

**them to БАРГУЗИНСКИЙ ЗАПОВЕДНИК,"** Valcomix reassures TSinged with a smile.

TSinged then smiles as well. Both recognize a bond through pain that the other wants to resolve. Comrades. TÖ-Slüdge is smiling for them as she is concerned about what Cretan had told her. The two then laugh, not understanding as to why.

**TO BE CONTINUED...**

# EPISODE 11: CULPRIT FOUND!?

## PART I

TSinged and Valcomix are both sore. Cretan is relieved that his expression has been pacified. Fürthrived is still a bit anxious but is gradually getting used to his presence. TÖ-Slüdge glares at the two boys. **"What happened to both of you to end up looking so beaten? You're wounded."** Fürthrived asks, and the two snicker. **"Just a tussle."** Valcomix answers vaguely with a smile. She accepts it, knowing it's deliberately somewhat true.

"**We should make our way through the rest of the Playgrounds. So, we're leaving tonight.**" TSinged informs everyone proudly. TÖ-Slüdge sighs. "**You're both injured, and you want to continue.**" She restates their decision as foolish. They both nod, understanding their predicament. "Now that the Black States been liberated, we can travel easily. Just got to be cautious. TÖ-Slüdge gives up.

**"No, you two will be a burden when it's time for us to run. You'll be at the rear, a target for the C.O.A.T.S.**

**So, heal up."** Fürthrived is serious as she gives the order, still with a quiet voice and a blank expression. TSinged smiles and looks to Valcomix. **"That sounds reasonable."** He says with a falsely disheartened tone, casting a smile. TÖ-Slüdge glares menacingly at him with a wicked smile.

Valcomix stands, gesturing for her to come with him. TSinged allows it. Cretan is confused and shocked. **"Cretan, let's go train a bit."** He tells him, and Cretan eagerly changes his skin to bright yellow with blue dots. **"Fürthrived, will you please join us? I'm not leaving you alone."** TSinged pleads with a soft tone. Fürthrived hesitates but stands. He offers her assistance, pulling her arms gently, braving the contact.

TÖ-Slüdge is now shocked and surprised with her mouth slightly agape. Witnessing him holding her hand and causing his own to smoke. Cretan grips his fists, noticing the painful sensation. Those three head up the river area. While Valcomix walks towards the small 3ft high water fall and sits in the water. Soaking his feet in the large hole. TÖ-Slüdge is beside him, leaning on his shoulder doing the same.

**"Why did you change your directive when Fürthrived gave her reasoning?"** She asks him calmly, pinching his ear. **"She finally spoke. Fürthrived hasn't**

**made an opinion or suggestion because she's afraid of us. So, it's best to subside an argument and submit to her valid reason, claiming to be right."** Valcomix answers seriously, with a sad smile.

*"Because she's unstable."* TÖ-Slüdge whispers, releasing her grip. **"You and TSinged got into a brawl. Cretan saw you two and came to me in a panic. When I arrived, both of you were lying down. Then, you two were laughing."** She sounds curious, confused, and concerned.

Valcomix chuckles softly. **"That's a sensitive subject. The two of us are struggling with something. I had made an outburst and frightened those I promised to protect. He almost did the same thing. Fürthrived seems to have been a victim. I don't blame her for it. It's just a difficulty that we have to deal with."** Valcomix shares weakly, with a smile upon him. TÖ-Slüdge looks at him with a sad expression.

He then stares into her violet eyes, seeing much concern, and then embraces her while wrapping his tail around them both. **"We'll be alright."** He says, attempting to ease her worries.

It's night, everyone is resting. TSinged and Valcomix remain awake. **"Do you want to talk about it?"** Valcomix asks with a serious tone. **"No."** TSinged answers with a sad expression. **"What about you?"** TSinged asks Valcomix. Valcomix looks up into the darkness, feeling the gentle, chilling breeze. **"Me neither."** He answers pathetically. **"When are we supposed to discuss our issues?"** TSinged asks, frustration evident.

Valcomix lays a gentle hand on his shoulder. **"When we've solved the problem or when we're comfortable."** Valcomix answers, swallowing guilt. They both sigh.

# PART II

Some days have passed; becoming history. Now, the light fades from the thick gray sheet of clouds. Valcomix carries one of the tusks in his left hand, the other is wrapped by his tail. Using the device with his free hand. A 3D compass rose is displayed, pointing east. He returns it to the home screen.

The time is 5:41pm of 08/18/3175

The battery life remaining is at fifteen percent. He shuts it down quickly. The sky darkens, bringing a colder night; the air is frigid, and the grass sparkles due to the layer of ice. Fürthrived is now alive, glaring at Valcomix, waiting for him to speak. He chuckles silently.

TSinged smiles as well, noticing her menacing glare as he carries the pack. TÖ-Slüdge isn't amused but is conflicted, mixed with emotions of annoyance yet joy that Fürthrived's attitude has returned. Cretan is at least eager. **"Are we heading out now?"** Cretan asks excitedly, prepared for the unknown. Valcomix puts the device back into the pack. TÖ-Slüdge chuckles. **"We are. We're heading across the ice."** Valcomix answers, heading forward.

## PLAYGROUND 10

The hazard suit-wearing soldiers are setting up a camp. Four C.O.A.T.S. soldiers make rounds of the perimeter, flashing lights around the area and gripping their rifles. One of them notices a blue sapphire light in the distance. Another soldier spots a pathway of grotesque sapphire flowers emitting glowing blue dust from the rot.

**"The scientists declared this Playground as safe, right? These flowers are growing around a majority of the Playground."** She says with disgust. Trying not to step on them **"They have been studied by them and are classified just regular plants."** Domony informs the rookies through their masks.

## SOMEWHERE SOUTH OF THE SAME PLAYGROUND

Sitting on a rock, staring at the sapphire plants, is Diim Sourn, occupied with his unit. **"Sir Sourn, I've been thinking,"** Criyo Domony says softly. **"Personal or business?"** Sourn sighs, asking his soldier. **"It's business."** Domony answers seriously.

**"Carry on."** Sourn permits for him to speak. **"We haven't had the being apprehended yet. It wasn't**

**recorded by them. Most of them are considered dead or lost, and their numbers are accurate. We were given the temperature recorded by one of the salvaged Arrow's data. It matches their kind. We are investigating the wrong areas."** Domony informs his unit leader.

**"This individual is wearing that uniform. They won't even consider trying it on. I hate the idea of us bothering them as well. But they wear that uniform, and this individual has it on. I have an idea that this individual is the reason we get to claim Playground ID. Now, only one more black state remains."** Sourn says with a scoff.

**"As heavy as a tank. I'm curious to know what it is but I don't want to be one to see it."** Domony shares with him as his voice lowers not liking the mode nor the word 'Giant'. Sourn bursts out laughing, causing the others to flinch from the loud sound. **"Sorry, Criyo. I'm just the same. I'm not that brave, either. For glory, for honor, and to die to protect. A sworn oath as a C.O.A.T.S. soldier. It's more fun just firing at Creates each day than dealing with higher threats. Easy jobs are the best."** He tells his fellow soldier, raising his arm to show off his armband.

Criyo shakes his head. **"You say that but became qualified supporting rookies. There was someone more**

**qualified and better than you."** he says with a mix of sadness and pride. Sourn then grips his friend's shoulder. **"Please, don't bring him up. Let's support the claiming of this Playground."** Sourn pleads with a trembling hand. Criyo nods. They're both still hurting over his loss.

## INSIDE DORM, A BUILDING IN TEXAS HOUSING A LABORATORY FOR THE SCIENCE FACTION

The hallways and corridors lead to rooms, each belonging to a scientist. One is marked with a golden plaque reading: **Hitomoni Free: Environmentalist, Botanist, Bioengineer, Biochemist**.

Within this lab workroom, plant specimens reside in terrariums with the addition of trees contained within the glass, variant lighting matching the outside times. Metal closets on the opposite side of the office, the desk which is positioned near the entrance, loaded with: devices, instruments, a laptop, a microscope, and six small cubed terrariums stacked in a pyramid, housing the mysterious sapphire blue flowers and vials of black ooze.

A young French/Russian/Caucasian female with vibrant pale blue eyes with dark circles around them. Studying the lab work, trying to gather solid evidence. Her ruffled, unkempt, short electric blue hair sways, her pale white complexion absent of vitamin D. Wearing a hazard suit, half-faced black gas mask, and safety goggles with magnifying capabilities, along with gold earring studs.

Her head throbs slightly, wincing from the pain. She runs a sample of the black ooze as before. The DNA scrambler still reads "Unknown." Hours stuck in her lab and still no classification for what she is studying. **"All the instruments are reading its properties, but no classifications. A complex gene code, that has a 48.1% Unknown read is bothersome. What creature is this from?"** Exhausted, determined, and serious, as she stares at the flowers, reading their biology from the researched information on her laptop.

Ivy-Rose: Invasive plant species vastly growing throughout Playground ID. Glowing bright blue, releasing pollen, asexually producing. Each flower is a genetic copy of the other. They can withstand harsh temperatures.

**"At least these flowers have been classified. I still need more to update. I should plant one of them inside a terrarium, just to see how invasive this discovered specimen is."** sounding a little livelier, she picks up one of the cubes from the top, gazing at its horrendous appearance yet entranced by its soft glow.

# PART III

**Metallic Rumbling** The double doors open. An average-height French/Russian man with short, electric blue hair and pale blue eyes enters the lab. He admires the collection of terrariums, wearing a hazard suit and a yellow half-faced gas mask that has a smile with the tongue sticking out.

The girl turns her rotating chair around, carrying a tablet as he stares at the trees. He then flashes his badge, showing a goofy picture of himself puffing his cheeks. The badge reads: **David Free: Biologist, Physicist, Chemist. Faction Term Leader.** She rolls her eyes. **"How may I assist you, sir?"** she asks with an angsty attitude. **"I haven't had any breakthroughs these past weeks. Have you found any evidence?"** He asks, ignoring her demeanor, focused on their professional exchange.

**"No. I've checked the genetic structure and searched various genetic codes and indexes. It still comes up as unknown. I was about to test how these flowers act when put in a live environment."** She informs him, playing with one of the cubes. He glances at her from behind as his neck is turned. Then focuses back on the huge terrarium. Then back to his fellow scientist. Noticing the black circles under her eyes and her pale, unkempt appearance.

**"I've ran the same tests. If you haven't found anything, then it must be unknown. We should put it on hold for now."** He says disheartened. She widens her eyes in surprise, understanding his perspective. **"We have another project to deal with. Our head lead wants our best group to reach Playground MI. Some are sick. The temperatures have dropped."** He informs her with a serious demeanor.

She stares at the ceiling, muttering her displeasure. **"I'll have to turn down..."** She starts to voice her objection. David Free glares at her, not accepting her refusal. She closes her eyes, takes a breath, and nods. **"You, few others, and I will have to set aside our projects and hobbies. So, please, go take a shower or bathe. Then, patiently wait for your next assignment."** He orders, visibly disgusted of her appearance then he dismisses himself from her lab.

She glares angrily as the doors close, then she cleans off her desk, organizing the substances and instruments and wiping the area clean with alcohol spray. She walks over to the metal closets and opens one. Inside, there's a cleansing shower with a hanger.

She removes her hazard suit and hangs it, watching it automatically wash off contaminants.

In another closet are her personal belongings: scientist's uniforms. She puts on a full set, including a white t-shirt, black slacks, black socks, slip-resistant boots, and a lab coat.

She clips on her badge, noticing a picture frame face down. Beside it are two golden rings: one on a thin chain that she puts around her neck and the other she places on her ring finger.

# PART IV

## PLAYGROUND IL, SECTOR 8

### The time is 11:24pm of 08/18/3175

A base housing many soldiers that are currently resting, while forty-two soldiers patrol the perimeter on foot or in vehicles.

***Beep*** A loud notification appears, resembling the sound of a digital alarm clock. Soldiers halt, staring at their screens. "**Pressure Plate Activated**." Following the procedure as taught, they seek shelter at the nearest base. Many awaken and enter the computer room. Hurrying as they play with game controllers. Now, thousands of arrows scan to assess the situation, displaying real-time video feeds on their screens.

After a few hours of flying, the fortified wall reveals a hole. A melted entry way tunneling through Playground IA. *Notification* All soldiers are receiving pictures and are on high alert.

Hours later, a single individual wearing the suspect clothing appears and is smiling. It's not camera shy.

Gaining attention. This information is sent to all C.O.A.T.S. military, leaving them stunned, surprised, and confused. One soldier... **Ranked: MD9QR**, sends out a message: "Apprehend that individual alive."

## HOURS BEFORE THE INCIDENT

The team of five reaches the wall. Fürthrived uses her ability to pass through the curved, reinforced perimeter. The heated metal drips orange, quickly cooling due the frigid, windy air. As the mist is becoming a creation of ice particles from the water vapor. TSinged and Cretan stay close to the walking hearth. Still bothered by the wind as they shiver. Knowing the C.O.A.T.S. have these sectors under siege, Valcomix looks back at the others. **"Once we reach the city, we'll find shelter in a building."** Valcomix tells them, and they smile weakly.

Fürthrived herself looks dimmer. The temperature has dropped drastically, affecting everyone. Valcomix's fur is laid flat, Fürthrived is even shivering, TÖ-Slüdge's complexion is pale and becoming ashy, while the boys are attempting to find warmth.

Pushing through dense trees, they reach a flat surface near a city with camps. Valcomix senses their distress. Walking on the hard ground feels odd, not the cold, nearly frozen soil he expected. He hesitates to dwell on it, focusing on reaching the city. They enter the nearest intact building, Valcomix is helping the boys first, then Fürthrived. They lean against the wall, shivering.

He turns to assist TÖ-Slüdge, who watches them with worry. Valcomix covers them with his tail, then turns to... Now, annoyed that she's fallen asleep. *"I forgot they had safety precautions in place if the giants were to enter these sectors,"* he mutters, wanting to share this with the team. Soon, Valcomix hears whirling and buzzing, reaching for his device, remembering it's at 8% battery life. Assessing the situation, he realizes they anticipated the giants roaming the claimed Playgrounds.

With the team exhausted and facing the freezing night, he rubs his forehead. Arrows hover, an annoying and concerning presence. Fürthrived is dimming and sleeping deeply due to the dropping temperature. Knowing that it's dangerous. ***"Traveling safely to Playground MI seems the best option but how?"*** Valcomix questions his goal without a plan.

# PART V

Refusing to rest, he tries to listen to every arrow around their location. They're scattering randomly, knowing they're being manually controlled. He gazes at his resting teammates, looking comfortable. He exhales and moves his tail slowly off the three. Fürthrived and Cretan latch onto it and pull it back, grumbling silently, clenching his tusk. Angry at himself for what he is about to do next.

*SCREEAHHHH!!!* The screeching yell alerts everyone in a panic; their hearts pulse fast. TSinged can feel the sweat as he stands in a defensive stance. **"We have to reach Michigan! From there, we can try to rest more. TSinged, pass me the device."** Valcomix orders as he approaches TSinged.

Reaching into the pack, Fürthrived glares at him. Cretan is confused. TSinged sees that Valcomix is serious, as well as TÖ-Slüdge. Now, turning on the device. **Beep Beep** He reads the warning. He opens it to the homepage and searches the map. There is a base near the fastest route. He then draws a line to reach the destination fast. *"The battery life is depleting, but minimizing its use should last when we reach Playground MI."* Valcomix concludes as he sets the device to rest mode

**"TSinged, carry Cretan. Fürthrived, get on my back. TÖ-Slüdge..."** He starts ordering, but they just stare at him for a moment. All confused and worried. Valcomix inhales quickly. **"We activated a pressure plate, a mechanism used to alert all C.O.A.T.S. about the giants if they ever enter other states that are claimed. There are multiple arrows flying, searching for us."** He informs them quickly and coherently, briefly explaining the situation.

**"Then, we leave immediately. But I'll carry Fürthrived."** TSinged tells Valcomix. He makes it over to her and lays a hand on her shoulder, unaffected by her heat but feeling a soft warmth. Everyone can tell that she is weakening. He then stares at Cretan, who jumps on his back. Valcomix places the tusk in his jaw, then rushes and lifts TÖ-Slüdge. He then heads for the exit.

TSinged follows suit. The air outside is calm, with a gentle breeze, but the temperature is annoyingly freezing. Valcomix leads them through alleyways, using what he is capable of doing. Seeing through the dark by sensing around him. After a while, it becomes a headache.

TÖ-Slüdge can see the anguish as he bites onto the ivory piece. Avoiding the camps as he runs onto highways taken over by nature. Soon enough, they reach a small town called Dixon, a barricaded area with debris-filled lands and trash piles. TSinged needs to catch his breath. The number of arrows has diminished, and he checks the device once more.

**The time is 5:13am of 08/19/3175**

TSinged sees a message... "**All C.O.A.T.S. of Playground IL are authorized to use heavy hitters.**" Valcomix looks to his team, mainly at Fürthrived and TSinged. He is here to replenish his stamina. The battery life is at 5%.

TÖ-Slüdge tries to read the notification over his shoulder. Then, she can see his frame with frustration and distraught but doesn't understand why. But upon reading it, it must be a terrible thing. *"There are four bases and many camps nearby. The most problematic one will be..."* Valcomix is growling angrily and seems under stress due to the message.

**"Valcomix, are you alright?"** she asks, and TSinged can see the expression on his face. Cretan clenches his parka tightly. Fürthrived is resting. He has an option but refuses on that action. Knowing that everyone is just as uneased and tired. Noticing that he is panicking he calms down. Then an idea. Another option but it's drastic and appalling. He lets down TÖ-Slüdge, gazes into her eyes, and kisses her.

TSinged is confused and awed, yet disgusted by this affection they're displaying. **"I'm going to do something foolish that none of you will agree with."** He says as he approaches TSinged with a lively smile. He passes the device to Cretan. **"Guide your team once more, but only through the cities. When you are on the highway, just go straight. Make it over the bridge and wait for me."** He tells Cretan. TSinged understands what he may be up to. He tries to reach for him but Valcomix dodges.

**"I will."** Cretan tells Valcomix, sounding strong. TÖ-Slüdge glares at him with an angry expression as tears well up. **"At least tell us what you are up to."** She declares. TSinged is worried and curious as well

**"They're permitted to use turtles and falcons. That is a term for tanks and bombers. The air is freezing, and you all are tired. We are slowly advancing. It will be best for you four to pace yourselves. Their attention will be on me only."** Valcomix informs them.

TSinged gulps at the terrifying knowledge. They're going to welcome the giants with these weapons. Seeing their condition and how the weather is, TSinged realizes that they aren't capable and their best girl is weak and heavily resting. TÖ-Slüdge then catches his hand. **"Meet them with a smile."** She orders him.

**"Six days. Then, we rush towards the ice. We'll unite in six days."** He tells her with a smile. Then, he rushes off. Leaving his comrades. He can hear the whirling again, stopping next to a camp. No soldiers are sighted and seeing the many arrows. Two of them notice his presence and figure. Circling around him, he has a smile, waving the ivory piece and showing off his tail.

## BACH IN DIXON

TSinged is calm as he watches TÖ-Slüdge who is saddened and worried, still watching the path he left from Fürthrived's light is really dim. Cretan is worried as well. *Notification* The dimly lit screen opens and has a message of urgency. Cretan then plays the message. Then, it plays... **"Apprehend that being alive."** Hearing a serious, raspy, and husky voice from the device, the two then chuckle and laugh while TÖ-Slüdge is confused.

**"They're going to have trouble."** TSinged says. Wanting him alive is a reassuring matter. Cretan is then points to the direction where the red line is directing. TSinged then makes steps. TÖ-Slüdge then follows suit.

# PART VI

## PLAYGROUND ID, ROTTING GROUNDS

Diim Sourn checks his device, seeing the messages consisting of commands. His hand is shivering. Criyo Domony notices his boisterous leader's silence. **"The culprit has been found. Also, Playground IA needs to be thoroughly investigated."** Sourn says with a shaky voice. **"Hey, you alright, Sir Sourn?"** Domony asks concerned about his pal after checking the messages.

**"All ranks 7's are to gather and head into the Black State: Playground IA. Massive bones have been sighted."** Sir Sourn informs, shocked by the update. Culprit sighted, pressure plate activated, now massive bones located. The two are both surprised. **"Our boss wants that thing alive. It's going to cause us an issue."** Criyo Domony shares his perplexing opinion. Diim Sourn shakes his head.

**"Criyo, for the glory. I want to thank this individual. You manage this area."** He tells his pal, punching his chest and sounding excited. **"Sir there must be a reason our culprit wants to found out now."** Domony tries to inform his superior but to no avail.

**"This is Sir Sourn. Rank: 7. Located in Playground ID. Sixth division loose camps."** Diim Sourn speaks into his mask with a loud, joyful tone. **"Received. Sir Sourn, your immediate pickup will be arriving soon."** a pilot tells him with a serious tone. The whirling of the engine can be heard in the background. He quickly heads toward the camp. Criyo Domony shakes his head and turns to his confused unit.

## PLAYGROUND IL

Soldiers from Sectors: 5, 8, 16, and 20 are leading their operatives into units all focused on the camp. The camp that the creature is occupying as of now. Arrows are keeping sight of the target. All are given the mission to apprehend it alive. Trucks and other vehicles are nearing its location. Arriving and has many sights on the being. Their lasers are bright but not brighter than his veins.

*"The term 'one versus an army' is supposed to be a metaphor."* He tells himself, feeling quite nervous, not wanting to be targeted. Gathering their attention with its smile upon their screen, feeling like it's taunting them. Soon enough, many more of them have arrived. Valcomix watches them carefully. He then inhales softly and launches himself with a rush, jumping over the vehicle.

**"That thing is agile?!"** A soldier yells, surprised. Valcomix is being chased through the city and its roads, keeping their vehicles behind him as he quickens his pace. **"The thing is fast and quick; our vehicles cannot turn fast, and it's leaving us behind!"** Another soldier informs the others with a frustrated and joyous tone. **"We'll cut it off ahead and trip it up somehow."** A male soldier says joyously and reassuringly.

Valcomix is serious as he's only been seeing trucks and moderate vehicles, not one tank or bomber sighted. Soon enough, there is a butterfly over him flashing its light. He patiently waits for its wrathful rounds. He then sees a blockade ahead. He jumps onto a roof and climbs up fast. The butterfly is still shining, giving away his whereabouts. Two more butterflies arrive over and drop nets. The creature dodges and is confused, examining the metallic netting.

**"This is used for capturing creatures alive. They just want me alive. Now that there are no dangers, then I can..."** He declares to himself with a vicious, menacing smile. His tail twirls lively.

Vehicles surround him, and he jumps off the roof, scaring a few soldiers. **"Be a soldier and take care of a threat."** Valcomix orders the low rank three that fell on his butt. The others shoot at him with soft rounds equivalent to a common ant bite. He makes his way to the vehicle driver's side, then buckles up.

They continue to shoot at him, and he snarls. **"Try a different method."** He informs them and then drives off. **"The creature took one of our trucks and is driving away."** A soldier informs. Similar information is shared. They have a visual of the stolen vehicle as the butterflies continue following him.

## ELSEWHERE IN AN OFFICE OF C.O.A.T.S. HEADQUARTERS

A senior aged bald Japanese/African/Russian tan-skinned male with vibrant green eyes is laughing about the situation. **"What's going on out there?"** the muscular gentleman asks, trying to keep his composure. Then, he makes it to the door. **"All C.O.A.T.S., I'm entering the fray! We'll execute its capture!"** He tells all that are manning their cubicle like a generic office on the top floor. Belonging to most overaged and/or injured soldiers, all bearing the rank NQ8R.

They leave their desk work and face him. They all bow to him as much as they are able to. **"Good luck, boss!"** They yell to him with much respect. He smiles and reaches for his coat hanging on a rack.

## PLAYGROUND IL, SECTOR: UNKNOWN

The sky is now dark. TSinged is more relaxed but concerned. TÖ-Slüdge is serious. Fürthrived isn't glowing as much as usual, as if her light is fading. Cretan grips tight onto the device. Valcomix is keeping them busy as they haven't seen an arrow nor a soldier yet. The three quicken their pace, facing exhaustion and the weather. To find shelter.

## ELSEWHERE

Valcomix is tired; the vehicle ran out of battery power and is parked. He is on top of a roof that he had to scale. Butterflies are still swarming him. Below, C.O.A.T.S. are launching pepper-filled balls, releasing black smoke. Valcomix covers his face to shield himself from the stinging sensation filling his nose. *Sneezing* *Coughing*

The helicopter then leaves, and another appears, dropping a net. Valcomix predicted it as he heard it coming. He snarls and jumps to another rooftop.

They shoot at Valcomix with tranquilizers but to no avail; they're ineffective. He still stands. Soon, another helicopter flies over and drops...

*Pitch* ***SCREEAHHHH!!!*** The cylinder opens on impact and releases a bright light. Valcomix falls off the roof and is surrounded. Chains are pinning him. He tries to struggle, swinging his tail, and many soldiers hold it down. Piling him as they chain the creature.

## INSIDE THE BUTTERFLY

The highest-ranked soldier is carrying a cylinder container. **"Sir Kiel, the creature is captured."** A ground soldier informs him. Sir Curesed Kiel witnesses it happening as they circle around the area. **"Transport it to the eighteenth division camp. I have questions for our lone soldier,"** He orders while mocking it with a smile behind the mask. Sitting comfortably with crates filled with flashbangs at his side.

Valcomix is still struggling with their numbers. Pushing the being into the trailer of a small compartment truck. Managing doing so and have tangled in chains. The creature is frustrated. They close the doors, leaving him in total darkness.

# TO BE CONTINUED...

# EPISODE 12: A CHANGE IN POWER

## PART I

Bound in chains within a truck, restrained in darkness, Valcomix is calm and collected. He understands that they may have questions for him, but their methods may be well-handled or violent. He isn't concerned for himself. He is thinking of their various questions and how he considers of answering them. His main focus is on his teammates.

*"TSinged, Cretan, Fürthrived survive the freezing nights. The battery, life should last a few days. I hope. Just make it there, and wait for me. Only five more days.* TÖ-Slüdge was crying for *me. You all need to be safe don't worry about me."* Valcomix says within himself and then bangs his head on the metal containment. The soldier driving the vehicle flinches and swerves a bit.

Valcomix feels responsible for her. **"Fürthrived, she burned herself out. Taking advantage of someone that fragile. I kept berating her when she finally started speaking again. Causing her mental strain**

**when she is already suffering from trauma. I'm sorry."** He announces his crime with a sad tone. He wants to rush toward them and join them, but this option is more than settling. Now, all their attention is on him. Whatever they may give him, he'll accept their wrath. They'll be busy. He now closes his eyes after long days without rest, exhausting hours, replenishing much-needed energy.

*Metal Creaking* The truck's doors open by the use of two soldiers. They see a slumbering being within the containment. **"This is that suspect we've been searching for?"** A soldier asks. **"The images are a match along with the uniform it's wearing. It's obvious."** The other clarifies. Then, the highest-ranking soldier approaches. The two now stand vast and bow making their back straight. Then they stand up straight. He sees their tags. Only a rank three. The two are falling short, but they're still just kids.

**"Return to your proper base."** The higher rank orders with a stern tone. The two excuse themselves without any regards for a reason. **"They forgot their manners."** Another soldier informs keeping watch of the compartment. The highest-ranking soldier then looks behind himself while chuckling. Seeing a rank seven soldier

**"So, I allow it. We're not around the public. Most of the bases act out anyway. As long as they are serious about the task, it's whatever. Even my own way of speaking is relaxed. But this creature is sleeping in the presence This is disrespect already. Wearing that uniform and giving us trouble of chasing it down. For now, we let it sleep until it awakens. Look at this creature looking comfortable when captured. I want to be the first soldier it meets."** He tells his soldier. The he turns back around and continues to gaze upon the troublemaker.

## PLAYGROUND IA

Approximately, three thousand soldiers bearing the rank of seven guard the carved hole. There are eyes inside. Arrows are hovering over gunning down every animal lurking unfortunate without sparring a single round. Tanks, grenade launchers, and other massive powered firing weapons are positioned near the wall. But inside are a few special soldiers as well. Eight ranked seven individuals all wear an armband with a gold star:

**Baron Roe, Victor H. Lune, Maira Devie, Trenton C. Calhous, Nikki Juan, Diim Sourn, Xin U. Mityus, and Lien Servia.**

These eight soldiers are traversing through the once claimed territory that belongs to giants. Each has their weapons drawn, following the swarm of arrows flying over them. Soon, they reach an opening of damaged grounds with pits. They stumble solid rocky flooring with huge bones scattered about.

**"Wow, these are massive."** says Lien Servia as she is awed. **"There's no meat left on them."** Victor H. Lune says as he examines them. **"Must have been our culprit's work."** Baron Roe concludes as he struggles to lift one of the femurs. Diim Sourn laughs. **"Use your legs. I'll give you some assistance."** He says, rushing to aid a fellow soldier. Even with both of them, it isn't budging. Nikki Jaun shakes her head, disappointed in her brothers' actions. She then checks her device.

The time is 7:37am of 08/20/3175

Reading the updates, now just appearing is the picture of the culprit in restraint, with the highest rank showing off his might with the being behind him. Disgusted, Trenton C. Calhous isn't pleased by the image, but others are amused. Then, a... *Notification* They begin reading.

"Playground IA. Giants have been eradicated. Ready to claim." Trenton C. Calhous searches for the sender around the group. Xin U. Mityus is the only one on her device moving her thumbs. She is now sending messages via group chat. "We should hurry up and claim this state. Transport these bones to Playground IL, camp division eighteen. Our respected leader wants us there fast." She texts. Trenton and the selected few members read it.

**"It's the eighteenth division camp of Playground IL."** Maira Devie corrects her with a snide tone. "Better correct that eating habit you have." *Notification* All seeing a receipt of a massive order of greasy and fatty meals. Then an image of a someone carrying a tray at full capacity that the face is blocked. "How was your meal miss wide hips?" Xin texts. Everyone backs away as the two approach one another. **"I'll call this in."** Says Lien Servia with an eager tone.

## EIGHTEENTH DIVISION CAMP

The highest-ranked soldier is bored, waiting patiently for his gold-starred children and the evidence to arrive. *Rattling chains* *Banging* Hearing movement from the compartment where it is restrained, the soldier rushes and has his focus on the beast. *Snarling* The creature's eyes slightly open and see a familiar band, but it is blurry. Coming into focus, **"Sir Kiel?"** it speaks in a confused and relieved manner, then closes its eyes, returning to sleep.

# PART II

Curesed Kiel ponders for a moment. This creature is familiar with him, and it can also speak. *"Then, it's capable of holding a conversation and answering my questions."* he concludes to himself. Staring at this beast, he remembers how it drove a vehicle until the battery died, and his soldiers still had trouble chasing it down. **"Remarkable."** he says with a twisted malice filled tone yet gives it credit. He now approaches it, standing just a few inches from its face. The beast's ears twitch.

**"Stand at once! You rest when given my permission!"** He yells with a thunderous roar. The creature awakens fast and is only capable of getting onto a knee. Tangled in chains, it becomes aware of what happened. Realizing that he got captured on the first day. He glares at Kiel with his sharp, scarlet eyes.

**"Step out."** He orders. The creature climbs down from the compartment. Curesed Kiel walks backward and then points to where it should stand. The beast approaches him, following his commands. **"Aren't we obedient?"** The soldier says with pride filled demeanor.

Now set where told to be placed, Curesed Kiel walks around the being, examining its stature. Sighting two solid white thick polished pointed stones curled within its tail. Notes down its appearance and the clothes: claws, and black fur coat, covered by the separated uniform. The creature is muscular but maintains a skinny body, and its feet have sharp nails as well. But what's disturbing to him is that armband. He now stands in front of the beast. The creature keeps his attention forward. Curesed Kiel can tell it's uneasy.

**"Before I get into questioning about you so that we can be acquainted, I have to tell you certain subjects of the matter. The reasoning for your capture is as a rogue soldier. But as a beast: a non-human factor. You'll be given the wrath from the C.O.A.T.S. Military. Understanding me so far?"** He asks with a serious tone. The creature nods. Curesed Kiel brings out his device and sends a message to all C.O.A.T.S. The message reads:

"No one is allowed to enter the eighteenth division camp. The only few who are permitted are the starred children. Those within this camp who are not of title are to return to Dorm immediately."

With the message read by all as it was sent as an urgency, the soldiers around them follow his order. It takes a while as they hear the scattering of boots among gravel, followed by vehicle engines, and then silence. They remain standing vast, focused on the other. Curesed Kiel takes a knee. Valcomix then sits on the ground, holding a knee while a fist is planted on his side upon the dirt.

**"Our arrows were scrapped. Playground ID is rotten. Playground IA has been recently released from the Giants' reign. Then, yesterday's fiasco. Soldier or beast?"** He asks with an upsetting, serious tone.

Valcomix hesitates but chooses the safest way to answer. **"A fallen soldier."** He tells Sir Kiel with a coherent voice, causing Kiel to ponder how he should justify him. *Exhale* **"Alright. So, are you guilty of the damages done on all occasions?"** Sir Kiel asks, keeping focus on it. **"Yes,"** Valcomix answers without hesitation. **"What's your name?"** Sir Kiel asks, and the creature, once prepared to answer, is now crestfallen.

**"I forgot,"** Valcomix answers, looking quite pitiful. **"What was your rank?"** Sir Kiel asks with a slight angered and annoyed tone. **"N2E."** He answers, focusing back on his interrogator. **"How did you take down our arrows and the apexes?"** Another question, but this one is meant to be answered with a story. Predictable questions.

**"I relied on my instincts. I didn't want to die trespassing in the wrong territory and areas."** Valcomix answers with a serious, calm expression. **"You're giving me a reason to consider you a beast,"** Sir Kiel warns the individual. Valcomix isn't liking this type of game, especially with the highest-ranking soldier. **"Traveling a long way; to where is your destination? But answer this question first; why be seen now?"** He asks with a cold tone.

Valcomix definitely hesitates to answer these questions. He then looks away. *Bang* Valcomix flinches as there is a small pit with a dented red bullet. The soldier now has a pistol at his side. **"Answer the question truthfully,"** He orders with a menacing tone.

**"I... I was..."** Valcomix hesitates. Having an issue to answer, Curesed Kiel gives it more motivation as he points his weapon at the creature. He is losing his patience. Thinking of his teammates, Valcomix snarls, ready to fight. But he also realizes the reason he came this way. He takes off the armband and glares at the respected man. Valcomix becomes proud.

**"I was leaving onto the ice to escape the Playgrounds because of my appearance. Those arrows were annoyingly loud, and my ears twitched, so I tried to escape, knowing that I couldn't. I was found out and became tired of running and fighting. I needed rest. Thanks for the peace."** He tells his reason, sounding kind of smart, using a fragment of the truth to fabricate a voiced lie with an honest temper.

Curesed Kiel is astonished by its attitude. *Chuckling* *Laughing* He listens to its drivel but only can hear... *Bang* **"I don't want to hear a beast barking like some common animal. If you were once a star child, then be honest. Also, no one is permitted on the ice."** He tells the creature, still maintaining a menacing, serious tone.

Shot in the shoulder but remaining focused, Valcomix's body can remember the strikes from various animals and his recent beatings. The red bullet falls from the wound and begins to self-heal Curesed Kiel is astonished. It was only a mere sting as if stepping on a thorn. Annoying. He inhales and exhales, calming his temper, remembering this soldier and his days as a part of the C.O.A.T.S. faction.

**"A soldier may not be permitted, but non-humans don't have to follow such a rule. Sir Kiel, I died protecting my comrades and am grateful for being given a second chance. I wanted to uphold the mission as a soldier for a final time. To liberate the Black States so that all of you can reclaim them. Humans aren't weak; they're resourceful. You gave me this band to be of the few. Representing and**

**becoming a new lead to be respected in order to take your place. But this armband wasn't meant to be worn for that privilege, not in my view. To remain vigilant, to prosper. An oath to guide, claim back the states, and protect our numbers and homes. I finished that mission. I'm now protecting something else, and you're in my path."** Valcomix says with a serious and a lifting tone, letting go of a burden that still lingers with guilt, but tears begin to fall.

Curesed Kiel remembers a day when a young individual entered his office that he called for. Asked simple but very tasking questions with the reward behind it. He tossed away the reward but kept the oath to only have fun while fighting alongside his brothers and sisters, losing many star children throughout his years. Now, eight of them stand after the loss of thirteen. One of them lost and was mourned by many C.O.A.T.S. and fought harder over his loss. He reaches out to lay a heavy hand on his shoulder where he injured him.

**"Valcomix, Valcomix. I thank you again, son. Still, I stay proud of you."** Curesed Kiel tells his lost soldier with a sincere yet serious tone, seeing the young brat. Valcomix tries to stay collected and strong, but tears still fall. This pain hurts more than all his fighting. Holding tight to the hand laid upon him.

# PART III

After the two gain back their composure, they are more relaxed. Valcomix is showing off the tusks as they he lays them crossed over the other. Kiel tries to lift it but struggles to even just drag it. **"Those were torn off the most massive one. Sir Kiel, I have to reach across ice to unknown territories. It's my selfish mission."** He requests with a serious demeanor.

*Sigh* **"Valcomix, I can't allow that to happen. You don't know those that inhabit such lands, and they won't let you roam freely with our uniform. And, when you do remove your clothing, I'll have to unleash the wrath of the C.O.A.T.S. on you and those who you are considering companions."** He warns him with a sincere and punishing tone. Valcomix is surprised, reading his expression.

**"Valcomix, back in Playground WA, Sector: 22, we have video evidence from our arrows. A lot of them were damaged by claw marks and heat radiation. Behind a glass is a ball of orange light. Sloppy work if you were trying to stay hidden. So, please explain all that has happened. It's only the two of us here"** He suggests with a kind tone, pleading for his soldier to be honest.

Valcomix realizes he couldn't beat him at interrogation. Surrendering, he tells his story. After listening to his detailed adventure, Curesed Kiel stands up and walks in a circle for a bit, pondering. ***"How could he have met those individuals, canisters filled with substances. They didn't leave behind any evidence. Or is it a cover up?"*** He asks himself remembering that awful court date. He focuses on Valcomix, who is now another victim. He then returns and takes a knee. Getting his device out, he bypasses his security and opens the home screen.

The time is 11:11am of 08/20/3175

Scrolling for files, he checks documents and sees a folder labeled "No Mercy." He opens the file with case files of information about many individuals with their names organized. Curesed Kiel puts away his device.

Giving Valcomix his attention. **"Beast or soldier? If you side with us, you can aid us so that we can quickly take back our Playgrounds. But this means separation from Dorm, but you will be respected. Gaining help from the scientists, they can cure you. Choosing beast, I would have to be the one to shoot you down. I can protect you and your friends."** He assures Valcomix trying to persuade him with a kind, proud demeanor. But this choice is one-sided and not very promising. He examines Valcomix's expression and can tell what answer he chose**. "Think more about it. Return to your confinement."** Sir Kiel orders.

Valcomix stands up and puts himself into the truck's containment haul. Curesed Kiel then closes the doors, leaving it in the dark, tapping his arms as he waits impatiently for his chosen children to arrive.

After long hours of playing 12x12 sudoku puzzles, he hears vehicles approaching. Coming into view is a heavy hauler truck with very odd wheels. Almost as if they're flattening. Able to haul two tanks on its flatbed. Placed upon it are bones. The remains of the giant that ruled over Playground IA for almost a millennium. The said creature was dubbed as heavy as a tank. Seeing the digital scaled weight on the side. The collection is:
9.51(US)tons 8,627.33Kg 19,020lbs

Finding an empty lot within the campgrounds, one of the soldiers steps out of the vehicle and points at the driver in the hauler. Curesed Kiel approaches Diim Sourn, and is directing him to dump. Massive bones are then lifted and scatter about onto the lot. Six other individuals exit out of the armored vehicle bow to their boss.

**"Sir, what must we do now?"** Nikki Juan asks. Curesed Kiel now focuses on his children. All of them wait for his next words of order. **"We're going to be quite busy, but first, I'm concerned about an individual who needs the aid of persuasion. Also, this fallen giant is getting my attention, and I want to know what it is. So, get those scientists outside with us."** He says while sounding fascinated but is hiding a purpose. The eight are not amused; confused about who to persuade and by what use of methods for needing to do so.

## ELSEWHERE

Inside a rundown building near the waterway of an alley, four individuals are trying to stay hidden. Cretan and TSinged are covered in dirty blue and green blankets as they continue to shiver. Meanwhile, Fürthrived is faded of light as she is covered with more blankets than the boys. TÖ-Slüdge is furious about their situation.

**"What are we going to do now?"** She asks as if complaining. Cretan grips the device with a depleted battery. TSinged takes off his pack and rummages for their rations. He tosses TÖ-Slüdge a lemon. She catches it and bites into it, but it doesn't ease her qualms. The temperature is dropping harshly by the hour. All see that Fürthrived bundled up to keep her from fading out. Despondency and guilt fill the room.

Valcomix was captured, the freezing temperatures are not safe to travel and the device is no longer of use. Deemed lost. And an ally is asphyxiating. TÖ-Slüdge tends to her, struggling to breathe as she remains slightly warm still. The boys approach the upset TÖ-Slüdge as she cries. They huddle around one another to keep warm and to ease her pain along with their own.

## EIGHTEENTH DIVISION CAMP

Curesed Kiel shares the story of the rogue soldier and spits out the creature's goal. The eight gold-starred soldiers are lined side by side. After receiving the information, they don't say words. Trenton C. Calhous, Lien Servia, Xin U. Mityus, and Baron Roe take out their devices.

**"You want us to persuade it to have it work for us. We don't know anything about it. It may have fought for us, but we must not allow it to travel onto the ice when it's wearing our uniform. When it removes said clothing, we are to conduct S.O.S. protocol. Shoot on sight."** Baron Roe tells Curesed Kiel, who already acknowledged the option because he already mentioned it to Valcomix.

**"Then, get to know its name first."** Curesed Kiel says as he pulls out the armband from his pocket, showing everyone. This surprises most of them as intended. Curesed Kiel turns from them and starts to make steps. They follow him, approaching the truck with a small trailer with double doors with a latch. He opens it, showing his children the rogue individual.

Seeing that it is heavily tangled in chains, the creature turns its eyes away from them, feeling pathetic. Curesed Kiel exhales calmly. **"Come on out."** He orders as he points to the area to be in front of them. The creature follows command. Many of the advanced soldiers are astonished that It's obedient.

**"It's adorable,"** Nikki Juan squeals as she stares at its face. Baron Roe laughs. Curesed Kiel shakes his head. The creature grumbles due to the embarrassment. Diim Sourn chuckles along with a few others. Trenton C. Calhous focuses on it. **"What was your name and rank, beast?"** He asks, and the beast stares at his mask with a serious and determined expression. **"Valcomix, Valcomix. Rank: N2E. Killed by roaches on 07/07/3175,"** he informs

# PART IV

Just mentioning his name was enough to shock them. Some could see the young soldier and remember their days of fighting, challenging, and talking. The young brat that had earned the gold star.

Diim Sourn swallowed the guilt of mentioning him as a beast and creature. Even looking different, his actions gave them victory. **"Valcomix."** Sourn calls him, wanting to talk more. Then, Baron Roe punches his old comrade in the arm. **"Still fighting the tougher battles!"** He yells with a boisterous voice, causing Valcomix's ears to twitch. **"You're always loud and heavy-handed. Be careful with the scrawnier ones."** Valcomix tells him with a smirk.

Then, his fur gets roughened up by Lien Servia. **"Good boy."** She says, teasing him as she wraps her arm around his neck. **"First treated like a rookie brat by you, and now I'm a dog."** Valcomix says with a grumble. Lien Servia continues to roughen him up. He looks for help from anyone.

Victor H. Lune stands in front of him. **"Managed to fall the giants and liberate the Black States but still got caught by us. Nice look for you but a better**

**achievement for us."** He says as if competing with such an opponent with an indifferent tone, focusing on one another, instigating.

Curesed Kiel shakes his head, remembering the constant bickering and tussling these soldiers have done. Now, he hears it once more. A nostalgic joy. Seeing the twenty-one soldiers that he chose just being themselves. Overwhelmed with joy yet guilt. Valcomix is smiling as they are lively around them, all playing around except for Diim Sourn, Xin U. Mityus, and Trenton C. Calhous. Trenton is focusing his attention on the highest rank. Noticing this, Curesed Kiel steps forward.

**"That's enough roughhousing."** He says, and Valcomix focuses his attention on him while the others back away from him. **"Sir Kiel, where are the other six?"** Valcomix asks with a sad smile. Kiel remains silent from his question. **"They fell ill due to the air outside. The same air you're breathing. They were forced to separate,"** he answers him with a serious tone.

Trenton gets his device out. **"Everyone, for I am relieved to know an ally is alive. We have to maintain our composure,"** he mentions as he gives Valcomix his attention. **"Valcomix, are you willing to fight for us?"** he asks with a serious tone.

Valcomix gives him a serious glance, clenching his teeth. **"I told him to think on it."** Sir Kiel informs everyone as he stands vast. **"He already has made his choice."** Maira Devie says with a hesitant tone. She also takes her device out. Now, everyone has their devices out except for Kiel. **"Once the scientists are called, we can cure him."** Sir Kiel mentions with a serious tone. Xin U. Mityus sends a text via group chat. "That's possible, but he committed a few crimes and missed his court date. Also, what he said to you first. Stepping on the ice is not permitted, and suggesting to do so is still treated as one who has done so." All reading her text. But having the troubled superior read it off her device's screen.

**"Dying has exempted him from the judging,"** Sir Kiel tells everyone. **"But he's alive and didn't want to be seen until yesterday. Valcomix, are you alive or dead?"** Lien Servia asks with a hopeful, cherishing tone.

Valcomix now gives her his attention. **"I greatly apologize. I lost my humanity and became like this. Besides, if I returned, I would have to be under constant watch and highly needed to work. Claim back the Playgrounds yourselves. I got comfortable being in my own fur."** He says, smiling brightly and proudly. Curesed Kiel is crestfallen.

**"Then, you are a beast. A threat to humanity and will be forced into the experiment of gaining back your old life. Valcomix, you'll be under submission to work for us, not requested. If you mention going across the ice again, then you'll be subjectively given the wrath of the C.O.A.T.S. Military."** Trenton C. Calhous says justifying the future for this creature with a serious tone as he sentences his forgotten comrade.

**"I accept the challenge."** Valcomix says peering at everyone. **"Valcomix, come on son you have to be reasonable here. You are suggesting to dire consequences."** Sir Kiel warns his lost soldier. **"Sir, you're showing kindness to a creature. You asked us to persuade it. Realizing he chose his option and is proud of it, you gave it time to think. There's no need to persuade, but only to take action and have it put down or submit to our faction."** Lien Servia informs her boss with a sad tone.

**"Anyone should agree that you're favoring this creature. Our comrade said something unforgiveable and can danger Dorm and itself. Under our submission it is protected."** Baron Roe mentions with a serious tone.

**"I making the right choice to save his humanity,"** Curesed Kiel says with a serious, calm tone. **"Then,**

**abuse your rank. You requested our aid. You should have forced him down and defeated it until he wanted to become human. We show no sympathy for all non-human species. Our law."** Baron Roe reinstates as he focuses on the creature, who is calm.

Sir Kiel understood his flaw yet considers that he is still in the right. Then, using this way of judging, many of them agree to set aside Sir Curesed Kiel. As the ones listening in are those with the status of power.

**"Curesed Kiel, Rank: MD9QR. Please, remove your rank and set aside your title for temporary measures until your court date has passed. You'll be having a hearing on 08/29/3175. Also, Valcomix, you are announced as dead and are to remain as such. But given that you liberated the Black States, you'll be confined as our purpose of a weapon as long as you keep wearing any of our uniforms. This is us being lenient. Do you agree to these terms?"** A woman with a calm, serious, yet raspy voice is heard from Xin U. Mityus's device.

She then sends another text. "Valcomix's situation is a complicated case. I agree that Sir Kiel was being lenient. Laws are broken, but he is an ally of profitable causes. We have to have the governmental faction justify these cases."

Reading her reasoning, Sir Kiel steps down, giving up his title for now.

Valcomix walks toward Xin U. Mityus, staring at her device. **"I agree to your terms."** The creature spoke into the device. Then, he returns, waiting for further instructions. **"Good. Now to the rest of you. You all, as the star children, are to appoint the highest rank at this moment."** Says the lady on the phone ordering them to do immediately as her voice is commanding and serious. The call then disconnects.

Valcomix bears his guilt as he focuses on Sir Kiel, whispering his atonement. "As protocol, we'll rely on the format of who has the better status." Nikki Jaun suggests.

They agree. They all open the app, and it shows all their number of completed tasks, highest threat levels subjugated, best achievement level of their units, and their positioning next to their name. At the top right corner is their profile picture. They then stare at their positioning and click on it. The leading child is...

**"Congratulations, Diim Sourn."** Trenton C. Calhous says with an indifferent tone. They all focus on him, including Valcomix, who is smiling for him, overwhelmed by the pressure and seeing a comrade's smile. Then starts remembering that day. **"No, no. I can't. Whatever he became, Valcomix saved our lives. He could have left us with the difficulty of fighting the massive beings on our own. I just can't lift my weapon to fire at him. I should have ranked to eight when first given the opportunity. I didn't know much of the responsibility nor do I want the burden."** Diim Sourn says with a regretful, disheartened tone, focusing on Valcomix, who is shaking his head as if wanting him to take back his words.

**"I'm disappointed in you, Sourn. To deny an honor is cowardly when years after effort and hard work is showing gratitude to reach high. It's difficult yet rewarding. Even as I am now, you all make me proud. Sourn, you yell to the rookies about the oath of being a C.O.A.T.S. soldier. Even Valcomix remains true when facing all of us. Don't be weak!"** Curesed Kiel yells with an upset and serious tone.

They all clench their fists as they receive his words. Valcomix clenches his teeth to keep his silence. Trenton C. Calhous stands in front of Diim Sourn. **"Ranking to eight. Behind a desk, helping no one. But to manage numbers of supplies and rations. A job for the old or broken. But you are neither, a coward, a burden, and weak-willed with a rank of the might as a C.O.A.T.S. top soldier. Pathetic, you don't deserve the title."**

He says, calling him such titles and then removes his armband...

**"I am what you think of me. Mostly, I am afraid to be the one in charge of all. I can lead units when the task is diminishing Creates or claiming. Borrowed power of those I consider a friend is what got me here. Having to reach higher statuses may sound rewarding but there is always trouble."** Sourn admits as he sounds relieved but serious.

Trenton nods, acknowledging his honesty. Valcomix remains silent and glares at him. **"Then, we can promote you. By whoever is appointed, you can rank to eight. Remain safe until you return to Dorm. Live happily."** Trenton C. Calhous says to him, and Sourn nods, turning his back to them.

**"Valcomix, I fell nearly four hundred Creates these past weeks."** Sourn says, holding his head proud. **"I feasted on many, including alphas, apexes, and hunted down almost thousands of Creates."** Valcomix shares with him with anger in his eyes. **"I'm not brave fighting against that. Valcomix, thank you for saving my life, and I'm glad you are alive too. I don't have to feel guilty anymore."** He shares with his old comrade then continues his walk.

Valcomix clenches his fist tight, causing his arms to shake as Diim Sourn walks away, heading towards a vehicle. **"Then, moving forward, we have a stalemate between Xin U. Mityus and Trenton C. Calhous. We are to vote."** Baron Roe suggests. The two then stand facing one another. Now that the remaining number is seven, the system can have a boss.

**"Raise your hand for Xin U. Mityus!"** Baron Roe yells as he raises his hand. Seeing another, she obtains two votes. **"You can vote for yourself,"** Baron Roe informs her. She then quickly takes out her device and sends a text just as quickly. "I cast my vote to Trenton C. Calhous, considering my condition." They read her message. The obvious reason...

**"Are you really considering that your condition is lessening your accomplishment."** Trenton asks and receives a message. A picture of a thirty-one-year-old African American/Russian muscular male sleeping on a black leather couch with a kitten in his lap while both are wrapped in a white blanket.

*Snickering* She even shows the picture to Valcomix. He chuckles. "Because you are much gentler and kinder than I am. Caring and nurturing, Sir Trenton." All of them admire the image. Getting teased...

**"I apologize for suggesting that you are inferior because of the incident. Valcomix, return to your confinement space until I let you out."** Trenton orders him as he sends a message out. Obeying the appointed highest rank, Valcomix enters the darkness.

# PART V

## TWO DAYS HAVE PASSED

### The Time is 6:01am of 08/22/3175

Hitomoni Free and a few others have returned. Sitting in the breakroom lounge with luxurious white leather couches and chairs with a coffee/tea maker and a half kitchen, there is a 70" plasma screen TV fitted into the wall. The group has saddened expressions, with a few of them bearing anger. Soon, two personnel enter the room. They show them a solemn look while one of them glares at them with detest.

David Free and Ovaiya Mist, as their badge reads. Portraying, their image and presenting their names. Her profession is mentioned as a Botanist, Environmentalist, Biologist, Med. Sci. Faction Lead. She is a German/African American with natural red unkempt hair sort of a style of rowdiness.

Ovaiya Mist has healthy peach-tan skin with freckles above her nose, soft teal pupils, gold and orange earrings (one on the right and three on the left ear), and she wears stylish black, thin-framed glasses. She gazes around the room and fixes her sight on the individual glaring at her, then back to where she can view all.

**"We've received a message from Trenton C. Calhous, who is now the boss of the C.O.A.T.S. faction temporarily. There is someone needing our urgent care and to bring hospital equipment. Also, they want us to examine bones that belong to one of the giants. The lot of you returned from Playground MI. Some of you want to make a complaint since conditions are worsening. Playground IL needs our expertise."** She voices loudly. Confused, worried, and/or serious murmuring fills the room. David Free scratches his neck.

**"They have medical doctors within their faction. How ill is this soldier?"** a scientist asks. **"We're not certain because they're not certain, but it's a profitable cause for us to examine our patient."** David Free answers. **"How do we intend to examine animal bones? No one in our faction is an osteologist."** Hitomoni Free informs her superiors.

**"We have instruments and scanners that have data on various biological informative structures of many different species. They should have data on bone cells as well. So, with this, we are going to need two more to assist us. Tingi Vendalic, Suviron Arc,**

**David Free, and I are already going."** Mrs. Mist informs all of them. Everyone is surprised upon hearing the names.

Hitomoni is wide-eyed as she stares at the two. Then, she becomes disgusted as she is winked at by Ovaiya Mist. Hitomoni stands up from the couch and approaches the two. Then, a scrawny, tan-skinned male approaches them. David Free leaves the room with the volunteers.

**"Are there any promotive advances for this type of job?"** the scrawny male asks. David peers down on him. **"No. Since there is an ice storm coming down in the Northeastern states, we have to work fast. They refused to relocate and were shorthanded on help. The trucks are already loaded with the needed equipment. Wear your thermals when you suit up."** He says to them in a panic, pushing the two down the corridors.

## INSIDE A BUILDING NEAR THE WATERWAY

TSinged and Cretan are shivering badly, feeling a rush of chill flowing through their very skin and stinging their joints. TÖ-Slüdge keeps focus on Fürthrived. She is depleted of her heat. Upset and wanting to cry but lacking the moisture to do so, she then walks away and stands outside. She stares into the vast sky, hating the calm, bright gray sheet of clouds with her pale violet pupils.

Her once deep ocean gradient flowing hair is now matching the frost. A pale blue shade becomes a silent white, lacking its luster. Yet, the violet strand of hair retains its sheen color over her right eye. Feeling the freezing temperature that is unleashing and listening to the howling, eerie whistling winds, her skin color is a pale tan. Her arms resemble ice and glass, yet pristine and stained with a small diamond-shaped pattern, the same as her legs. Her nails shine pink.

Filled with pain and rage, Fürthrived is dying, and the boys are struggling. Food supply is scarce. Valcomix is captured. Yet she is alright and unaffected, in a way that isn't harmful. Such despondency has its grip upon her. Scared for her friends and with no one to rely on, a torturing emotion is stabbing her chest.

*HIGH-PITCHED SCREAM* Releasing aggression, yet the sensation remains. TSinged hears her tortured screams and casts his head down, clenching his teeth as *"TÖ-Slüdge, I'm sorry. We should haven't left from that place Fürthrived called a haven. We just weren't comfortable there.*

***I couldn't find comfort there too many nightmares. Now everyone is suffering. Fürthrived, is silent and unmoving."*** He says within himself. Burdened by guilt for the scenario. Holding onto Cretan who is suffering beside him, also refusing to stop her.

TSinged braces the cold as he tends to Fürthrived due to her moment of absence, ready for the worst. Deserving of her fury instead of her screaming. Placing his hand upon her cold wrist, no longer glowing, breathing, nor warmth yet the pulse is beating lively. He smiles, knowing she is still fighting. Relieved. He then notices that she is no longer screaming.

## OUTSIDE

TÖ-Slüdge gets herself discovered by a unit of C.O.A.T.S. A pack of six soldiers just making their rounds, ranking at level 4. Four of them have their rifles drawn, aiming at the head of the mysterious female. While two of them approaches her cautiously. She notices them and remains still, watching them carefully. Getting a few feet closer, she breathes out angrily, creating a cold mist. Feeling the stabbing sensation within her chest as they continue to approach her. A few of the soldiers can see a formation of dust clouds surrounding her using infrared scanning. All white around blue.

# PART VI

Surrounding and speaking to her, but TÖ-Slüdge doesn't know what they're saying. [Combined language] "Why are you out here? Where did you come from? What's your name?" one of the soldiers asks, but he is glared at.

**"Suspicious female is showing hostility."** One of the soldiers tries to pin her down, but she quickly does a reversal, slashing through the hazard suit and pushing the body into the other. Twisting her body to avoid hits, two others leave and are ready to fire but don't want to shoot their allies. She pierces her nails through cloth and then skin. The four of them scream in agony, feeling a burning sensation as their hazard suits are ripped open.

They see their skin dissolving around the infected area, terrified. One panics and angrily tackles the girl, only to get kicked in the chin. Due to the use of her ice-skating like skill for combat purposes. TÖ-Slüdge then slides toward the two as they fire at her. Limber and agile, she dodges rounds using combative dancing. She inflicts wounds on both, piercing a neck and an arm. One dies instantly, while the other screams in her own language. TÖ-Slüdge then reaches into the fallen soldier's pocket, pulling out a device. Corroding the metal and screen, she tosses it away.

Ripping the clothing from the fallen soldier, she wraps her left arm with the material and approaches the one still alive. The soldier stares at his own pockets and then at the murderer. Then, TÖ-Slüdge reaches into the soldier's pockets. The soldier holds her arm. The thief glares angrily.

Seeing that her nails are ready to stab another area. The soldier lets go of her. TÖ-Slüdge proceeds to search the soldier's pockets, pulling out a device, a bundle of white ash sticks, and a flare. She removes more cloth from the fallen soldier. Placing the stolen items onto it, she rushes toward the building.

TSinged can hear fast-paced steps. Watching the stairs cautiously, TÖ-Slüdge appears and places the cloth in front of him. **"What did you do?"** He asks with a serious expression, guilty and angry. "**There were six of them, and I defended myself. Valcomix may be disgusted with me, but I'm just managing our survival."** She tells him with shaking hands.

TSinged looks down and can see a device, a flare, and white ash sticks. Cretan is wide-eyed and quickly picks up the white ash sticks and flare. He snaps one stick and watches it burn slowly. Placing it on Fürthrived and burning the covers, he snaps a few more, creating a fire on her. Amazed at how warm the fire feels, TÖ-Slüdge is still upset with herself. **"Thank you,"** TSinged tells her with a serious, sincere smile.

As long as she is okay, he can be as well. Knowing they are going to have attention to them and Valcomix's capture now became futile, they watch the fire grow. While Cretan opens the device and starts to read the messages, they focus on Fürthrived. *Gentle Breathing* Her eyes twitch and slightly open. Seeing her smile, TÖ-Slüdge holds her tightly, embracing her. TSinged is surprised by her recovery, and Cretan is crying. Her bright, fiery eyes are gentle and confused. **"What happened?"** She asks kindly.

## EIGHTEENTH DIVISION CAMP OF PLAYGROUND IL

Left alone in the dark and chained, unknowing of his time in containment, he scratches at the metal. Restricted as he is bound in chains inside a small space, he hears his hunger fill his ears and echo.

Feeling uneasy, restless, and hungry, Valcomix is annoyed by this sensation as something roars and cries from inside his mind. **DEVOUR. EAT. ROAM.**

**WHAT DOES A... TASTE LIKE?** He shakes his head to remove the thoughts from his conscience.

Afraid, he remembers his first encounter with Sevulix but pictures a different perspective. He bangs his head to knock away the thought. **"Please let me out,"** he begs for salvation as such thoughts slowly swarm his mind.

**TO BE CONTINUED...**

# EPISODE 13: A NEW Coat/C.O.A.T.S. FORGED FROM BONE AFTER IRON

## PART I

Trenton C. Calhous' first act as a boss is already being overworked. A soldier lost an arm, and his subordinates were murdered in the same Playground he is in. A frosty female was located around Sector 16. Sending a search team was effortless. No one was found except for the bodies with melted flesh. The pictures are horrific. His allies became sick, and the weak-stomached are in the bathroom crying. He is furious.

**"Have all arrows on the search! Victor and Maira, lead your units through the Playground and shoot on sight anyone that doesn't have our uniform!"** Trenton yells with rage in his voice. Once a calm yesterday, but after hearing their recording and the survivor's report, this woman is relentless and dangerous. Sadistic.

**"His device was stolen by the frosty female. We can pinpoint it by giving specified orders. We can have our faction shut theirs down and leave ours on. This would give us sight to see who is using the stolen one outside."** Baron Roe implies while readying his device. Trenton C. Calhous makes a call. **"C.O.A.T.S. faction office headquarters. This is... rank: NQ8R speaking,"** a male's calm and strict voice informs.

**"This is your appointed boss, Trenton C. Calhous, rank MD9QR, ordering you to keep an eye on your computers for all active devices. Then, you are to update me on its location."** He orders with a strict tone that is ruthless.

**"Yes, boss."** A voice says through the device. Acknowledges the order but sounds confused. Trenton then sends a message to all C.O.A.T.S. A must do order.

ELSEWHERE

TSinged, Cretan, and TÖ-Slüdge share the situation that the team is in with Fürthrived. **"I was burnt out, Valcomix got captured, you murdered a few members, I woke up, we're on the run also we're going to save him and then leave all of this madness behind us."** Fürthrived summarizes to clear away her confusion, all while traveling the narrow alleyways.

**"Yes, that's the gist of the events. We still don't know where Valcomix may be incarnated. At least we do know his location, just not its whereabouts."** TSinged informs her as he cautiously leads them through the passageways. Checking for any soldiers around the corners.

*Notification* Cretan stares at the screen and reads the urgent message. **"Shut down your device. Obey."** He shares out load. Then has a serious expression. **"TSinged, they're telling us to shut down the device. What should I do?"** He asks, showing the screen to him.

TSinged ponders, trying to see how he can take advantage of it, but it may put Valcomix at risk. **"Shut it down for now,"** TSinged orders him, and he does just that. The screen is now black. **"We should stay put and hide elsewhere,"** Fürthrived suggests.

Seeing Fürthrived glowing once more and feeling her radiative burning them, they realize that they can be discovered easily. TÖ-Slüdge is joyous and the same time afraid because she is radiating heat melting the snow. Leaving a trail behind them. **"We have to hide somewhere. Fürthrived is already giving us away."** She informs pointing at the ground behind them.

TSinged pinches his forehead. Smiling that this is a good headache.

## BACH AT THE CAMP

Trenton C. Calhous is informed that there are only seven active devices outside. Also, the C.O.A.T.S. in other Playgrounds are returning to the nearest camps and bases. He is disappointed, but he has a being that may know the transgressor corrupting their grounds is. Tainting his ground with her hate. He focuses on his comrades. **"I depend on you,"** he says to them calmly. The four give him their attention.

Now, in front of the hauler truck, opening the doors, Valcomix takes a breath. Looking quite tired and defeated, he sees five soldiers in front of him. They then pull his chains and tighten his restraints. He snarls, glaring at Trenton C. Calhous.

**"Valcomix, who's your travel companion!?"** Trenton asks with a roar, and Valcomix turns his sight from him, refusing to speak. The highest rank nods his head. Lien Servia kicks the creature in the stomach, but it doesn't even flinch. *Rumbling* Hearing only its hunger being disruptive, Baron Roe and Xin U. Mityus tighten his restraints by pulling them much harsher now. Valcomix lies on the cold dirt.

Nikki Juan approaches, proceeding with the interrogation. Beating it with a series of kicks, **"Something happened?"** the creature asks, bored of her attacks. Then, Trenton shows him pictures of the fallen soldiers, now his eyes are wide and showing a surprised and compassionate expression. **"I don't know who did it. Some animals do have poisonous saliva,"** Valcomix informs them. They all know that he is lying. **"It was a female with a frosty complexion, wearing a black t-shirt and skirt with a silver chain."** Trenton informs, trying to hide his fury and anger.

Valcomix snarls angrily. **"If you manage to catch her, I'll punish her for you,"** he tells him. His eyes are furious. Knowing he's telling the truth. **"Drag this creature,"** Trenton shakes his head and begins walking. Valcomix closes his eyes. ***"TÖ-Slüdge, please have a reason. Please."*** He says in his mind begging for a justifiable cause. Disturbed by a feeling of betrayal as they drag him away.

# PART II

## PILE OF BONES' LOT

Feeling his back against a hard, cold wall and his arms tied, still, his legs are free. He then wakes up from a blunt hit to his cheek. Baron Roe punched him. Valcomix is unfazed because there are creatures that has hit him harder without much effort.

**"I don't know that individual."** He tells the five of them as he sees that his arms are chained around the curvature of a massive bone. Baron Roe walks away from the creature.

"**Valcomix, you're neither protecting yourself nor her. If a proper beating is ineffective, then maybe this will suffice."** Trenton says as he gets out a pistol and fires at him. Valcomix's tail reacts quickly, shielding the main body from being shot. He is surprised as much as they all are. Copying a certain beast's skill. **"Tie down his tail as well, along with his feet,"** Trenton orders, and the four surround the beast.

Struggling to hold down his wavering and free-flowing furry ligament, Valcomix just watches, enjoying them work. He moves it a bit. The four are putting their weight on it, finally getting it pinned. Now tying it to the huge bone. Now secured in its bondage.

Trenton then accosts him, carrying the tusk that was placed nearby. Valcomix's stomach rumbles once more**. "Sir Kiel said you removed this from its skull. You devoured the meat from this massive apex. But you left the bones. A creature like you shouldn't be this wasteful when your stomach is rumbling this much."** Trenton C. Calhous tells the creature and drops the heavy ivory onto his right leg.

Valcomix winces from the blunt pain. A sharp sensation, then a harsh throbbing. His heart rate speeds up. Breathing hard while in agony, as if kicked in the shin by a steel-toed boot, is what he is feeling.

**"Now, who are you traveling with?"** Trenton asks calmly, and Valcomix remains silent. He then lifts the heavy object carefully to his chest and drops it onto his other leg. Bearing the pain, Valcomix clenches his teeth, showing him his dull whites. Trenton kicks him in the jaw. No effect. Valcomix moves his head, pushing his leg off his face, and snarls at him with an annoyed glare.

**"Even when dead, this being can still harm me. Yet, you're alive, putting in effort, and harmless.**

**Soft. I don't know the individual. I perhaps have seen her, but I thought she came from a separate base."** Valcomix says, gazing at the boss of the soldiers. Furious by his comment, he repeats the tortue. **Snarling* *Wincing* *Cries of agony**

The time is 3:28pm of 08/22/3175

Trenton C. Calhous has his device out after receiving a message from the scientists. "**Arriving soon**," he then focuses on Valcomix and sees that his legs are shaking. Tired from heavy lifting, his arms are aching, and still, the creature glares at him. *Stomach Rumbling* *Snickering*

**"Remain outside in the icy temperatures. The cold should aid the swelling and for you to think of a better answer. If you're hungry, chew on the bones."** Trenton C. Calhous says as he turns away from him. **"Baron Roe. Keep watch until 6 pm. Try to open him up. Use any method to do so,"** the boss says. Now left alone with the brawniest member from their group.

After the others are no longer seen, Baron Roe sits beside Valcomix and pets his fur. **"You're still just as brave as when you were a low rank. You faced a bird nesting in Playground NY and led it into a trap. Commanded the higher ranks. No one should be so**

**eager to do something so stupid. Again, you remain foolish. Valcomix, why do you want to go onto the ice?"** He asks, and Valcomix hesitates to answer but takes a breather.

**"I betrayed the C.O.A.T.S. This is my way of atonement. For a while, I wanted to throw away my life to be rid of the guilt, pain, and those I inflicted my violence towards. The opportunity came that day on both occasions. I hated myself. When I was gone for a moment, there was peace; now given a new form. But this uniform was an accident. I didn't want to wear it again. I was filled with fear, regret, and anger. Remembering all of my days as a soldier are very warm and welcoming, and I didn't want any more of you to feel weak, so I did what I did. Then, it became bizarre because I was having fun. So, you all should reclaim back your states. Shortly, I won't be where you can reach me,"** Valcomix shares with him, with tears in his eyes and a bright smile. Baron Roe embraces the strong being. Valcomix can feel a pain in his chest rather than his legs.

**"Remain strong, kid. Even when I'm the one firing, you are to fight. As long as we are alive, we have to fight. I'm proud of you, even when I hate you right now for protecting a murderer. I will miss the brave soldier you once were. Beast, I will put you down for**

**the murder of our little brother,"** Roe tells him with conflicted anger. They both have something to be proud of now and those to protect. Fellow enemies as of now.

## The time is 6:02pm of 08/22/3175

As Baron Roe checks his device for the time, seeing that it is time to leave, he does just that. Walking away from the creature that fell his little brother, they both mutually despise the other, as the two don't share any more words. Now that he is left by his lonesome outside, the night's freezing winds brush his fur. The sensation relaxes him until... **Stomach Rumbling**

Valcomix's four scarlet veins emerge from his back, and he moves his tail out of the restraints. Lifting one of the tusks to his jaw, following the suggestion of Trenton's, he chews on the piece of ivory. He is hurting his own teeth, but his hunger needs to subside. The piece is too tough and dense. Not noticing that one of the veins wrapped around the base of it is molding the material. The tiny bit is entering his bloodstream, overlaying one of his fractured bone cells.

# PART III

## WATERWAY TUNNEL

The water is frozen, and most of the walkway is slippery. A short passage leads to the other exit. Due to Fürthrived's heat, she helps TÖ-Slüdge into the wet medium, enjoying a warm soak and aids her. Regaining her usual appearance. TSinged and Cretan have their backs turned from them since both the girls are exposed. TSinged checks the pack and finds that their supply has diminished only a few fruits left. He passes two lemons to the girls, offers a pear to Cretan, and eats an orange himself.

Holding onto the device and staring at its inactive screen is Cretan. TSinged ponders with a calm expression. **"Anyone else want to speak of a plan?"** he asks, believing someone must have a better idea. The three notice that he has one, but is doubting it. **"We can fight them,"** TÖ-Slüdge says with a serious glare. **"No. Valcomix will be at risk. We'll tire ourselves out as well,"** TSinged tells her, knocking away her plan.

**"We can turn on the device and have someone instruct me on how to use the map."** Cretan says with a positive and prideful smile. TSinged raises an eyebrow while Fürthrived is concerned, and TÖ-Slüdge shakes her head, refusing the idea.

Now, the attention is on Fürthrived. She ponders for just a moment and smiles at them. **"We can activate the device, set it aside somewhere, and then ambush those that come. Ask for the whereabouts and have it mapped on the device,"** she shares. TSinged is stunned. Cretan is surprised, and TÖ-Slüdge is confused. **"I somewhat came up with that same idea,"** TSinged announces with a calm, surprised tone. **"The problem is, how will we get it done? Considering that they can gather their numbers rather quickly. Valcomix did get caught on the first day,"** Cretan informs them, and he is right. Knowing that they sent a swarm of arrows to their previous location, they're cautious.

Nobody is blaming TÖ-Slüdge because TSinged could have stopped her screaming but didn't want to be her pacifier, knowing she was hurt and furious. He exhales. Everyone is all right, and, well, now he is concerned about Valcomix.

**"Fürthrived, we'll go with your idea. But as a team, we have to compromise to make it a plan,"** he says as he lays himself down before causing himself to have a major headache. No one voices out. Cretan is tired as well. The boys had to go through sleepless nights because of the freezing temperature. The two then fall asleep rather quickly. TÖ-Slüdge smiles warmly at them, and Fürthrived hugs her and kisses her cheek, feeling warmth once more.

## THE LOT, SCATTERED WITH BONES

Sleeping soundly even in the freezing temperatures as the howling winds are rough, the clouds coalesce, creating a dark plume of darkened gray with a blue overlay.

**Sneezing** Valcomix awakens due to the chilling itch from his nose. Using his tail to scratch it, he stares at the vast sky and growls at it, irritating him. Remembering their condition and wanting to move, but his legs are rendered useless, his ears twitch. *Growling*

**Rumbling Engines** Five trucks arrive, each driven by a star child and the appointed highest rank. They open their doors and unload the vehicles. His eyes widen and fill with fear. They transported a hospital, sighting syringes, scalpels, saws, and other necessary tools and instruments. The six scientists scramble around to organize the tables. A computed tomography scanner is unloaded by four people. Monitors are connected to the generators.

Finishing setting up the area, the C.O.A.T.S. and scientists collaborate on the tasks. **"Suviron Arc, your team of specialists is protected by four of the most experienced. If the creature causes a disturbance, they will put it down in regard to your safety."** Trenton C. Calhous says, holding out his hand. Suviron Arc grasps it and gives it a quick shake.

**"We'll start the operation and see if curing is plausible. What is the name of this ill soldier since you're so concerned?"** Arc asks, and Trenton removes his hand. **"That's confidential to our faction. Let them work. I'm going to check up on Maira and Victor."** He tells everyone as he turns away and steps on. **"More serious than usual,"** David Free comments. **"Lives of our soldiers fell yesterday, and shifting command is difficult. We're in a predicament,"** Nikki Juan informs them as she holds out her rifle, aiming it at the patient. Then, the other three do the same.

He remains calm, but seeing the sharp objects laid on the tables causes him to feel uneasy. **"Hitomoni, you go scan the huge bones. We adults will intend to the patient."** Ovaiya Mist tells her. Doing as suggested, she grabs a bone saw, a test tube, and a tablet. Walking past Valcomix, upon seeing her name tag, he clicks his tongue and is angry. The five examine the patient's appearance.

**"Adorable!"** David Free says out loud in a perverted tone. Valcomix is afraid. His colleagues stare at him and block his sight of the ill soldier. **"Ovaiya Mist, can you engage using your field of expertise?"** Suviron Arc asks, but in a nonnegotiable manner, as he steps towards one of the tables along with the others, leaving her to work alone.

**"Can you let free one of his arms, please?"** She asks the nearest soldier with a kind voice. Approaching close is Lien Servia, unbinding his right arm and stepping back quickly to regain her aim upon the ill patient. Miss Mist then pulls over a table. Valcomix is nervous.

**"Be easy now. Let's check your blood pressure first."** She then wraps his arm with the needed instrument with a digital gauge. *Calm inhale followed by an exhale* Knowing the procedure, he calms down the tension from his mind and body, lowering his heart rate. Feeling a slight squeeze and the thumping through his arm, then a release.

**"Way higher than the regular number of hypertensive rates. How are you alive with 235 above 120?"** She asks with a surprised and concerned tone. Seeing the condition that the patient is in, he shouldn't generate this much of a risk factor. She then grabs the stethoscope off the table that is attached to a small monitor to measure sounds within the body. Lifting up his shirt and placing the cold metal on his chest, his rate is fast-paced, abnormal.

She is shocked witnessing the waves created. **"How did you get like this?"** She asks surprised with a concerned tone. **"Complicated mishap,"** he answers briefly. She then pulls a band off the table. Valcomix knows exactly what is coming next and is shivering. Baron Roe is chuckling, and he growls at him.

**"For a creature that withstood torture, a grueling journey, and defeated apexes, you have a fear of the wrong things. Want a wiggly?"** Nikki Juan says, teasing the individual while snickering. He growls at her, too.

**"I got swallowed by one and was close to being strangled by another! Needles remind me of their teeth!"** Valcomix lashes out. Baron Roe is chuckling hard, holding his stomach. Xin shakes her head, disgraced by their attitude.

Miss Mist pulls his arm hard, surprising him. **"Relax, close your eyes, and dream of pleasure,"** she suggests. He looks away and does as she suggests. Daydreaming of a life that can no longer be obtained, his eyes are filled with moisture but gone with a quick blink. Seeing around him are old friends, but he has to rely on the new meaning they are to him now.

Miss Ovaiya stares at the black blood swirling in the test tube. She rushes and places a sample onto a glass slide under the microscope. David Free is next to her. Everyone is now curious. Using the biometric system data bank, the readings are...

**"The black ooze spreading around Playground ID and growing those Ivy-Roses are matching his blood!"** she says loudly, surprised. The scientists are shocked. The four soldiers become serious. **"What?"** Valcomix asks confused as to what just happened.

# PART IV

As the scientists gather around the monitor, witnessing the 100% match, they murmur excitedly. The four soldiers look to Valcomix, who just shrugs his shoulders. Emerging from behind the scattered bones is Hitomoni, seeing the adults cluttered up in front of the monitor.

**"What's happening with them?"** she asks the civilized folks. **"They discovered that my blood is matching the rotting of Playground ID, and it is growing flowers. I was surprised at first. I informed Trenton, Kiel, Baron, and the others that the fox threw me in a bed of thorns, and I got tangled in it. They laughed at me."** Valcomix shares with her, and can hear soft giggling.

**"You hunted down an African Bush Elephant. The age of the bones is approximately eight hundred years of hardening, consisting of ivory and concentrated calcium. Given the scaled weight, the giant's appropriate actual weight could have been 35.3US tons as a whole. Adding the organs and blood of the creature of course."** She informs the soldiers and the patient as she shows them the scanner.

**"It lived that long only to be done in by a scrawny, adorable little pest."** Baron Roe says, feeling sympathetic to its tragic end. Valcomix glares at him but with a calm demeanor, hiding his animosity. **"It did give me much of a stomachache when I finished devouring it, yet a new craving came about."** the patient says, and they give him their attention as they become more cautious.

Then, accosting the rare being, Suviron Arc examines the stature of the specimen, gripping its chained arm. Holding a scalpel, he quickly inflicts a light cut. Valcomix snarls at him. Gathering the black fluid into a vial, Suviron Arc says**, "We're going to need more of your DNA to find a cure, as well as to create a biological weapon."** He informs him as he stares at its facial expression. Its teeth are brilliantly white.

The wound closes. **"I am not a source of supply. This is not an illness. It's a change,"** Valcomix tells the scientists, noticing that the incision should still be draining but isn't. **"Fast healing properties. What are you?"** Sir Arc asks, fascinated by what they captured.

**"Hungry,"** Valcomix says viciously as his stomach grumbles. Hitomoni steps away, and the four soldiers take aim at his vitals. Suviron Arc remains brave, putting his face near Valcomix's. **"Take a bite,"** he says with a serious, indifferent tone. Tempted to, as the little voice whispers in his ear, Valcomix shakes his head.

**"Your humanity can be salvaged,"** Arc tells the creature, seeing the innocence within its eyes. The other scientists are bewildered as they focus on the two. Seeing all becoming frightened or just wary of him. Valcomix whispers to Arc with a sad yet angry expression, **"Please don't try to save me."**

Following where his eyes are gazing, the four soldiers now express anger and guilt from inside their mask. Suviron Arc stands and peers down at the lost soldier, trying to figure him out. Putting on a scene, the individuals were enjoying the company even if the situation was dangerous. Noticing that its legs are not moving, he gazes at the creature and the soldiers. *"A shoot-on-sight target is accepted to only be captured."* He steps away and returns to his colleagues.

As time progresses, Valcomix is treated with caution and given silence. Working to develop a cure to reverse the effect of what caused him to become the way he is now; ignoring his plea for he works for Dorm. Suviron Arc is curious about the patient's name as they are familiar with one another, it seems. David Free is working well with Hitomoni, hopefully. Being observant of others, Suviron Arc is then tapped on the shoulder.

**"Sir Arc. It's four pm,"** the tall scientist informs with an emotionless tone, holding out his device. **"Everyone, clean off the tools and head back inside the camp!"** Arc yells as he reaches for the alcohol spray bottle. Soon enough, Trenton is approaching.

**"I told you scientists to be gone by four,"** the appointed boss says with a disappointed attitude. Sighting some needles and scalpels on a table. **"I'll be using these,"** he says to David Free, holding the table. He takes it from him and lifts it towards the patient. Nikki Juan steps towards the scientists. **"I'm escorting you all,"** she informs them.

Leaving their sterilized equipment tools after turning off the generators, Suviron Arc turns his head back. The soldier blocks his sighting. **"Don't look."** She orders with a pained, saddened tone.

Now, sighting reinforced metal building structures of many single-floor houses, residing within them is a bunker. Before entering the opposite door, they pass through a long, wide quarantine area. Placing devices and other loose items on the shelf, they press the red button that is on the door they entered from. The area fills with a mist creating yellow soap bubbles on their hazard suits, then scalding hot water rains down. They wait for five minutes. Then, scanned by an arrow, it blinks blue. They then remove their suits and proceed through the next door, entering a platoon-like home. Twenty bunk beds, ten lined up on each side. Placing their hazard suits in the metal cabinets, they see the bathroom on the left and the entertainment center on the right.

**"Get comfortable. We're going to be roommates with all of you for the next couple of days."** Nikki Juan, an Indian/African American/Polish woman with long, lush white hair halfway down her back, caramel-colored skin, and has dull gray eyes, says while heading to her claimed bunk and reaching into the footlocker for her cleansing kit and clothes. She then heads towards the bathroom with the many toilets and sinks. From the side, she enters the shower area.

Ovaiya tries to have a conversation with Hitomoni. David Free lurks at the entertainment center and begins to play a first-person shooter-type game. The tall Chinese/African American/Italian scientist with pure white shining hair, brown eyes, and a light, healthy tan complexion, wearing a red shirt and black slacks and shoes, Tingi Vendalic, joins him. Both now play a co-op mission.

The bald Caucasian/Hispanic/Italian man with lime green eyes, a pale peach complexion, a slash mark on his nose, and a burn injury from his neck to his right cheek, wearing a gray shirt, black sweats, and brown boots, sits on his bunk holding the device in his scarred right hand. Pondering the complex events of the C.O.A.T.S., invested in researching the individual who is probably being tortured by now. Interrupting him is an individual with black flowing hair, peach skin with freckles, blue eyes, and wearing formal clothes. Suviron meets his eyes and looks at everyone as they get comfortable.

**"Is anyone else curious about the events? Even she recommended for us to be here and to keep why we are here confidential."** He asks everyone, and they ponder, knowing that it is a complex order because they share research with the faction, but to be asked now to keep the details to themselves is...

**Sighs** **"Suviron Arc. This is our problem, and it is personal to our faction."** Nikki clarifies as she wipes the water from behind her ear with a serious look aimed at all of them. **"Personal to the faction or just with the star children since he was one?"** Suviron asks as he calmly looks over her to read her expression, looking quite crestfallen.

**"Be curious all you want, but don't ask Trenton any questions concerning it."** She warns them and makes her way to the entertainment center, joining in as a third player. Then, she easily overtakes the two in completing the mission and has headshot the two.

Suviron Arc glares at the kid beside him, and he backs away slowly. Then, focusing on the device, he says, *"Your faction can separate those infected by the outside world without remorse. Send our starters for field testing experience to aid them unless it gets serious. But this one is getting special treatment. Of course, I'm curious. He requested to remain the way he is, feeling quite guilty."* Suviron Arc says to himself, looking into the files of fallen soldiers and having it specified to "Gold star bearers."

Listing of thirteen individuals with reasons for death, only seven of them had their bodies recovered and buried near Dorm as the honored. There were witnesses of the others falling, but one wasn't fully seen to have fallen. Surrounded by roaches, he said his final words. His eyes widen and begin to swell, letting a single tear fall with a smile on his face. Hiding his discovery from everyone, including his broken smile as he enters the bathroom area.

## OUTSIDE IN THE DRY FREEZE

Trenton is finished with his questioning. The three others couldn't bear to witness such an extreme measure of cruelty. Trenton remains peering down on the creature. Valcomix withstood his fingers pricked by needles as they remain in. His legs are gashed open, along with his free arm. The smallest bone from the massive is forced into his shoulder joint, and one of the tusks is pierced through, near his stomach. His eyes are half-open as his head is down. *Staggered breathing* Trying to breathe slowly so the suffering in his body can subside, he is soon left alone to whimper through the freezing night.

His body throbs violently, and immense pain surges. His four veins bore through the femur. Appearing through the other side. The tail moves about and begins to remove the tusk. His body is doing such actions alone. The removal was quick and very painful. His tail is dangling the collection of ivory dripping his warm thick black vital fluids; lifting it toward his jaw. Hunger defeats his pain as he takes a bite...

**Bone Shattering Crunch**

# PART V

## PLAYGROUND IL, SECTOR: 13

Maira has her troops searching the alleyways by the dozen. Occupied by her squad, with the many arrows overhead hovering about. Using the map app of the Playground's schematics, they see many areas where they can take cover: bridges, buildings, and sewer entrances. C.O.A.T.S. are already searching the dark areas. Buildings are being run through, with them busting doors, windows, and other closed-off spaces open. Her squad moves on, placing vehicles over bridges. Then...

**"Maira. They activated their device in sector 28. Head there with you and your troops, along with Victor's. I already fed him the knowledge. Now, enjoy your hunt as well,"** Trenton informs, speaking into her mask.

She then presses a button on the side of her mask. **"Everyone, sector 28. We're meeting up with Victor and his troops. This is not a competitive matter. We are brothers and sisters ready to unleash our might upon the enemy that fell our kin. Show no mercy."** She says with a steady tone, ready to kill.

**"Yes, ma'am!!!"** A roar from the soldiers as they yell, their boots kicking up dust. They gather into vehicles and rush towards the destination. The first flake of snow falls, carried by the whistling gust, followed by many more swaying gently.

## SECTOR: 28

TSinged is out in the open on a park field along with his teammates with evident anticipation, nervousness, and preparedness. Cretan is watching the two green dots approaching fast towards the green standing dot. A cluster of green dots is on the top left of the screen. They all stare at the device.

**"I hope this plan is effective. We're putting both our lives and Valcomix's at risk."** TSinged says calmly. Fürthrived and TÖ-Slüdge both glare at him while Cretan remains focused on the screen. **"I'm turning it off now."** He does as he says it, then quickens his steps, bursting into a roll. The three then follow after him, keeping up with him. Soon after, the C.O.A.T.S. arrive, searching the area. Maira and Victor are close by.

**"We have lost the signal on device. Trenton, how should we handle this?"** Victor asks, annoyed and feeling a chill through his body due to the weather. **"With caution. The arrows will need to hover at a**

**wider radius while you all keep searching through the hidden areas. Sector 28 doesn't have any waterways nor bridges."** Trenton answers calmly and provides them necessary information. After a while, Victor H. Lune checks his device.

The time is 6:52pm of 08/23/3175

Feeling quite cold and with normal visibility down, relying on night vision mode, he can see a few of his soldiers shivering. Maira comes up to him. "**The temperature is dropping rapidly. We'll charge up our vehicles and warm ourselves up quickly. Going forward, we should do shifts,"** she suggests, showing him the back of her hand. He clasps it with his. **"I agree. Return to the nearest base to rest and recharge."** Trenton says to them through their masks.

The snow starts to pile up fast. Soon, there is a blizzard. Thanks to Fürthrived, they don't feel the freezing air, and the snow is evaporating from their path. Thankful that she is alright and very much helpful.

Cretan leads them, then stops, remembering the cluster of green dots, but the route is complicated, and he stares at his teammates. TSinged nods. He then turns on the device, sighting the cluster of green dots at a slight right from the top center. He quickly turns it off and leads them forward.

## WITHIN THE HOUSING

Trenton C. Calhous, a brawny male with brown eyes, has black slick hair. A dark tan complexion and a combination nationality of Caucasian/Indian/Greek, is staring at his device. He saw a green dot just at the bottom of the screen before it disappeared. He sends a message. Noticing that everyone is asleep around him but himself. His main focus is on an individual.

## OUTSIDE

The creature is almost buried in snow, feeling a burning sensation from his stomach flowing through his body. Immense pain throbs from his chest, tail, arms, head, and fractured legs. His veins are glowing their pink brilliance once more, shining through the snow layered on top of him.

The chains remain gripped to his wrist, but the bones that were scattered behind him are gone. Tossing and turning as he whimpers, feeling sick and in agony, his four burning, shining pink veins exhume from the snow and melt what they touch. They wrap around his neck, legs, torso, and tail, burrowing through the flesh and the meat. ***SCREEAHHHH!!!***

## ABOVE ELSEWHERE

The night sky's weather is relentless. The arrows are doing the emergency landing as programmed. Some of them break on impact due to frozen propellers or torn apart by the strong winds. "**Not safe for butterflies.**" is alerted from them. The blizzard continues piling snow and covering pathways. The blue crystal substance lays on top of frozen water. The howling rushing wind breaks through the windows, shattering glass.

Soon, the night's cold rage subsides, and it begins to calm. Now, the snow falls softly, and a gentle breeze flows through the freezing Playground. What was agreed on is discordant. Maira's and Victor's troops are plowing away the snow with their heavy and charged-up vehicles. The many are heading to a certain location.

## INSIDE THE HOUSING

Trenton is putting on his thermals, both a gray shirt and pants, and then a black beanie. **"You and your colleagues are to remain inside here. As a safety precaution, we have a threat to handle with our set skills and name. With this, you are all excused from**

**work today."** He notifies the scientists as he puts on his hazard suit and then his black boots.

Now, his gas mask latches it to connect it to the hazard suit. Checking for any areas of exposure, he puts his device in his right pocket along with a bundle of white ash sticks and a flare. Four magazines are put in the left pocket. He then straps the rifle over his right shoulder, now ready.

Heading down the tube, he enters the outside world. The sky is thick with dark grey and heavy blue clouds, and visibility is low. His team was waiting for him. Trenton then leads them away from the platoons towards a different area with an open field used for training purposes. There waiting is Victor and Maira with all their troops, all armed and ready.

**"What isn't human, unleash wrath."** Trenton orders as he watches the device. A green dot appears south of him, and it is close by. Ahead of them are structured buildings with four passageways. Trenton sends an alert to all C.O.A.T.S.

## WITHIN THE CITY'S MAZE

"**Approach the exit or get rushed**," reads the message. TSinged clicks his tongue angrily. Cretan is nervous and scared. **"They figured us out?"** he asks. TSinged snatches the device from Cretan's grip and tosses it forward. **"Valcomix should be ahead if they're all gathered here. We avoid being sighted. Take to the rooftops."** TSinged says, stretching his arms to reach the flat, sturdy top of a building. With a jump, he pulls himself up. He then aids Cretan next, then both the girls, his arms feeling unpleasant as usual.

**"TSinged, we shouldn't hide nor run,"** Fürthrived suggests with a gentle smile. **"We're on their grounds, and they are heavily searching for me. Playing at stealth isn't a skill we developed,"** TÖ-Slüdge mentions, glaring at him. TSinged nods, agreeing with her but reluctant to face them.

*Snow crunching steps* A soldier finds the device, but no traces are left in the snow. They return with the obtained item. Trenton is then notified. Three soldiers are carrying a platform. Two others bring out a specialized upgraded toy and its load of ammo inside a backpack. The modified M224 is placed on the platform. They turn it on, and Trenton connects to it via Bluetooth. The targeting map shows up on his screen. It automatically adjusts itself, aiming at a set location. Loading it up for a single shot, they move around it while ducking their heads, clearing a way. He presses the green check part of the screen. It launches.

**Explosion** A building is reduced to rubble and debris. Snow is now steam. The four sight the cloud of smoke. The soldiers load another shot, moving away. He sets another location and presses the green check. The red tail is sighted in the air and disappears. **Explosion** Another building is reduced to rubble.

Maira chuckles. **"Trenton's favorite toy,"** she says, and Victor scoffs. **"We want to blow something up as well!"** he yells. Then, more soldiers hurry to place platforms on the snow. Bringing out FGM-148s (Javelins), attaching them to tripods and turning them on, connecting all of them to their devices wirelessly. Assisting to load them up and back away, they unleash wrath. Some explode before impact, sighting a bright orange bubble on one of the standing buildings' tops.

## ELSEWHERE

Piled over snow is a being lowly grumbling, causing the frozen substance to vibrate. It quickly jumps out of the snow and focuses its dull magenta eyes towards the sound of destruction, then disappears.

# PART VI

The troops and Trenton continue to fire their wrath at the bubble. He then raises his fist. All is silent but the sound of the howling gentle breeze. He then readies his rifle, and the others do so as well. Four individuals approach them. TSinged is furious, and his arms are glowing a dark orange. TÖ-Slüdge is angry as well.

Fürthrived stands in the front, protecting those behind her, shining. Her fiery hair has more of a yellow shine with a greenish tint to it. Her complexion is now a brighter orange to yellow. Her eyes shine gold in color with a pinkish hue that flickers red a bit.

Cretan stands behind everyone else, covering his head with his hood. The snow evaporates. So does the air that surrounds her. The ground is smoldering. Trenton fires his weapon without any hesitation upon sight. The troops rally and manually control the ranged weapons while many of the other soldiers take aim at the individuals approaching them.

Unloading ammunition from their barrels, spiraling bullets are fired and reach her. The rounds melt early before hitting the individual, reduced to cinders and melted metal before evaporating. Black smoke covers the snow.

Trenton steps back; realizing what he just did. His heart is racing from anger and him retreating, biting away the embarrassment. He steps forward and continues to do so. Victor looks to Maira. **"This is our job,"** Victor tells her with a nervous chuckle as he follows Trenton. Then, the other star children accost into the danger. Maira joins her brothers and sisters, feeling an uncomfortable heat through their bodies as they get closer.

**Screaming** Soldiers are terrified of something. The being moves too quickly and swiftly through their gathered numbers. The dark, glowing pink, slender figure traverses smoothly and then pass the higher ranks.

Fürthrived is surprised as her arm is pulled, soon embraced by a creature she recognizes. TSinged is surprised and shocked. TÖ-Slüdge is wide-eyed with her mouth slightly agape. Cretan is joyous with a full innocent smile upon seeing it. The soldiers continue to fire at it, but the bullets and ammunition seem to bounce off or fall due to the quick movement of its tail. Within time, they can no longer unleash wrath. Trenton C. Calhous, Baron Roe, Victor H. Lune, Maira

Devie, Nikki Juan, Xin U. Mityus, Lien Servia, and the gathered troops are focused on the being.

Fürthrived is let down and has cooled, becoming her usual appearance. The burning magenta eyes peer down at the C.O.A.T.S. It is growling lowly and showing off its bright, white, sharp teeth. Trenton aims his rifle at the creature. Valcomix then remembers the day he first encountered Sevulix. But the roles are reversed. His eyes soften, seeing his new form along with the others witnessing his change.

Sighting a tall 6.7ft, slender, slightly muscular creature, its claws are longer and jagged with a lustrous sheen of white. The hands have white, sharp knuckles, with a plate from the knuckles to the surface area of its hands. The palms have small, rounded plates near the thumb and wrist. Two lines of thick white fur curve all the way from its wrist to the covering plates shielding its shoulders.

Its feet have bright white, sharp nails and thick plates around the foot. Solid white legs stretch from the ankles to the end of the knees. Its chest has solid plates as well. From its back there are three lines of thick white fur reaching the shoulders that curve the shoulder blades down to the tail. The line in the center reaches from the center lines around its neck, curving its spine and reaching its tail.

The tail is longer, lengthening to 6.5 ft, swaying its three-spiraling thick white bumpy lines and its sharp sickle end. The eyebrows are plated as well, and its ears are lined and protected, too. Its veins shine pink, causing the layers of white to brighten. It is now wearing black and white shorts with green biohazard symbols and a white armband with a gold star inside a black monster jaw. No shirt though.

Finishing up seeing his new change and feeling heavier but strengthened, remembering the elephant's body and how it moved, the speed of the rhino and how it rammed him. Then Sevulix. He as well sways his tail in an intimidating way, flashing its sharp-edged bladed end. Valcomix stands vast in front of the leading soldiers.

**"I'm crossing over the ice. Take back your states and claim victory,"** he says as he turns his back on them. He then lifts Fürthrived and approaches his teammates, who are still in shock. Refusing such a phrase, Trenton pulls his trigger and fires at his back. Valcomix quickly rushes at him, moving smoothly and taking a bite, rendering his rifle unusable. He even cuts the other starred children's weapons with ease.

**"Humans are weak,"** he says to them as he reaches into Trenton's pocket, taking his device. Disrespecting the leading soldier in front of all, then pushes him aside. No one is able to stop it. The four approach Valcomix, led by TSinged. Valcomix passes the device off to Cretan.

All are witnessing five monsters just trespass on their grounds. No one acts brave. They disappear as they all watch them do so. Baron Roe kicks at the snow. Victor holds his head to remove a headache. Maira looks up at the sky.

*Chuckling* **"That monster is challenging us and allows its friends to just disrespect our territory!!! Do we allow that?!!!"** Trenton C. Calhous shouts loudly and proudly, waking those who felt lost to their loss. **"No, we don't!!!"** The C.O.A.T.S. yell out, feeling riled up. "**My brothers and sisters, we will fight using all we have!!!"** he yells, riling up everyone as they scream in anger. Valcomix's ear twitches, and he smiles proudly, hearing their war cry.

# PART VII

TSinged notices there are tears falling from his eyes. **"Want to talk about it?"** he asks with a gentle tone. Valcomix is confused, but his eyes feel hot, and then he notices the tears, confused as to why. **"I don't even know why I'm crying,"** he says with a soft chuckle, wiping away the moisture from his face with his arm.

TÖ-Slüdge is crestfallen and feels pitiful for him. Cretan is smiling, knowing everyone is safe. Fürthrived is astonished by his new appearance and the softness of his fur, even though it looks rough. **"Are you really alright?"** TÖ-Slüdge asks Valcomix, who then takes a breath.

**"No, I was concerned about you all. You murdered a few soldiers and then all of you stood against their army. What were you all attempting? At least no one else is injured, and everyone is bright."** he says with a serious, disappointed tone. Seeing that TSinged's arms are glowing, the candlelight has gotten brighter, and TÖ-Slüdge is glowing as well. Cretan is still himself. Looking at himself lighting up with a pink hue, he feels guilty, but they consider it a good cause.

**"We were going to rescue you. Fürthrived lost her glow, and the boys were shivering and hadn't slept for two days. I went outside to vent and got discovered. I did it. They were saying something I didn't comprehend and attacked me. I defended myself. Thanks to that, I stole a device and sticks that can burn. It helped her regain life. Then, we relocated and came up with a terrible plan. Our supply diminished, and we decided to act. To get you, how can you get yourself caught?!"** TÖ-Slüdge yells angrily, guilt biting her as she stares at the one upset with them, burdened by the pain as tears fall from her eyes. TSinged grips his shoulder. Cretan focuses on the device with a sad expression. Fürthrived dims down, sharing the blame with her team.

Valcomix glares at her as he wraps his tail around her. TSinged is furious, and is focuses on him. **"Don't, I am punishing someone. The rest of you can go ahead. Unless you want to challenge me."** Sounding confident as he glares at TSinged. Remembering how he moved, he steps back and scoffs as his arms continue to glow. Cretan obeys, and so does Fürthrived. He relaxes his fists and follows after the two. Now given privacy with the true perpetrator, he wipes away her tears, which causes her to flinch.

**"I'm upset. I betrayed my old ranks and witnessed the pain it caused. Hearing about your murder, you put**

**others and yourself at risk. I said six days. A storm will be hitting these Playgrounds soon, and I will rush to find you all. Not rushing to save those humans wasn't the plan. I'm thankful that all of you wanted to rescue me, but I am no damsel."** He notifies her and pinches her cheek. Then he sets her behind his back and wraps his tail around her and himself, trapping her in his grip.

**"You're going to have me stuck to you. For how long?"** she asks, struggling to free her arms. To no avail, as his tail tightens its wrapping, squeezing her. Feeling uncomfortable already, he then begins to walk on, not answering her question. Listening to her complain, he catches up with the team. TSinged raises an eyebrow and chuckles, worried for nothing.

**"Some baggage you're carrying,"** TSinged taunts her. Fürthrived looks behind and sees her friend's facial expression struggling. She has a smirk on her face. Cretan sighs, relieved. **"As a team, all must be given a deserving punishment. When we find a place to resupply, all of you are in for it."** Valcomix shares with a serious expression. Now, the two in front shiver. TSinged raises an eyebrow and then sights four thin pink veins emerge from its back, spiraled by the white covering much of the main body. At the end is a needle-like point. TSinged gulps and steps away from his newly formed ally.

## ELSEWHERE

The empty lot. Seven individuals are investigating the area. Xin U. Mitys discovers a chain belonging to their escaped prisoner. Not a single bone is found. Remembering the appearance of Valcomix's newly formed body, **"He ate his way free?"** Nikki Juan asks unbelieving something can devour such a pallet.

**"His stomach capacity has no restrictions. It would've been a ferocious, yet an amazing sight to see him consume that much calcium."** Baron Roe says, sounding both proud and disturbed. Maira Devie focuses her attention on the silent leader, noticing her staring. Victor H. Lune waits for the leader's words as well.

**"That's no longer Valcomix. That's a monster. Just an it. And it needs to be put down. There are five of them, and they are considered a threat to all of the C.O.A.T.S. As a threat and mucking up our grounds with their dirty feet and causing violence, we deal with them. After the storm, I want the beaches barricaded. I want all of us to evolve as well, with upgraded weapons that can shatter its layers. We will fall them."** Trenton C. Calhous appointed boss announces with a serious, menacing tone. Declaring the truth that threat must be dealt with. A betrayer of humanity and a murderer. The seven of them saw its armband, angered by it. Creating their own conclusion of its meaning but sharing a similar concept that it's challenging them. They march on toward the housing. The sky darkens, and now ice falls heavily, along with thunder rumbling in the distance.

**TO BE CONTINUED...**

# EPISODE 14: VIOLENT ICE, DEADLY DAMAGE, AND AN UNSETTLING ENCOUNTER.

## PART I

### FREE ZONE: HALAMAZOO, PLAYGROUND MI

Taking shelter in a structured museum with plentiful plant life and vegetation that glows vibrantly violet. Orange moss growing on the walls and flowers bringing in beauty. The museum houses raccoons, squirrels, small reptiles, amphibians, and a variety of rodents. The trees are even growing through the walls.

An abundance of different fruits are being picked by TSinged and Cretan. A small snake lands on TSinged's shoulder, and he brushes it off fast. Feeling as if his own is crawling. And then shivers. **"We've been here for a few days, sharing shelter with pests."** He says, glaring at the slithering being as it hisses at him.

Cretan rolls his eyes and lays his hand on the slender thing. The animal just goes past him and slithers back up the tree. TSinged is astounded as of how Cretan is willing to chase them. **"They're cute."** Cretan says as he continues to pick fruits off the tree. Then has small thin scaly friends wrapping around his arm. He begins to play with them. TSinged's expression is exposing his fear and disgust of such a vile existing reptile. *Bang* TSinged jumps quick and sees only...

Valcomix carrying the device in his soft paws and the pack as he is standing upon the railing. Appearing suddenly as he dropped from the tree. **"We invaded on their grounds, so we're the pests. Keep complaining, and I'll let you attempt to sleep outside once more. The hail is bigger this year."** He warns TSinged, who steps back from Valcomix. **"I'm not complaining. I just want these things away from me when I'm sleeping."** TSinged informs him while he glares upsettingly at the snakes around the place.

Cretan places his picked fruits into the pack. **"There are none them outside."** He says protecting his friends. **"He is right"** Valcomix agrees with him. TSinged is outnumbered and decides to quit. Returning to pick fruits and has a scaly friend on his wrist. Cretan removes and puts it around his neck like casual.

Valcomix's ears twitch and he chuckles silently. **"Keep up with the work you both are doing outstanding."** He says with no enthusiasm. TSinged isn't amused hearing that and watching Cretan's over zealous demeanor to gather more of them is creeping him out. They're even slithering in the bag. Valcomix jumps to the bottom floor and moves swiftly.

## IN A SPACEOUS ROOM

TÖ-Slüdge is rubbing her arms as they are still stiff, residing in an area that has water mainly reaching three feet and soaking her sore feet. Hearing rustling from the sound of the grass being stepped on, she leans supported by her arms as she turns head to see who is behind her...lurking behind the orange moss-covered door...

**"What is it, Fürthrived?"** She asks with annoyed tone after sighting the orange luminous light that is also emanating such warmth. *Giggling* The walking hearth is finally seen and is approaching TÖ-Slüdge who is refusing to give her anymore attention. Now setting her sights on her reflection on the water. Feeling a tight embrace around her waist.

**"I'm bored TÖ-Slüdge,"** Fürthrived answers resting her head upon her companion's shoulder. Now adding some weight. Causing TÖ-Slüdge to lean more to the right. Captured. TÖ-Slüdge grumbles, understanding where her attitude came from.

TÖ-Slüdge now feels free as the heat is now off her back. Gazing at Valcomix with an appreciative smile, she sees him using his tail to carry the annoyance as he disapproves of her cute smile.

**"You're a bad influence. This is your fault next time you will have to deal with her."** Valcomix tells TÖ-Slüdge with a serious demeanor. *Tch* She clicks her tongue with such attitude and turns gaze from him. Valcomix shakes his head annoyed by her behavior then focuses on the source of his headache.

Fürthrived is entertaining herself by playing with his fur and surging her heat. Hearing her giggle, he orders, **"Calm down,"** annoyed by her actions. She then hugs his fur and nuzzles her cheek on it. **"So fluffy and soft,"** she says joyously and playfully. Ignoring him, he quickly snarls at her and glares. These past few days, she has been disturbing the others. TSinged was accidentally burned, and Cretan suffered as well, being hugged by her. TÖ-Slüdge was almost preyed upon many times.

Causing trouble but remains innocent, only showing affection. Most times it's too much. Continuing to glare at her, she gazes into his eyes, seeing some flickers of red. Grabbing his attention, she continues to release waves of heat in an alluring pattern.

Valcomix then wakes up from the trance and realizes her condition. He became a victim of similar gazes. Seeing her smile mischievously, she speaks softly. **"TÖ-Slüdge had your attention the other day, right? Valcomix, do you see me that way as well?"** She asks looking quite envious with such innocent sorrowful eyes. He hesitates and looks at TÖ-Slüdge who is serious. **"Valcomix, please take good care of her."** TÖ-Slüdge says with a gentle smile at him

He sighs as Fürthrived is excited and is gazing into TÖ-Slüdge's vibrant violet eyes. **"Thanks for sharing."** She says appreciating her kindness. Valcomix then carries her. Nods his head to TÖ-Slüdge and adds a smile. Understanding what she intends for him to do. He then exits the room with Fürthrived to go somewhere more secluded for private affairs.

## SECOND FLOOR

Cretan is chasing after a squirrel that stole a plum. TSinged is shaking his head. *"The pack is almost filled for tomorrow's leave. No more sharing shelter with these serpents and thieves. The days have been*

***hectic. Fürthrived's actions resemble TÖ-Slüdge's, concluding that she copied her influence."*** He says within self as he puts a plum upsettingly into the pack.

Remembering how TÖ-Slüdge got ambushed, he begins to snicker and then continues to pick fruits. Stunned. There is a black snake wrapping around his arm. He shakes his arm, but the thing isn't being thrown off. Cretan stops his arm and gently unwraps the slender reptile, which then wraps around his arm. Saved again. Then is surprised...

**"Cretan you were just chasing after a squirrel. How fast did you get covered by them!"** TSinged yells and gets hissed at by the many. Cretan's devotion to reptiles, amphibians, arachnids, and silkworms is upsetting him. Cretan smiles at him while confused and its innocent as another snake slithers across his arm.

## DOWNSTAIRS

TÖ-Slüdge is now bored, staring at the orange mossy ceiling. She then stands and wanders around, sighting vast trees, raccoons chasing after mice and squirrels, and other small creatures surviving within this structured building. The plants are glowing and growing vast, and so does the moss. A wondrous area claimed by the new nature housing the smaller critters.

Continuing her walk to alleviate her boredom, TÖ-Slüdge sees a familiar glow. A orange light and a pink hue behind a tree. With a mischievous smile, she lurks closer and then blushes as Fürthrived's clothes are scattered about. At an angle, she witnesses a rousing scene. Fürthrived is enjoying herself as she is holding on tight. TÖ-Slüdge chuckles holding her voice, *"She definitely was influenced by my behavior,"* sounding quite proud of herself as she continues to watch.

## UPSTAIRS

The two are finished filling up the pack. TSinged zips it up, ready to head down, but Cretan is playing around with the serpents. Disgusted by the sight, he avoids his fun having time as he carefully walks away. **"Cretan, I'm going downstairs to the usual spot,"** he informs him and receives a thumb-up.

Walking the spiral mossy and slippery staircase, the railing is in the same condition. Treading carefully, he enters the room with a water preserve. Setting the pack in a corner, he lays down against the wall, protecting the supplies from masked, cunning thieves. Closing his eyes, he takes a nap.

## ELSEWHERE

Fürthrived has finally calmed down and rests in his arms. TÖ-Slüdge comes out of hiding, holding onto their clothes. She then glares at Valcomix. He smiles at her and scoots over a bit. TÖ-Slüdge now sits beside him, looking at Fürthrived's expression. **"Finally, she has calmed down. Such a dangerous behavior."** TÖ-Slüdge mentions to herself seeing her satisfied. Stroking her hair as she leans against Valcomix.

**"I appreciate that you dealt with her, but you ravished her like some beast,"** TÖ-Slüdge says while pinching his side. He laughs softly as she gazes at candlelight's frame. Then gazes upon TÖ-Slüdge. Noticing that she is lightly blushing and her softened, curious eyes linger with jealousy. He then whispers in her ear. She nods quietly.

After a while, the three return. Fürthrived remains asleep in his arms, Sighting TSinged who is resting and snoring softly. Valcomix then lays her down on the opposite corner as gently as possible. Now he attends to TÖ-Slüdge. Wrapping his tail around her.

# PART II

Awakening from his nap, TSinged views the area around the room and sees three comfortable individuals. Upset, he glares at them but mainly at the creature the girls are clinging to. Cretan isn't around. He doesn't want him to witness this. Sighting that its tail is draped around them.

TSinged doesn't want to think about the actions, knowing something is going on between them, especially when TÖ-Slüdge goes to coddle Valcomix. Now, Fürthrived has joined. *Scoff* He shakes his head with an attitude showing detest. He exits and notices Cretan surrounded by serpents, just enjoying himself. He is disgusted by the sight, but at least Cretan is happy. When they cross over the ice, there will be a better chance for them. *"I'm grateful that he can manage to quell their mischievous behavior when they act out. However, satisfying such desires is not approved of."* Standing near the exit, he looks up at the ceiling covered in moss.

Outside, the sky continues to unleash harsh droplets of ice. Vicious freezing winds are howling. Thunder is rumbling louder after sparks of blue light flash through the thick cover of heavy, dark gray clouds.

Fürthrived is providing a shield over them, clinging to Valcomix's soft fur while TÖ-Slüdge is walking beside him. Cretan is lagging behind and yawning, eyes feeling quite heavy. TSinged can see that he is tired. Valcomix notices as well. **"I told you to rest up, but you kept on playing,"** TSinged says, nagging at him.

Cretan rolls his eyes. **"It was hard to rest with Fürthrived around, and then your snoring got louder."** Cretan informs with a drowsy, annoyed tone. Fürthrived apologizes to him silently with a smile. TSinged sighs with a serious expression. Cretan trips and falls forward. TSinged reacts but is slow to aid. Valcomix's tail catches him in his stead.

**"TSinged, just carry him. It's a two-day journey to the next Free Zone by our pace. Or should I carry all of us,"** he suggests. and TSinged decides to lift Cretan quickly forming into a white plastic ball. After some distance traveled, Valcomix pulls the device from his left pocket.

The time is 5:03pm of 08/28/3175

Following the red line towards their destination, Fürthrived is breathing softly into his ear as she sleeps. He scratches it. TÖ-Slüdge giggles and smiles at him with a smirk. He snarls at her playfully. Watching them playing as he is following behind them. TÖ-Slüdge is enjoying herself, conversing with Valcomix. He doesn't realize his own expression. Valcomix notices and is concerned.

**"TSinged, you alright?"** he asks, genuinely caring for his teammate. **"Yeah, I am,"** he answers, but his expression shows anger. He sighs and asks again using the combined language. TSinged is now serious after hearing this dialect. **"Are you intimate with the girls?"** TSinged asks bluntly.

With a serious expression, Valcomix answers, **"Yes and strongly attached to them at that."** He admits. TSinged admires his honesty. He inhales and exhales silently. **"Okay, what are your intentions."** he asks, hoping to be answered with another honest-to-heart answer. Valcomix becomes serious.

**"Don't have any. I just got attached due to their kindness and I want give back. Is it wrong to have such desires?"** Valcomix asks not feeling as he committed any wrong doings. **"Were you after them yourself?"** Valcomix asks with a surprised tone. Caught him off guard with such a question. TSinged smiles upon hearing that and begins laugh.

TÖ-Slüdge is confused as to what they are speaking of or even about. During his laughing fit

TSinged stumbles onto his knees due to a misstep. TÖ-Slüdge bursts into laughter. Valcomix is concerned. TSinged quickly regains composure and shakes his head frantically. He then sees the look of concern on Valcomix. *Inhale*...

**"No, definitely not. Because of their perverted behavior. And yours adding in, it became much more unbearable and disgusting. To watch knowing that you're all playing with each other's emotion. But seeing you care about them. I accept but do keep it moderate especially in front of Cretan and I. Please."** TSinged requests with a plea. Valcomix nods his head with a gentle and a serious smile.

**"I will do that. TSinged, you sound like a mom not wanting to have her daughter marry,"** Valcomix clarifies as he turns back his head now facing forward. **"I have been their nanny for some years so you better understand."** TSinged says half-jokingly. Valcomix faces forward. **"Thank you."** He says smiling at TÖ-Slüdge. But is showing gratitude to TSinged who is now smiling with pride.

Soon enough, they reach a frozen canal of a small wasteland, with no signs of life, just rubble and damaged buildings tattered by age. **"Is this a Free Zone?"** TÖ-Slüdge asks, examining the area. **"No, a**

**weapon-targeting area."** He answers while staring at the sky. Stopping here for a small rest. His ears e twitch. *Notification* Expecting it. And it reads.

"**All C.O.A.T.S. are to remain inside during the ice storm.**" Reading the message as if he knew. He then looks over the walkway out to the solid ice canal. **"Our checkpoint is on the vast waters of Lake Erie near the Free Zone,"** Valcomix informs them. The two approach him and join him. All starring out to the frozen canal.

TSinged is sanding lose by to stay warm while TÖ-Slüdge is leaning on him. The sky gradually gets darker, and the ice is falling faster, as well as increasing in mass. Then, a red bolt of intense electricity breaks the ice. The infected radius is glowing, and red currents scatter around the ice. Underneath, something is chasing after the light.

Witnessing the strand strike the canal, TSinged jumps back. Valcomix's ears twitch. **"We are done resting. Let's go,"** TSinged says as he steps off the walkway. TÖ-Slüdge agrees and follows behind him. Valcomix growls at the sky. His veins emerge from his back and tangle TÖ-Slüdge. He lifts up, TSinged, securing everyone in his grasp. His hairs are raising, and he rushes on, launching himself with a single step.

The lightning is attracted to heat, and they're a target. Running through the ruined town for shelter, avoiding the strikes as he runs and jumps off the icy grounds. Moving quickly and still unable to find cover, he hardens his hands. The layer of bone is thick. His knuckles are ready.

He punches through a wall and shields everyone at the furthest wall. The sudden storm has all of them scared. Fürthrived is awake, and so is Cretan.

**"This is not an ice storm as predicted. It's the beginning of something much worse!"** Valcomix yells, flinching from all the lights flashing and striking from above. The wind is swirling violently. Soon, the lightning storm subsides and only zips through the clouds.

**"Valcomix, what storm is coming?"** Cretan asks, concerned and curious. Standing still, they can feel rumbling from the earth. **"An earthquake?"** TSinged asks, questioning the strange phenomenon.

**"This is the mass buildup of the collected trade winds and cloud pressure approaching from the North. We have to reach Playground NY's subterranean subway system."** Valcomix mentions as he puts the destination in the device. **"We have to**

**escape this storm by any means. The Quadricane is starting."** He informs them, angry at the sky.

The four are confused. **"What's that?"** Fürthrived asks, tapping his shoulder. He glares at the uneducated bunch. **"Remember the twin funnels back in Playground, WA?"** he asks. They nod their heads, answering him. Relieved. **"This storm is just double that and can last for thirty up to forty-six days. It's their month,"** Valcomix informs them, and TSinged is ready to leave. **"Can we go now?"** TSinged asks as a statement, and they follow him out. The sky's winds are steadily increasing in speed.

# PART III

## EIGHTEENTH DIVISION CAMP OF PLAYGROUND IL

Within the housing quarters where the C.O.A.T.S. share their residence with scientists, everyone is giving Maira Devie their attention. A blonde, short-haired, Japanese/Korean/Hispanic, muscular yet slender woman with hazel-colored eyes and a light tan-brown complexion, wearing black sportswear, who is now addressing the group.

**"We have been updated on the occurring storm building up outside. It's a Quadricane,"** she informs them, showing them the device. Displeased by the news, some groan.

**"What about our equipment?"** Ovaiya Mist asks, sitting on the polished floor. **"We had our troops gather them to one of the bases. What about our supplies, including meals?"** Baron Roe asks, concerned and anxious. Baron is a bald, very brawny, Caucasian/Russian/Japanese male with green eyes and a peach complexion, wearing a plain blue shirt and black and grey shorts.

Coming from the side door of the entertainment center are two individuals. Victor H. Lune, a Greek/German male with long black suave hair, pale blue eyes, and a pale peach complexion, is wearing a white cat onesie. Nikki Juan is wearing gray sweats. Most of them laugh at the onesie.

**"What? It's an adorable creature. Don't you agree with me, Sir Trenton?"** Victor asks, putting his hands on the hood and covering his face with a new one. Bright blue shining eyes.

**"Purr up to him so he doesn't feel lonely,"** Maira says in a degrading tone, teasing him. Everyone enjoys the teasing. The scientists can see that their faction can, in fact, have fun. Trenton grumbles.

**"Honestly, my wife and two daughters decided to switch out my casual nightwear for this one to match our cat. For our supplies we are well stocked. We have food to last for at least three weeks if rationed correctly. Since the updated storm is unexpected, we have to minimize the kitchen's use. Other than that, the two generators are fully charged, and there are many necessities to clean ourselves and the fabrics, but it's the cheap products. We should log what is used, then have it replaced."** He informs with a serious tone as he looks at the listing on his device.

**"Also, we ordered the headquarters using your title, Sir Trenton, and had all C.O.A.T.S. activate their devices. Then, we sent out the alert. Most of the bases free from the storm will try to provide needed groceries when in dire need. Most bases within the proximity of the Quadricane's trajectory need them now,"** Nikki informs the appointed highest-ranking soldier. Trenton inhales deeply and exhales calmly.

**"Yet we're sheltering inside a platoon. We don't have a basement, but we can manage. Suviron Arc, I do apologize for having you and your team left in this condition. Also, taking extreme accountability. That creature and its team are outside, probably looking for shelter as well. Can Dorm engineer upgrades on our weapons, along with traps?"** Trenton C. Calhous requests from the leading scientists.

**"They can, but what about those in the Northern bases?"** Suviron Arc asks Trenton, who looks crestfallen by his question. Xin U. Mityus, a French/African/ American female with short platinum-blonde hair, silver-colored eyes, has an ebony skin tone, is wearing a graphic t-shirt with a wolf devouring zombies and graphic lounge pants with pink roses set on fire. She shows Trenton her device.

"No confirmation." Her expression is emotionless, but he notices her eyebrows twitching, just as annoyed as he is. **"No response. Alright, everyone, we're going to be left here together. There should be rules,"** he says with a menacing glare.

**"No snoring, be courteous to others while they are at peace, men on one side, women on the other. Share the TV. Bathroom rules apply as normal. Everyone cleans and shares tasks, and if anyone becomes insane, we toss them outside. Any complaints?"** Lien Servia announces with a stern boisterous tone. Her violet eyes are glaring at everybody as her short white hair sways. She is a Caucasian/Russian female with a muscular body and a pale peach complexion, wearing black sportswear.

**"What do you mean by insane?"** Hitomoni asks, confused. **"Small place to roam. Limited entertainment. Sharing a space with others. Limited food. Anyone can get anxious. A few fights can break out, whether physical or verbal. After some days, you're going to want to go outside, so instead, we take cold showers. Awaken the mind. We all went through it,"** Baron Roe answers as he sits on his bunk, ready to read a book. His comrades agree.

## MONROE, PLAYGROUND MI'S FREE ZONE

### The time is 8:46am of 08/31/3175

Vast areas of crops host vegetable gardens and abandoned greenhouses. The food is frozen, and the glass on the greenhouses is dirty and damaged by age and weather. The streams flowing through the crops are frozen as well. The land is ice blue and sparkling. Those that thrive in this area are three-horned, bush-tailed, thorn-haired gray rabbits, hamsters, gerbils, common field snakes, and other small creatures.

**"How is this considered a Free Zone if there is no shelter?"** TSinged complains as he feels the rumbling of the earth. Small animals are all just walking over their feet and gathering food, then returning underground. Valcomix leads the group and chuckles as he feels the small critters scampering, tickling his feet.

**"Free Zones are abandoned lands, properties, or other areas that were owned by people who tried to remain outside. Yet, they just couldn't. Now, it belongs to lower threat levels sometimes a 3 but mainly a 2 and under. Raccoons are an exception as the highest accounted predator. Why are you interested in the Playgrounds now?"** He asks as the freezing winds howl and push back.

The other three are focused on TSinged. **"Just curious because there are mainly snakes around us,"** he answers while kicking the scaly serpents away from him. Some hiss at him.

**"Snakes are actually harmless in the Playgrounds, thanks to thick hazard suits. Not even the venomous ones could penetrate through it. Swamp areas are hazardous and eerie. Leeches are a top concern. Dirt fields that are wet can house the deadliest of worms. I hate both, especially worms. Too many dragged. They hate alcohol, so we dropped tons of salt and isopropyl on them. Then burn them. Their squirming and screaming were satisfying to watch and hear,"** he says with a depraved, violent smile as he reminisces the scene, scaring his teammates.

Now, they reach solid ice, so cold that the top layer is covered by a mist. Valcomix takes the first step. His feet slide a bit, and his white layers of fur harden, forming sharper claws and nails. Managing to walk easily, he sees himself just as he becomes new.

Fürthrived tries to step on the ice, but her radiative aura causes the frozen surface to crack. As she approaches the lake, the ice breaks. TÖ-Slüdge pulls her arm, giving her friend a scolding expression. Fürthrived laughs nervously.

TSinged and Cretan step on the ice, and they both slip. Valcomix catches them both before they fell, lending his veins to them. TSinged is skeptical and disgusted to even take hold of it. Cretan is surprised by its warmth and stickiness. By the touch, it is smooth, dry, and firm, similar to a snake's skin but it's not scaly.

**"Fürthrived, jump on my back. TÖ-Slüdge, take my tail. Cretan keep hold on my vein. TSinged, do you want to hold my vein, or would you rather hold my hand?"** Valcomix offers his hand out gentlemanly to TSinged while the girls do as they are ordered, happily cuddling his soft fur as they whisper sweet compliments.

TSinged steps away from his hand and veins, not trusting that needle. TSinged lays his grasp on his hand. The two are embarrassed, hating this type of physical bond. He pulls all of them onto the ice. For some time now, as the storm is growing and becoming more violent, the ice is rumbling and loud popping harmonizes with the whistling howling winds. Something is stalking them under the ice.

# PART IV

It is difficult moving forward due to pulling everyone when the ice is slippery and managing to grip the surface of it with each careful step. The winds are roaring and swirling, pulling them back, and the rumbling effect on the area is quaking.

The ice is cracking as clumps of shattered pieces are carried by the approaching vortexes. Cretan is tightening his grip, fearing for his life as his eyes are shut. TSinged is kneeling as he cannot get to a standing position. TÖ-Slüdge, as well, as she is grasping his tail. Fürthrived is increasing her heat, radiating a barrier to no avail as the strong winds reach in and push them back.

Valcomix snarls. He uses his veins to wrap up TSinged and Cretan firmly at his sides. Then, he pulls his tail to set TÖ-Slüdge on his back and secures the two girls with the use of it.

He then slams his hands onto the ice. With a powerful kick, he starts to run. The movement upsets TSinged's stomach. Cretan is wide-eyed and terrified. Fürthrived is excited. TÖ-Slüdge is keeping her head down. Valcomix is smiling menacingly, leaping and sliding away from the clumps of ice. Then... **Breaking* *Cracking* *Shatter**

Freezing cold water pushes them back a few feet. A wide opening is ahead of them. Valcomix snarls angrily, growling at the ice below him. A silhouette bangs the ice from underneath them. Their hearts are beating faster, as something underneath is sending them towards the opening. Having trouble gripping the ice, the creature comes up with an idea.

**"Fürthrived, TÖ-Slüdge, maintain a tight grip."** he orders them, feeling a strong pinch on his shoulders and neck.

He then swings his tail. The sharp-bladed tip stabs the ice, hooking them. Using it to pull himself and the team he carries away from the opening and to escape the vacuuming winds, the being from underneath slams into the ice, weakening the surface of their location.

Terrified. He then releases the grappled end to slide sideways towards the right. Arms are raised, and legs bent, using a powered press to jump. Bending his arms under his chin, he lands roughly and uses his tail to anchor. Setting the weight to slow himself down, the creature then gets an idea as he feels the bladed edge tip grace the ice.

Now able to keep sturdy and stand on the slippery surface, he kicks off, running while sliding his tail across the ice, keeping the edge flat and cutting into the ice.

The being underneath creates another opening, and a huge spiraling of bone plates layering at the spine of its tail emerges, splashing about, widening the created opening and wetting the surface area and them. Fürthrived's heat is soothing as she helps dry her teammates.

Keeping focused, the creature changes direction with the weight of his tail as it hooks and anchors. Pulled back by the vacuuming winds, he digs his nails into the ice to avoid being dragged further behind. The being from underneath attempts its strategy again.

The creature quickly swirls its tail, then whips it ahead of him, causing it to move forward. Kicking off once more, the opening is made behind them. Feeling the ice rumbling, cracking, and splitting, everyone witnesses what is chasing them as its armored head is meters behind them, swimming through the thick water while breaking the ice.

**STURGEON:** Freshwater boss fish that can have an average length of thirty feet. But can reach up to thirty-three and a half. They are orange-bellied, with dark grassy green scales, and their spine is sharp and rigid protruding from their backs are gray. Mainly armored, they have tough scales that can bounce back hammers. Their bulky round heads are reinforced with concentrated calcium, and their eyes are so small that they seem eyeless.

**2**-Avoid the tail by any means. The tail acts as more than just a rudder and a useful kick. It can vibrate fast enough to have the head smash through solid earth. They can jump out of the water, reaching meters high. These creatures mainly swim at the bottom of most lakes and rivers, eating the vegetation, but as the weather changes, their diet changes to other fish, and they can perform cannibalism. Attracted to shiny things, like most fish, also they are an endangered species.

**3**-Threat level: Uncategorized. Avoid lakes and rivers, and they're no threat. Avoid swimming in such territories if you don't have the gills.

The massive fish is thrashing through the ice. Soon enough, Valcomix can feel the snow under his paws. The storm is approaching and becoming terrifyingly louder while the Sturgeon is eating ice just to keep up its chase. Meters away from it all, Valcomix trips from the change in terrain. TÖ-Slüdge lands on her side near

Cretan, whom she accidentally touches. Fürthrived laughed hysterically as she kept her grip on his fur. Valcomix is snickering while half his body is in a pile of snow. TSinged...

**Retching* *Coughing** The torsion of his stomach feels unsettling. At least there are no contents coming out, but everyone else is becoming sick as they look at him with disgust. **"We're finally on..."** TSinged says, relieved but noticing the coalescing clouds swirling heavily, pulling in snow and huge chunks of debris and ice. Wide-eyed and scared, Valcomix pulls out the device and checks the map. They left the lake too early.

## MILLCREEK, PLAYGROUND PA

## The time is 11:10am of 08/31/3175

Annoyed by the location and how close the storm is, Valcomix quickly tosses the device to Cretan as the map remains open. He then takes everyone and secures them where he settled them. Rushing fast along the side of the lake through the town destroyed by worldly natural disasters, loose and light debris is carried over his head.

Running along the lake's shore, they witness a phenomenon that continues to grow more dangerous.

A dark, thick gray, and blue mass built of gathered clouds is swirling in a violent cyclone, pulling ice, debris, and water into its body. It is a wondrous and terrifying sight. Red flashes of light can be seen as well.

Valcomix returns his focus to seeking shelter from what's approaching. Reaching his fastest pace while keeping near the shore, he eyes the youngest member seriously. Cretan keeps a tight hold on the device as he shows Valcomix. They're close, but so is the storm.

Now, entering the downtown district of their destination, he searches frantically for an underground entryway. Sighting rubble creating a blockage to their safety, Valcomix slashes the heavy chunks of structured blockade with teeth and claws. TÖ-Slüdge considers that mostly unnecessary as she raises an eyebrow. Biting his way through; it's expressed on her face that she is surprised. Fürthrived and Cretan are both awed by his strong jaw. TSinged's stomach is unsettled.

Valcomix enters the underground area and, using her light, Fürthrived exposes the infestation of giant cockroaches. They accost the group, unwilling to share space with the surface dwellers. The team is prepared, but TSinged is on all fours, touching the dirty, mucked, moist, and cold flooring. This time, he does release some contents from his stomach. As he does so, the others quickly exterminate the roaches without the need of effort. Valcomix then pulls everyone deeper into the area where the tracks are. Now, all safe as some dust falls from above.

## BUFFALO, PLAYGROUND NY

### The time is 2:01pm of 08/31/3175

Relieved, but a new concern is expressed on Valcomix. His teammates are mentally exhausted, and TSinged's stomach wasn't feeling well as he was holding it. Staring at the device, he shuts it down.

# PART V

The team remains quiet. All of them are nervous. Cretan changes his skin and balls himself up into his heaviest form. TSinged leans on the wall while holding the rail of the track. Fürthrived is holding TÖ-Slüdge's hand and gripping it tight. Valcomix's heart is beating fast as his arms are folded. His body aches due to overexertion.

Just hearing the horrid winds and feeling the earth rumbling, he takes a silent breather, waiting patiently. Their found shelter seems to be sturdy enough. Valcomix exhales with relief, placing a hand on his chest, feeling his heart pound. Then, he relaxes his stiff body and lays himself on his tail.

TÖ-Slüdge relaxes as well. Fürthrived chuckles, then rests her head on her lap. TSinged wants to relax, but his stomach growls. He then rummages through the pack filled with fruits. Valcomix growls at him with menacing, scarlet, bright eyes. **"How long can those fruits last us? We're going to be sheltering here for a month or over. Our supplies need to last,"** he informs TSinged.

TSinged passes him the pack filled with a variety of gathered fruits. Valcomix puts effort into getting up from his position and then lifts the pack. Its weight is acceptable. He looks inside, *"There is enough but the fruits don't last more than a week they'll spoil."* He then inhales as he closes his eyes, using only hearing, smell, and touch.

Sighting strong bluish-white figures of four beings, the earth rumbling is interfering, but he slightly senses the skittering of many creatures crawling. Snarling as his head starts to throb, he focuses on the skittering. A vague static of dark blues pictures something alive.

The pain is unbearable as he shakes his head and then stumbles. He gives TSinged back the pack and returns to his resting position, rubbing his aching head, exerted both mentally and physically, exhausted. TÖ-Slüdge pets his head and softly scratches his fur. With a caring smile, she asks, **"Are you okay?"** in a gentle tone. Valcomix nudges his head, giving into the pleasure.

**"Just overexerted myself. TSinged, try to have it last for about a week"** He requests with a quiet yet coherent tone, resting his eyes. **"I'll do so. Now, go to sleep,"** TSinged orders Valcomix as he takes a plum from the pack. Valcomix is already slumbering along with Cretan, who is still in ball form. Fürthrived is resting on TÖ-Slüdge's lap while she is lying on top of Valcomix. TSinged is the only one awake, staring at Valcomix, awed by his new appearance. His mind is swirling with questions to ask about his current evolution and their situation, also about those people he saved.

*"What is your reason, pup?"* he asks, keeping watch on him and the two that are attached. Finishing up satisfying his stomach, he then lulls to sleep as he sees everyone else at peace.

After a good rest, Fürthrived is the first to rise, rubbing her right eye and slowly opening it. Sighting from her position, she sees TÖ-Slüdge resting her head on Valcomix. It's a cute scene to see, but she is bored. Understanding that the storm is going to continue for a while and that if she roams around freely, the two boys are going to freeze. Seeing her friend slumbering but exposing her navel, Fürthrived smiles mischievously, poking at TÖ-Slüdge's side and listening to her mumble, giggling as quietly as possible.

After some more light teasing and playful actions, she feels a sharp jab at her side. Rubbing away the ache as she continues her play, she feels another sharp poke at her side. She then sees sharp teeth and bright eyes glaring at her upside down. Smiling nervously, she apologizes silently.

**"Bored again?"** Valcomix whispers as he chuckles. She blinks once and nods her head. **"We're going to be here for a while,"** she says, rolling her eyes, offsetting the gesture as a misuse. Using one of his veins, he pokes her side. TSinged is awake due to the two individuals acting adorable. It's annoying. He returns to sleep with a groused expression.

Fürthrived lifts her head from TÖ-Slüdge's lap and then walks slowly to Valcomix's other side. Pulling her closer, he engages in a word game. The rules are: one starts a word, and the last letter of the said word is used as the first letter of the next one. Repeated words are a forfeit, and more than three seconds of thinking is a loss.

Already smiling victoriously, she thinks she has won. Whispering back and forth for some time now. *"Several,"* Fürthrived says fast. *"Lime,"* Valcomix says back just as quickly. This is the two-hundred-forty-third word said. *"Electric,"* Fürthrived says with a raised eyebrow, ready to predict what his next one may be. *"Citrus,"* he says with a relaxed tone. She then pinches his cheek. *"How come you've only been using food-based names, scents, and flavors? Spheritic,"* she asks with a menacing smile as she tries to win this game. He then whispers close to her ear. *"Because of how you tasted. Candlelight,"* he says, using her nickname. She blushes and warms up the area.

*"Trapped,"* she says, feeling in such a predicament. *"Deep,"* he says with a chuckle, knowing exactly what the next word is going to be. *"Pervert,"* she says nearly silently with a smile. He laughs and says, *"Tame."* She then closes her eyes. *"Emergency,"* she says, looking around for help.

Valcomix winces as he feels his ear being pulled. TÖ-Slüdge is wide awake and a bit upset. **"Enjoying a private game without me,"** she notifies them, her jealousy evident. He then pats her on the head, soothing her. Fürthrived smiles victoriously. Valcomix grumbles.

**"Can you three please relocate your affection elsewhere? I'm directly in front of this,"** TSinged is disturbed by their noise-making tendencies. Begrudgingly tired of witnessing such actions that are leading to depravity. He is still surprised and fascinated that a member of theirs is still able to sleep. They look at him as if he ruined their playtime. TSinged is glaring back at them.

After a moment of rest, they move from the spot and journey through the subway's tunnel. Cretan walks beside TSinged while the two girls flank Valcomix. Still having to view such annoyance, he relaxes his glare and hesitates a bit. With a deep inhale, he follows up with an exhale.

**"Valcomix, how did you gain your new appearance, and why were you set to be captured alive?"** he asks such questions bluntly. Valcomix is caught off guard. He looks behind himself and sees that TSinged is curious. Cretan is also curious.

**"I finished my leftovers. The giant beast has been consumed bones and all. But the reason why I was captured alive is because of my old clothing. I was wearing their uniform. Now I am another target."** Valcomix shares with everyone listening. Cretan then realizes that his style did change. **"How, we cannot modify the appearance even the color we desire."** He informs Valcomix with a wide eye fascinated expression. TSinged is surprised as well. *"He ate that much calcium so his fur is layered with bones. What!?"* Screaming in his own head.

They soon discover an adjacent tunnel, unlike the subway's, with the wall still wet. Remembering the nest, they're ready. Exploring the warm depths of the tunnel system, they descend towards lower levels. A few roaches are found, but they escape the light illuminating from Valcomix and Fürthrived. No other insects, just roaches sighted. Not as many as from the entrance blockage though.

Soon after, they listen to the sound of dripping. They find an infestation. Thousands of them, touching antennae, communicating with the hive. Valcomix doesn't hesitate as he approaches them. They move out of his way and allow him to drink their water.

Almost resembling the queen's nest schematics, a huge opening is on the other side. At least this place doesn't have a stench. Fürthrived leads the rest, and the roaches bother no one. **"Our food supply is stocked,"** Cretan says joyfully as if he knows the predicament. **"Cretan, you heard us last night?"** TÖ-Slüdge asks him, and he nods his head. **"Valcomix sounded upset with TSinged about it. Also, eating fruits is nice, but I'm craving meat or such things that will suffice just as much,"** he admits, waiting for Valcomix to attack one. Valcomix approaches the darker opening.

**"There is a queen,"** TSinged says, sounding surprised about the huge roach coming out of its nesting area. Without hesitation, Valcomix slashes the huge pest with his tail and claws. Stabbing his syringe-like veins into its hard-layered skin, he renders it legless first, then kicks its head, breaking the outer skin and exposing the muscle and tissue of the meat.

Only taking what is needed to satisfy his hunger, he is not as voracious as at other times but still brutal. He peers down at it with no remorse, respect, or emotion. The roaches scatter into the nest area, leaving the vast side of this room to their invaders. They just look at him as if he did something wrong, shaking their heads.

The room is big and somehow clean. Even the water is pure and clear. From the other side, the huge queen is dragged into the dark. Valcomix is snickering. **"Third time I witnessed cannibalism by them,"** he says, soaking his feet.

TÖ-Slüdge goes in for a swim. Cretan rolls around and changes his skin while doing so. TSinged is dodging his attacks. Fürthrived settles into the water to splash TÖ-Slüdge. All are able to push aside boredom. Valcomix chuckles, remembering the old days. Those times, he went insane and started instigating fights and had to be put in a cold place.

# PART VI

## PLAYGROUND WV, SECTOR: 32

### The time is 3:16pm of 10/16/3175

Trenton C. Calhous is checking his device for a sent message listing their equipment. Soldiers are opening trucks and checking off inventory. All C.O.A.T.S. ranked 4 and higher are issued new rifles and given a manual. Butterflies are taking off into the sky. Arrows are operational. Trenton is answering messages and sending mission plans.

"All beaches are blockaded. Falcons and turtles are in the streets. Planted weeds are set."

Reading this message while seeing the pictures of five dangerous individuals, he notes, "5DBs. 5 Deadly Bios. Shoot on Sight. Last located in Playground NY." He sends, bearing the band on his right arm with three golden stars. Now officially titled... **Trenton C. Calhous, Rank: MD9QR.**

## LABORATORY'S CORRIDOR

Walking down the clean white hallway are Ovaiya Mist, Tingi Vendalic, David Free, and Hitomoni Free. They approach the office of **Suviron Arc: Nuclear Specialist, Bioengineer, Physicist, Chemist, and Science Faction Head Lead**.

Ovaiya knocks on the door, and it opens. The four of them enter and see many people, numbering sixteen. Eleven are from the engineering/manufacturing faction, four from the governmental faction, and one individual who bunked with them. The scrawny male They all leave the main office of his lab, which resembles a high school classroom lab with the same layout.

The four find a seat and place themselves in front of the room. The scrawny individual is upset with a twisted, angered expression, quite ugly. **"You'll have to excuse the boy; he was not offered a promotion to become my probationer,"** Suviron informs them, feeling just as disappointed. He allows them entry and has them seated. Now, he stands in front of his colleagues.

**"From before, they have received their new toys. The soldier that we were told was killed by the storm is a hoax. This is between only us, for we were once close with him as well."** Suviron Arc informs and then coughs for a moment. The four wait patiently for him to continue.

**"Valcomix, Valcomix is the soldier they wanted us to cure; now he is the main target for his crime. He intends to cross over the ice,"** he informs them. Tingi is astonished, showing anger, yet he is relieved. Conflicted by emotions, David Free is indifferent. Ovaiya Mist is smiling. Hitomoni Free is furious. **"We cannot help him now,"** David Free mentions.

**"I just wanted to let you all know. It is also thanks to his blood that we have a plant killer. It was given approval."** Sir Arc shows them the document with the seal of approval by the madam. David Free is excited. Tingi nods his head. Ovaiya Mist leans back in the chair, folding her arms.

**"Then we should work to spread that blight. Also, you shouldn't favor that fallen soldier like Mr. Kiel who is facing trial now these past few days. Valcomix is now their target, and they will not allow him to leave and surely kill the creature. Those five are going to fall,"** Hitomoni says with evil in her eyes, spitting out malice and misfortune. She then removes herself from the room.

Ovaiya Mist is baffled by how violent her tone is understanding where her anger and hate is coming from. Suviron Arc is joyous and smiling. It's a bit offsetting by his appearance, but Mrs. Mist is happy for him. Valcomix became something adorable and very much troublesome. Staring at the sign documents with a satisfied demeanor. David Free is disgusted by the atmosphere of the room and wants to get out.

## PLAYGROUND NY, UNDERGROUND SUBWAY TRAIN STATION

### The time is 4:52pm of 10/16/3175

Valcomix is scrolling through the messages, checking the map app, and seeing their announced infamous names. The beach directly east is occupied by them. All of Playground NY is occupied. The Free Zones are as well. Trying to draw out a line, but each direction is heavily occupied by them. Cretan looks worried as he stares over his left shoulder. TSinged's arms are glowing.

**"Can we get into Canada?"** TSinged asks, considering the best option. **"No, there is a border wall. Playground ID has an opening along with VT and ME,"** Valcomix answers him as he still tries to draw a line. Then TSinged glares at him with an expression of, 'That kind of information is late.'

TÖ-Slüdge can see he is frustrated. **"Which direction is the least worrisome?"** she asks, knowing the situation is unavoidable. Fürthrived hugs him from behind. **"They started their actions first; we are eight days late,"** Valcomix snarls angrily. **"Pick the less dangerous path or the shortest one that is most difficult. I'm ready to fight."** TSinged suggests, knowing Valcomix doesn't want to fight.

Valcomix understands the choice he made. Abandoning humanity and telling Trenton what he intends to do, he zooms in on the map, sighting various checkpoints. The destination, Playground MA, Sector 38, is four hundred eighty-two miles away, while Playground VT, Sector 23, is three hundred ninety-five miles away, but they are heavily occupied. Butterflies, turtles, falcons, and weeds are set on the routes.

He understands they have to preserve their energy for the long journey over the ice.

Then there is an idea. There are forests and lakes on a route to Playground VT, Sector: 23. Playground ME is less occupied, but it will take longer to reach one of the beaches. He sets variable checkpoints, remembering that he got captured on the first day. Trying to plan their escape while thinking about his opponents' probable moves, the team can see that this is going to take a while.

**The time is 8:51pm of 10/16/3175.**

Valcomix finally stands up, approaching Cretan, who is rolling around. He catches him and watches as he unravels himself. Then he passes him the device with four drawn lines reaching Playground ME's many beaches. Looking at it with a scared expression, Valcomix kneels and lays a gentle but strong grip on his shoulder.

**"Cretan, don't be pressured. It's still my burden to give you this. They know me well, but the C.O.A.T.S. doesn't know you. I cannot use the device when I'm going to be protecting all of you."** Valcomix says to him with a pleading smile. Cretan is having trouble making a decision. But seeing the smiles on the four individuals around him he hesitantly takes the device.

**"You all are meant to protect Cretan and yourselves. This is my stand to fight them, when necessary,"** he announces to everyone standing at the ready. Valcomix then goes into the dark room. His lit body is swallowed into it. TSinged saw him smiling evilly. He then looks at everyone. **"Be ready,"** he orders, and then...

***SCREEAHHHH!!!*** That sound terrifies all except for Fürthrived, who is excited.

## OUTSIDE

C.O.A.T.S. are still walking the city with heavier ammunition. Vehicles that have an enhanced, upgraded GAU-19 attached to the top. A soldier taps her mask and holds a game controller. The machine activates and then moves remotely. Easy controls. Automatic lock-on settings. With many C.O.A.T.S. roaming this location, they got caught off guard...

*Hissing* Soldiers ready themselves. Thousands of roach's surface above ground. Butterflies shine light, getting them to move in a line. Ground soldiers shoot them down with ease. Their upgrades made a difference.

Then they notice something bright moving fast. They try to chase it, but the pile of fallen roaches does not give them a chance to do so. Valcomix is again carrying everyone and rushing, launching himself as he runs, gliding swiftly. Butterflies are on the move, firing missiles, and Valcomix dodges them. Firing heavy rounds rapidly, he then jumps onto the ice of Lake Ontario. Six butterflies are above him. The searchlights keep sight of his movements. Valcomix smiles viciously...

*Crack* *Shatter* Sturgeons break through the ice. Valcomix keeps running while the butterflies turn back, retreating. Valcomix is now the only target for these fish.

Two sturgeons are working together to have a satisfying meal. The creature is rushing, digging its claws into the ice for a firm grip, sliding, and anchoring his tail. TSinged's stomach is unsettling once more. Cretan shows him the device map. Valcomix can see that he made a choice. TSinged is uncomfortable.

Valcomix kicks off stronger, gliding longer distances. Cretan is amazed, TÖ-Slüdge is awed, and Fürthrived is still excited, feeling the rush of the cold air even though she is to remain warm. Valcomix feels lighter. The sturgeons give up their chase. They then reach an island named Galloo.

**The time is 2:29 am on 10/17/3175.**

Cretan shuts down the device. Valcomix is exhausted and is resting. TSinged is picking the fruits while the girls are out hunting. Cretan stares at the screen, remembering the routes he made. Knowing the next time that the device has to be activated, he is going to have to lead them.

# PART VII

## PLAYGROUND VT, SECTOR: 23

### The time is 6:03am of 10/17/3175

It is raining heavily. The weather is horrible. Trenton and his gold star-bearing individuals are in a room within the base. Just a room with luxurious black leather couches. All of them are sending messages to their units.

## IN THE SKY

Butterflies are firing missiles on the island. It is set ablaze. They position themselves for anything to run for safety. Animals rush towards the beach only to fall to their wrath. Brutally gunned and blown up.

## PLAYGROUND NY, SACHETS HARBOR

Valcomix is breathing heavily and is exhausted. He is dimming, losing his pink hue. TSinged eases him down on the bank of the lake. Fürthrived is concerned, along with the rest of them gathered around him. TSinged then passes some fruits to Cretan, TÖ-Slüdge, and Fürthrived. Valcomix is asleep, slowly gaining back his pink hue. He had eaten heavily already on the island.

Soon enough, he awakens, still kind of groggy as he stumbles a bit, still managing to stand even though his body is aching and sore. He nods at Cretan, who then activates the device and shows it to Valcomix. He snarls at the time...

**The time is 11:44 pm on 10/21/3175**

Now, he is rushing. Soldiers are on the roads, firing at them. Butterflies are firing at them as well. Valcomix's arms are aching badly. He trips, and they see his arms shaking. Valcomix lets down the boys and stands up slowly as the girls get off his back. With no more load, he then rushes towards the bullets, unaffected by their rounds. Slashing the vehicles, ripping metal with ease, knocking others on their side, and ripping off their weaponry, he continues his assault. The butterflies are the most annoying.

Valcomix relaxes his hands, pulling back his claws, and then holds the machine gun from one of the vehicles he shredded. He unleashes his wrath and takes care of them easily by destroying their tail rotor. The main rotors cease their spinning, and the pilots jump out of the aircraft, spread their wing suits, and deploy their parachutes.

All of them land safely, with a few minor injuries such as twisted ankles and road rash. The helicopters go to the scrap yard for recycling. Valcomix tosses away the carried weapon and takes another one that is fully equipped.

Soldiers aim their rifles at him. **"Check each other for injuries,"** Valcomix orders as he returns to his teammates. Many of them want to take him down, but they have sustained damage. The soldiers focus on what is most important: getting the vehicles upright and attending to one another. TSinged pats him on the back, and they continue their route on foot.

## PLAYGROUND NY, LOWVILLE

An abandoned wood and textile factory. Industrial field. Cretan turned off the device. TSinged is tired, Valcomix is exhausted, and Fürthrived and TÖ-Slüdge are concerned.

Cretan is hungry. Hearing his rumbling stomach, TSinged passes him the pack. All are hiding inside the dirty area of the factory.

## PLAYGROUND VT, SECTOR: 23

Inside the same room with the couches. Most of them are annoyed, but they are all upset and frustrated.

## The time is 6:48 am on 10/26/3175

No casualties thus far. Nikki Juan is scratching her head, envisioning a plan. Baron Roe is sending a message, seeing that the arrows are deployed and swarming Playground NY. Knowing that the 5DBs are still within the area, planting weeds randomly will not suffice.

**"Do we know a route they're taking?"** Victor H. Lune asks with his head back and arms folded. **"No, and with our comrades on the search, we cannot have them shut down their devices. The butterflies gunning them were hunted. We can wait for them here or at the beaches,"** Lien Servia suggests.

**"It is us against Valcomix, but these actions and movements are random. They are approaching a center point, though. There are three exits,"** Maira Devie informs.

Then, with wide eyes, Xin U. Mityus checks the map and scrolls through the messages of their sightings. Placing pin marks, she sees that their route is random on an expanded scale. Minimizing the map to view a better-drawn line, C.O.A.T.S. covers majorly named cities and those with hidden alleys. There are sectors above the thirties: Sector 46.

She sends a message stating their next action and a plan. Upon reading it, most are a bit skeptical. Trenton glares at her. **"We'll follow through with this,"** he announces with a serious tone. He stands up and walks out of the room. The rest follow.

## PLAYGROUND NH, KEENE

### The time is 4:12pm on 11/02/3175

The five of them are exhausted. Chased for days and had protected themselves while Valcomix fought back without causing any casualties. Fürthrived is dim. TÖ-Slüdge holds her friend. Valcomix roughs up Cretan's black spiky hair.

TSinged checks the pack. Their supply is limited. They are surrounded by a vegetable farm that is mainly growing corn. But they're frozen solid. **"I understand how you were caught on the first day,"** TSinged says, sharing the fruits with his team.

**"They could have been using worse artillery on us,"** Valcomix says, lying on the soft, cold ground. **"Persistent bunch. Valcomix, are there any more apex creatures?"** TÖ-Slüdge asks, frustrated by the constant days of them pursuing her team. She is ready to...

**"Hopefully, we can reach the ice soon."** Fürthrived says with a tired expression, chewing on an apple.

**"We're close to the route. When there is an opening beach, we are then free. But the device is at five percent. I already shut it down,"** Cretan informs. TSinged punches his shoulder lightly. **"Best guidance than our furred menace,"** TSinged announces, feeling proud of the kid. *Laughter* Valcomix can see that this is a moment to relax, but... **"We mustn't celebrate early. Our destination is located in unknown territories,"** he informs them, and they understand.

**"TSinged, I'm ready to speak."** Valcomix announces with a serious expression. TSinged understands, but the others are confused, now facing him. **"I'm listening,"** he says with a gentle smile.

Valcomix chuckles a bit. **"I'm fighting my brothers and sisters. I saved them from Fürthrived because they're still family to me. I'm willing to fight without causing any casualties. Sevulix took away the lives of my unit. I failed to protect them and fight for them. I was spared because of my refusal to fight. Shown sympathy by a beast. That was after the day when I was able to meet them. Humans aren't allowed on the ice because they're weak. It was just an easy get in get out mission. Sevulix, that hawk and other apexes was**

**my goal. I was to raise humanity higher than all other species. I hated what you wanted me to be. I also hate them for creating this an issue. Given a second chance I am forgetting what it means to be human. I'm terrified of this change. I never intended for them to become an adversary. You may say capability isn't strength. Then how do I win? I became this and still lost against those apexes besides the hawk. I was human then. I forgot what my face looked like before this. Looking back just several months went by. Next month is winter. Playground ME, Rockland, is the location of exchanging gifts. I want to be seen by everyone there that I am stronger. You may say it's selfish but they stated this and I want them to fall. Our destination is Playground ME, Rockland on the ice."** He shares this with everyone and feels lighter as tears fall. Releasing pent up rage, anguish, and hurt. He now smiles. TSinged is furious.

**"Are you requesting to remain here another month? We cleared the black states! You now share valuable information that there are lives across the ice! Other strong?! Do we ask for permission?!"** he shouts at him. The others are surprised and can only watch.

**"Yes, if a proud leader such as Sir Kiel wouldn't use the C.O.A.T.S.' wrath against this enemy, then**

**they must be dangerous. Also, permission is needed. You have to face them on the ice"** he tells TSinged with a serious expression.

**"No. I knew I doubted you for a reason. TÖ-Slüdge, Fürthrived, Cretan, go somewhere else for a moment,"** he orders with the same glare of hate/ hell. Valcomix remains calm. **"I'll do so without your privilege. I'm thankful you saved my life. But they had me in a stronger bond. You continue to protect them while I fight. I thought I could prolong this journey. Cretan, pass me the device, please,"** he requests, and the eyes of TSinged terrify Cretan. Valcomix approaches the youngest member with a kind, gentle smile, giving up the device to him.

TÖ-Slüdge is glaring at TSinged. Fürthrived is scared. **"Calm your yourself down,"** Valcomix tells TSinged. He then turns around, hiding his look. Glaring evilly at Valcomix as he holds the device, knowing that it is late and conflicted that Valcomix was hiding information. Who remains calm and collected while appearing to them as some good pup. TÖ-Slüdge is continuing to keep glaring at him. He walks away with his arms shaking and glowing.

Soon, the team is resting. TSinged is awake, still furious, and is away from them. Valcomix is sitting next to him. **"TSinged, want to talk about it?"** he asks with a sincere tone. **"No, you?"** he asks, still angry. **"Yes... I hated the weakness of myself and unleashed my frustrations on those close to me. I lost those that I said I would cherish,"** Valcomix explains his reasoning. TSinged now listens to his story. TÖ-Slüdge is hearing his tale and shedding tears for him. TSinged understands. Valcomix chuckles for a moment, feeling lighter. **"Do what you want; I'm not interfering,"** TSinged tells Valcomix, patting him on the shoulder, still frustrated with him but can relate.

The next morning a blizzard has started. Valcomix sends a message and then leaves the device in the snow. TSinged then leads them away from the area. Valcomix walks behind everyone with a serious expression but proud.

## PLAYGROUND VT. SECTOR: 23

### The time is 9:07am of 11/03/3175

Within the base's cafeteria, Trenton C. Calhous is ready to eat until... **Notification** He checks his device, then reads the message personally sent to him and the golden-starred children. "**I declare war on Rockland. One game. Pick your flagship wisely.**" Upon reading such a message, it doesn't surprise him.

Then another message from... "We'll be ready, all of us are going."

As the days pass, there haven't been any sightings of their military. Their exhaustion is recovered, and so is their food supply. Then Valcomix's ears twitch. He smiles at his teammates. TSinged then blocks the other three from following him or try to persuade him.

PLAYGROUND ME, SECTOR: 46

Xin U. Mityus texts, standing surrounded by her elite army along with her comrades and their elite units. Butterflies, falcons, and turtles are residing here. All C.O.A.T.S. under the chosen are camping here. Then, from afar, a few of the soldiers sight a figure approaching them. Maira Devie checks her device.

The time is 12:44pm on 12/24/3175

A butterfly flying about in the sky gives him the spotlight. Inside of it is the highest rank. The creature then snarls, and then... ***SCREEAHHHH!!!***
*Firing Rounds*

**TO BE CONTINUED...**

# EPISODE 15:
# Fallen Arrival

## PART I

Missiles and heavy rounds are fired by the second, directly aimed at their target. To no avail are they keeping a lock on it. Moving so swiftly avoiding the heavier attacks. On all fours is...

**VALCOMIX:** a beastlike creature, a terror that fell three apex monsters and the leader of the 5Deadly Bios. Disruptor of the Playgrounds. Threat level 14.5. Shoot On Sight.

Trenton is tossing cylinders at it while the pilot is using the butterfly's effect. The equipped barrels spin rapidly unleashing massive rounds upon it. Shells fall and the creature smiles menacingly within the clouded smoke. They are relentless in firing. The spiraling piercing bullets cease, but the explosions continue their song.

A cloud of violent black covers it. Now all is quiet. Arrows are sent to uncover the beast. Their mini propellors beat away the smoke. Uncovering a clump of rough white ridges. *Bones cracking and popping* Black liquid seeps from its wounds that heal instantly. Its four burning pink additions and its sharp ligament start to sway rapidly. Cutting away through weak metal. Destroying the drones. They unleash wrath once again. Trenton is barking orders while yelling, **"Keep firing, use the turtles!!!"**

Tanks take position ahead of the squads. Ninety-six at the ready, moving to confront it. Valcomix welcomes them. Rushing towards them. They have a lock on it and unload violence. Valcomix relies on hearing; dodging rounds that are close to a size of a house cat. He makes it to one of the leading turtles and takes a bite.

Bits of hot metal burn its tongue as it now stands on top of it. The tank's barrel is removed. Using its claws, teeth, bladed edge, and piercing veins to shred an opening. Now three soldiers are sighting their target. *Snarling* Its saliva is spilling onto their technology. Frightening the soldiers inside. Causing one of them to quiver and then a heavy scent of ammonia. Valcomix is disappointed. **"Soldier did you really?"** He asks staring at the person. **"Get out."** He orders making a wider opening for them to escape. Now the three of them lay flat on their stomach upon the sand covered stones.

Valcomix jumps quick and headbutts another turtle. Giving himself a slight headache. Understanding that he himself is not heavier than a tank. But he does manage to put a dent in it; his claws are enough. Now rubbing his head.

Quickly working to remove their long barrels, along with scaring them with his adorable face. Valcomix is having fun. Smiling mischievously. Until the butterflies shine concentrated lumens on to him. Burning his eye sight. Twenty butterflies are firing upon him. Running randomly now and then feels a jolt of electricity surging through him. **"He tripped on a weed!"** Trenton informs with a serious yell. Sighting a furred menace being shocked by a field of electricity connected by four rods. Valcomix is struggling by the weird sensation. His four veins are unbothered by the effect. Wrapping around one of the rods and pulling him out to safety. His muscles are still spasming

Coughing up vital viscous liquid. His fur is flickering pink and scarlet. The fired heavy rounds feel like droplets of hail. Another round from the missiles and other explosive projectiles. Valcomix takes a breath. Feeling a pause in time relying on other instincts. Remembering his moments with his brothers and sisters, his praise worthy accomplishments. Then envisions on his days outside. Free. That is all he ever wanted to be. But his weakness didn't allow such a thing. Now he has to prove it. *Heart beating* Remembering those apexes. With an innocent smile upon his face, he exhales calmly with his claws and bladed edge ready.

Disowning his humanity as he once again stays on all fours. Sighting blue, white, and black. Using his quick moving tail and veins like Sevulix. One of the butterflies got close to aim straight at its face. With a powerful press the creature lunges and wraps its tail and veins for a hold. The aircraft rolls left. The pilot and a soldier in the passenger's seat now sight the creature cutting through the aft. Letting itself in. The soldier is ready to fire but Valcomix catches his rifle. **"It isn't smart to fire rounds in an aircraft."** He warns the individual. Then a few minutes pass and they lost sight of it. **"Yeah, it's aboard our aircraft. Butterfly-GA. #3628-MID is occupied. What should we do? No, it's not attacking us. Creepily staring at us sir."** The pilot is conversating with his superior. The others are surrounding this butterfly. Soon the door opens. The force of air rushes in. Trenton has sights on the creature and it seems excited.

# PART II

**"Take us down near ground level."** Valcomix orders with a laugh. **"Sir, this creature is telling me to go hover a few feet from the ground."** The pilot says informing his lead.

## Near the beach

Standing on rough edges of rocks and sand just a mile from the frozen salt. Xin is keeping a close watch using her specialized rifle's scope. Observing the centered butterfly descending and the surrounding ones are doing so as well. She quickly texts her comrades. They begin reading the messages. **"It took down all of our turtles and now it's after the butterflies. Get Trenton away from it."** Lien says with an angered tone. **"At least he isn't spilling blood."** Baron mentions. **"But, indirectly it did. We lost five of our kin and one had to separated. He lost her arm and was exposed to the toxic air."** Maira reinforms Baron with a crestfallen and serious tone.

Feeling remorseful. Nikki is sending a text. Then hears static, she taps her forehead's mask, pressing a button. **"You came up with a plan?"** Trenton asks with a despondent tone. Sounding as if he lost the battle. She looks to everyone else and, no one has a plan. **"No one has one. Why, Sir Trent, go claim us that a victory."** Nikki sounds with a cheerful tone and they shake their head. He chuckles. **"Trenton, you can either sacrifice them by friendly fire or to retreat and be put on standby. We have weeds planted here."** Victor tells him and everyone is mad with him. **"That still means to forfeit, all lives are precious. That will bring fear to our faction of my name. We're facing one and there are five of them. Then tomorrow is our meeting."** Trenton informs them and they are low in mind set. Xin texts fast.

## Trenton's Piloted Butterfly

He reads the message. Sighting the individual creature that is maintaining a proud smile. Frustrated. The creature is passed a device and puts it to its right ear. **"Give up. Valcomix, you and your team will fall here. You do know about tomorrow."** Hearing a threatening and agitated voice. **"Yes, and I want to meet with them. Sir Kiel allows them to stand upon the claimed Playgrounds. Yet no one is allowed to step on the ice. I became an enemy of the C.O.A.T.S. and no longer human. Take back your Playgrounds and focus on that victory. You ran a creature off. Log that and you'll deemed a higher title."** Valcomix says with a serious tone, snarling.

Trenton is upset. Watching it give up the device and is given two flares. It then jumps onto the butterfly in front of him. Using its veins to stab through the glass. From behind it shoots off both flares. The sky is lit by a bright white and red light.

Then surprised, it punches the glass and pulls the main rotor emergency brake lever. Then kills the engine. As the blades stops spinning. With a movement of its bladed edge, it cuts off the main rotor. Rendering it flightless. Valcomix does the same routine rather quickly rendering all of them unairworthy. Glaring at them with a smirk. Approaching the traps as he walks on heavier sands and stones. Using his veins to pull up the weeds and his tail to cut the rods. Valcomix is waiting for them to unleash another round of wrath.

From a distance they see a glimmer of orange and yellow. Their bombers are locked on target but the furred menace is also in front of them. It is a calm breeze on a delightful day where the sky is relaxed but very chilling as frozen mist blow pass. With a serious expression Valcomix walks through their numbers once more. Only facing forward.

## Rockland Harbor, Salted Ice

The time is 5:19pm of 12/24/3175

Valcomix's heart is beating rapidly. The cold sensation isn't new but the mental cost is frightening. Now he can no longer be targeted, but now has to approach them. Valcomix is shivering and TSinged lays a firm grip upon his shoulder. Fürthrived hugs him and TÖ-Slüdge is smiling while Cretan smells the salt in the air. **"So, we finally made it onto the ice."** Fürthrived says looking at the vast frozen flat of sea water. **"Valcomix, you shouldn't be so nervous."** TSinged says to him but he cannot help but be so.

The C.O.A.T.S. have lost. Now gathering equipment and tending to one another. Setting up loose camps and clearing away damage. While the 5DBs share food from the pack. All waiting for the next day to happen.

### Clarkes Harbour, Nova Scotia

An individual is pulling a metal and wood cart that has three sections filled with minerals and metals. Resting against the front of it on the pier with their feet touching the ice. *Snickering*

The sky over the harbour is heavily cloudy as if it has descended. Slumbering under white feathers and fur. Then is bonked on the head. Quickly awakening staring angrily at the older individual. Now pulling the cart across the frozen salt to the destination.

# PART III

## Rockland Harbor, Salted Ice (BEACH)

## Time is 7:22am of 12/25/3175

Trenton is focused on five individuals that can no longer be attacked. Him and his comrades are waiting for their yearly meeting with them. Staring at his device agitated but focused forward. Valcomix's ears twitch. Someone is approaching from the North West. TSinged awakens everyone else. A silhouette who seems to be struggling, then stops. Taking a few minutes and continues.

Sighting a person cloaked in white fur and feathers. Bones sticking out of the hood. Seeing that there are beings on the ice. *Tch* **"No one is allowed on the ice." [Gibberish]** Hearing the individual speak none of them can comprehend yet Cretan is mad. Valcomix takes a step forward. **"We're not humans."** He says using a serious tone. Everyone is surprised except for TSinged. The individual then let's go of the cart and removes his hood.

**"Humans are weak. So, prove your strength."** The guy says with a challenging demeanor with a smile as he gets into a stance. TSinged smacks his face, annoyed by another interaction. Sighting this light tan brown skinned, with dark green eyes, violet and gradient silver hair, skinny but well-toned muscular male that just removed his cloak. Wearing a bone plate on his chest, arms, legs, and gloves that are over a blue furred shirt and black furred pants.

Getting back into stance and excitingly hopping. Valcomix is welcoming this challenge as he now stands in front of him. **"If you die from my hands, I will wear your skin."** He says with depraved intentions but sounds innocent. Valcomix chuckles as he glares at him.

TSinged is annoyed. TÖ-Slüdge is smiling nervously while Fürthrived is pumped to see them fight. Cretan is pondering if Valcomix is going to devour this person quick. Then all are surprised as the person's skin tone just darkened but his eyes are brightening a lime-green color and his hair is lighting up as well. Valcomix and this person clash fists. *Bone Shattering Crunch* The sound made them flinch. Valcomix's knuckles are pushing against his. Both are smiling menacingly as they push the other as some measure of strength. Valcomix is winning.

Black blood mixes with dark crimson on the salt of the frozen ice. Dripping from their direct connection.

The individual swiftly kicks Valcomix into his side. It was harder than those rounds of bullets, it is similar to a light fall. Valcomix then swings his tail and punches his shoulder. Receiving the hits. He just brushes them off like they were nothing. Still, he rolled his shoulder. Now done measuring their opponent they both get serious. Valcomix gets on all fours and exposes his veins. **"That is not fair, you must be abnormal."** He says as he keeps sight of all possible attacks. Counting each limb, ligament and its very stature.

He goes on the attack first watching all attacks coming and deciding to approach cautiously. Valcomix's surprises are failing. His quick speed is the only advantage. Borrowing attacks form other animals. The guy has a smirk and quickly dodges then counter with a kick to his jaw. Valcomix then slams his jaw down causing him to pound his heel on the ice. That actually hurt. Now standing unbalanced. He rushes at him with teeth, fur, veins, and claws. The guy is forced to protect his face. Now he is laid down sprawled out defeated. **"You cheated."** He says sounding sore then begins laughing.

Valcomix chuckles and stands him up. He points to the cart and Valcomix aids him to it. Then his smile is put away as he looks to the side. *Tch* Valcomix as well, feeling nervous. Finally witnessing the being that now threatens humanity. A dark skinned, red veined, yellow eyed induvial wearing gold silk shorts and fangs of apex beasts around his neck. Approaching the two boys and peering down on them.

Showing a menacing glare. **"I'm doing my work. We were just finishing up our sparring."** He tells the intimidating old crone. **"Spilled blood on the ice is not considered sparring if not sharing the same nature. Now who are you?"** The old man asks Valcomix.

**"Valcomix."** He answers strongly. The older individual raises an eyebrow and then notices the other four. He stares down at the short person that is stepping on the ice. **"Humans are not allowed on the ice. Step back on the land and receive your gifts. I'll discuss how to punish you with your lead."** He warns using the old dialect. Valcomix is annoyed as he growls at him showing off his teeth. **"Go complete your errand."** He orders the younger individual. Upset and disappointed.

Then is glared at angrily as the boy pushes the cart towards the beach. The older male turns sight back to the person. **"If you want to act like a mutt, you won't survive long. I put dogs down."** He threatens Valcomix. **"Try it Virit."** Saying that with a smirk. The other guy is snickering and bows to him. Then quickly heads off the ice then he is glared at again. Valcomix swings his tail, the old man catches it.

Using the mutt's bladed edge to cut into the ice and steps on it. **"Trying to use sneak attack, you have no honor as a human. Only beasts use any attack to ana advantage."** He teaches the mutt while glaring at Valcomix. Now holding his neck. But Valcomix remains smiling. "All tactics welcome." He mentions and then Cretan rolls into the old individual. The old guy is pushed off him, he then elbows Cretan. Cretan does a reversal to have TSinged barrage punch him. Blocking every hit and then catches his hands. Bending back his wrists. TSinged is struggling.

Fürthrived then brightens releasing a surge of heat. Valcomix headbutts the old man. The heat in ineffective. **"Young immature delinquents. Your battle prowess has no coordination nor the function of taking me down. Just weak attacks. And if you're going to use heat, make sure it outburns the other, you lukewarm brat."** He shouts and then kicks her in the side with a glowing leg. Fürthrived wails in pain as there is a burn mark on her. TSinged and Valcomix are upset both showing their hate filled glare. TÖ-Slüdge attends to her.

Valcomix is relentlessly swinging all of himself to fall this old man while TSinged is using an explosive barrage. Cretan is ready to roll once more with his spiky skin. The old man catches both their arms. Tosses TSinged at Cretan. Breaking off a few spikes and slightly piercing TSinged but one goes fully through his shoulder. Then drops his elbow onto Valcomix's head making him fall flat on the ice. **"Humans are fragile beings that are sensitive. You all will not survive."** The old man says to them. TSinged recovers but the spike remains causing some complications for him to move his left arm. Cretan is at the ready in his lightest skin.

TSinged lifts him up and throws him. Then shifts to his heaviest skin. Right into the old man's shoulder. TSinged has a grin. Valcomix stabs his hurt shoulder with his needles. TÖ-Slüdge digs her nails into his hurt shoulder. The old man is smiling. He then rolls to the right and kicks fast. Doing a horizontal spin. Ready to slap the girl but Valcomix takes the hit.

**"You brats are not able to go across the ice. Trail the snow it's easier. You won't survive out here. But you may journey if you can convince me."** The old man informs them glaring down at all of them. Valcomix is upset. **"We traveled from the Washington to Maine."** He shares with this old crone. The old man is actually surprised and starts to smile. He gestures for them to go on. **"Whatever happens I did warn you."** He reinforms them, but at least they're allowed. Aiding one another up and venture forward without looking back. The old man chuckles as he watches them, and from a few meters away the brat pulling the cart has a smirk.

# PART IV

The old man glares down at the young degenerate. **"What brat?"** He asks with an angered tone. Seeing him beaten up. **"You went easy on them, but never once treated me kindly."** He says pulling the cart. Then receives a brutal punch on the top of his head. The young lad just laughs rubbing his head as he delivers the cargo. Rolling his arms. The old man is annoyed gesturing for him to speak. The boy snickers nervously. Trenton and the golden starred chosen children stand lined up greeting the individuals.

**"Where is Sir Kiel?"** The old man asks with a disappointed tone. **"Demoted to eight. It was time for his retirement. What is with the kid?"** Trenton asks with an annoyed and serious tone. **"I'm passed my prime. Retirement is nigh for me as well. So, this brat wants to do the meetings."** The old man says with his arms folded. Now their attention is on the brat who is picking out his ears. The old man is glaring more angrily at him. The kid smiles evilly ready to fight his...

But realizes they're patiently waiting for him. **"I got this, so keep watch."** He says showing the leader of the C.O.A.T.S. the cargo he hauled now facing their numbers. **"Again, it is a pleasure to know that you**

**are all surviving strong. But as you know the world you remembered is gone. Soon enough humanity will diminish and become extinct. You are all weak to the world around you. Consider to lose and abandon such pride. But since it's a gift giving day. Accept this: tungsten, titanium and diamonds. Build your mediocre tools and thrive for another year."** The brat voices with a kind strong voice, almost boisterous. The old man is astonished, *"The brat managed to do it properly"*. That smirk annoys him so much. Now he wants to act smug.

**"We appreciate the offer. But we humans aren't as weak, we claimed back our states and soon enough we'll move forward."** Trenton says with a threatening tone. The brat's attitude is now menacing. **"Stay off the ice."** He warns them and turns his back on them. *Bang* The kid turns around and sees a red bent bullet at his feet. Picking it up and examining it closely. The old man takes the thing from his hand. His veins are burning and his darkened skin is becoming lighter. **"Hey, teach. I'm alright."** He tells him trying to pull him back but is only glared at. **"Don't take threats kindly."** He tells him sighting the culprit. Trenton keeps forward and those around him do so as well.

The soldier is only a rank four as the person is singled out. Everyone else around the soldier had stepped aside. Turning a head to the right. *Burst* No: skin, organs nor bones, just vital hot boiling red liquid is splashed around. The rocks around the old man's feet are melted. Speed, power and heat obliterated the soldier. He turns away frightening the many. Standing near the leaders. **"Protect the remaining."** He tells them and then pushes the brat who has an apologetic expression. Trenton is clenching his fists.

## Laboratory

Inside the lab of Suviron Arc's office. Ovaiya, Tingi, David and Arc are labeling a vial of black ooze. "Zion-RTFQ". All congratulating one another as they shake hands. **"We are able to mass produce this."** Ovaiya says proudly. **"It's now subscribed as a biological environmental weapon. The many Playgrounds' fields are rotting and growing the ivy-roses."** Tingi informs reading the data and watching the videos. The North Western states are the targeted. **"We still have work to do my fellow scientists, we should help the northern bases. If Valcomix can do it, why not them?"** Arc questions while putting a request to their faction through his device. **"But if you do manage to get the support to do so we'll need his medical records when he was human. His DNA is the qualification to go forward."** David tells them. Now all eyes on Ovaiya. She smiles and nods then leaves the room.

## C.O.A.T.S. headquarters

Bottom floor main desk. Diim Sourn and Curesed Kiel are named on their platinum prisms. Sitting far away as the desk can go. Both at each of the end. On the right; wearing a pressed dress shirt with a clip-on black tie, black slacks and polished black shoes is Diim Sourn. Looking quite presentable. While Mr. Kiel a: Caucasian/Polish male with pale blue eyes, short cut grey hair, pale white skin. Slender but well-toned. Wearing the same type of clothing but his tie is violet is on the left end.

**"Want to go to the gym after work again?"** Diim Sourn asks staring at the computer screen. **"Might as well, if we can get drinks after the workout and some wings. That kid is probably out of the Playgrounds by now."** Mr. Kiel says with a disheartened tone. **"I'll pay."** Sourn offers. **"Tell you now drinking isn't my best choice."** He says seriously. **"It's how us kind of men can talk."** Sourn tells him with a saddened serious tone. They both indulge themselves in their work.

## On the ice

The five are struggling to journey forward. The clouds are denser and closer to the ground. Violent winds are blowing them back. Fürthrived is trying to keep everyone warm. Valcomix pushes himself forward and blocks them from the winds, slightly. They understand. Once more he carries everyone. The weight helps their gravity. Digging each nail into the ice. Each passing day is draining.

Fürthrived's light is diminishing as she exhausted her ability trying to keep everyone warm. The freezing temperatures are worse. Causing Valcomix to feel frostbite. TSinged and Cretan fell asleep. TÖ-Slüdge's grip has weakened and so has Fürthrived. He quickly wraps his tail around them including himself. Bearing anger and concern he begins running digging his nails into the ice.

# PART V

## Suviron Arc's lab room

## The time is 3:10pm of 1/03/3176

The head faction lead is annoyed seeing an individual sitting in front of him along with other governmental workers of the faction. Electronic documents supporting his projects and even Trenton C. Calhous is present. Signing this off. Arc signs it next and bows to them. Seeing that innocent smile is angering him. Then all of them exit except for Trenton. **"Sir Arc. How long will this project take?"** He asks in a serious tone. **"I do not have that answer. But my colleagues and those under them will begin working. Zion-RTFQ is a stable compound but we are missing the 'unknown' factor. Once we are given his records we can proceed. I assure you it may take a while. Just take care of them, they're still our people."** Sir Arc tells him with a serious tone turning his sights from the leader of the C.O.A.T.S. faction as he escorts him out of his office.

Trenton gets up from his chair. Heading out of the door opened by Suviron who wants him to leave as well. **"I'll be relying on your faction more frequently**

**along with the engineering faction."** He says exiting. Suviron Arc closes the door.

## Elsewhere

Valcomix's abandoned home. The cautioned taped door is pried open. Given clearance is an African American/Korean/German female that has a rich light brown complexion. Medium length shiny black hair with red & violet dyed tips. A simple gold clip over her left ear, while her right ear has three silver earrings. Vivid violet eyes, Black polished nails with a silver serpent on both her thumbs. Wearing an official pressed black work dress with a white buttoned shirt underneath. Stockings, covering her silver snake tattoo with a red eye on her right leg. Still noticeable. And black polished flat shoes.

Escorted in by two of the C.O.A.T.S. soldiers. Using their flashlights. Sighting the dusty house. The intelligent female flips the switch by the entrance located on the right. Making them look rather incompetent for not trying the light. Exploring the single two bedroom, a small kitchen, and two full baths. Just a dirty bed, antique furniture, and barely any décor except the frame. The house is more similar to a Holiday Inn hotel with a double sized open closet and extra room that was left unkempt. The Soldiers are searching through the area. She heads straight opening the closet space. Viewing the brilliant old-fashioned birch wood desk. Opening the drawers and hidden compartments. Empty. She then turns on the light. Dimly lighting up the space. Setting her sights on the trashcan.

She examines the cinders and ashes. She then flashes light on it and shakes it and saw a number. Rummaging through with her hand. Then feels something small, flat and familiar. After some minutes she discovers an 8TB SD card. Her expression is furious. She gets out her personal device with a wolf devouring zombies red case. Opening the slot and places it in the free spot. Counting all four occupied spaces. Nodding with a joyous grin. She then marks the area as clear on the device and sends the message. She then exits the room and then the house.

## Lège-Cap-Ferret, Nouvelle-Aquitaine, France

A vast beach washout of clumps of sand and debris. The wind is calmer but the air temperature is far below freezing. Valcomix is covering his teammates as he is shivering as well, laying his tail and body on them. Soon his ears twitch. Trying to stand but his arms and legs give out. His heart is beating weakly.

Dull eyes sighting individuals wearing cloaks made of white feathers and fur. Carrying weapons, he growls at them. Standing with a quaking body. Salivating black ooze. Soft vibrant yellow eyes are focused on his teammates. Valcomix snarls. Dripping more of the black ooze staining the sands. **"Don't worry they must be our guests' products by the looks of them. Can you understand me?"** A gentle male's voice asks attempting to reach out for one of them.

Valcomix backs away. The male feels them, testing for a pulse. Smiling victoriously. **"They're all alive."** The male informs him. Valcomix is relieved and finally relaxes and sleeps with a smile on his face. The many others are called to aid. Muffled speaks are heard, then so faint until silent.

## Bordeaux, France

TSinged is recovering in a building and has just woken up feeling warmth from a being that is similar to Fürthrived. Shivering still as his body is cold and stinging. Relieved to see that his team is sleeping, covered in a cloak that they must have given them. Yet one is missing. **"Where is Valcomix?" [Old Dialect]** He asks with an annoyed tone but a grin. The individuals look to one another and the male that saved them puts a gentle hand on his shoulder.

**"Your friend couldn't recover. His pulse stopped days ago. You all have been asleep recovering for a while now. We buried him already in our garden."** He informs him. TSinged eyes are wide, not believing such a thing. Shaking his head. Remembering Valcomix carried all of them continuously for days on the ice and only ran. His arms were weakening but he managed to stay firm on the frozen salt. He thanks him silently. Now he looks to his teammates with a sad expression feeling guilty.

## Laboratory of Hitomoni Free

## The Time is 2:05pm of 01/07/3176

Experimenting with the Zion-RTFQ as she is supposed to. Staring at the tablet. No one still haven't solved the 'unknown' factor and it is crucial to the project. Reading the reports of animals behaving weird and unsettling when the areas started to rot. Watching videos of her colleagues spraying the substance on many materials. Even sees it being set on fire. But it's not. She attempts the DNA scrambler once more. Given the results and then that 'unknown' factor.

She has an idea and places a thin filter into the black ooze. Attempting the process and given the same results. Pulling out the filter and sees hardened black crystals attached to it. Examining the thin wire under a microscope. Tiny bristles of needles are reaching and stretching. This phenomenon is very familiar and only happens in...

Her eyes are open wide in shock. She then quickly sends messages. "We cannot keep spreading this. It's not a blight. Valcomix is a..."

**CONTINUED NEXT SEASON...**

Milton Keynes UK
Ingram Content Group UK Ltd.
UKHW041653151024
449742UK00004B/11

9 798822 961517